Praise for
O'Brien's Broken Play

"A visceral, compassionate story about the hope of the 1960s and the heartbreak of America's favorite sport."

—**KATHERINE HILL,** author of *A Short Move*

"You can feel the tense divide between expectation, promise, destruction, and recovery. *O'Brien's Broken Play* is a novel rich in historical details and a deeply moving character study of one man's journey to revitalize his self-worth and heal past traumas. An adventure not to be missed."

—**JODY LULICH,** author of *In the Company of Grace: a Veterinarian's Memoir of Trauma and Healing*

"With *O'Brien's Broken Play*, Robert Johns crafts a lovely, tender portrait of a young man's search for meaning after his football dreams are dashed. From the 1970 shootings at Kent State to a hippie commune in Hawaii, this engrossing coming-of-age tale is set against a fascinating historical tableau. It's sure to satisfy those who lived through the period and those curious to understand its complicated, far-reaching legacy."

—**MAYA HLAVACEK,** creative writing faculty member, Minneapolis College of Art and Design

"The main character in Robert Johns's debut novel will immediately draw you in and carry you through the many shifts of his journey. An authentic seeker, he travels through the late '60s and early '70s—a time in American history that is wrought with painful divisions and seismic reckonings. That backdrop is an integral part of Tom O'Brien's challenges as he navigates stardom as a talented athlete, an injury that changes the direction of his life, explorations into anti-Vietnam war protests, and the subcultures of those times. It's a historically meaningful story told through the personal lens of O'Brien who, in response to the changes all around him and his own broken dreams, deepens his search for identity and connection. A suspenseful page-turner, this novel will invite you to remember or learn more of those times and to accompany this memorable character as he reinvents himself in ever-surprising and meaningful ways."

—**PATRICIA HOOLIHAN,** author of *Hands and Heart Together: Daily Meditations for Caregivers* and *Storm Prayers: Retrieving and Reimagining Matters of the Soul*

O'BRIEN'S BROKEN PLAY

A NOVEL

ROBERT JOHNS

River Grove
BOOKS

Published by River Grove Books
Austin, TX
www.rivergrovebooks.com

Distributed by River Grove Books

Design and composition by Greenleaf Book Group and Anna Jordan
Cover design by Greenleaf Book Group and Anna Jordan
Cover images used under license from ©Adobestock.com/ Augustas Cetkauskas

Publisher's Cataloging-in-Publication data is available.

Print ISBN: 978-1-63299-750-0

eBook ISBN: 978-1-63299-751-7

First Edition

For Linda

PART I:

1965–1966

1

Tom ignored the slight twinge in his calf from the previous play. The night air was colder than usual, even for November, and he could see his breath coming out the front of his face mask. He allowed himself to peer toward the Massillon section of the packed stands where he knew his family was watching, but he couldn't make them out in the blur of orange and black.

This was a big night. Canton was Massillon's archrival, and there seemed to be as many fans from Massillon as there were from Canton in Canton's Fawcett Stadium, a standing-room-only crowd of over 22,000. The Massillon fans were there to watch Tom's team take on their archrivals in the tenth and final game of the season, and some college scouts had come to see if he lived up to his reputation as the best offensive lineman in the state. Tom thought he glanced a flash of a scarlet cap on a man—maybe the Ohio State Buckeyes scout—but he couldn't be sure because the Canton McKinley fans were also there in droves of red.

His girlfriend Cindi yelled his name from the sidelines, her voice the clearest among the cheerleaders. It was the third play, and he needed to focus, but he couldn't resist looking over at her for a split second to see if he could catch her eye. She winked at him.

He settled into his stance with the other linemen, squaring his shoulders, planting his feet, tensing his calves. At 6-foot, 3 inches and 230 pounds, he knew he stood out for the scouts watching. More breath was visibly coming out the front of his helmet. He tried to slow it.

Curt stepped behind Tony.

"Hut one, hut two!" Curt shouted. Tony hiked the ball, and Curt pitched it to Vince as he headed around the right.

Tom pulled out of the line to the right and took off in front of Vince, his legs pumping, his face reddening. He collided with a linebacker and moved him back to create a hole for Vince to run through, then targeted the Canton cornerback running up to tackle Vince.

The noise from the stands was deafening as Tom and his teammates barreled down the field. The cheers from the Massillon fans—the students of Massillon Washington High, the residents of Massillon and its surrounding community, and his family and teammates' families—drowned out the Canton cheers.

Tom surged forward, ready for his next collision. He lowered his shoulder and slammed with full force into the cornerback, easily moving him aside while other defenders rushed in. He could feel Vince pressing against his back, trusting Tom to pave the way for him to carry the ball for more yards.

Tom charged ahead at a forty-five-degree angle, continuing to move defenders back. He shot forward as another linebacker got close, throwing all his weight into a powerful lunge and bracing himself for contact. He pushed hard, his head up, his eyes open, his right leg fully extended. He could see the beads of sweat on the linebacker's face.

At that moment, the defensive safety flew in from the side to help the linebacker and was shoved to the right by another player. The force of impact caused him to lose his balance, and he careened, his body out of control, toward Tom. He fell hard onto Tom's extended leg, hitting first with his upper torso, before landing in a heap.

The back of Tom's right ankle popped and he screamed. He hit the ground, his face mask planted into the grass. He lay in the same position he'd fallen in, comprehending, for those first few seconds, only the sharp, excruciating pain in the back of his ankle and lower leg. After a moment, he realized the defensive safety was trying to get up. Tom moaned as the weight of the player shifted on his leg.

The action on the field came to a standstill, and the stadium became eerily silent. Tom could see the cleats of other players around him. He remained down, breathing heavily, continuing to moan.

He became aware that some of his teammates were kneeling next to him. Cindi had run over, dropping her pom-poms on the ground a few feet away.

"Tom! Tom! Are you hurt?" she asked, her lips a few inches from his. But the trainer had arrived at the same time and was ordering her and the other players to move back.

"O'Brien. Where do you feel the pain? O'Brien, look at me." The trainer pulled Tom's helmet off. Tom tried to reach toward his calf.

"My l-l-leg," he stammered.

Kneeling next to Tom, the trainer pressed down on Tom's calf in the area above the heel. Tom groaned loudly in agony. The trainer pulled Tom's sock lower, pressed along various points, causing Tom to moan.

"Let's get him up," the trainer said. He asked Curt and Tony to help lift him to his feet.

Coach Bruce had come over and the trainer was whispering to him. After a second or two, Coach nodded.

Tom struggled to balance himself on one leg so he could stand, holding onto Curt's arm. The stadium lights were bright, and the stands were still. His teammates on the sideline were all looking at him. Cindi stood between a couple of other cheerleaders, hugging herself, receiving their sympathy, unaware her eye makeup had created a dark smudge on her cheekbone. Tom scanned the sidelines for his father.

"Son," the trainer said next to him. "You looked good, but you're done now."

Done? What did that mean? Tom couldn't think straight. He stared at the trainer's chapped lips. His calf throbbed. Done tonight? Done for the future? What about Ohio State? Beyond that? Hopefully the Buckeyes scout couldn't see his face from the stands. He turned his head away from the crowd.

The trainer motioned for Curt and Tony to help him off the field. Tom didn't want anyone to carry him, but when he placed weight on his right foot, he grimaced—the pain was unbearable. He put his arms around their shoulders, so he could hop off the field on his good leg.

"It's going to be all right," Curt told him, as he supported Tom from the left.

The fans began to applaud.

"We'll win this, O'Brien!" someone shouted from the Massillon side. "This one's for you!"

Cindi helped bring him the rest of the way. She sent a radiant smile up to the stands to communicate her appreciation for the crowd's support. Tom winced when she nearly knocked him off balance, but he was grateful to have her by his side. When they got to the benches, his teammates helped him onto a stretcher.

Coach Bruce clapped him on the shoulder.

"O'Brien," he said, looking at him with sympathy. They were enveloped by several assistant coaches and players.

"Damn shame," one of the assistant coaches muttered to someone. The other person cleared their throat.

The referees blew their whistles, and the coaches directed the players back onto the field. Play began again, and the crowd turned its attention back to the game.

Tom watched his father stride toward him from the stands, not hurrying, but walking deliberately, his ramrod posture influenced by his years of military training. He stopped to talk to the trainer, while Tom's mother, grandfather, and younger sister, Kara, quickly went toward Tom.

"You'll be back," Tom's grandfather said, bending down to him and placing a gloved hand on his shoulder. "Don't worry, my boy."

"I knew this would happen! I always knew this would happen," his mother said, in tears, kissing Tom on the top of his head and doing her best to hold him.

"Mom, get a grip. That's not what he needs right now," Kara said. "Look at him. No matter what, Tom's going to be okay."

"I think it's his Achilles," the trainer said. "An ambulance is on the way."

"Will he be able to play football next fall?" his father asked.

"We need a doctor to take a look," the trainer said.

Tom's eyes flitted to his right leg, his grass-stained pants, the sock that hadn't been pulled up. The area near his heel felt swollen and enormous, and he didn't know how his shoe was still on. He looked at his father.

"We'll fix this," his dad said, approaching. He stopped and stood a few feet away.

"But what if we can't?" Tom blurted out. "My scholarships! What would I do?" He hated that his voice had cracked, but his father appeared not to notice.

"You're going to be okay," Kara said. "He's going to be okay," she told the others. Everyone ignored her, and Tom's mother started crying again.

"No matter what, everything will work out as it's meant to," his grandfather said, patting him gently. Tom's father shot his grandfather a look.

"You'll work hard to get back," his father said firmly, his eyes locked on Tom. "Schools will wait for you." A vein stood out in his forehead. Tom's grandfather handed him a cup of water, and the four of them waited in silence for the ambulance. Behind them, the crowd roared as the game went on. A man with a scarlet cap came down from the bleachers. At the bottom, the man turned toward the exit and disappeared from view.

———

Tom was lying on his stomach, his feet hanging over the edge of the exam table, when the ER doctor confirmed that his Achilles tendon had ruptured and his injury was serious. From Tom's angle, he could see his mother's grip tighten on the rosary beads she was holding, Kara shift her weight, and his grandfather put his hands in his coat pockets. His father wasn't in his line of sight, but Tom was aware of his proximity to his good leg.

"His tendon is completely torn," the doctor said to his father. "It will require surgery to repair it." Tom's lower leg had been jostled when he was brought in, his swollen calf muscle had been prodded and squeezed, and he was still in a great deal of pain, but it was this news that caused him to react the most strongly. "Surgery? But . . . what does that mean for football? Will I be able to play?" His father wore a grim look on his face.

"How long before he can play again?" his father asked.

"After the surgery, if he does what the physical therapist says, he could be back to normal in four to six months," the doctor said. "We'll need to see how the tendon heals, but he could be able to play football again if he strengthens his leg enough."

"I have scholarships!" Tom said. "The colleges will want to know *now*." He had trained so much, worked so hard, and he hadn't gotten a scholarship offer yet from Ohio State.

"Will he be back in the same form?" his father asked. Tom's grandfather placed a hand on his back.

"That will depend on how the tendon heals and how much Tom can re-strengthen it," the doctor said. "Time will tell, but it's not out of the question."

Tom thought of the scouts who had come to visit them in their home. The handshakes, the letters, and the phone calls. He thought of his teammates and their run for the state championship. He pictured the students at school screaming for the team in the pep rally, Cindi locking eyes with him after ending a cheer with a cartwheel. He remembered all the people in the community who had gathered in town for the homecoming parade. The image of him in a cast did not fit with this. The idea of him without football was unfathomable.

"He'll do it," his father said.

Tom kept hearing the doctor's words, *Time will tell.* His mother moved her rosary beads around in her hands.

They were able to schedule the procedure for early the next morning. Tom's father insisted that the recovery needed to begin as soon as possible.

———

Tom awoke groggy after the surgery, but sensed a heaviness on his right leg—he was wearing a stiff plaster cast that started below his knee and extended down to his toes. It seemed like something that didn't belong on his body. Then he remembered why he was there.

Tom felt his stomach drop and heat rise up from his chest to his neck. He knew his freckled cheeks were becoming red, and he thought he could hear his heartbeat. He wanted to swallow, but his throat was dry. His grandfather's coat was slung across the arm of a vinyl-padded chair in the corner. A few feet away, the curtain had been pulled back to let in the sun. There were muffled voices nearby.

In the hallway just outside his open door, Cindi was standing with his mother, his younger sister Kara, and his grandfather. Cindi stood with her back to him and still wore her cheerleader's skirt from the night before. She'd let her long blond hair out of her ponytail, and it moved as she sniffled and shook her head. Tom's mother patted Cindi on the arm, but he knew his mother agreed with his father that Cindi was a distraction to him.

Tom's father came into view. He was speaking with a doctor Tom didn't recognize, and gesturing toward the doctor's clipboard.

Tom felt sweaty. He closed his eyes, so it would seem to others as if he hadn't yet regained consciousness. He was tired and didn't want to have to talk with anyone.

The night before, Cindi had told him that his team had wrapped up a perfect season and the state championship with an 18–14 victory. When some of the players stopped by to check on him on their way to a post-game party, they told him his backup had played a hell of a game. Tom wondered if anyone had even missed him on the offensive line. He'd worked hard to be the best right guard he could be, and he didn't like thinking someone else had taken it over in his absence.

Trying to ignore the whispers of Cindi and his family in the hallway, Tom thought back to his first memories of playing football—when Grandpa had given him a small leather football for Christmas when he was four. Football ran in the family, and although it was cold and windy outside—and his mother had been against it—he, his father, and Grandpa had gone into the yard, slightly covered with snow from flurries, to throw the ball back and forth after dinner. They'd only lasted fifteen minutes in the cold, but after Tom threw the ball a few times, his father exchanged a surprised look with Grandpa, and they both smiled broadly. Tom carried the ball with him the rest of the evening, even sleeping with it in the crook of his arm that night.

When Tom was in kindergarten, his father began taking him to Massillon football games. Tom loved sitting in the stands next to his dad, gazing out on the huge green field. He appreciated the orderliness of the white yard markers, the crisp, clean look of the painted numbers, and the precision in the lines that ran down the length of the field.

When, not long after that, he began participating in Pop Warner football teams, his dad attended every single game and practice he could, only missing the one weekend a month when it was mandatory for him to report to his drills and training camp for the National Guard.

When he was twelve, Tom's coach walked with him over to his father after the last Pop Warner Pee Wee season.

"I think Tom's future is in the offensive line," the coach said. "He's going to be big, and he's strong and fast. Plus, he's smart and a quick learner."

"What do you think, Tom?" his father asked, placing his hand on Tom's shoulder. "I think Coach might be right."

Tom liked football, he liked making his dad proud, and he knew the right answer. He'd nodded and smiled at the men.

"Okay, little man," his dad said. "That's what we'll work toward." He tousled Tom's thick, reddish-brown hair, still sweaty from his helmet, and then patted him on the back. The coach and his dad continued to talk about him, and he basked in the attention. His dad had never called him a man before.

After that conversation, Tom's goal was to become the best offensive line-man in the state. Setting goals, his dad had always told him, would give him direction, help him become successful, and hold him accountable to what was most important in life. Tom set his sights on football. He loved the game's techniques, the teamwork needed, the joy of winning, and the admiration he received when he excelled. His father wasn't the kind of person to holler and clap when he did well, but he'd jumped to his feet on more than one occasion to give him a silent nod.

In the hospital now, Tom thought about all of the practices he'd attended, all the hits he'd taken, and all the plays he'd memorized. He thought also about all the advice his father and grandfather had given him before and after games. They'd both played on Massillon teams in their time and were part of the legacy, helping Massillon become recognized as one of the best football programs in the country. Their football experiences in high school were high-lights of their lives, much more than their subsequent jobs in the steel mill, and Tom knew they loved nothing more than seeing him play.

Tom had not disappointed them. After his junior year of high school, he was chosen to join the first-team all-state. It was the first time he'd seen his father's eyes become watery, but then his father had turned away, making Tom wonder if he'd imagined it.

Going into his senior year in 1965, Tom couldn't have been more prepared for the season. He played nine great games before his Achilles injury, helping his team toward their undefeated season and state championship. Several col-lege scouts had visited his home, trying to sell their programs to him and his father. They'd offered scholarships right at the kitchen table. Tom was excited, but he was hoping to hear from Ohio State.

———

Tom's eyes popped open in the hospital room. He stared at his cast. If he couldn't heal properly, what would his future be? Would he be able to return to football? If not, what would he do if he needed to find a completely different path for his life? He and his father hadn't invested so much in football just to have him be mediocre, and his dad didn't want him to just work at the steel mill.

"He's awake," a nurse said, entering the room. Cindi and Tom's family hurried in.

"Hey, Tommy, how are you feeling?" his grandfather asked, coming alongside Tom's bed.

"We thought you'd be sleeping for longer," his mother said. She leaned over to kiss his forehead, her rosary beads clinking against the metal of his bed rail.

"Nice cast," Kara said, crossing her arms and leaning against a counter. Tom knew she tended to cross her arms when she was worried or nervous, and he watched her uncross and recross them again.

Tom's father moved closer, standing tall over him. "The doctor said the surgery went fine. They stitched the tendon back together again. Now it just needs to heal."

Cindi swooped in, her hair falling onto Tom's face as she leaned over to kiss him fully on the lips. Tom felt her breasts press against him.

"Don't worry, Tommy," she said. "I'll be with you. Nothing can stop you, not this or anything else."

The nurse moved in to check Tom's pulse and used a small light to peer into each of his eyes. "Are you uncomfortable anywhere?" she asked, adjusting his pillow and folding over the top part of the bedsheet.

Tom didn't answer.

"He looks alright," Cindi said after another moment. She adjusted his pillow also, pulling it up higher than it needed to go.

"The doctor said you were a champ," the nurse said, as she brought the tray with water on it closer. "If you follow the instructions from your physical therapist, you'll have a good chance at recovery."

"That's your goal now, Tom," his father said. "You've had a setback, but you can still win if you put everything into your recovery."

Tom thought about the countless times he'd looked down the field to clear a path, using his body to push his way through defenders. He expected to take hits and prepared for them. This one, however, he hadn't seen coming. The sharp pain of the night before was still with him, and he felt like he was still on the ground, caught under the weight of what had happened.

He looked at the thick cast on his leg. It blocked his injury from view. He couldn't tell if his leg was bruised or swollen or if it appeared as it always had. The cast, with its hardened plaster, blocked from him a clear view of his future, and he felt confined to it.

2

Tom was exhausted but unable to sleep in the first week following his surgery. He'd been told to get a lot of rest, but he could only lie anxiously on top of the blanket, his right leg propped up on pillows, worrying about whether he'd be able to heal fast enough to play again next fall. Occasionally, he would lie downstairs with his leg up on the arm of the couch, but he was too big to be comfortable on it.

His daily routine had become receiving meals from his mother, appearing agreeable when his father spoke of rehab exercises, and thinking about how his pain medications were making him sluggish. He no longer wanted to elevate his foot above his heart. He didn't want to tape a plastic bag around his cast to take a shower. He resented the constant itchiness under his cast.

Kara, after checking in with Tom's teachers, brought him his assignments and updates from classmates. She appeared next to the couch one afternoon, looking amused. She liked to give him a hard time on occasion. Unlike Tom, she was extroverted and opinionated, often clashing with people, including their parents. A junior in high school, she'd grown to be taller than many of her friends—about five feet eight that year—and with their Grandma O'Brien's unmistakably Irish red hair and green eyes, Tom's football friends had asked him about her. But he still saw her as a kid.

"What is it?" he asked. She reported that Cindi had attached a photo with Tom, in full football garb, onto a poster near her locker, and many of his teammates and fellow seniors had signed it. She said their principal had mentioned Tom's name in an all-school assembly that week. She told him kids had bugged her all day asking questions about him.

"And this," she said, holding out some paper she'd been hiding behind her back. The student newspaper had run an article conjecturing about Tom's future. Tom read it with a sick feeling in his stomach.

—

One evening, Tom's father called from the bottom of the stairs that Tom's friend Jack had come to see him. Tom, busy with the football season in prior months, knew he hadn't spent as much time with Jack as he used to. He felt sheepish about this, although he recognized his history with Jack went back far enough that their friendship could take it. Almost like brothers since grade school, when they'd played pickup football games with other neighborhood boys, they understood each other, even after Jack decided in junior high to focus on baseball, feeling he didn't have the size or skills for competitive high-school football in their town.

Tom slowly got out of bed. His father and Jack were talking downstairs. Tom imagined Jack looking intently at his father through the dark plastic frames of his glasses, which were often crooked and needing to be cleaned. Tom used the back of a chair to stand up, then reached for his crutches that had been splayed across the top of his desk. He made his way toward his bedroom door, swinging his left foot forward, his crutches following, keeping his right foot off the floor.

". . . and you're waiting to hear back from three more colleges, then?" his father asked Jack. Tom, emerging from his room, thought about how his father had often gone out of his way to ask Jack how he was doing, chatting briefly with him about his studies at school or his home life, and later on, about his part-time job pumping gas or his play on the baseball team. Tom knew his parents had been concerned for Jack ever since his father had abandoned his family to go to California when he was in second grade, but Tom sometimes felt over the years that his dad showed more concern about Jack than about him.

—

Once, in grade school, he and Jack had gotten into a fight. After Tom's mother had made them sandwiches, and Tom's father had asked Jack about his favorite subject in school, Tom and Jack went outside to throw a football back and forth in the front yard. After a few minutes, Tom's father stuck his head out the front door to remind Tom to wind up the hose.

"Good pass, Jack," he'd said before closing the door.

On top of all the attention his father had already given to Jack, this comment irritated Tom. Tom's passes had *all* been good. Had his father not seen a single one from the window?

Tom told Jack they should have a contest to see who could catch the football the most times without dropping it. After a few back-and-forths, Tom hurled the football with some extra force, and it had bounced off Jack's fingers and dropped into the grass.

"No way. Doesn't count!" Jack said. "That was a bad throw!"

"No, it wasn't. How would you know?" Tom said, running to scoop the football up from the ground.

"I saw you throw it."

"You don't know what you saw," Tom said. "You don't even know the right way to catch."

"Give it," Jack said, trying to swat the football out of Tom's hands.

"I can't help it if you're lousy at football," Tom said. He held the football high above his head. When Jack jumped up and accidentally swatted Tom's arm, Tom pushed Jack with his free hand, and Jack stumbled back a few steps.

"I'm telling your dad!" Jack yelled.

"Tell your *own* dad!" Tom yelled back.

Jack's nostrils flared and he made a guttural noise trying to tackle Tom. But Tom stepped out of the way and tackled Jack from the side, using his weight to get Jack onto the ground. He sat on Jack, pinning him there for several seconds before he realized Jack had started crying.

"Stop it!" Tom's father said as he came out the door. "This isn't how a friend behaves." He ordered Tom off Jack and helped Jack stand up, brushing some dirt off his back.

Jack's glasses had been knocked askew and his face was smeared with tears. All at once, Tom was keenly aware that he stood almost a head taller than his friend. What would Jack's dad in California have thought to see his son on the ground?

"You owe Jack an apology," Tom's father said.

Tom knew his father was right, but the lump in his throat felt huge. He did his best to swallow, and then in a thick voice said, "I'm sorry, Jack."

"Shake his hand," his father said. Tom stuck out his right hand.

Afterward, his father invited Jack for dinner. His mother cooked meatloaf and mashed potatoes, Tom's favorite. Tom's father asked Jack about his baseball card collection while Jack finished off the last of the potatoes. Jack promised to bring some of his cards to show Tom's father the following day, and when he did, he also gave Tom one of his favorites, Rocky Colavito of the Cleveland Indians.

——

Nearing the top of the stairs now, Tom adjusted his weight and accidentally knocked against a picture frame in the hallway. Jack came bounding up the stairs, and stopped at the top of the landing. Jack was one of the few boys in high school still wearing a flat-top haircut and it seemed shorter now than ever.

"Come on, let me save you a trip," Jack said, motioning him to return to his room. They made their way down the hall, and he took Tom's crutches as Tom settled against the pillows on his bed. Like he had a million times before, Jack paced slowly around Tom's room peering here and there at Tom's posters and football trophies through the dark frames of his glasses. "Your dad says you're starting to be able to get up more?" he said, standing next to an Ohio State pennant.

"A little," Tom said. He knew it would still be months before he would have complete use of his leg and ankle, and the thought made him a little crazy. He stared at his foot, propped high on some cushions Kara had brought up from the family room.

"That's good," Jack said. "What have you been doing while you're resting?"

"Nothing." It was quiet.

"Cindi been by?" Jack asked, ignoring Tom's obvious moodiness. Tom gestured toward the stuffed teddy bear on the desk next to him. It had a pink heart sewn onto its stomach and, just yesterday, had been pinned under Tom when Cindi was on the bed with him. "It's weird to see her walking around school and not hanging on your arm," Jack said.

Tom shrugged. Jack paused near the punching bag mounted in the corner by the closet, folded his arms, and looked Tom in the eye.

"How are you feeling?"

Tom followed Jack's eyes to the unopened schoolbooks on the floor near his bed, some crumpled get-well cards around the trash can, and a slightly discolored indentation and splotches on the wall across the room where he had hurled a soup spoon a few days before. His room was usually tidy. He was aware that he and Jack had been friends too long for Jack not to know exactly what was going on.

"I dunno," he said.

Jack nodded and sat down at Tom's desk.

"So, O'Brien, what are you going to do if you can't play in the fall?" he asked. Before Tom could shrug again, Jack added, "No matter what happens with your scholarships, you should still apply to some colleges. Even if the worst happens—no scholarship—you could eventually get better and play."

The worst? Tom's heart jumped up into his throat. He didn't want to talk with Jack or anyone else about his situation. Plus, they weren't close anymore.

"Look, you can't just stop living," Jack said. "You're a smart guy. You have a beautiful girlfriend, a family who cares, everyone in town wrapped around your finger . . . You can do whatever you want."

Tom's right leg itched, but he didn't try to reach into the top of the cast to scratch it.

Jack looked down at the desk. He tapped the space bar on Tom's typewriter with his index finger a few times. They watched the carriage move right.

"Remember when your dad took us to the Ohio State game against Michigan?" It was a day that Tom and Jack had declared the best of their fourteen years. When they, along with Tom's father and grandfather, had pulled up to Ohio Stadium in their old Ford Country Squire, Tom and Jack had stopped whooping and cheering from the back seat, falling silent as they took in the giant horseshoe-shaped structure of concrete before them. After finding their seats, they gazed out at the fans in scarlet filling every bleacher and chanted "O-H-I-O!" with them, as the Buckeyes defeated the Wolverines 28-0. Tom had vowed to do everything he could to one day play on that field and have the crowds screaming for him and his team.

"I wasn't into football as much as you," Jack said, returning the typewriter carriage to its original position. "But that day made me feel like family. I remember telling you after the game that I wished I could be as sure about something in life as you were about football." He looked at Tom's cast. "You said I could do whatever I wanted."

Tom nodded. He didn't remember having that conversation, but the words made sense to him. His father had always taught him that if he had a plan, stayed disciplined, and did the work, he could make something of himself. He had set a goal to be the best lineman on the field and had succeeded. He was a son his parents were proud of.

"You can too," Jack said. "You've had a setback, but you can do whatever you want."

Tom was silent, staring at his feet, and Jack said he had to take off. He went back downstairs, and started chatting with Tom's father again. The more Tom heard them talking, the more irritated he got. He lay back on his bed and closed his eyes.

3

The following week, Tom returned to school. Because he couldn't yet drive, two guys from the team, Vince and Tony, gave him a ride. They asked him how he was doing, what the doctors were saying, and when he thought he might be back on the field. These were the same questions a few of the colleges he'd received scholarships from had asked when they called in prior days.

"I'm right on track for fall," Tom said with more enthusiasm than he'd intended. "I just need to choose a school." He quietly cleared his throat a few times and tried to keep his face relaxed. From his view in the back seat, he saw Vince catch Tony's eye as they pulled onto the main road and began to pick up speed. Tom looked out the window and pretended to notice a passing car.

"That's great," Vince said.

"Yeah, it is," Tony said over his shoulder without looking back at Tom. After a moment or two, he turned the radio up.

Vince drove the car up to the front of the school where students were streaming in. Cindi, who was waiting with a small group of Tom's friends, opened the car door. Curt took his crutches while he climbed out of the car. He stood stiffly, balancing on his good leg, until Cindi took the crutches from Curt and handed them to him. Several students stepped closer to pat him on the back.

"Welcome back, Tommy," Cindi said, brushing his ear with her lips and placing her hand on his chest. She was smiling at everyone around them, including the students who were passing by. He wished he were back at home where people wouldn't look at him or attempt to size up his situation. He'd feel better if he could just be alone with Cindi, but she liked being in crowds.

"I don't think I'm up for this," he whispered as they turned to enter the school.

"Don't be silly," she whispered back. "Of course you are."

Tom was greeted by students and teachers alike as he made his way into the school with his small entourage. In his first-period class, the teacher had a boy move to a different seat so Tom could elevate his foot. The class took a test, but Tom, who wasn't yet caught up, was given permission to read a book instead, or in his case, stare at a book.

Throughout the morning, Tom was asked to recount his version of what had happened during the football game. He kept his telling short, ending by letting people know he was still deciding among colleges in the fall.

The nurse stopped by to check on him at one point.

Kara passed him in the hallway during a passing period and waved.

He saw, next to the front office, the student who'd written the article about him in the school paper and glared at him. What did he know?

By lunchtime, over half of his cast had been signed with Get Betters, smiley faces, tiger paw prints, hearts, and other well-wishes. Cindi read all the messages while sitting close to Tom among their friends in the middle of the cafeteria. People kept asking him about his leg, and Cindi told them that, knowing Tom, he'd probably be playing again by summer's end.

Tom's armpits were sore from his crutches. He was hot in the sweater his mother had him put on that morning. He had a slight twitch under his right eye that wouldn't go away. And his cast pressured his calf and ankle from their swelling.

Tom decided to go down to the weight room after lunch instead of class. He wanted to be alone. He made his way to the locker room, the sound of his crutches alternating with each slow step. Several hand-painted banners announcing Massillon's championship win hung on the wall. The trophy case had been rearranged to make space for the new one, which, Tom had heard during lunch, was still being engraved. There was his name on a plaque from the previous year—Tom O'Brien, First-Team All-State, 1964.

Cindi had come up to him about a year ago, shortly after he was named all-state. They were at a house party thrown by a student whose parents were out of town. She was his same year and a member of the cheerleading squad, and he'd already noticed her blond hair, firm body, and short cheerleader skirt that revealed her flashing athletic legs in her leaps and cartwheels. At the party, she'd walked right up to the circle of players surrounding Tom, and they'd immediately moved back to make room for her.

"I think you and I have something in common, O'Brien," she said, smiling radiantly at him. She cocked her head and met his eyes.

"We do?" he asked. She smelled like flowers or some kind of sweet perfume. The other players seemed excited just to be standing so close to her.

"Yeah, we both know what we want, and we like to win games." She put her hands on her hips, like she did when she had pom-poms. "I've watched the way you play, and you're amazing."

"Thanks," Tom said, unsure of what else to say.

"Congrats on getting all-state," Cindi said. "I can't wait to see what else is going to happen for you." She moved a little closer, touching his forearm with her hand. It was clear to the other players she wasn't there to engage with them, and they began to disperse. Cindi said she was looking forward to cheering for him the next year when she would be captain of the cheerleading squad. She looked up at him with her bright blue eyes.

Heat rose up through Tom's face as she leaned into him to say into his ear that she loved watching him play. Taking his hand, she led him to a living room away from all the noise and settled down on the couch right next to him. She turned toward him, her leg touching his. The directness of her gaze was intoxicating. She smiled, tilted her head up toward him, and ran her hand slowly up his forearm, bicep, shoulder, and the back of his neck.

"All muscle," she said, drawing him in for a kiss. Her lips were soft and moist. His hands ran up and down her sweater and the curves underneath while they kissed.

The following week, Cindi would occasionally show up at Tom's locker or at the lunch table where he sat with other football players. She seemed to have set her sights on Tom, and he was excited by it. She was a catch, and people were talking about them. He started walking her to class. She started calling him at home in the evenings. They would make out in Tom's old Ford after going to a restaurant or movie.

"Lucky," Vince said one day after she leaned in for a deep kiss before getting into a friend's car after school. "Let me know if that doesn't work out." He play-punched Tom on the arm and shook his head admiringly.

Tom learned Cindi had spread the word that he and she were pretty much officially an item. They hadn't talked about this, but when, after a few weeks, Cindi asked if he wanted to go steady, he gladly agreed. They were in his car, and she climbed over into his lap so that she was facing him, her arms encircling his neck and her body pressed against his. She kissed him, and he returned her kiss, his hands cupping her face, his fingers entangled in her hair. He slid his hands down her sides, passing his thumbs over her breasts and then pulling her hips closer toward him. He couldn't get enough of having her body next to him.

"It's like watching royalty go by," Cindi's friend Cheryl said one day as they passed her in the hallway. "The football king and the cheerleader queen."

———

But all of that was last year, a time when college scouts were contacting him, and a scholarship offer from Ohio State was a possibility. Now he secretly worried Cindi might not look at him the same way if he couldn't get back to playing in top form.

Tom used one of his crutches to push open the weight room door. How many times had Cindi waited for him after practice or a game? How many times had she stood outside the locker room, chatting with friends while he showered and got dressed? He made his way over to the machines, dropped his books and crutches to the ground, and lowered himself onto the bench. Cindi understood what football meant to him, and he needed her now more than ever.

He set the bench press weight, peeled off his sweater, and took a deep breath. He would show those colleges what he was made of. He lay back on the bench and began sets of bench presses, gradually increasing the weight. Sure, he was injured, but did that mean he had to stop training? No, it didn't. He could do this; he knew he could. He would show his dad that he was as disciplined as ever. And he would show Cindi that he was the same guy she believed in.

After bench presses, he moved to the machine for curls. He sat with his triceps on top of the foam cylinder and began sets of pull-ups. He grunted as he increased the weight. The vein running along his right bicep and disappearing into the sleeve of his T-shirt began to bulge. He broke a sweat. He had found a rhythm.

The weight room was quiet. It felt calm and familiar. He stayed there for the rest of the school day.

———

Tom kept doing upper-body workouts, going to school, and spending time with Cindi while he waited for the appointment when the doctor would finally remove his cast. Cindi often took Tom to the school gym to lift weights early in the morning.

"We need to decide on the college we're going to," she said one morning, looking up from the novel she was reading for her English class.

Tom paused. He had not heard from Ohio State—or any new college, for that matter—since he'd been injured, and he knew his father had been contacting the colleges that had offered him scholarships.

"We're still waiting for OSU," he said, gripping the bench press handles a little more tightly, "but it could be any day now."

"It's taking longer than usual, isn't it?" Cindi asked. She bookmarked her novel and closed it. "We have to make our plans."

Tom was no longer sweating just from lifting. He felt uneasy with Cindi's questioning.

"I have a lot of good schools to choose between," he said.

"I know we do. I just want to know which one."

"We still have months," he said, "then we'll pick one together." He didn't know what else to do except start lifting again. Cindi frowned. She looked as if she was about to say something else when a few guys from the basketball team came in.

"Hey, O'Brien. Hey, Cindi," the starting center for the basketball team said, slightly taller than Tom but probably fifty pounds lighter. "Up early, aren't you?" Tom smiled and continued to lift. He looked at Cindi, who said she would find him before first period.

She picked up her books and left.

———

After six weeks, they finally removed his cast. His leg was pale and dry. It had tingled when the cast was being sawed off, which was scary, but the doctor said the tingling would pass. He'd lost muscle definition in his leg.

It was clearly smaller than his other leg, and the dead skin on it was flaky and smelly.

The doctor put a temporary walking cast on Tom's foot until his limping improved and sent him and his father back to the waiting room for his physical therapy session. After reading the doctor's notes and examining Tom's foot, the therapist showed him a series of exercises to help his Achilles tendon heal and recover. Tom began the exercises at home immediately and was able to do them multiple times a day over Christmas break.

Once school started, Tom dedicated himself to a daily routine of exercise. He continued to get up early to go to the gym to lift weights before his classes. As soon as he got home, he went down to the basement and began his therapy exercises of stretching, strengthening, and icing, gradually increasing his repetitions. He often continued after dinner, sometimes stretching in his room before bed, facing his Ohio State poster.

Tom's father periodically asked about his treatment. Every once in a while, his father's shadow appeared at the top of the basement stairs, and Tom knew he was standing there. Tom's mother continued to prepare the kinds of meals she did during the football season, and Tom, disciplined as ever, kept his diet healthy.

Cindi sometimes came by when he was doing his rehab exercises and sat on the basement couch, watching TV, tackling bits of homework, or making plans for their college years. She would live in the women's dorm; he would live in the men's dorm for athletes; she would become head cheerleader, and they would travel together to his away games. When Tom would be named to the All-American team, she would be by his side, and they would eventually move in together. And then, after graduation, he would be drafted by an NFL team.

One afternoon when Tom's parents had left the house, he sat next to Cindi on the couch and kissed her, pushing her down gently to recline her back.

"You haven't done your therapy yet," she said matter-of-factly. Cindi monitored his progress even closer than his father did.

"I thought we could take a break," he said, smiling and going in for a kiss again.

"No, I don't think that's a good idea," she said. "The only way to get back is to do the work."

Cindi was right. He reluctantly got up and started his exercises. She smiled at him and returned to her homework. When he was done, she came over, put her arms around him, and kissed him.

Before long, they were making out and breathing heavily. He started taking her sweater off when the sound of the door opening downstairs startled them from their reverie.

"We're home," his mother called near the top of the stairs. Tom quickly helped Cindi pull her sweater back down and then leaped up from the couch. There was a small but familiar twinge in his calf, but it was probably just because of the way he'd jumped up, or the way his leg was healing.

He had noticed the twinge occasionally when he did particular stretches and once when he was walking in town with some of the other football players. But hadn't he done everything the doctor and therapist had asked him to do? The students at Massillon Washington High School still treated him as one of their finest athletes. His relationship with Cindi was more intimate than ever. And people in Massillon were still interested in his future.

"We're going to see you on TV one day, young man," Mr. Byrne said, peering over his wire rim glasses when Tom popped into the drugstore on an errand for his mother.

"Thank you, sir," Tom said. He hoped that was true.

By late April, four months since the accident—Tom felt he still had every reason to feel positive. He'd been disciplined in completing his therapy. His tendon was still tender after walking, but what could he have done any better?

———

Tom and his father waited in the exam room for the doctor. The room of bare, white walls was colder than Tom remembered, and he almost shivered in his gown. He felt nervous and exposed under the fluorescent lights. His reflection was distorted in some of the chrome equipment near him.

"How does it feel?" the doctor asked as he opened the door.

"Good. It hurts a little when I walk." He hadn't meant to lead with that information. He'd wanted the doctor to do an independent assessment. Tom's father looked at him, and he felt guilty that he had kept the pain to himself.

The doctor motioned for Tom to move back on the table and straighten his legs. The paper crinkled beneath him. The doctor rubbed his hands together to warm them, then took Tom's right foot and gently rotated it to the right.

"Tell me when it hurts."

Nothing. Tom was quiet.

The doctor stopped rotating and moved Tom's foot slowly up and down. When the doctor applied pressure, pulling Tom's toes toward his knee, Tom winced. His father became very still.

"That hurts?"

Tom nodded, his throat suddenly dry.

The doctor gently pressed the tendon above his heel, moving around his calf. When he reached the center of the calf, Tom inhaled and groaned quietly.

"Do you feel that pain when you do your stretches?" the doctor asked.

"Once in a while."

"You said it gets worse as you walk?"

"Yeah, after a half-hour or so maybe."

The doctor turned to his father, who had been staring at Tom intently.

"He has Achilles tendonitis, which causes microtears. He needs to reduce his stretching and walking until there's no pain."

Microtears? Tendonitis?

His father looked around the exam room and then turned to face the window.

"When can I start working out?" Tom asked. He was afraid of the answer.

"You need to scale back for at least two months," the doctor said. "Then we'll resume your therapy after that."

His father turned back to the doctor. "He has scholarship offers to play football in the fall, I think you know." His voice was quiet.

"That may not be possible."

"They'll want a doctor's statement. What will you say?"

"I would need to put down Achilles tendinopathy, needing six months of rest and therapy."

Tom quickly counted the months. That was October! His stomach dropped. That meant he probably wouldn't be able to begin football practice for the fall 1966 college season. He knew his father was thinking the same thing.

The room was silent.

The doctor told him to return in two months, shook both their hands, and left the room. Tom's father went into the hallway while Tom changed back into his clothes.

His father looked straight ahead as they walked down the hall afterward. "You overstretched," he said.

"I did what they told me to do!" Tom said. His father did not respond.

Tom felt a stinging in his eyes and was embarrassed they were wet. He realized he had just lost his dreams and plans, and he hoped he wasn't partly to blame. He felt sick to his stomach.

4

As instructed, Tom cut back on exercising and tried to avoid stretching his calf. He stopped going down to the basement to stretch and took a break from early morning upper-body exercises at school. But it was hard to do nothing. His future depended on his leg getting better. Why couldn't he heal and be like other seniors who were accepting offers to colleges?

Cindi, when she heard he wouldn't be able to play in the fall, looked exasperated. "Wait. What does that mean for us?" He reached out to pull her close and reassure her, but she drew back. "Is your leg actually going to heal?"

"Yeah," he said, surprised by her reaction. "It's just taking a little longer than planned. We have nothing to worry about." He bent lower to give her a kiss, but her lips were not very responsive. She furrowed her eyebrows and sighed.

She continued to have questions the next day when Tom walked with her to her locker. "We've put a lot of work into getting you stronger," she said. A group of kids walked past, and she straightened up, smiling and stepping closer to Tom. After they passed, her smile faded a little. "What are we going to do?" she asked under her breath.

"We'll be all right," he said.

"I hope so." She closed her locker more loudly than usual. "Right now, I don't even know where I'm supposed to be in the fall." She gave him a pointed look, then walked away.

Tom focused on doing what he could—keeping his grades up to help hold onto his scholarships, returning to upper-body workouts, and trying to please Cindi. But she didn't have as much time to spend with him. She said that with graduation approaching, she had a lot on her mind and needed to make sure she finished strong in her classes. He understood that, but why was she so distant? He missed her driving home with him after school, sitting near him on the basement couch, or sidling up to him in his room. He couldn't shake his loneliness and dreaded thinking about a future without her.

———

When the first of Tom's scholarships was withdrawn, he was in the kitchen helping his mother get a platter down from a high shelf before dinner. He turned around to hand the platter to her and his father was standing in the kitchen doorway.

"We need to cross one off the list," his father said quietly. The phone had rung about ten minutes earlier, and he knew his father had been talking to someone in his study.

"Cross one what off the list?" Tom's grandpa asked from the living room. He was there to join them for dinner that night, and his father frowned at the question. Rather than answering, he looked directly at Tom. Tom's heart went into his throat.

"One college," Tom said to Grandpa in the other room. Tom's mother held the platter to her chest.

"It's just one, Tommy," she said. "You have others."

Tom felt dizzy. Through a haze, he listened as his father described the call. The admissions officer had told his father how much the college regretted the decision, but they needed someone who was ready to play on the team in the fall. His father's eyes stayed focused on Tom.

Tom's grandpa appeared in the doorway with the whiskey he'd been drinking. "Don't you worry, Tommy boy. You're going to be just fine," he said.

Tom's father glared at Grandpa impatiently. "You won't be fine if you don't do what's necessary," Tom's father said, turning his eyes back to him. "This could have been prevented, but you overstretched."

Tom breathed in, slowly filling his lungs and taking in his father's words. He was breaking into a cold sweat.

With the exception of his mother saying grace, they ate dinner in silence. Tom's father chewed slowly, his face expressionless as he cut through a pork chop with precision. Tom's grandpa shook his head from time to time and took drinks of his whiskey, the ice clinking in his glass. Kara, when she heard the news, had said, "Those idiots!" but she was otherwise quiet, seemingly to let the situation play out between Tom and their father.

Tom wanted to escape to his room to sort out his thoughts and get his emotions in check. His stomach was churning, and he was not about to get any food down. But he stayed planted in his chair—sitting there with the people who had poured themselves into him and his future—he owed them that at least, after the disappointment he had caused.

———

By the middle of May, Tom's scholarship offers had all been withdrawn. He never heard from Ohio State. The only college that had called him—in addition to sending a short form letter like the others—was Kent State, a football program that had not interested him because its conference was at a level below the Big Ten. The Kent State coach who called asked Tom to let him know when he was fully recovered. It was nice to have that, at least. Tom felt the weight of his father's frustration every day.

Cindi frowned when Tom told her all his scholarships had been withdrawn. She had seemed as frustrated as Tom's father as the letters from colleges came in that spring. When she and Tom were together, she didn't embrace him as closely as she used to. Her kisses lacked the same passion and enthusiasm, and she often suggested they hang out with friends in town rather than do things by themselves. While out with others, she laughed more at things other people said than at what he said. He began to feel alone even when he was with her.

Cindi passed Tom's mother on the front walk one afternoon as she was leaving and his mother was returning from a weekday mass. From the front door where Tom stood, he watched his mother study Cindi's face.

"How's Cindi?" his mother asked Tom when she reached the top of the steps.

"She's fine," he said, feigning a smile. "Just busy—meeting up with friends to study." He didn't actually know where Cindi was headed. She'd simply said she was late and needed to go.

His mother held his arm and gazed at him when he opened the door for her. She had put her graying hair up into a bun, and she wasn't wearing her usual housedress. "I know losing your scholarships is hard on you," she said, looking up at him with concern, dark circles beneath her eyes. "I've been praying for you." She reached into her purse to remove her rosary beads.

A lump rose up in Tom's throat. He wanted to tell his mother that he had no idea what he was going to do with his life; that with everything he'd prepared for now gone, he wasn't sure what he had to look forward to; that it was like the end of who he knew himself to be. But he stayed silent.

"In hard times in my life, I've always had church and prayer to fall back on," his mother said. "Why don't you try it?" She pressed her rosary beads into his hand.

Tom nodded, not surprised by her religious faith. "I'll think about it," he said. But he didn't see how church could help him. Other than the Hail Marys his mother had taught him when he was young, he didn't feel prayer would make a difference. He had dutifully attended church on Sundays with the rest of the family, but he didn't see the point. He loved his mother, but he hoped she would drop the topic.

She seemed to understand this and hugged him.

"You'll get through this," she said, giving him a small smile and entering the house. But would he? He was supposed to be a freshman starting college with a full-ride athletic scholarship. But without football and a team to play for, he was at a loss. How long was he going to be stuck in Massillon with a leg that wouldn't heal, while Cindi and his friends moved on?

———

"I hear they took back your scholarship offers," Jack said one Saturday evening. He had popped by unannounced.

"Yeah," Tom said, his eyes on the TV screen. His parents were at a dinner party, and he was watching an Indians baseball game in the living room. He had hoped to be alone with Cindi that evening, but she wanted to go to a party, so she had gone without him. He'd turned on the TV but wasn't really paying attention. The room had grown dark around him as dusk set in, with only the glow of the TV on his face. He sat with his arms folded and his feet on the coffee table.

"It's not the end of the world," Jack said, taking a seat in the armchair Tom's father usually sat in. "You can still apply to colleges without a scholarship."

Tom was silent. Jack had been accepted into the engineering program at Miami of Ohio. Vince, Tony, and many of his other friends had also been accepted by colleges and were making their final decisions for the fall. They were probably celebrating and talking about their plans at the party Cindi was attending. Tom continued to stare at the TV. He didn't even know who was ahead.

"Look," Jack said. "People are worried about you, and I don't like seeing you like this. Why don't you come over tonight? My mom's out on a date, and my brother bought some beer for friends he's having over. He said I could bring a friend."

"I don't think so," Tom said, but the thought of not being alone had some appeal.

"C'mon! You're being stupid. I'll drag you out if I need to."

Tom hesitated, thinking if his boring friend could have some beer, so could he. "Okay," he said. "But I don't want to talk about college tonight. And I don't want to talk about my future."

"Alright. Deal," Jack said. "Now hurry up. This is just depressing here." He stood up to flip off the TV, turn on some lamps, and wait at the door with his keys.

Tom got up, his mood suddenly changed about the prospects for the evening. He had been out of sorts ever since the injury, obsessed with getting better, and he'd been way too intense. "Hold on," he said, and went over to the liquor cabinet. He took out the bottle of Irish whiskey that only Grandpa used when he was over. He had poured glasses of it for Grandpa before but never tried any.

"What are you doing?" Jack asked.

Tom had watched Grandpa relax many times with a glass of whiskey. Why not try it? If it helped him become more easygoing and understanding like Grandpa, that would be fine with him.

"I need to be a little more free and easy," Tom said out loud, more to himself than to Jack. He opened the cap and took a small swig straight from the bottle. It tasted like fire, and he coughed violently for a second or two. His eyes watering, he quickly replaced the cap. "You?" he asked with a gravelly voice, holding out the bottle. Jack shook his head disapprovingly.

"Come on, O'Brien. Let's go." Tom replaced the bottle, coughed several more times, and left with Jack.

Tom used to bike to Jack's house when he was younger and would pass the playground with the two seesaws, the mailbox shaped like a barn, and the field where he and Jack would play Pop Warner football games. He and Jack had a lot of history. Jack pulled his car into the driveway behind a couple of other cars. The basketball hoop still hung above the garage.

The house was warm. Tom was a little light-headed from the whiskey as he carefully followed Jack down the stairs. There was laughter in the basement as they descended. At the bottom, Jack led Tom to the basement bar, where Jack's twenty-two-year-old brother and friends were drinking beer and watching the same Indians game Tom had been watching at home.

"Hey, O'Brien," Jack's brother said. "Long time, no see." He gestured to one of his friends to hand Tom a beer. "That's a tough break, man, but don't worry—you'll recover and play football again."

"That was a hell of a season you guys had," one friend wearing a blazer with neatly combed hair said.

"Shit. How tall are you?" another friend asked, a short and heavy-set guy with bloodshot eyes. His words were slurred, and he looked unsteadily up at Tom.

"Thanks for the beer, fellas," Jack said, grabbing a beer of his own and pushing Tom away from the conversation.

Tom sat down on the same striped couch he remembered from his youth. He opened his beer and touched it to his lips. He liked it a lot better than the whiskey. He took a big sip, leaned back against the cushions, and let the alcohol work on him while Jack's brother and friends argued about whether the Indians would win more games than they would lose this season. Jack sat down next to Tom and sipped his beer.

"How's your dad?" Jack asked.

"Why?" Tom immediately grew wary.

"He encouraged me to apply for engineering school. I haven't talked to him since I was accepted."

Tom was silent, annoyed as usual whenever he heard how encouraging his father was to Jack.

"Your dad is one of the good ones," Jack said. "Ever since I was a kid, he's watched out for me. He told me I could learn about life from sports, and he's a huge reason why I stuck with baseball all those years once I figured out football wasn't for me."

Tom had heard this many times before and was sick of it. "How's your dad doing? Is he still in California?" he asked Jack.

Jack's face became more serious. "I don't know. I haven't talked to him in a long time." He adjusted his glasses and looked at the game on the TV.

"That's a home run!" Jack's brother yelled. Jack jumped up and went to the bar as the TV announcer said it was hit by Rocky Colavito, tying the score in the ninth inning.

"Looks like extra innings!" Jack said. "Rocky came through again." He climbed onto a barstool.

Tom lay back on the couch again, glad that the baseball game had interrupted their conversation. He sipped his beer and closed his eyes while Jack and the others cheered on the Indians. His thoughts turned to his early elementary-school years, when he continued to enjoy throwing and kicking his football with his father and Grandpa. They often disagreed on how to coach him, so the advice he received was usually from just one or the other, never both at the same time.

More than once, Grandpa had reminded Tom's father that he had played on an undefeated Massillon team that won the state championship, unlike the Massillon teams that Tom's father played on. It was a sore point that seemed to bring out anger about all sorts of things between Tom's father and Grandpa. On one rare occasion when they'd both had a glass of whiskey, Tom had heard his father shout at Grandpa that Grandpa never saw his good points.

Tom felt the same way. His father seldom seemed to comment on what Tom did well. Tom wanted to feel close to his dad, but he just heard his father's criticisms—whenever he threw a ball wrong, scored too low on a test, forgot to put away sports equipment, or didn't say something politely enough.

"He does love you. Very much," his mother had told him on numerous occasions, but Tom never heard this from his dad. She said that sometimes his father didn't have time to show his love because of his job and his obligations with the National Guard, which he had joined after World War II because he had been too young to fight in the war.

Once, when Tom was thirteen, he cried angry tears all the way home from a game after being chewed out by his father for causing his team to be penalized twice for being offsides. They drove home in silence until his father went into the house.

"Your dad had a hard time growing up," his mother said. She and Tom remained in the car in the darkness, and he could see her silhouette turned around in her seat. "Grandpa expected a lot of him and wasn't always the best example."

"What do you mean?" Tom asked. He'd wiped his nose too roughly with the back of his arm, and his nose felt raw.

"You know. Grandpa likes to drink his whiskey and beer, and your dad had to be more like the grownup sometimes. Grandpa would come home from working long hours at the foundry and then he'd drink whiskey for most of the night. Your dad had to figure things out younger than some other kids did." She shifted against the vinyl seat. "He went straight from high school to his job in the steel plant, and unlike Grandpa, was promoted out of the foundry. I know Grandpa loves your dad, just like your dad loves you, but Grandpa never took it easy on him."

Tom supposed he could understand his father's frustration with his own father. But Tom valued his grandpa, who, no matter how much he drank, had always encouraged Tom through the years. He would rather have a drunk Grandpa who showed him love than a sober father who didn't.

Tom's thoughts were interrupted by Jack sitting down beside him on the basement couch. "What are you dreaming about?" Jack asked. "You're missing quite a game. The Indians are ahead by one in the bottom of the tenth."

"I was thinking about playing football with my grandpa when I was a kid." Tom finished his beer and stood up. "But now I'm ready for another beer."

Tom and Jack went over to Jack's brother and friends, and Tom opened a beer. The Indians needed two more outs to win the game. Tom joked and laughed with the group, cheering and commenting on the Indians' fortunes along with everyone else. He was enjoying himself, more relaxed than he had been in weeks. Nobody was asking him to make a decision about his future.

When the Indians won, Jack's brother turned off the TV and announced it was time for them to go to the bars to look for women. He and his friends got ready to leave. Too young to join them, Jack and Tom headed out.

"Do you want to go to the party where Cindi is?" Jack asked after they got in his car. Tom pictured being around people who would talk about graduation and college and ask him questions about himself. He was wearing sweatpants from earlier and he was disheveled. Cindi would be embarrassed by him.

"How about we hang out in the basement at my house?" Tom said. The beer had left him in a mellow mood, and he didn't want to deal with the usual high school crowd.

Jack nodded and drove back toward Tom's house. They had each had two beers—enough to feel something, but Tom knew it was not enough to be obvious. When they entered through the front door, Tom's father was watching TV.

Tom's father smiled at them from his armchair, but it quickly became apparent that his father was mostly pleased to see Jack. He and Jack chatted about Jack's engineering program in the fall and when Jack would be moving to school. Tom shifted his weight, waiting for their conversation to end, feeling ignored, and becoming increasingly more irritated. "You've come a long way," his father said to Jack. "You've worked hard and have a lot to be proud of."

Tom stared at his father.

"Thank you, sir," Jack said, his face becoming flushed. Tom felt betrayed. He caught Jack's eye and frowned. "I mean, we both have," Jack said to Tom's father. "Tom's one of the hardest workers I've seen, and if it wasn't for what happened, he'd be playing this fall for sure. I've encouraged him to apply to college anyway. Even if he can't play yet, he can still start school."

Why wouldn't Jack just shut up? He didn't need this kind of encouragement.

"We'll see," Tom's father said, looking at Tom. Tom couldn't hide his anger from his father. "Right now, he's feeling pretty sorry for himself."

Tom clenched his jaw and moved toward the stairs.

"See you later, Jack. I'm going to my room."

"Okay," Jack said slowly. "I'll talk to you tomorrow."

Tom didn't answer as he made his way up the stairs. He could only imagine the looks Jack and his father were exchanging. When he finally entered his bedroom, he slammed the door behind him.

Tom sat down on his bed, still seething with anger. He didn't know *what* to think. Did his father care about him or not? Why was he always knocking Tom down when Tom needed his help? Why had it always been so much easier for his father to show support to Jack instead of him? It was suffocating to have his father expect so much of him, when he just wanted to be close. Tom balled one of his hands into a fist and brought it down onto his mattress. Where was the kindness and understanding that dads were supposed to give their sons?

He lay back against the pillows propped up on his bed and stared at the ceiling. He could still taste the beer from earlier. Getting a little buzzed again would be better than what he felt now. Besides having an uncaring father, he didn't know his future; he was losing Cindi; and he still couldn't walk without favoring his leg. He was tired of constantly thinking of and worrying about these things. And there was no one to talk to about it. No one truly understood what he was going through.

Tom tried to think of something positive, something to stop his downward spiral. He'd had a good time with Jack's brother and friends. It had been easy to hang out with them, and he had been a happier version of himself—untroubled by his college situation and unencumbered by anyone else's expectations. Those guys didn't know him that well, just that he was a good athlete.

He closed his eyes. He was on the field again. No leg injury. No pain in his calf. Just running and blocking, pushing people aside, making holes for Vince to run through, picturing the green of the field, the yellowish hue of stadium lights on his uniform, the colors of his school, orange and black, giving way to scarlet. Tom breathed deeply and his thoughts drifted. He was exhausted.

5

When all else failed, Tom did what was automatic to him—setting some new goals to get himself back onto the football field and committing himself to them. This had always served him well in the past.

But as the days went by, this became harder and harder. He tried to stay in shape by using his father's stationary bicycle and weights, but regular exercise that wasn't tied to the team took a kind of self-motivation he lacked at the moment. He didn't have regular games to look forward to, a real prospect for the fall, or anyone really pushing him. His father seemed frustrated with him all the time, and they had exchanged only a few words since the night Tom had slammed his bedroom door while his father talked to Jack. Tom's workouts became sporadic.

By the beginning of June, Tom had gained a bit of weight and grown lethargic from watching hours of TV. He was sleeping more, studying less, and skipping school here and there. Kara complained about his wet bath towel and dirty clothes on the floor of their bathroom. His mother reminded him to bring down the used dishes in his room. He could hear the two of them talking about him in the kitchen sometimes, their voices hushed and worried.

His father, one evening, went up to the TV to change the channel from the baseball game Tom was watching to the world news, presumably to get Tom to do something else. Tom fumed from his position on the couch, then went upstairs, with only the sound of the report on Vietnam trailing up behind him. That was the most his father had acknowledged him all week.

When Tom did leave the house, other than for school, it was to go to drink beer with friends, some of them former Massillon football players who'd already graduated. He and his buddies would drink while they drove down gravel roads in the country, throwing their empty cans into roadside ditches as they went. Tom liked the feel of the wind through the open window and the smell of the country air. Nights like this were an escape from the pressures of his situation. He didn't need to do much more than just enjoy his beer and laugh with the guys about old times playing football.

Tom often stared in the bathroom mirror. His body was becoming rounded and fleshy. What would he look like if he kept this up? Without a college that wanted him—or a girlfriend who wanted him—he'd let his therapy completely fall by the wayside, and he was no longer the strongest version of himself. Graduation was around the corner, and he had no plans for what to do next. His stomach ached when he thought about it.

———

In the hallways at school and around town, everyone knew he'd lost his scholarships. People were supportive at first. They spoke to him as if it were a given he would play college football at some point. But as word spread that he hadn't applied to any schools, most everyone avoided talking to him about his future.

"What are you doing?" Cindi asked one day as they sat in a booth at the Burger Grill, surrounded by noisy students.

"What do you mean?" he asked. He hadn't wanted to go out in public, but she'd insisted.

"You've stopped physical therapy, you're not in shape, and you're barely studying."

"I just need a little time to get my act together. I can't help it that my leg isn't cooperating."

"I thought we had something special," she said, her eyes on the saltshaker. When she looked up, she didn't have the usual big smile he'd always loved. Instead, she was studying him, as if trying to figure out who he was.

The waitress arrived with their burgers, and Tom sat back.

"We do. You know how much I love you," he said as soon as the waitress departed. The smell of the burgers was making him nauseated.

"You can show me you love me by deciding what colleges you'll apply to."

"I'll do it this week," he said quickly.

Cindi sighed. "I have to know what you're planning. I applied to Ohio State because I thought they would give you a scholarship. They just sent me an acceptance letter. I've been waiting to see where you're going and maybe go with you. But you still haven't told me if you're even applying to colleges." Tom froze at the mention of Ohio State. He knew he should be happy for Cindi, but a part of him was intensely jealous. He also realized her plans to go to college might mean she would leave him.

"I'll figure it out soon. You're pushing me too much," he said, his throat tight. He didn't know if he wanted to yell at her or cry.

"I don't like the smell of beer on your breath every weekend," she said. "I think you have more plans to go out drinking than you do for your future. Am I even in your future?"

"Of course!" He tried to reach across the table for her hands, but she didn't return his touch. Her eyes were glistening, but her face was defiant.

"Then show me," she said, then she got up to leave.

Tom watched her as she exited the restaurant, her tight blue jeans and sweater, her blond hair curling at her shoulders, her confidence. She was the girl who had always beamed at him and caught his eye from along the sidelines. He knew she wanted a future with him as a successful football player. But there was no guarantee he'd ever be able to play like he had in his days at Massillon. Would that even be enough for her? He wished she could understand his pain.

Students and other customers went past Tom's booth in the busy restaurant. They finished eating, made their plans, and got up to go, moving on to the next place. All the while, Tom sat there alone in his booth with two uneaten burgers, feeling life go on without him.

———

Tom didn't apply to any colleges that week. He kept to himself in his room, often sitting at his desk trying to do homework but instead rereading his letters of rejection. He couldn't see a future for himself at any particular college if he wasn't going to play football. At school, he waited for Cindi at her locker at their usual times, but when she didn't show up, he took to avoiding her in the hallways.

Toward the end of the following week, he found Cindi waiting for him in the parking lot after school. She had been sitting on the hood of a car, talking with some other cheerleaders and football players. Her arms were folded, and when she saw Tom, she got up and came over to him.

"Can we talk?" she asked. Tom's heart started racing. She gestured toward the side of the parking lot near some bleachers, and he followed her, a few paces behind.

"Hey, O'Brien," someone yelled out a car window as they drove past. The music from inside the car grew faint as it made its way down the row. He saw Curt, Vince, and a group of friends walk up to the car where Cindi had been sitting.

Tom stopped when Cindi turned around to face him.

Her lips were pink and frosty with lip gloss, and she pursed them together. "Look, I thought you were for me. I really did," she said. "But I can see now you're not." It sounded to Tom like she had rehearsed it.

Though Tom had prepared himself for this on some level, he still felt like he'd been hit by a blow harder than any he'd ever received on a football field. "Why?" he asked her, his throat dry. He tried to search her eyes.

"I wanted to go to college with you—to have a future with you," she said, looking at him squarely. "But you never even applied. You just mope around." That was like a second blow.

"You know I'm having a hard time." The afternoon sun was harsh, and he began to sweat. His collar was scratchy. "Why can't you stay with me while I work this out?"

She stepped closer to put her hand on his forearm. "I wish you hadn't gotten hurt and things were different, but you're just not you anymore. I can't do this with you." She turned from him to go.

Tom watched her cross the parking lot and get into one of her girlfriends' cars. When the car was out of sight, he went to the far side of the bleachers and struck down on the wooden bleacher with the fleshy side of his fist, his eyes closed tightly, trying to stop his tears.

In his last weeks of high school, Tom spent most of his time in his room with the door closed or with his friends, often driving and drinking beer on country roads. Maybe his injury was a sign that he wasn't even supposed to go to college. If that were true, it meant he would need to get a job after graduation, but he made no move to find one. He was stuck in a holding pattern, and his whole family was waiting to see what he would do next.

Tom wallowed in his room. His football career had ended before it even began, and Cindi, the most gorgeous girl he'd ever been with, had left him. He pictured her at parties, her beautiful eyes broadcasting her availability to other boys the same way she'd always used them to draw him to her. In a sorry state one Saturday night, he hurled a football at the opposite wall of his room. His trophies on the bookshelf rattled, some pens rolled off, and the photo of Cindi and him from the homecoming dance fell over.

Tom barely passed his last high school courses—surprising his teachers, who had always been used to him getting good grades. When he walked across the stage to receive his diploma, the vice principal didn't have the name of the college Tom would be attending, so he instead touted Tom's athletic achievements. People cheered, but Tom couldn't help feeling their enthusiasm was somehow more subdued than if he had plans to play college football in the fall.

Tom saw his mother, Kara, and Grandpa applauding him, but his father sat quietly. It stung, and he felt heavy as he slowly made his way back to his seat.

After the ceremony, he threw his cap into the air like everyone else and took the requisite photos with his family, his father standing stiffly next to him. The Massillon Tiger band played the school song as everyone shuffled out of the building. The song had once filled him with tremendous pride as he stood along the football field with his helmet in his hand. Today, it made those days seem far away, his once illustrious high school experience now literally a thing of the past.

—

With nowhere to be that summer and nothing really to do, Tom started hanging out with a larger group of ex-football players whose plans varied—some preparing to go to college or technical schools, and others, like Tom, undecided. The friends all loved to party, so drinking soon became a regular weekly ritual. They would have beer and laugh for hours, and no one gave him a hard time about what he should or shouldn't be doing.

These parties got bigger after graduation, with the biggest ones held on a nearby river sandbar. It was at one of these sandbar parties that Tom spotted Cindi from a distance. She was standing close to his friend Curt, quarterback of the football team, who had his arm around her shoulders. Cindi's arm was around Curt's waist, pressing her body against his.

With a sharp pang in his chest, he began to move backward in the crowd, trying to make himself inconspicuous. He knew he stood taller than many of the people there, so he found his way to a campfire on the other side of the sandbar and sat down on a log. Jack had seen Cindi too, and followed him.

"Sorry, buddy," Jack said. "I heard they'd started seeing each other but didn't know they would be here." He reached into a cooler and handed Tom a beer.

Tom tried to control his emotions, but he couldn't speak. He downed several cans of beer in a row while Jack sat next to him, drinking quietly. Though Tom tried not to look, his eyes kept lingering in the direction where he'd spotted Cindi. At a certain point, he abruptly stood up, staggered toward the woods, and vomited, telling Jack when he returned to the campfire that he'd need him to drive him home later. He then had another beer and spent the rest of the evening staring at the fire, not caring that the smoke blew toward him and at times seemed to envelop him, stinging his eyes.

——

The next day, Tom came down to the kitchen for a late breakfast wearing a wrinkled T-shirt he'd found balled up in his covers. He hadn't yet combed his hair and still had pillow lines on his left cheekbone. The light from the window over the sink reflected off the laminate tabletop and intensified his already splitting headache. He was incredibly thirsty.

Tom's mother was standing at the counter, biting her fingernails and watching him as he entered. Tom moved past her to get orange juice from the refrigerator. There was a newspaper splayed out on the counter.

"Hi, Tommy," she said. "You sleep well?"

"I slept alright," he said, taking out a glass from a cabinet and filling it to the top with juice.

"Did you and Jack have a good time last night?"

Tom, gulping down the juice, paused and said, "Mm-hmm," into the glass. Her face was distorted through the glass, but he could still make out her worried frown.

"I saw an article in this morning's paper about some kids being arrested for underage drinking last night," she said, turning the newspaper on the counter so that it faced him. "They were at the sandbar. Weren't you at that party?" she asked.

"No," Tom said, thinking the arrests must have happened after he and Jack left. Tom finished his juice, poured a bowl of cereal, and sat down with his back against the window, hoping his mother would change the subject. She looked at him without speaking for several seconds.

"I know the disappointments you've had this year," she said, moving to put two slices of bread into the toaster for him, "but I want you to know that you are a wonderful person and a wonderful son. Your whole life doesn't have to be about football."

"But what if I want it to be?" Tom asked, looking at her.

"It already is. I'm letting you know there's more to you than just that." She went to get his toast, brought him some butter and jam, and sat down across from him at the kitchen table.

"Like what?" he asked.

"Like you have to go find out," she said. "You've graduated now. Your father . . . we . . . are wondering what you're going to do." She waited, but Tom didn't answer. "You can go to college and not play football, you know," she said after another moment.

Tom couldn't conceive of going to college without playing football. His spoon slipped from where it had been balanced against the edge of his cereal bowl. "College doesn't need to happen right away," he said.

His mother sighed. "I know your father wants to help," she said. "Your injury has been as hard on him as it has been on you." Tom was caught off-guard hearing this. He sincerely doubted it. His father's harsh words and condemnation always rang in his ears.

"If Dad is having a hard time, he has a hell of a way of showing it," Tom said. Her face became still.

"Your pain is his pain, Tommy. He's so disappointed . . ."

". . . by me," Tom said.

". . . *for* you," she said. "He wants to help but doesn't know how. He doesn't like what he's seeing happen with you right now."

Tom loved his mother, but this was getting to be annoying. It felt like his father going through his mother to criticize him. "Well, college isn't happening yet. I think I should get a job first. If he wants to help, he can help me with that," he said.

She frowned but then seemed to recover. "Okay, Tommy," she said. She got up to pour him more juice. "Then ask him. He only wants what's best for you." She filled his glass to the top and kissed him in his smoky hair.

Tom cleared his throat slightly but didn't say anything more. He hated himself for having been short with his mother. He reached out to hug her for a moment.

——

After supper a few nights later, Tom took the dishes to the kitchen for his mother and Kara, so he could create an opportunity to speak with his father. When he returned to the table to pick up the bread plate and last few utensils, his father was there reading the newspaper. Tom stood uncomfortably next to him, but his father didn't acknowledge him. Tom saw a headline about increased military forces in South Vietnam. He moved the spoons around in his hand to make a little noise.

"Do you need something, Tom?" his father asked without looking up.

"I need to find a job. Do you have any ideas?"

"I'm glad you're finally thinking of that," his father said. He flipped to a different page. "You've been moping around ever since you lost your scholarships."

Tom felt a wave of anger. He stayed silent, trying to quickly collect himself, so he could behave like his mother would want him to. But this was not a good start to the conversation.

"I know your injury is a huge blow," his father added, breaking the quiet after a few moments. "I'm struggling with it myself, not knowing if I'll have a chance to see you play football again." Tom glanced at his father. He hadn't heard words like this from his father in a long time. He started to feel himself softening a little. "But life isn't easy," his father said, picking up the newspaper and folding it in half. He finally looked up at Tom, but he wasn't smiling. "You can't just give up. I've taught you better than that. You have to keep plugging away."

The warm feelings Tom had quickly evaporated. He didn't need to be lectured. "That's why I'm asking you about a job," he snapped. His tone caused his father's jaw to clench.

"Have you given up on college this fall?"

"I don't have plans for that right now."

"Remember what we've always talked about. You need to have purpose, and you need to have discipline. You can't get anywhere like this."

"Right. What about a job?"

His father looked down at the table, his chin pointing toward his chest. "There's a contractor the steel plant hires for remodeling and construction," he said. "I think they're looking for laborers. I'll give you the foreman's name and number." He straightened his shoulders a bit. "I think you can do better than this, but I suppose you'll figure that out. If you can't find a job, maybe you should join the army—it's been good for me, and I believe it would shape you up the way you need."

Tom's mother entered the dining room and asked if they wanted ice cream for dessert. Tom shook his head and rolled his eyes to signal to his mother his annoyance with the conversation he'd just had with his father.

Tom took the remaining dishes to the kitchen. He appreciated the lead for a job but couldn't believe he had to sit through yet another lecture. His father worked a job he obviously hated. He was angry at Grandpa all the time. He had a son who, despite his best efforts at raising him, had turned out to be a disappointment. Where had all his father's goal setting and discipline gotten him? And what had the army done for him except to give him a supreme sense of self-righteousness?

Tom didn't want this for himself. He didn't yet have a clear plan but at least he knew he needed to get out of his rut in some way—to do something different—and a job seemed like it was a start.

6

When Tom arrived at the job site, a worker made him wait, sizing him up for a few moments before finally calling for Dan, the foreman, from one of the upper levels of the three-story apartment building the crew was framing. Dan's head appeared, and then he descended, his thumbs hooked into his tool belt. He looked about forty and was average-sized; he squinted at Tom beneath his hard hat. He had a cigarette tucked at an angle in the side of his mouth. There was a ruddiness to his unshaven face, likely from working outside year-round.

"So, O'Brien, you're the football player," he said, his cigarette moving up and down as he spoke. It wasn't a question, and Tom didn't know if he was being positive or negative.

"Yeah."

"Are you just looking for a summer job before college?"

"I'm not going to college."

Still squinting, he dropped his eyes to Tom's leg. A few ashes came loose from the end of his cigarette. Had his father told him about the injury?

"That works," he said after a second or two. "I don't care for high school boys who leave when we've finally got them trained. You'll be available in the fall?"

"Yeah."

"You're definitely big enough," he said. "We could use some muscle to help with these materials." He jabbed a thumb at a big pile of lumber behind him.

Tom nodded, his interest in the job increasing. He wouldn't mind being valued for his strength again.

"If things work out, we'll train you to be a carpenter."

"Sounds good," Tom said. Presumably, becoming a carpenter would mean an increase in his pay.

"Okay," Dan said, throwing his cigarette into the dirt and putting it out with his boot. "I expect you to show up on time every day. No exceptions. This can be a challenge for high school kids, but I don't care what else you've got going on in your life. Just be ready to work. All right?"

Tom could get on board with that. He liked how Dan was so direct with him, how he was willing to let him prove himself. Everyone else in his life had been acting like he'd already let them down.

Tom shook Dan's hand.

For his first few days on the job, Tom made sure to show up early. When a truckload of lumber arrived, his task was to unload it and move pieces to different locations at the construction site where carpenters continued to frame the apartment building. The guys on the crew had apparently heard that he was all-state. They were mostly older than him, and none of them was built like him. They'd rib him about his youth and size, referring to him as "the baby giant," while he unloaded lumber next to them, and they'd make raunchy jokes about all the girls he'd supposedly had in his football years.

"How many?" one overweight carpenter called Smitty asked Tom just as Dan came up the ladder.

"How many what?" Dan said.

Smitty hesitated, looking down at the plywood floor. "We just wanted to know how many girls All-State has had."

"Boys, why don't you mess around on your own time," Dan said, taking a deep drag on his cigarette and exhaling. "Let's get back to work."

That's all it took. They were friendlier after that and mostly left him alone, though they still called him "All-State." Tom was okay with that, although he preferred not to be reminded of his football achievements at work. It was still too soon and too raw, and he was trying to begin a new chapter.

Dan took Tom under his wing, entrusting him with more responsibilities. Maybe he could actually learn something from a guy like this? The job did give him structure, at least, and he liked working with his hands, focusing on the task in front of him, and not thinking about football or girlfriends.

But then, after a couple of weeks, he started checking his watch more frequently, and wishing the time would go faster until his lunch break. Even if his dream of playing college football was over, shouldn't he be aiming for something more challenging than spending his days unloading two-by-fours?

He couldn't help but think about how, if he'd been accepted into a college football program, he'd be getting ready to train on a college campus in preparation for the fall season.

"Hey, All-State," Smitty said one afternoon. "Buck up. Whatever you got on your mind can't be *that* bad. Throw me those gloves."

Tom got back to work. This is what he'd signed up for, and he was determined to follow through. His days were filled with a combination of hard labor, self-contemplation, and joking with the other guys on Dan's crew. He knew these men were working for a paycheck and liked to relax in the evenings with some beers. He was in a different phase of life than they were, sure, but he began to wonder if maybe this was all he had to look forward to.

———

Before heading to a party they'd heard about one Saturday night, Tom and Jack went to the truck stop café on the highway known for burgers and brats. It was a summer gathering place and pre- and post-party hangout for students, and Tom was already a little buzzed from drinking before they got there. He'd turned to check out girls in different booths when he spotted Sam Peterson, a second-team football player he knew. Sam was a good guy, a high-energy linebacker who always wore his blond hair combed down over his forehead.

Sam came over to Tom and Jack, smiling broadly. "O'Brien, I heard you're working now. Good for you." He gave Tom a high five and perched on the stool next to him. "What are you guys up to tonight?"

"Party at the other end of town," Tom said, grateful that the first thing out of Sam's mouth wasn't a question about his leg. "Some guy's house we don't know. Come with us if you like."

Jack turned to a group of girls he'd been talking to while they waited for a booth and said, "Why don't you ladies come too?"

Sam smirked. "Looks like you guys might be busy. I'm already headed somewhere else with a couple of other friends." They chatted for a bit about his own job in the steel plant, and Sam said he and his friends were thinking of going into an apartment together. He helped himself to Jack's fries.

"We're looking at a four-bedroom apartment," Sam said, dipping a fry into Jack's ketchup, "so it might not happen unless we find a fourth person to go in with us."

"You're staying in town this fall?" Jack asked, swiveling around on his stool and tuning in. He scowled to see Sam eating his fries. The girls were talking to another guy as they moved to a booth.

"Yeah. I'll be right here," Sam said.

Tom was feeling like himself again. The atmosphere was relaxed in the café, and it was nice talking with his old friend. It felt almost like things had felt before his injury—but then a couple of Cindi's friends walked in. They had on the same pink lip gloss Cindi wore. He didn't want to talk to them.

"I think it's time to head to the party," he said. Jack nodded and crammed the last of his burger in his mouth. Tom slapped a few bills onto the counter, told Sam they should meet up again, and handed Jack the keys to his car.

Tom often let Jack drive his car that summer. It was his nod toward responsibility, given how much he was drinking. As soon as he got in the car, he opened a beer.

———

It was typical at a Saturday night party that after hours of drinking, listening to music, and laughing with each other, some guys and girls would pair up. By the time Tom and Jack pulled up at the party, some couples were already making out in cars parked outside the house. Inside, Tom grabbed a fresh beer, navigated around a couple embracing near the stairs, and settled down on a couch. His head was fuzzy from the drinking he'd done in the car. He blinked and looked around the room.

He finished another beer and noticed a girl smiling drunkenly at him from where she sat on a pillow on the floor with some friends. He didn't recognize her and assumed she was from another high school. Her skirt was hiked up a little higher on her thigh, but she didn't seem to notice. She took another drink of her beer, then stood up unsteadily and made her way to him.

"So, you were first-team all-state," she said, plopping onto the couch next to him and gazing up at him with bright eyes. Her skin looked smooth and soft, and her hair fell invitingly onto her shoulder.

"I guess I was," Tom said, smiling back at her. He moved his empty beer to his other hand and put his arm across the back of the couch. Without missing a beat, she moved under it, her body touching his. She felt warm against him, and they moved closer together. He realized he didn't know her name. She kissed him, and he pulled her toward him.

They continued to kiss, their mouths mashed together, her leg on his. She tasted like beer. When she got up to lead him down a hallway, he followed, sipping from a new beer as he went. He passed Jack, who was laughing loudly with some guys in the kitchen. Tom and the girl tried several rooms upstairs, all of them occupied, until they found an empty one at the end near the bathroom. As they entered the room, the girl stumbled and held Tom closely. They fell onto the bed, kissing and caressing each other, eventually taking off their shirts and her bra.

As the girl was fumbling with Tom's belt buckle, she suddenly said, "Wait, my head is spinning." She turned over to lie on her back and put her hand on her forehead. "Oh . . . too much beer." Tom drew back from her and asked her if she was all right, but she had fallen asleep.

Tom lay still in the dark with the girl sleeping beside him, breathing through her mouth. His head was spinning too. What would have happened if she hadn't fallen asleep? Was this the kind of sex he really wanted? He didn't even know her name! They'd barely spoken. Maybe he wasn't much different from any other drunken guy looking for sex.

His mind drifted to Cindi, and he pictured her making out with his so-called friend Curt, doing the same things with him that she'd done with Tom. He felt a sorrow set in. As much as beer could make him high, it could also bring him down, and he'd had more than usual that night. He sat up, moving slowly, and after turning his shirt around and around in his hands a few times, managed to pull it on. He found his shoes, then checked on the sleeping girl. She was snoring slightly. He placed her shirt and bra next to her on the bed and brought the covers up to cover her. He stumbled toward the bedroom door, bumping into a desk along the wall.

Out in the hallway, he passed by the open door of the bathroom where someone was loudly throwing up. He wanted to go home.

In the living room, he gestured up the stairs to let the girl's friends know where she was, but they seemed as drunk as he was. Where was Jack? There were too many other faces. He tried looking for him in the kitchen, but somehow ended up outside. He almost fell over as he stepped down from the entryway to the front walk.

Jack, the group of guys he'd been talking with, and a couple of girls were on the porch.

"O'Brien!" Jack said, his words coming out too loud. "We're going to another party. Wanna come?"

"No. Give me my keys."

"Are you sure you can drive?" Jack asked, digging around in his pocket. "Why's your shirt on backwards?" He peered at Tom through his glasses, but his eyes didn't really appear to focus in one place. He lurched to the left.

Tom didn't reply; he just took the keys out of Jack's hands and stumbled down the drive to his car. One of the girls said, "He's really drunk."

Tom got in his car, shook his head vigorously, and started the engine. He drove home slowly, taking back roads, not wanting to risk getting pulled over. He was worried he might nod off, so he opened the window to feel the night air on his face. He just had to get from one streetlight to the next until he was home. He didn't know how long it took him, but eventually he saw his house down the street. Relieved, he let himself relax, dropping his head and closing his eyes as he turned into the driveway.

He was jolted awake again as his car smashed into the mailbox and glass exploded from the right headlight. The car continued to push the steel mailbox and supporting pole over, the metal on metal emitting a screeching noise as the pole ended up underneath his car.

The porch light came on, and Tom's father burst out the front door. He could barely keep his head up, but he knew he was in deep shit. He searched for his father's eyes, his head wobbling back and forth, but he could only see a dark silhouette against the glare of the porch light.

"You're drunk."

"Big fucking deal!" Tom said out the window. He struggled to get out of the car, finally managing to stand after getting his shoe unstuck between the seat and the inside of the door.

"Don't you ever talk to me like that again!" his father said. Tom still couldn't see his father's face clearly in the darkness, but he could sense that his father was gritting his teeth as he spoke. "Get in the house. *Now!*"

Tom left the car door open. He was aware that he probably should have turned off the engine, but he followed his father's orders and lurched unsteadily to the porch, stepping into some rocks that lined one of their garden beds. He glanced back at his father, who was watching him silently. His father strode to the car, got in, and backed it off the mailbox. The scraping noise was terrible, but Tom didn't care.

Tom went up the porch steps, gripping the railing with both hands. The living room curtains might have moved. He opened the front door, and his mother stood inside in her bathrobe.

"Oh, Tom," she said. "Are you okay?"

His eyes dropped to the floor. "-M sorry." He didn't want his mother to hear the slur in his words. He was so sleepy.

Tom moved past her and clutched the railing as he climbed the stairs to his bedroom. He heard his father come inside and say, "I told you so."

Kara stood in the darkened hallway just outside her room. Her hair was messy. She'd clearly just woken up.

"You ran over the mailbox," she whispered. She was trying not to smile.

"It happens."

"Uh, no. That's not normal," she whispered. She studied his face while he struggled to stay awake. "I don't want anything else bad to happen to you," she said after a few moments.

He paused, then lumbered down the hall to her. Kara was a good kid. He grinned. "I'm pushing through it. That's what I do," he said.

She furrowed her eyebrows.

"I'm all right," he said. He went down the hall to his room. He fell into his bed and was out cold.

———

When Tom awoke the following morning, he rolled over in bed and realized his shoes were on. He stared at them, squinting and blinking, looked at the clothes he was wearing, and then remembered what had happened the night before. He groaned.

He hadn't closed his door all the way. Had his parents passed by or stood there watching him while he slept? It pained him to have to face them in the aftermath of what he'd done. He couldn't believe he'd driven all the way home without trouble, only to hit the mailbox in the last twenty feet. Now his parents knew how drunk he'd gotten, and he'd have to face more of his father's disapproval and his mother's disappointment.

He unlaced his shoes and let them fall to the ground. Perhaps from hearing the noise through the ceiling, his mother called up the stairs a moment later, saying it was time to go to church.

Tom found some clean clothes, brushed his teeth a couple of times, ran a comb through his hair, and went downstairs where his father was seated at the breakfast table as if waiting for Tom. His mother was at the counter putting dishes away; she said he would have to eat after church.

"I hope you understand how foolish you were last night," his father said, staring straight ahead. The collar of his father's button-down shirt was crooked, and he had dark circles under his eyes. His mother's eyes, Tom noticed, were puffy.

Tom was silent. He knew his own eyes were bloodshot, and he didn't have to be told how foolish he'd been.

"I want you to pay for a new mailbox and for fixing your car."

"Okay," Tom said. He'd already planned on doing that, but to hear his father demand it was grating.

"If you're going to drink, I don't want you living here."

Tom stared at him. Was he kidding? It had never occurred to him that his father might kick him out of the house. And to kick him out for drinking? Grandpa would have glass after glass of whiskey around them, and they would all pretend it was normal.

His mother put a hand on his shoulder. "I want you to think of this in your prayers at church today," she said. "And also go to confession next Saturday. I'll be praying for you. This is very serious."

Tom nodded. He turned around and went to the front porch to wait until they would be ready to leave for church. He knew he deserved their disappointment and anger, but he couldn't take his father's lecturing or harsh directives. He didn't want to be around that anymore.

Tom looked at the old neighborhood where he'd lived all his life. The houses were nearly identical—starter homes for young couples today but permanent homes for families like his who couldn't afford to move. Who said he *did* have to live at home? Hadn't he started making some of his own money? If Jack and others were old enough to move on and start something new, why couldn't he? His mind went to Sam's apartment, and he pictured not living with his parents, free to be who he was without anyone breathing down his neck.

———

On Saturday, Tom went to confession, standing in line at the church to wait his turn. He confessed his sin of disappointing his parents by drinking. The priest talked to him about the evils of alcohol and said his penance would be to recite an Our Father and Hail Mary twenty times each. Tom kneeled in the sanctuary and said the prayers twenty times. He didn't like being lectured, even by a priest, but he did enjoy the comfort and ritual of the prayers. He closed his eyes and relaxed as he repeated the same Hail Mary cadence over and over. When he was done, he knew what he was prepared to do.

Tom called Sam late that morning to see if he and his two friends were still looking for a fourth person to share the rent of their four-bedroom apartment. Sam said they were, and Tom counted up his savings from his paychecks, confirming that he could afford the rent.

He found his mother and father downstairs, having lunch in the kitchen. They looked at him silently, and he could feel the tension that had been brewing between the three of them all week.

"I just went to confession, I replaced my headlight, and I'm on my way to buy a new mailbox—I'll put it in after lunch," he announced. He folded his arms.

"That's great," his mother said, wiping her mouth with a napkin. "We hope you learned your lesson, and this won't happen again."

His father just looked at him and nodded.

"It won't," Tom said. "I've also decided to move into an apartment with Sam Peterson, a football player I know."

His mother turned abruptly to look at him. "You don't have to do that," she said, her voice going to a slightly higher pitch. She looked at Tom's father, then back at Tom. Her eyes grew wet. "We love you here. You can stay here and save money."

Tom hated to make his mother sad, but he didn't want to continue with things as they were. He had outgrown his parents' house.

His father didn't say anything, but he gazed intently at Tom, his sandwich hovering above his plate.

"I'll only be four miles away," Tom said. "I can still have dinner here some nights and Sundays . . . if you guys want me."

"Of course we do, Tommy. All the time!"

"I remember Sam," his father finally said. "He was a linebacker. He seemed like a hard worker."

"Yeah, he was," Tom said. Had his father just signaled his acceptance?

"Even though you'll be on your own, we want you to behave," Tom's father said. "No more drinking. You'll need to keep working hard at your job because we won't bail you out if you don't have enough for rent. And make sure you get that mailbox in *today*."

Tom's mother dabbed her eyes with her napkin. She got up and started to make Tom a sandwich.

Later that afternoon, as Tom installed the new mailbox, he saw his parents watching him through the front window. He felt a twinge of sadness and love for both of them, but it wasn't enough to squash his excitement about living without them.

7

That summer was a nonstop party. Living in an apartment with roommates who didn't care what he did and having an income from his
construction job was the most freedom he had ever experienced. Sam's two
roommates—Paul, a tall, slender student at Stark State College, and Jason,
one of Sam's coworkers, short with a half-grown mustache—were already
twenty-one, and they kept the refrigerator stocked with beer. Tom got into the
habit of having a beer every night when he got home from work, particularly
after long hot days of laboring in the sun.

He and his roommates lived for the weekends, and their apartment became
known for its parties on Friday and Saturday nights. The people who stopped
by drank heavily, and as the night went on, the beer would lessen everyone's
inhibitions. Getting blitzed offered Tom an escape from thinking about his
future, and he sensed it did the same even for his old high school friends who
had plans for college. Maybe everyone was feeling their way into a new phase
of life where success was uncertain.

One Saturday night, a couple of former Canton football players showed
up at the apartment. Paul knew one of them, shouting his last name, "Kolar!,"
as they entered. Kolar had a thick neck with a vein standing out on one side
and what Tom thought was a stupid, smug expression. Tom had already had
two beers by the time the Canton players showed up, and he and Sam eyed
them as they reached into the cooler full of beers in the middle of the living
room. Like everyone else, the Canton guys drank steadily, and eventually, the
cooler ran low.

Tom had been programmed to hate Canton since he was a young boy.
He didn't like these guys drinking the beer and hanging out at their party.
He filled the cooler up with more beer, then sat back down on an old beat-
up couch near some other former Massillon friends. An Indians baseball

game played on the TV in the background, and the conversation inevitably turned to the Massillon and Canton game the past fall.

"You know, O'Brien, you weren't blocking our best lineman," Kolar said to him from behind the couch. "He was injured that night." Tom had never heard of Kolar before, but apparently Kolar knew about Tom. Tom looked over his shoulder at him and took a long drink from his beer can.

"He's got a scholarship offer to Akron," Kolar said, his voice growing louder. "I think he could've beat you pretty good."

"Are you shitting me?" one of Tom's friends said. "Tom would've rolled over him just like he did the sub." Kolar shrugged and took another drink, his vein bulging as he swallowed. Tom didn't want to engage, but all the same, he sat up taller.

"That's the past," he said. "No way to tell now, so I don't know why you're wasting your breath."

They kept drinking, all of them cursing the TV as the Indians lost another game. The two Canton guys were becoming incoherent as they harassed some of the other Massillon guys and hit on some girls Tom knew from high school. Tom's head was spinning, and he tried not to pay attention to the slurred banter until Kolar asked, "Where your cheerleaders at? That blond beauty with the nice ass and tight tops? Cindi, right?" A few of Tom's friends stopped talking and looked at Tom. His face grew hot. He knew he should probably be careful, but he found himself gripping his beer can more tightly before setting it down on the table.

"She wouldn't be interested," Tom answered slowly, giving the guy a steely gaze.

"You so sure about that?" Kolar said. "From what I heard, she'd be plenty interested in what I have to offer her in one of these bedrooms."

A surge of anger shot through Tom, and he flexed his knuckles. He'd had enough of this asshole. "Why don't you just shut the fuck up," he said.

"Who are you talking to, *All-State?*" Kolar set his beer down, missing the counter. The can fell to the carpet, and beer leaked out.

Tom was already lightheaded from all the beers, and he stood up so fast he almost blacked out. Kolar faced him, wobbling but looking fiercely at Tom. He was big, but Tom was bigger.

"It's time for you to leave," Tom said. His hands instinctively became fists.

"Fuck you, asshole!"

"Fuck you!"

"Wait a minute!" Sam said, He took half a step forward, but Tom barely noticed. He was already rushing toward Kolar, barreling forward with his full weight. Kolar tried to swing at Tom, but Tom crashed into him, shoving him back until he slammed into the wall. He hit the wall so hard with his back that the plaster broke off. Kolar continued trying to bring up his arms to fight, but Tom just kept flailing drunkenly and crashing around the apartment, knocking into furniture, sending people scattering, overturning the cooler. Though Tom started to drift in and out of darkness, he was aware enough to know at some point that he was straddling Kolar, pounding him in the face, his knee in Kolar's spilled beer. Kolar's nose was bleeding. Tom swooned and began to black out. He felt hands around him, pulling him back.

———

When Tom woke up on the floor near the couch, Sam, Paul, and Jason and two other Massillon guys were the only ones left at the party. A lampshade was turned sideways and cracked. Some kitchen chairs lay on their sides. Tom stayed where he was on the floor. His hands hurt, and there was dried blood on his knuckles. He groaned.

"You about killed that Canton guy," Sam said. He was listening to music and smoking a cigarette.

"How'd it end?" Tom asked with a low, gravelly voice. His throat was sore, and his lips felt chapped. The music made his head pound.

"That bastard didn't stand a chance. Lucky for him . . ." Sam took a long drag. ". . . we pulled you off. His friend picked him up, and they left quick. You passed out before we could get you to the couch."

Tom closed his eyes but could still make out the light in the room. It was too bright and too loud. He felt lousy and annoyed for wrecking his apartment, drinking too much beer, and letting himself be goaded by some idiot from Canton. He wasn't the kind of guy who wakes up on the floor with blood on his knuckles, was he?

———

"You look like hell," Jack said on Sunday afternoon at the softball diamond. One of Tom's favorite things to do that summer was to play on his construction crew team in a slow-pitch softball league. When, earlier in the season, Dan had said they could use some subs, Tom had asked Jack, who wound up becoming the best shortstop in the league. Both Tom and Jack had made an impact, and their team became something to be feared, especially after it beat the first-place team.

"Last night's party got a little out of control," Tom said. His eyes were bloodshot, and he was still hungover.

"I heard."

Tom didn't like Jack's critical tone. They were standing in the dugout in the bottom of the third inning, leaning forward against the chain-link fence. Jack shuffled his cleats around in the dirt, appearing like he had more to say, but then he paused and gazed back out toward the players on the field. "Think that will be us in twenty or thirty years?"

Tom welcomed the deflection. "I hope I'm not that beer-bellied or that addicted to cigarettes."

Jack smiled, repositioned his baseball cap, and turned to face Tom again. "Could you do that life? A construction job, drinking beer every night, maybe a family—although it seems like half of them are divorced." He kept his voice low, so the guys on Tom's crew wouldn't hear.

"I don't know," Tom said. Had Jack been talking to Tom's father? "This way of life may be as good as any."

"I guess so," Jack said. "But the highlight of the year for these guys seems to be how well they're doing in this softball league."

At the other end of the dugout, Dan clapped his hands loudly to cheer on one of the guys. "That's right! That's right! Way to run, Walsh!" His cigarette bobbed up and down in the corner of his mouth.

"What are you getting at?" Tom asked, frowning at Jack.

"Both you and I know this isn't where you should end up." Jack gestured around the dugout.

Tom shook his head. Here we go again. He was going to have to listen to Jack's views on life and their implications for Tom. Tom sighed and said that not everyone had to choose the college path. Jack agreed, but then stung Tom by saying an alternative life of drunken fighting could land him in prison.

He had no idea how to respond. Jack understood Tom's dreams better than anyone, and he understood how devastating his Achilles injury had been, but honestly, Tom still didn't know what he wanted to do. It seemed that the closer Jack got to starting college in the fall, the more separate their lives became.

"Look, you have to be smart about your future," Jack said. "At the very least, you have to watch out for the draft. You're vulnerable if you don't have a student deferment this fall."

It was true that the president had called for more ground troops to be sent to Vietnam, a thought that only added to his stress about life. It created in him a sense of helplessness, but he simply said to Jack, "I'm aware of that, and I don't care."

"So . . . you're okay fighting the Viet Cong in rice paddies?"

God, here he went again. Jack could be a self-righteous asshole when he wanted to be. "My father would be happy if I was in the army," he said.

Jack sighed and shook his head. "Do what you want, but I don't think that's a reason to risk getting killed. Not when you have a choice."

"O'Brien, you're up!" Dan called. Tom turned abruptly away from Jack and picked up a bat. The guys on his crew clapped and yelled for him as he stepped onto the field. He smiled at them, took his place by home plate, and got into position, raising the bat behind his ear and waving it slowly as he stared at the pitcher.

Jack didn't know what he was talking about. Tom wasn't the same guy since his injury. He couldn't be, whether he liked it or not. He had lost his football dreams and his girlfriend, and his focus now was only on living day-to-day. He could do that—manage the present rather than try to control an unpredictable future.

The pitcher, a middle-aged man with a beer belly protruding beneath his jersey, lobbed the pitch, and Tom hit the ball so hard it went into the parking lot.

———

As the summer continued, the parties at Tom's apartment grew larger and wilder. Paul and Jason proposed getting a keg of beer and charging people at the door to drink all they wanted for five dollars—a bargain, they said. Tom laughed at the idea, but when Saturday night came, Paul opened their apartment at seven o'clock, and people were already lined up at the door. Tom recognized students from Massillon Washington High and heard some of the crowd had come from the other surrounding high schools and community colleges.

"This is *your* place, O'Brien?" a short student wearing a Massillon baseball cap asked as he entered with his friends. "This party's a great idea!" He clapped Tom on the back and nodded his approval.

"I can't exactly take credit for it," Tom said, "but I was first in line when we tapped the keg."

Two hours later, the apartment was rocking with an increasingly noisy crowd. Music was blaring, and people were dancing and singing at the top of their lungs.

Tom was in the kitchen getting more beer when a girl rushed by and slurred something about the police. She was pitched forward ever so slightly as she spoke. She might have just been out of her head, but Tom made his way toward the living room to check. The Massillon student with the baseball cap, hurriedly exiting from a bedroom, careened into him in the narrow hallway.

"The police!" the student said to no one in particular. "My parents are going to kill me!" He and others edged toward the sliding patio door in the back.

Two policemen were standing just inside the front door. Except for Paul holding small bills, there was a wide berth around them. Word had spread throughout the apartment, and everyone was trying to get out the back door. One of the policemen pushed his way through the crowd to block the door.

"Turn the music off!" the other policeman yelled. It was suddenly quiet except for the panicked voices of the retreating partygoers outside. Tom's heart beat rapidly in his chest. He tried to sober up.

The policeman said they were responding to a noise complaint from the neighbors and had everyone move to one side of the living room, so they could all have their IDs checked. Tom joined the group and when it was his turn, pulled out his identification.

Before even looking at Tom's ID, the policeman's eyes widened. "No, O'Brien. You? How'd you get mixed up in this?" Tom's breath caught in his throat. The policeman grimly took Tom's ID and had him move to the side, along with Sam and some others.

At least a dozen kids, including Tom and Sam, were cited for underage drinking and told their parents would be contacted to pick them up at the police station. Paul and Jason were arrested for providing alcohol to minors. Tom couldn't believe this was happening. He pictured the fury on his father's face at receiving the phone call and imagined the sobs of his mother in the background. He felt lower than he ever had before.

Tom watched as Paul and Jason were loaded into the back of a squad car. He, Sam, and the other minors boarded a police van. A girl with disheveled hair cried the entire way to the station, wailing more when the driver asked her to stop. When they arrived at the station, they all waited their turn to be questioned and make their statements. Then, they sat in a holding area until their guardians came for them. In the chair next to Tom, Sam leaned forward with his head in his hands.

"They were *arrested!*" he said quietly at one point. "What's going to happen to *us?*"

When Tom's father strode in, he walked calmly and deliberately, unlike the other parents who rushed in and started yelling at their kids right away. He didn't make eye contact with Tom but instead stopped at the front desk and spoke quietly with the officer. Tom was unnerved.

"O'Brien," the officer called. "You're released to your father." Tom got up slowly and went to the front desk. His father was signing some papers, applying more pressure than necessary with his pen as he wrote. He kept his back to Tom.

"You're being charged with a misdemeanor," his father said stiffly without turning around. He handed back the papers. "Because it's your first offense, you'll most likely have to do community service, take a class, and pay a fine. If you haven't broken the law after a year, your charge could be dismissed." He turned to go, and it was clear Tom was to follow him. Tom shot Sam an unhappy look as he walked out with his father.

In the car, Tom's father did not speak for sixteen blocks. Tom counted them one by one. As they passed beneath streetlights in the darkness, his father gripped the steering wheel and wore a dour expression. His knuckles were pointed.

"This was your first and last offense. Your nonsense needs to stop now," his father said out the front window. He turned left and continued down the street. Tom stayed silent, ready to accept whatever was to come, but his father did not say anything more. To Tom's confusion, he drove past their neighborhood, went around the outskirts of town and over the train tracks, and then pulled up to the front of Tom's apartment. He'd assumed he'd be taken home—to his parents' home—where he would be confronted.

"Dad, I'm sorry," he said.

"You're still drunk. You need to sleep it off, but you're not doing it at our home." His father had not looked at him once. Tom heard only the sound of the car idling. He hesitated, then got out. His father drove away as soon as Tom shut the door. Tom watched the taillights grow smaller in the distance, then returned to his apartment and surveyed the mess.

——

Tom slept fitfully for only a few hours that night. He was shaken, and he knew he needed to change his life. He needed a direction, and he could no longer avoid it. When he emerged from his room early the next morning, he looked with disgust at all the beer cans, garbage, and overturned furniture, now clearer in the light of day. He was the only one there, and as if to shed the effects of the night before, he impatiently took off the clothes he still wore, dropping them to the ground in the hallway as he made his way to the shower. He took a long shower using the hottest water he could, then dressed himself in his sports coat and slacks, his church clothes.

He drove to his parents' house, wanting to catch them before they left for church. Tom found them in the kitchen, silently drinking coffee. His mother jerked her head in Tom's direction when she saw him. "Tom! You said you wouldn't drink anymore! How could this happen?" The coffee in his mother's cup rocked from side to side.

"I'm sorry." Tom kept his eyes on the table. Wanting to stay silent until his father responded, he remained motionless.

The sound of his father's chair scraped on the ground. "Your sorry isn't good enough anymore. You've been on a downhill path for a long time," his father said, standing up and looking Tom in the eye. His voice was loud.

Tom hung his head. "I made a mistake, and I'm admitting it."

"You bet you did!" his father said, jabbing his pointer finger at Tom. "One mistake would be bad enough, but *twice* in a matter of months? And a misdemeanor charge? This is not how we raised you! You're better than this!"

Tom's eyes narrowed, and his jaw clenched. He'd gone there to tell his parents he was ready to change, but his father was leaving him no room to do it. He needed help and direction, not his father's condemnation. "*I* don't need to be lectured," Tom said. "I don't talk about Grandpa's drinking or the fact that you can't deal with him because of it."

His father glared at him, and his face grew red. "Get out of this house!"

"No! We're going to church!" his mother said, rising quickly to her feet and looking from one person to the other. "That's the first thing Tom needs to do. Tom, how *could* you say that to your father?"

Tom and his father glared at each other, both breathing heavily. His mother put her hands up, as if to hold them back from each other. Tom continued to meet his father's gaze, but then they both quickly shifted their eyes when Kara came down the stairs.

"What's all the yelling?" Kara asked, appearing at the entrance to the kitchen. She was wearing a blue dress and holding a hairbrush. Tom's father exited the room. She watched him go, then looked questioningly at Tom.

Tom's mother seemed uncertain about what to say. She was still standing in front of her chair, but then she sighed. "Your brother was taken down to the police station last night for underage drinking, something *you* should *never* have happen, and charged with a misdemeanor. He's gotten himself into serious trouble, and I want you to learn from this." She sat back down, her shoulders slumped.

Kara turned to Tom, her eyes huge. "*What?*" This was different than her usual teasing expression, a look of pity. It was surprising, but he deserved it.

"I can't tell you how sorry I am, Mom," Tom said. He regretted disappointing his mother, Kara, his grandfather, and others who thought better of him. His mind went to the policeman who had recognized him.

"What's happening with you, Tom?" his mother asked. He didn't know what to say, but he could see Kara watching him.

"I'm figuring it out." Tom knew it was like his father had said. He had been on a downward path ever since his injury. He'd been limping through life in more ways than one.

Tom cleared his throat. "Maybe let's drive separately to church today." He looked toward where his father had stormed off. "I can pick up Grandpa and meet you guys there."

Tom's mother nodded. He cut through the family room and picked his keys up from the table by the front door. As he stepped out onto the porch, Kara appeared behind him.

"Hey," she said. Tom turned to look at her. "As your sister, I feel I should tell you that people talk about you in this town." His stomach dropped to think of how his reputation had changed. "I don't believe everything I hear," she said. "You know why?"

"Why?"

"Because I know you."

"I don't even know who I am."

She smirked. "Well, I do. And you and I both know who you're *not*."

Tom gazed at Kara, surprised by her support. It was awkward to be having this conversation with his younger sister, but she was the only one who had said anything of comfort to him in months. Her words caused him to feel strangely lighter. He searched for a moment for some sort of appropriate response that wouldn't embarrass either of them.

"Shut up," she said, hitting him on the arm with her hairbrush before he could say anything. She smiled and closed the door.

Backing his car out of the driveway, Tom glanced at the mailbox. He remembered with shame how he'd run over the old one in his drunken state, but now it was fixed. As he set out down the street, he wondered how he might go about fixing himself.

—

Grandpa, dressed and ready for church, opened his door to Tom's knocking. "Tommy! This is a surprise. Are you driving this morning?"

Tom grew nervous, but his grandfather would find out what happened soon enough. It would be better for the news to come from him directly. "My roommates and I had a huge party last night that got out of hand," he said. "The police came, and I was charged with a misdemeanor for drinking as a minor."

Grandpa started to laugh.

"It's serious," Tom said, "My parents are really upset. I wanted to tell you before they did." Tom's grandpa hesitated and looked closely at Tom. He reached out to give him a bear hug—and his embrace caused Tom to choke up. Tom's father hadn't even looked at him last night.

"Are you okay, my boy?"

"No. I mean, yes. I will be," Tom said.

"Then what's the problem?" Grandpa asked, smiling widely. They got in the car. "You're just eighteen, sowing your wild oats. That's what you should be doing at this age! I tried to tell your dad this after you hit the mailbox, but he was too bent out of shape."

His grandfather's words were a relief. Tom drove them toward the church. "I've been arrested twice for drunken driving, even though I wasn't that drunk," Grandpa said. "When a cop sees you swerving a little, you're in trouble, so just be careful."

"I wasn't driving, but I was drinking. And two of my roommates were selling beer to underaged high schoolers."

Grandpa laughed again. "That sounds like quite a party—something I would have gone to when I was your age."

Tom smiled. Last night had clearly been a bad idea, but his grandfather gave him the ability to see some of the humor in it. He always felt better after talking to Grandpa, who understood him in a way his parents just didn't.

"You learn from doing stupid things, Tommy," Grandpa said. "It won't be the last time—you're only eighteen. Your parents will be upset, but don't worry too much about that. Just don't do the same stupid thing more than once. That's how you learn how to live."

When Tom pulled into the parking lot, he watched his family getting out of their car. They all entered the church together, but he and his father sat at opposite ends in the pews and avoided eye contact during the service. The service ran long, and after it ended, they returned home for Sunday dinner in their separate cars.

Tom watched his father and Grandpa at the grill out the kitchen window, finishing up the steaks for dinner. He couldn't make out all their words, but his father looked stern as Grandpa sipped his whiskey, smiling and laughing a little too loudly. Tom heard Grandpa say, "Just give him some extra rope," as they turned to come inside. "He's learning! He'll be fine." But Tom's father didn't give him any rope that day or any day after that leading up to Tom's appearance before the judge.

On the phone the next day, Kara told him their mother hadn't come out of her bedroom all morning. Their father had told Kara that their mother

was praying and fasting for Tom. When Tom heard that his mother had finished her fast on the third day, he stopped by the house that evening to try to
smooth things over. His mother hugged him close, but his father just glared
and went to another room.

At Tom's sentencing that week, Tom stood before the judge in a small,
mostly empty courtroom, with only his father and mother seated in the gal-
lery behind him. The judge had deep wrinkles on his forehead and frown
lines. He peered at Tom over the top of his dark-framed reading glasses and
said that he would need to take an alcohol education class on the weekend,
perform three days of community service mowing and cleaning city property, and pay a $100 fine. Tom tried not to squirm in his suit, but he was
sweating and shaking.

"If you were not a first offender, there would be no leniency for you," the
judge said, Tom heard his mother's sharp intake of air behind him. The judge
said if he could remain law-abiding for a year, his misdemeanor charge would
be dismissed.

"Yes, sir. I will," Tom said. The court reporter typed Tom's words.

As Tom and his parents departed, other kids from the party were sitting
with their parents on benches along the hallway, waiting their turn to go
before the judge. His father's steps reverberated in the space, and Tom could
tell by the sound of the tread just how angry his father was.

In the car, his mother said he was blessed to have a chance to redeem
himself, but his father dropped Tom off at his apartment without a word. It
was as if he didn't want Tom near him or at the house, and this didn't change
by Sunday dinner or any of the next few mid-week dinners after that. Tom
gradually stopped eating with the family except for Sunday dinners, which he
continued for his mother's sake.

———

In the later part of the summer, Tom spent more time with Sam and occasionally got together with Jack. Paul had moved out of the apartment, and
Jason, Sam, and Tom didn't throw any more parties. They still got their hands
on some beer and drank together on weekends, but always in the privacy of
their apartment and no more than a couple of beers at a time. None of them
wanted to risk getting caught again. Tom kept working hard to earn money,

taking on extra hours to ensure he would have enough to pay his increased rent. He didn't want to have to move back in with his parents.

He'd worried that Dan might fire him when he let him know he'd been charged with a misdemeanor and needed to miss work for three days to do community service, but Dan had just smiled. "You don't even want to hear about the drinking mistakes I made at your age," he said. Tom offered to work on tasks that could be done on the weekend or evenings, but Dan told him not to worry about it.

As Tom picked up trash around Massillon and mowed the grass on city property, he was keenly aware that people in town were watching him. He was required to wear a neon orange vest as he performed his community service hours, and it made him all the more visible. He was humiliated when he saw Cindi and Curt drive past him one day.

As August rolled around, Jack and many of Tom's other former classmates prepared to leave for college. When Tom ran into them or even worse—their parents—they often asked him what college he would attend. For a while, he wasn't sure how to answer. A few knew he wouldn't play football, but they all assumed he was still going to college.

He finally made up an answer that seemed adequate, telling them he was working to save money for college. If anyone pressed him, he would say he'd been counting on a scholarship, but his injury had ended that possibility. But no matter how often they asked, he felt exposed and conspicuous, imagining that people could see he had no real direction. Their questions also struck somewhere deeper, reminding him of his lost football dreams, and it was usually following this that he would retreat to his apartment in search of a beer.

Jack came over on one of these days. It was his last visit with Tom before he left for college. Thankfully, he hadn't made Tom feel any worse about the misdemeanor charge.

"Maybe once you get partying out of your system, you'll decide what comes next," Jack said, eating out of a bowl of chips in his lap as they watched an Indians game on TV.

"Too bad you won't be around to keep me out of trouble," Tom joked. He'd finished his beer—it made him feel mellow, and he was already missing Jack.

"You'll be okay, once you figure out what you want to do," Jack said. He groaned at the TV as the batter struck out.

Tom had known the day was coming, but picturing Jack at college with new friends and experiences, a program of study and academic goals . . . he was jealous. "I'll see you at Thanksgiving. Maybe you'll bring a sorority girl home with you."

"Yeah, right. I just hope you don't get drafted before that."

"Ha-ha, very funny," Tom said. But it was a sobering thought.

The Indians lost, and Tom and Jack stood up, then awkwardly shook hands at the door to say goodbye.

"Good luck," Tom said.

"Good luck yourself," Jack said. "I'm stopping by your house to say good-bye to your dad also. Anything you want me to pass on to him?"

"No," Tom said. He hoped Jack wouldn't push the issue and ruin things. Jack nodded, and Tom felt a deep sadness as his friend walked away.

That Saturday morning, he went to mass—alone, without anyone knowing. He closed his eyes as he smelled the incense and listened to the rhythmic Latin prayers spoken by the priest. He wanted to replace his loneliness and misery with peace, hoping to feel some of the comfort from the church his mother received. He waited, but nothing came.

8

Tom climbed down the ladder from the second floor of the apartment building he was helping to build. A drizzle of rain had begun, and his shirt and jeans were getting damp. He entered the site trailer, where Dan was studying the blueprints. Dan looked up while reaching for the pack of cigarettes he kept in his shirt pocket.

"Why the long face, O'Brien?"

Tom had been unable to shake the feeling of melancholy that hung over him the past few weeks. Jack and several other people he'd considered friends had left for college. Though Tom was learning new carpentry skills and techniques from Dan that fall, his sense was that everyone was moving on without him—getting on with their lives—and he was getting left behind. Even Kara was busier with her high school semester in full swing and field hockey season underway.

Tom shrugged, trying to get a rain jacket out of a locker. "Some of my good buddies have left for school."

"I tried college for a while," Dan said, lighting a cigarette. "I can tell you it wasn't for me."

"Why not?"

"I couldn't see spending money to learn a job that would put me behind a desk all day. I like being outdoors, working with my hands, producing something I can see."

Tom did like being outdoors, just not today. It was different being cold and wet on a football field, lining up with his teammates, thinking how to run a play. Tom missed it. But he agreed with Dan; he couldn't see himself behind a desk for the rest of his life.

"This line of work could suit you if you wanted it to," Dan said. "You're good at it. Quick learner. Hard worker. Solid skills."

"You really think there could be a future for me in this?"

"You'd be welcome on my crew anytime," Dan said. He placed his hard hat on a corner of the blueprint that had curled up. "Maybe you'll run your own crew someday. Then we'll be softball rivals, and I'll beat your ass." He smiled, then returned to studying his blueprints.

———

Since Jack had left, Tom and Sam had been hanging out together even more. Like Tom, Sam had not enrolled in a college, choosing a job in the steel plant instead. They often went to the truck stop café, listened to music in Tom's car while driving through the country, or met up with other friends who had also taken jobs in town. Tom felt like he could talk freely with Sam; maybe their police station experience had made them closer. Plus, Sam didn't have the annoying connection with Tom's father that Jack had.

In late September, Sam got a letter from the draft board. Without student deferments, Tom and Sam had known they were at risk of getting drafted, but Tom was shocked to see the actual letter. He took the news harder than Sam, who just shrugged and said he hoped he wouldn't be sent to Vietnam. Tom was losing one of the few good friends he still had, and he still had no plans of his own. He knew he could get a letter himself any day.

When his mood darkened, he saw himself living a lonely existence, working a mind-numbing job during the week and drinking beer on the weekend, then doing it all over again the following week. But the thought of physically going to Vietnam to fight in the war was just as bleak. He'd seen enough footage of the war on TV to know he didn't want to go. Jack said he should think about a student deferment, but Tom hadn't been—and still wasn't—in a place to do anything about it.

After a going-away party for Sam some weeks later, Sam departed for basic training. He looked too young, as he waved goodbye to Tom from the front seat of his sister's car.

Tom struggled to get out of bed and go to work after Sam moved out. He began to leave frozen dinner trays on his bedroom floor, where they accumulated and piled up, and throw his clothes on his bed or chair instead of hanging them up. He stacked dirty dishes in the kitchen sink until Jason yelled at him that the apartment smelled like rotten food. He showered less and slept more.

Tom reflected on how much he'd lost in a year—football, Cindi, Jack, and now Sam. He thought of the ongoing rift with his father, the change in the trajectory of his future, the loss of his ability to play football for a Big Ten school. Afraid of receiving a letter like Sam's, he started leaving the mail unopened on the floor by his closet. He felt empty inside, and stuck. What could he do? He spent his evenings drinking beer in front of the TV, oblivious to everyone around him.

———

Sunday dinners after church had consisted of awkward silences and stilted speech for a while, except for Grandpa, who kept a steady banter the more he drank. Tom was grateful to have Grandpa act as a buffer between him and his father, particularly because his father still seemed so livid. His mother would sometimes ask Tom about his job, new roommates, or apartment, but Tom felt this only opened him up to his father's quiet criticisms.

During one of their dinners, his mother broke the silence by trying to focus attention on Kara. "Are any of you planning to watch Kara's field hockey game this week? It's at three-thirty Friday," she said, passing the gravy bowl to Tom. Kara looked at each person sitting at the dinner table. Any sports talk in the past had always focused on Tom or a game on TV, never Kara, and in their household, field hockey just wasn't taken seriously.

"I won't be able to leave work," his father said. "We have to do inventory on Fridays." Tom thought of his father's attendance at many of his football practices after school over the years, including Fridays.

Grandpa fidgeted in his chair, looking as if he was debating what to say. "I'm not much of a fan of field hockey," he finally said. "I don't know the game." He got up to pour himself another drink.

Kara's face grew still. She appeared to study the gravy. Her nostrils flared.

"I don't know how you girls even follow the ball. It's a blur to me," Tom's mother said quickly.

"It just takes proper stickhandling," Tom's father said. "With practice and repetition, anyone can learn it. It's not hard. You need to keep your eye on the ball." Tom couldn't help but feel that last part was directed at him.

"There's more to it than that," Kara said. She chewed angrily. It grew quiet again.

Tom knew his father had trouble seeing Kara as an athlete. He also knew what it was like to be on the other side of his father's good opinion. "I'll come watch," he said. "I can get off work early this Friday." Kara narrowed her eyes at him, but Tom could make out a slight twitch at the corner of her mouth, which he took to be her look of gratitude.

His mother put her hand on his.

Tom realized he couldn't remember ever having gone to any of Kara's activities, maybe a tap dance recital once when she was in elementary school, but that was short-lived because she'd hated it. He knew she played in sports after that, but by then, he'd become consumed by his own participation in Pop Warner football. She'd come to plenty of his football games over the years, and he felt like he could easily show her this kindness now. Besides, he had nothing more interesting to do on Friday.

———

Tom arrived at the field for Kara's first game of the season on a Friday in mid-September. He sat with a handful of the players' friends and family members in the small bleachers, and was surprised to see that Mr. Barnes, a high school math teacher and part-time coach, was coaching Kara's field hockey team. He had coached Tom as a shot-putter on the track team, and Tom had liked his supportive approach. Mr. Barnes turned briefly to talk to one of the parents in the stands and saw Tom. He paused, waved, and smiled, and Tom returned the wave before the coach huddled with the team.

Tom, leaning forward in the bleachers, watched the girls warm up. The grass was lush from recent rains, and he breathed in the smell of fresh turf. The ref blew the whistle, and the players got into position. Tom hadn't felt this kind of energy or pre-game anticipation in a while, and he found himself really looking forward to the game. Kara called something out to her teammates, her stick ready.

Kara moved up to the center of the field when her team was attacking with midfielders and wings rushing toward the goal. When an attack stalled, players would pass the ball back to Kara, who would decide where to restart the attack and make a pass to a running teammate. Tom watched his sister also position herself on defense to protect against their opponents' crossing passes to their forwards running to the goal.

It soon became clear how significant Kara's presence, communication, and decision-making were for the team. She seemed a natural out there, comfortable and focused. It was a tied game as the seconds wound down. Kara maneuvered the ball while waiting for a teammate to get open. She shouted, "Peggy!" to a short but lightning-fast forward who was in the clear, and then smoothly passed her the ball. Peggy slammed it in for the winning goal.

The whistle blew to end the game and the girls jumped up and down and hugged each other. Tom cheered and clapped along with everyone else. The game had given him a rush of adrenaline he hadn't expected. He also had no idea that watching his sister win a field hockey game would make him emotional, giving him the same type of elation he'd often felt from winning football games. Is this how his father and grandfather felt when they watched him play?

He stepped down from the bleachers and stood on the sideline while the girls huddled with Mr. Barnes. The redheaded girl beside Kara said, "That's Tom O'Brien," and several of the girls looked over. The teammates each put an arm into the middle of the huddle and yelled, "Go Tigers!" Kara walked over to Tom, smiling broadly. He hugged her, and she looked surprised.

"You were incredible out there," he said. "I had no idea!" She was uncharacteristically at a loss for words, but she looked up at him—her eyes glistening. The team was headed toward the bus, and she needed to go. Tom reached out to hug her again before she left.

"I'm sweaty," she said, smiling. "I'll see you Sunday. Thanks for coming." She carried her gym bag and walked to the bus with her stick over her shoulder, looking back at Tom once or twice.

After Kara boarded the bus, Mr. Barnes came up to Tom. A small man with intense eyes, he wrote a final note on his clipboard before greeting Tom.

"I'm happy you were here. Kara had a great game," he said.

"She did," Tom said. "The whole team did. I have a new appreciation for field hockey."

Mr. Barnes smiled at Tom. "I think all the girls knew that Kara's all-state brother was watching them today."

"I'm not sure how big of a difference *that* made, but if it helped . . ." Tom smiled back. "I'll come to more games this season when I can. I enjoyed it."

Mr. Barnes was silent for a few seconds. "I was sorry that you got injured.

I was at the Canton game. I know you were on your way to big things in football." Tom felt a pang in his chest.

"Not much I can do about that now." Tom's eyes went down to his right leg.

"I heard you're working right now to save up for college?" Kara was right. People talked. Or had Mr. Barnes heard this from Kara?

Tom nodded. "Until I decide what to do."

Mr. Barnes was silent again. "I have a proposal for you," he said. "These girls need to be in better shape. Today, we were the favored team, so we got by with the win. But it won't be so easy when we play Canton and Cleveland." Tom waited. "How would you like to assist me in practice? I'd like you to lead the girls on speed and endurance drills."

"Why me? Don't you want someone who knows field hockey?"

"For starters, I can tell the girls idolize you. They know you're first-team all-state and would probably be playing for the Buckeyes if you hadn't been injured—Kara talks about you a good deal. I also know from experience you're the most disciplined athlete I've ever coached. You know how to practice—I believe that's what these girls need."

Tom looked casually down at his feet to hide the flush of pride he felt blooming in his cheeks. "I guess I could give it a try."

"Excellent, let's plan on at least once a week. Two days would be ideal, if that can work with your job."

Tom nodded. Surely he could figure out a schedule with Dan that would allow him to leave work for practice. He would start earlier in the mornings if he needed to. He was no stranger to being up before the crack of dawn.

He thought about it on his entire drive home, and realized with a chuckle that he was kind of excited. Hopefully Kara and her teammates would be receptive to the idea, and he could actually do some good for the team.

As usual, Tom's mother tried to start a conversation at the dinner table that Sunday. She asked Tom what was new with him.

"Kara's coach asked me to help him with her field hockey team," Tom said, glancing over at Kara.

"What?" Kara said.

"He wants me to work with your team on speed and endurance."

His father's eyes flickered to him for a moment, then away. He didn't say anything, but Tom registered an interest he hadn't seen for weeks.

"But you don't know anything about field hockey," Grandpa said, wiping his mouth.

"That's true, but the coach thinks I can help get the team in better shape through some drills. He was my track coach, and I used to train under him," Tom said.

"I've seen you practice," Grandpa said. "Kara, you better watch out—Tom's going to have you and your team running laps."

Kara didn't say anything, but her mouth still hung open. Tom thought he understood what she was feeling—a mixture of interest and concern that he'd be intruding on her world. After dinner, she took him aside. "I'm not sure what Coach Barnes wants, but we have a good team, and we're in good shape—you saw how well we play."

"Don't worry," he said, and put a hand briefly on her shoulder. "I'll only be helping the coach with some things I learned from football. I don't want to disrupt your team's success." She frowned and narrowed her eyes at him. Of course she was still skeptical, but he would show her. That night, he started planning his drills.

———

At Tom's first practice, Coach Barnes explained his role to the team and the girls gave him their full attention. He was more nervous than he thought he'd be, feeling their eyes on him and knowing they were probably just as skeptical as Kara. He described his plans, doing his best to behave like the many coaches who'd guided him in the past. He wanted them to jog two laps—a half-mile—to warm up before each practice. Then, they would alternate with sprints, longer runs, and weight training to improve their speed, endurance, and strength.

After the girls completed their warm-up run, Tom let them know his plans to have them run repetitions; they would increase the number of reps over time. He started them with wind sprints, having them run as fast as they could for fifty yards, to help them build their breath capacity and speed. By the time the girls had completed their fifth rep, they were gasping for air, doubled over with their hands on their knees. They looked at each other in disbelief, their eyes going to Kara.

"If you work us this hard every week, we're not going to have anything left for the games," Kara said, breathing heavily. The other girls nodded, their faces flushed.

Tom remembered the younger players on his football team having the same reaction at the start of the season. He'd run alongside some of them during practices to encourage and pump them up, and he'd found it satisfying to see the way they improved. "If we do these drills, your games will be easier," he said. "I promise. You'll be a lot less tired and have more speed."

The girls looked to Coach Barnes for help, sitting on the bench, but he ignored them, scribbling away on his clipboard. The team would move on to regular practice when Tom was finished with them. When the girls took a water break, Mr. Barnes caught Tom's eye and smiled.

———

A couple of days later, Tom had the girls run quarter-mile reps—three reps, with a half-lap walk in between. Again, the girls ended up bent over with their hands on their knees. Some of them shook their hands.

"Your brother's going to kill us," Peggy said to Kara. "I'm still sore from the other day."

He assured them that those quarter-mile reps would improve their endurance. "Don't worry," he said. "You'll find them easier over time."

After practice that day, Kara caught a ride home with Tom. "Your workouts are torture," she said flatly. We're not runners on the track team. We're here to play field hockey." She took an impatient swig of water from her thermos.

"Do you guys want to just play hockey, or do you care about winning?"

She swallowed. "Of course—we want to win."

"What else besides winning?"

She furrowed her brow at him and blinked. "We want to go to state."

"What do you want to do at state?"

"To win it!"

"That's a great goal. Keep that in mind when we work out."

She shook her head, took another swig from her thermos, and said, "This better be worth it."

Instead of going back to his apartment for a frozen dinner and beer, he drove to a bookstore in town where he looked through some books on field hockey.

——

That Friday, Kara's team had a game with the Cleveland Benedictine Bengals, always a tough opponent. Would any of the training he'd done with the girls that week make a difference? From the sidelines, he monitored the speed and endurance of the Massillon players and observed Mr. Barnes as he coached the girls on defense and got them to run plays on offense. Tom was the only one from his family there to cheer on Kara and her team, and he yelled and clapped for all the girls.

At halftime, they were ahead by three goals. The girls all smiled at each other and strode confidently around the field, but he noted the speed of the Cleveland attackers and anticipated that Kara's team might be in for an unpleasant surprise.

The second half started with the Massillon girls looking strong. However, the momentum changed midway through the half when the Bengals started increasing their attacks. The girls were no longer smiling. One particularly athletic attacker on the Cleveland team dribbled the ball around Kara and then smashed it with surprising ferocity into the corner of the net. With five minutes left, Massillon was ahead by only one goal. Mr. Barnes called out instructions to the girls, all of whom were bent over with their hands on their knees or walking in slow circles with their hands behind their heads, trying to catch their breath. It was clear they needed more endurance and more sprinting capacity, and Tom had an idea how he would tell them.

The final two minutes were dominated by Cleveland players who made one attack after another. Tom couldn't help clenching his jaw and rocking back and forth on his heels as the clock ticked down. Massillon's goalkeeper managed to stop a flurry of shots as the whistle blew to end the game, giving Massillon the win by one goal. Tom leaped into the air and swung his fist.

The girls slowly made their way off the field, happy but exhausted. They could barely speak to one another, they were so out of breath. Mr. Barnes had them circle up and told them it was a good win, and that they would talk about the game at the next practice.

While the girls put on their sweats and gathered their gear, Mr. Barnes went over to Tom and asked softly, "What did you see?"

"They're only in shape to play half a game."

"Right. I don't think they're aware of it."

"I have ideas. "

"Good. Be ready to talk to them at practice."

Kara was silent as Tom drove her home. She looked beat. He held back on his observations, instead congratulating her on their win against a formidable team. But when he went over on Sunday for dinner, Kara wasn't so quiet, particularly after she was goaded by Grandpa.

"So, what do you think of Tom as your fitness coach?" Grandpa asked.

"He's clobbering us. We were so worn out from his drills, we almost lost our game." Tom looked at his sister.

"Maybe you almost lost because you're not in shape," Grandpa said.

"We wouldn't be one of the best teams in the conference if we weren't in shape." She glowered defiantly at Tom.

Tom decided to stay out of this conversation but watched it with a half-smile.

"Who's the best team you'll play?" Grandpa asked.

"Probably Canton."

"You better not be worn out for that game."

"Tell that to Tom!"

There was no need to respond. She'd learn soon enough.

"Tommy, you better go easy on the lasses," Grandpa said. "They're not football players."

Tom laughed, which drew an angry look from Kara.

"I'm finished talking," she said. She got up from the table to help her mother in the kitchen.

Grandpa looked at Tom, thinking for a few seconds. "Her fire reminds me of you," he said. "I may have to come watch that girl play."

"You should," Tom said. "Kara's quite an athlete." He looked at his father, who remained silent, but Tom could tell he'd caught his attention.

———

At practice the following week, Mr. Barnes had the girls sit down on the field so they could talk about the Cleveland game.

"Tom, you mentioned something after the game. Can you tell the girls what you thought?" At this, Kara narrowed her eyes.

Tom stepped forward. "You guys have told me you're after the state championship, right?" Several of the girls nodded. He cleared his throat. "To be champions, you need to act like dedicated athletes—with the same desire and drive—not just good friends playing a sport together. I think you'd be a stronger team if you were in better shape. I've seen it again and again in football—there are no champion athletes who aren't physically fit." Some of the girls lifted their heads to look at him more fully.

"But we won," Kara said. "We didn't hold back—we left everything on the field." A few other players nodded.

"I agree," Tom said. "But that Cleveland attacker went right around you, Kara, and scored near the end of the game. That kind of thing didn't happen in the first half when you were fresh—early on, you always stayed between the attackers and our goal." Kara appeared to process this. Tom looked at each player.

"Champions are usually fitness fanatics, often going beyond what a coach requires," he said. "They know that if they can push themselves through hard workouts, they'll be the ones who have the momentum at the end of the game."

As Tom worked with the girls in practice that day, he heard a little less complaining and saw some of them push themselves a bit harder. Kara even ran a faster lap. Standing in the evening sun, he felt proud and satisfied in a way he hadn't in a long time. Was it because he was starting to get through to the girls? That Mr. Barnes had valued his experience and opinions?

The more he thought about it, the more he realized a lot of what he'd said were things he'd learned from his father. He knew these words were true and important, but they also came from the same person who'd always made him feel like he wasn't enough, the person who'd withdrawn his support, turning a cold shoulder after his run-in with the police. How did his father reconcile his behaviors with his noble message about purpose, goals, and discipline— the "rules for living," he'd always impressed on him? Tom knew the way he thought about sports, football, and life had largely come from his father and now Kara and her team were hearing the same kind of message from him.

He wanted to deliver it better, kinder, but hoped it would help her, as it had helped him.

When he got back to his apartment, he went into his bedroom and looked around at the dirty clothes piled everywhere, the empty beer cans, dirty dishes, and fast food trash. He was tired of feeling like a slob, someone who didn't care about things. He picked up his dirty clothes and put them in his laundry bag, then brought his dirty dishes to the kitchen and threw away a bunch of fast food cartons.

He started doing the dishes and Jason popped his head into the kitchen. "Holy shit," he said, "I wondered what that noise was. What's gotten into you?"

"Just cleaning things up."

"You've been living like a pig ever since I met you. Who are you?" He laughed.

As he rinsed the dishes, Tom reflected on the experience he was gaining. Mr. Barnes's idea had come out of nowhere, kind of like a Hail Mary for Tom. Maybe he wouldn't mind his construction job so much if he knew he could also be helping Kara and her team. It was similar to playing softball on Dan's team. He wondered how many carpenters felt that the softball games were as meaningful as their jobs. Jack had mocked the carpenters for possibly feeling this way, but Tom realized now that he was wrong.

At work the following morning, he searched for Dan around the job site and found him next to the newest construction, peering over blueprints.

"I wanted to thank you for letting me leave early in the afternoons to help coach field hockey," he said.

"Field hockey, huh?" Dan said, grinning. "Interesting line of work for an all-state football player. Is that with a puck?"

Tom made the rounds to the carpenters, asking them what help they needed. Some were still drinking coffee, not even ready to think about work. "Aren't you bright-eyed this morning," one carpenter said. Tom smiled. Maybe he was going overboard, but something had changed in him, and he liked it. Although he still had no idea about the direction of his life, he'd reached some sort of turning point. He wondered what would come next.

9

The girls had finished their third quarter-mile rep and were walking a quick half-lap around the track before beginning their final rep. They were silent except for their panting. Tom knew this was a challenging work-out for them, and he clapped his hands to encourage them. He timed each rep and urged them to make their final lap the fastest. The girls, led by Kara, started fast and pushed themselves, grimacing and gasping as they ran the last hundred yards.

"Great work," Tom said. "Remember this during your game Friday. You can outrun them, especially in the second half."

At the job site the next day, Tom found himself going over the drills and training in his mind. He was excited to see how his methods might affect the girls' performance.

The game on Friday turned out to be their best game of the season. They won by three goals. Tom noticed the team's increased effort in the second half. He hadn't expected miracles after only two weeks of training, but he could tell the girls were playing with more confidence. He believed it was influenced by his grueling practices.

The girls were ecstatic, and most of them came up to thank him afterward. Kara, surrounded by her cheering teammates, caught his eye.

"I doubted you," she said over the noise, "but it's possible you might know what you're talking about."

Bolstered by the win, Tom was feeling good, mentally and physically. Watching the girls improve their conditioning made him wonder if he could start working out again. He had stopped his physical therapy exercises at the beginning of summer, but his Achilles tendon no longer felt tender. He decided to see if his leg could handle a light workout. Tom came to practice in his sweats and running shoes the following week, telling the girls he would try to run with them. He'd debated whether to do this, not wanting to look foolish in front of them, but he thought if they were willing to put in the kind of effort he'd been requiring, he could maybe give it a shot also.

His therapy had called for him to run for five minutes every other day, stopping to walk if he felt any tenderness in his Achilles tendon. The muscles in his leg felt tight, but he was surprised to be able to complete the five minutes without discomfort. He increased his runs to ten minutes a day and then to fifteen. He was encouraged. He still had more work to do before fully testing his tendon, but he was regaining some of his former strength and endurance. He soon joined the girls in their repetitions.

As he kept in stride with a few of the girls in the back one day, he wondered what was motivating him to push himself like this. Did he still have some hope that he might play football again? He had to be careful to guard against unrealistic dreams, but his newfound confidence motivated him to follow his instincts and keep training. He joined the girls in their weight room workouts as well.

On Monday, he ran three fifty-yard wind sprints with the team. He was cautious, wanting to protect his tendon. The girls enjoyed beating him each time, asking him if that was the best he could do. Mr. Barnes looked up from his clipboard a few feet away and watched Tom with interest. On Wednesday, Tom ran two quarter-mile reps and felt more confident with their pace than with the speed of the wind sprints. But he was winded, and the girls again teased him as he took deep breaths at the finish line.

"So much panting," Kara said, standing with her hands on her hips as Tom finished after her.

After a few more practices, however, Tom matched most of the girls in both the sprints and the quarter-mile reps. One day, he noticed the girls whispering with Kara as they were gathering their bags after practice, and he saw Kara look over to study him.

On the way home when she and Tom stopped at a drive-in for a milkshake, she blurted out, "The girls and I were talking—do you think you could get in good enough shape to play football again?" She wore a Massillon baseball cap and peered at him from underneath the bill.

His pulse quickened. It made him nervous to hear his sister say aloud something he'd been wondering himself. He was aware of his current limitations.

"I'd be fooling myself to think I could ever play at a Big Ten level," he said, moving his straw around in his shake.

"What about teams not in the Big Ten? Who else was interested in you?"

Tom waited until the whir of the blender behind the counter stopped. "There was one coach who told me to call him after I had recovered," he said. "From Kent State." He knew exactly where the Kent State letter was in his desk. He'd placed it on top of the rejections.

"Why don't you call him? You have nothing to lose," Kara said.

That night Tom looked out his apartment window at the streetlights and cars passing by and wondered whether he was ready to play football again. Could his leg be strong enough to allow him to compete at the college level? And, most importantly, was he prepared to deal with the risk of finding out he *couldn't* play football again?

———

Tom waited three days to act on Kara's suggestion. He stared at the phone, rehearsing what he was going to say before dialing. His conversation with the Kent State head football coach was short. The coach said he remembered him and his excellent record at Massillon Washington High. He was glad Tom had called, and he asked about Tom's physical therapy and how his tendon felt.

Tom was honest. "I feel good, but I'm unsure if I can play—I want to try." He didn't want to set himself up for disappointment or mislead the coach.

"Let's check you out then," the coach said. "I'll have my line coach, Coach Peters, call you to schedule a visit with our trainer." Tom hung up, feeling shocked and strangely elated, but he reminded himself to be cautious.

Coach Peters called him that evening. Tom chided himself for answering too quickly, but the coach sounded friendly and relaxed. He and Tom scheduled a date and time to meet with the trainer, and he told Tom he was looking forward to meeting him.

Tom had a hard time sleeping that night or concentrating at work the next day. He decided not to tell Kara or his family about his upcoming trip to the university in case nothing came of it, but he mentioned to Dan that he had a morning appointment in a few days and would need to start work late. Tom was a mess of nerves.

Later that week, he made the one-hour drive to Kent State. He tried to drown out his fears by blaring the radio, but he didn't really hear the music. He pulled up to the training facility, got out of his car, and just stared at the building for a few minutes before going in.

He was directed to walk past the indoor football field, the weight room, and the trainer's room to Coach Peters's office. Several players were playing catch and lifting weights. The chatter among the players, the clanging of weights, and the smells of athletic balm and sweat brought back memories of what it meant to be a football player—a world he loved. He again tried to temper his joy. At the coach's door, he took a deep breath, steadied himself, and knocked.

The door opened, and Coach Peters shook his hand, standing as tall as Tom and several pounds heavier. He had an engaging smile, and Tom immediately liked him. He brought Tom into his office and had him take a seat.

"So, you want to try football again? We felt for you when you were injured in high school," Coach Peters said, facing Tom from where he was perched on his desk.

"Thanks," Tom said, trying to keep his voice steady. "I wish I was playing somewhere right now."

"You'd probably be playing in the Big Ten if you weren't injured. We didn't have much of a chance to recruit you. You think you can play now?" He studied Tom, still smiling as he spoke.

Tom was flattered that Coach Peters thought he could actually have played in the Big Ten. This made him realize how close he'd probably been to achieving his goal. "I've been working out and conditioning myself, but I honestly don't know."

"Let's go see our trainer," Coach Peters said. "He's helping players prepare for our game Saturday, but he'll find time for us." Tom followed Coach Peters to the weight room.

The trainer, in the middle of helping a player with some sets of triceps dips, looked up and greeted them. Coach Peters introduced him as Ralph Jones, but said everyone called him Jonesy. Jonesy had Tom take off his right shoe and sock and sit on the table with his legs horizontal. Tom held his breath. With Coach Peters watching, Jonesy held Tom's foot and slowly rotated it back and forth. He asked if there was any pain.

"I don't feel any," Tom answered.

"Look at the size of that scar," Jonesy said to Coach Peters. "That was major surgery. Tell me about your physical therapy," he said, still rotating Tom's foot.

Tom described his months of therapy, his overstretching, and his occasional stretching since then. He told him he recently had begun wind sprints and quarter-mile repetitions, and his leg felt strong.

"What do you think? Can you fix him up?" Coach Peters asked Jonesy.

"You never know about these types of injuries. But if we could work with him this spring, there's a chance he might be ready next fall." Tom's heart leaped.

Coach Peters nodded, looking pleased, and walked Tom back to his office. Two players about Tom's size were waiting outside his door. Tom felt their eyes on him, sizing him up.

"Be with you in a second, fellas," Coach Peters said. He looked at Tom. "Jonesy and I will talk with the other coaches, and I'll get back to you. I want to make this work."

Tom exited the football facility in a daze, with the coach's and trainer's words playing over and over in his mind. He was excited, but he needed to prepare himself for any possibility.

On his drive back to Massillon, Tom pictured himself running down a football field, leading blockers in a college stadium full of fans. A college stadium! But he also imagined a phone call from the Kent State coaches saying he was too much of a risk.

When he arrived at work, he thanked Dan and said nothing more about his morning. He intended to keep the visit to himself, especially from his family. He remembered his father's and Cindi's expectations, like his own, that he would be ready to pick the scholarship of his choice after four months of physical therapy. Their disappointment multiplied his own when those expectations proved to be false.

For the rest of the week, Tom did his best to follow his daily routine of work and practice, waiting for a call from Coach Peters each evening. When he still hadn't heard anything by Thursday, he slowly began to let go of his hopes. He'd been stupid for thinking it might happen, impractical. But he did think about the Kent State campus and the possibility of being a student. Maybe that was a direction for him, regardless of football. He tried to envision himself going to college, sitting in lectures, studying, eating in cafeterias, talking to girls.

He was watching TV on the couch late that night when the phone rang. He jumped at the sound. Jason answered and said it was for him.

"Tom, this is Coach Peters. Sorry I didn't call earlier—we've been busy getting ready for our game against Toledo."

Tom's mouth was dry. "No problem at all," he said. His heart thumped in his chest as he waited to hear what the coach would say.

"We want you to enroll for our spring semester." Tom's eyes bulged. "We can't offer you a scholarship at this point, but we can offer to work with you to strengthen your tendon, so you can begin practicing with the team. How does that sound?"

Practicing with a football team? At the college level? His mind was spinning. "That sounds good," he said, playing it cool, resisting the urge to shout.

There might have still been an obstacle, though—his misdemeanor charge for underage drinking was still on his record. He steeled himself. "But there's one thing I need to talk to you about."

Tom told Coach Peters what had happened that summer, and that his charge would be dismissed after a year if he kept his record clean.

"I appreciate you telling me," Coach Peters said. "You're not the first high school football player who got caught drinking. What would you say you've learned from it?"

Tom was quiet. Images of the past eleven months—the Massillon game, his leg in a cast, his father, Cindi, his drunken fight, his appearance in court—flashed quickly through his mind.

"I'd say that getting hurt and then having to lose football brought me to a low point," he said, "I didn't cope well with it. I'm still not sure how everything will work out, but these past months taught me a lot about what kind of person I don't want to be."

It was quiet on the other end of the line. Tom waited. *That's it. I blew it,* he thought. He'd been so close.

"I saw something special in you your senior year," Coach Peters said. "I still see that in you now." Tom blinked. *What?* "If the other coaches agree, I'll put in a good word for you with the admissions counselor who helps us. She'll flag your application to show our interest in you. Are you there?"

"Yeah," Tom stammered. He leaned against the wall next to him.

"Good. I'll call you this weekend."

Tom thanked the coach, and they hung up. He went over the entire conversation again in his head before sitting down on his bed, stunned.

He tossed and turned all night.

———

On Saturday evening, the phone rang. Tom had been sitting next to it after listening to the Kent State game against Toledo on the radio, which Kent State won. He let it ring twice fully before answering it, so he wouldn't sound too eager.

"Sorry for another late call," Coach Peters told him. "We had a big win today. I spoke with the coaches, and we're prepared to move forward with you. Has anything changed for you since we last spoke? Are you still interested?"

Tom realized he was pressing the phone to his ear harder than necessary. "I'm definitely interested," he said. "I listened to your game today and wished I was playing."

"Great. We'd like you to get your application in for the spring semester as soon as possible. I'll give you the name and number of that admissions counselor I told you about."

Tom closed his eyes and took a deep breath. It had been so long since he'd felt this kind of excitement. He wanted to shout a cheer to Coach Peters, but he tried to keep his emotions under control.

"We can't promise you anything, but if you're admitted and good enough to play in the fall, you could be a candidate for a scholarship the following year."

"That would be great." His heart was beating fast.

"I know you'll be able to do it, Tom. Get that application in—I want you in my offensive line."

Tom was at a loss for words. He could only say, "Yessir." He was ready to do anything to please Coach Peters. After thanking the coach and hanging up, he exhaled a huge breath of air, and his whole body relaxed. He now had a sense of direction that he hadn't had for months.

———

Three weeks later—three weeks that seemed like forever—he received an admissions letter from Kent State. He ripped the envelope open and regretted that he'd mangled the letter a little. He couldn't believe they had accepted his application. It was one he wanted to keep on top of the rejections.

Tom decided he would announce the news to his family at their Sunday dinner. He'd keep the secret to himself for a while and couldn't stop smiling to himself, thinking his mother wouldn't expect his answer when she asked what was new with him that week.

He was right.

"Oh, Tom, what a surprise! I'm so happy for you!" she said, jumping up from her seat and coming over to embrace him. Her eyes were wet.

"Kara deserves the credit. She saw me getting back in shape and put the idea in my head," Tom said. "I don't think I would have been motivated enough to call Kent State without her."

Kara beamed at him from across the table, and started to open her mouth, but before she could say anything, Grandpa interrupted.

"Tommy boy, that's fantastic! Forget the Buckeyes—we're Kent State Golden Flash fans from now on!" He raised his whiskey to toast Tom. Tom smiled and toasted him back with a glass of water.

Tom slowly turned to look at his father, who had been quiet. Rather than averting his eyes, his father returned Tom's look with a rare expression of pride. He seemed both tired and relieved. "Congratulations, son."

"Tell us how it happened," Kara said. As Tom described his conversations with the coaches, the excruciating wait for a decision from the university, and his observations about the training facility and team, he knew he couldn't wait to get to the Kent State campus to begin a new life as a student and football player.

———

Tom worked up the nerve to tell Dan a few days later. He planned to stay on with Dan's crew through December, so he could save more money for college, but he felt strangely disloyal for making plans to leave. Even though the job hadn't always been interesting, it had been a lifeline for him, allowing him to move out of his parents' house, develop skills as a carpenter, and become more independent.

"So, you're off to college," Dan said. He'd been scrawling on a schedule but now he put his pencil down to look at Tom.

"Yeah, I'm going to see if I can play football again," he said, then nervously added, "I don't know how I'll like college. I'm mainly going there for football."

Dan smiled, and the lines on either side of his mouth deepened. "Football is getting you in the door—you should take advantage of the chance to get a degree. I like being a carpenter, but I also would like the salary of an engineer." He arched an eyebrow, as if to make sure Tom got his point.

"Yeah, but I'm sure there will be times when I wish I was a carpenter again," Tom said.

"There's always a need for carpenters, and you have skills now that you can use on demand. It could be your fallback."

Tom nodded and reached out to shake Dan's hand with a firm grip. He began to feel emotional. It could have been much worse for Tom had Dan not taken a chance on him. He knew he would miss Dan's leadership, his fellow carpenters, and the daily routine at the construction sites.

"All-State, you left your thermos up here," one of the guys on the crew said from the top of a scaffold. He tossed the thermos down to Tom. Tom didn't know at what point he'd stopped being annoyed at his nickname at work. He was going to miss it.

———

Tom continued to work out after the end of field hockey season. The times for his repetitions continued to improve, though his tendon would occasionally feel a little tight on cold mornings. He didn't want to jeopardize anything, so he'd rest it for a few days, going to upper-body workouts in his parents' basement instead.

He also got his life in order, so he could move to Kent State in early January. He informed Jason he would be moving out of the apartment: he found a carpenter who agreed to buy his car, and he made plans to temporarily live at home during the holidays before leaving for Kent State. Since he would not be on a scholarship his first semester, he knew he had to reduce his living expenses and wisely use his savings to afford tuition and room and board.

Because he was still in the apartment during Thanksgiving break, Tom invited Jack over to watch football games with him when Jack returned from college. Jack glanced at the sparse, secondhand furniture when he arrived as if he couldn't believe Tom still lived there. Perched on the dingy couch, he talked about his college experiences. To Tom, Jack appeared a bit cocky about having experienced something outside of Massillon. He wore a cardigan Tom had never seen before, and mentioned professors he liked, an honors program he'd been invited to join, and a new girl he was seeing.

When Tom showed Jack his wrinkled acceptance letter from Kent State, Jack said, "That's great. Going to college is the smart thing to do. You'll finally have a student deferral and won't have to worry about getting drafted."

"In some ways, I'm glad I didn't go to college this fall," Tom said. "I've learned things from working as a carpenter that are different from what I'm going to learn in college—not just carpentry but also about the lives of construction workers who don't go to college." Tom talked about how carpenters got up every morning to work in all kinds of weather, risking injuries with construction equipment and worrying about making mortgage and car payments. He felt he knew realities of life that he wouldn't have learned about in college.

"That's fine," Jack said, "but I'd rather *design* what carpenters build instead of hammering nails in the rain."

"I still think it was a good choice for me," Tom said simply. He started to look back at the TV, but saw Jack shake his head and roll his eyes.

"It was also a choice that risked you being sent to Vietnam, plus your drinking could have put you in jail instead of mowing city boulevards."

Tom kept looking at the TV, squinting his eyes in reaction to Jack's words. "I don't need to be lectured. What are you, my father?"

Jack turned to Tom. "Fine. You're confident now that you get to play football again. Like before in high school when you were on cloud nine. Just don't forget how low you sank this summer."

Tom shook his head. Jack was his oldest friend, but how was it that they always seemed to arrive back here, arguing like they had as boys in the yard? "I don't recall you having the ideal life," Tom said. "In fact, I remember you coming over to be in our lives all the time."

"All I'm saying is don't let football delude you," Jack said, his nostrils flaring. "You feel secure now that you have it back, but what if Kent State didn't want you? Would you go to college somewhere else or just continue moping around, drinking every night, and most likely getting drafted?"

"How do you know what I'd do?" In spite of his best efforts, Tom felt his knuckles tightening.

"Because you haven't proven that you can live up to your potential without having football as your main goal in life."

Tom stared at Jack, clenching his jaw. Deep down, he feared that Jack might be right, but Tom wasn't about to give his friend that satisfaction. Jack was just like his father. Tom didn't need someone to rob him of the sense of pride he felt about the first positive thing that had happened to him since his football injury.

"You've always been such a condescending asshole," he said.

Jack stood up, matching Tom's glare for an instant, but they both knew that any sort of shoving match or fight would always work in Tom's favor.

"Good luck," Jack said dryly as he walked out the door.

"Good luck yourself!" Tom yelled. He sat on the couch for several minutes longer, fuming.

Tom thought of Dan's words—about how football was getting him in the door and he should take advantage of the chance to get a degree. It was true that Kent State was the best option he'd had since graduating. Maybe it could help him live up to this *potential* that Jack—and his father—kept going on about.

PART II:

1967–1970

10

On a cold and cloudy day in January 1967, a month before his nineteenth birthday, Tom packed his parents' car full of clothes, school supplies, and a bag of toiletries his mother bought for him, hugged his sister goodbye, and drove with his parents to Kent State. The forty-minute drive was quiet, except for the occasional piece of advice from his mother. Her eyes were red-rimmed as she talked about how much they would miss him, especially at their Sunday dinners. Tom's father focused on the road ahead. When they drove past the stadium upon their arrival, he said they hoped to come watch him play there in the fall if Tom made the team.

Tom's new home was a dormitory where several other football players lived. As he and his parents brought his bags into his room, they met his roommate, who was unloading some shirts and jeans from a box. He was considerably smaller than Tom, but muscular, with thick brown hair falling over his ears. He introduced himself as Kevin Valenta from Chicago, and they learned he was a freshman defensive back on the football team. He held up his chin and smiled engagingly at each of them.

"Welcome to Kent State," Kevin said as he shook Tom's hand. "You're now a Golden Flash." Kevin carried himself with confidence and joked easily with Tom and his parents. He even made Tom's dad smile with a corny joke about how the coach had to go to the bank "to get his quarter back." He would be fun to live with.

Tom noticed the poster over Kevin's bed; it depicted a giant peace sign along with the title "Peace Now!" His father looked at it, too. Tom imagined his father disapproved, given his support of the military as a National Guard member. But he was quiet as usual.

It was midafternoon by the time Tom had finished moving in and walking his parents around campus. They cleaned and set up Tom's side of the room so that it was neat and orderly, noticeably different from Kevin's side with its already unmade bed and toiletries strewn across the desk. Tom's mother held Tom's arm as they toured the campus grounds. When they reached the football training facility, Tom's father nodded his head and suggested that Tom not waste his opportunity.

Afterward, Tom walked his parents through snow flurries to their car, where they said goodbye. Tom's mother held him close and said how proud she was of him. His father shook his hand. Tom was more emotional than he thought he would be as he watched them drive away. He was only thirty-some miles from home, but their farewells felt like a rite of passage.

That evening, Tom and Kevin filled their trays with food from the cafeteria line and walked to a table of loud football players, where Kevin introduced Tom to everyone. Tom wasn't sure what to expect; the guys had already played through the fall season together, and he wondered if they'd accept him in their ranks.

Kevin started with Ron Wozniak, one of Tom's fellow offensive linemen. "Woz, you better watch it," Kevin said. "I think Tom might take your position."

Woz laughed, seemingly unthreatened. He had broad shoulders, a block-like torso, and a small head covered by short curly black hair. He wasn't quite as tall as Tom but appeared to weigh more. He looked like a tough football player.

Other players welcomed Tom, shaking his hand, giving him a nod, and chatting with him. One guy said he'd gone to a Cleveland high school that played Massillon and knew that Tom had been first-team all-state. Tom looked at them, one by one, and felt any remaining nervousness wash away. They were going to be good teammates.

———

Coach Peters blew his whistle. His offensive linemen had ended their practice with wind sprints and he asked them to gather on the sideline of the indoor practice field. This was Tom's first practice, and he hurried over and sat down in the front row. At Jonesy's direction, he hadn't run the wind sprints that day, even though he felt he could have. Jonesy wanted him to gradually build up to speed work. He cautioned Tom to be conscious of any tenderness in his tendon, and to stop immediately at any sign of pain.

As the players around Tom guzzled water and wiped sweat from their faces, Coach Peters told them he would mix first-year players with the varsity players during the spring practice sessions. The fall games for first-year players had been a good test, he said, but now everyone would be competing for positions on the varsity team. How they played in the spring and fall practices would decide who would be the starting players next season. He then looked at Tom.

"You no doubt see we have a new addition to our team—Tom O'Brien. He's working with our trainers to get his Achilles tendon in shape for the fall."

Tom glanced around, feeling self-conscious. He was glad when he caught Woz's eye and Woz gave him a nod. "We'll have to see how he does blocking Richie," one of the guys said, grinning at Coach.

Coach laughed. "That's a challenge for every single one of you. Richie could be named all-American next year."

Coach was clearly close with his players as their offensive line leader, and the players genuinely seemed to like and respect him. Sitting there, Tom realized how much he'd missed being a part of an offensive line—it was a unique fraternity of football players. Unlike the more exciting ball-handling and defensive positions, an offensive lineman had to focus more on techniques and less on reacting athletically. He needed to be skilled at positioning his body, using his arms and hands, and leveraging his strengths.

Offensive linemen were often underestimated by people who did not fully understand the game. But their coaches and teammates knew how crucial the offensive line's performance was. Tom had never played to be noticed or celebrated; he played to perform at his best and to elevate the team. The position matched his personality, and he was relieved to be able to return to it after such a long time away.

As much as he'd resented it when his father had told him not to waste this opportunity, he'd been right, of course. He needed to do everything he could to play again at the high level he was accustomed to. Walking to the locker room with Woz after practice, he asked about Richie.

"Oh, that guy? He's our best defensive lineman, but a bit of a jerk. He had a *monster* season last fall as a sophomore," Woz said, setting his gear down on a bench. "He'll be a test for you, O'Brien. But one step at a time."

Tom was motivated for that test. He already planned to do a light run that evening.

———

That semester, as Tom attended classes, adjusted to college life, and practiced with the team, he found himself spending the most time with Kevin and Woz. They were easy to hang out with, but he also sensed that he shared a seriousness with them that went beyond football. Other first-year players appeared to have only two goals: keep a passing grade point average, so they could continue to play football, and have fun pursuing girls. Kevin, Woz, and Tom wanted more. Kevin and Woz, already thinking ahead to life after Kent State, had declared their majors—history for Kevin and business administration for Woz.

Kevin always had a stack of books on his chair. He loved his courses and talked of going to grad school somewhere after Kent State, possibly following the academic path of his father, who was an economics professor at the University of Chicago. Like Kevin, Tom enjoyed learning, especially about topics he hadn't studied before. He was intrigued by his course on Western civilization that semester, and Kevin laughed when he saw the textbook on Tom's desk. "Great—you're learning about the foundations of American imperialism," Kevin said. Tom liked to hear Kevin's views, and they would occasionally talk late into the night about the influence of the US government on other countries. They were intrigued by the Vietnam War protests beginning to take place at Berkeley and other universities, and they would watch news coverage about them on a TV a student down the hall had in his room.

Woz was different from Kevin in that he saw his football scholarship as a means to get a college education that would lead to a good job. He didn't want to work in coal mines as his father and grandfather had done, which had led to his grandfather's death in his fifties. Tom could appreciate Woz's perspective on the practical benefits of college. He too wanted to come out of it with knowledge and skills to help him pursue a career. He thought about his father's and grandfather's work at the steel plant and how they each may have had dreams for something else beyond that. Maybe the reason Grandpa drank and Tom's father was so demanding was due partly to their dead-end jobs.

Tom watched the ways Kevin and Woz handled their classes and worked toward their goals, and he kept at his own studies to ensure he would be ready once he figured out what to do beyond college. Near the end of the spring semester, he met with his adviser to discuss his major so he could identify the required courses he would need to take. Going with an area he knew about from his summer job, he chose the College of Architecture and Environmental Design, with a potential major in construction management. He wasn't sure if that was the right decision, but he felt pressure to choose *something*. It was a mystery to him how some people knew exactly what career path to pursue.

———

At one of the last spring football practices, Tom met with Coach Peters and Jonesy in the training facility. His focus that spring had been to carry out the exercises designed by Jonesy—a combination of running, stretching, and weights. Tom had increased the speed and repetitions each month, always stopping if there was tenderness in his Achilles. Jonesy also had him do some drills using a blocking sled. Coach asked him to demonstrate, and Tom pushed the sled about twenty feet, using the blocking techniques he had learned in high school.

"His techniques are solid," Coach said to Jonesy. "His hips are back, elbows squeezed, and he pushes without swinging his body."

"You saw what's lacking, though," Jonesy said. "He doesn't have an explosive start. Tom, are you favoring your injured leg?"

"Yeah. It hasn't been tender, but it hasn't felt as strong as before the injury." Tom had worried all spring that his leg wasn't where he wanted it to be, but he'd done everything Jonesy had asked.

"How do we get him there?" Coach said.

"He's come a long way," Jonesy said. "Without weeks of exercise, he wouldn't be able to move the sled that well. We need to keep on that path: increasing his reps and weights, depending on how his tendon feels."

"Good. What do you think, Tom?"

"Sounds good, Coach." Tom was committed to following Jonesy's guidance. He knew how to meet goals related to playing football but still felt nervous about his leg.

"One more thing," Jonesy said. "Some of this is mental. Work on increasing your confidence as well as your reps. Once your leg is at full strength, there's no need to feel cautious."

"Yeah," Coach said. "Go for it like you did in high school, if your leg feels good."

Jonesy left, and Coach and Tom stood up. Coach smiled warmly at him and clapped him on the back.

"This is going to work," Coach said. "I'm excited about you playing in the fall."

Coach's enthusiasm was contagious, and Tom felt a rush of adrenaline. He knew that Kent State had taken a risk in encouraging him to play football again and investing in his training. He wanted to prove to them that they had made a good decision. He wanted to earn praise and approval from Coach Peters as he had from his high school coaches and his father. And he wanted to have everything he'd gone through in the last year and a half lead to something good.

He was anxious, though, when he thought about playing in the fall. He could remember the moment his tendon ruptured during his high school game as if it had happened yesterday. He'd gone over it a billion times since then. There was always the chance of it happening again, and he didn't know how to get past that. But he would try to put his faith in Coach and Jonesy. He would keep on their path and see what would happen.

———

One day after practice, Coach Peters asked Tom for a ride home since his car was at the dealer for its annual maintenance. Tom said he didn't have a car, but he was riding in Woz's car back to the dorm and was sure Woz would swing by Coach's house to drop him off. Tom caught up with Woz in the shower and Woz agreed.

The three of them left the training facility and walked to Woz's used Plymouth Valiant. Its paint was faded and its doors were chipped, but Tom was glad Woz had it because, not being on scholarship yet, he was using all his savings from his summer job just to pay his college expenses. Woz gave him rides everywhere and sometimes let him borrow his car if he needed to buy things at the mall.

When they pulled into Coach's driveway, Coach invited them in for a coke, saying he wanted to introduce them to his wife and son. Coach and his family lived in a split-level house on the edge of Kent, a larger home than the house Tom grew up in, with a much larger backyard. Tom imagined growing up in that neighborhood of suburban professionals, a class above the mix of blue- and white-collar workers in his parents' neighborhood of bungalows.

Tom and Woz followed Coach into the kitchen, where he introduced his wife, Jill. She was attractive, probably in her mid-thirties, wearing makeup that drew attention to her eyes and lips. Jill greeted them warmly and turned to introduce their four-year-old son Jimmy and a new puppy. She motioned them out to the back patio and said she would bring them some cokes and snacks.

They walked through the house, side-stepping toys, with the puppy jumping after them, and opened the sliding glass door to the backyard patio. They sat down, and Jimmy wanted to sit on Coach's lap while Tom played with the puppy. Jill came out with a tray of crackers and cheese and three cokes, and Coach stood to help her. Her hair fell softly around her face as she leaned over to give Coach the tray, and Tom felt like he was getting a glimpse of a family living out the American dream. A football coach, his loving family, and food on a patio that looked out on a beautiful back yard.

Coach wanted to hear their plans for the summer, and Tom described his carpentry job. Woz said he would be working for a furniture moving company.

"I'm glad that neither of you are going to sit behind a desk all summer," Coach said. "We want you coming back in good shape in August. I'll be sending each of you a weekly workout schedule."

Tom and Woz smiled, not surprised at all by this news.

"Also, I don't want you to lose weight," Coach added. Tom smiled again. The large cafeteria meals provided to the football team, combined with all the weight training he'd done that spring, had made him gain ten pounds, to 240.

"You don't have to worry about our appetite," Woz said.

They finished their cokes and stood up to drive back to the dorm. When Tom led the way through their kitchen, Jimmy jumped out from behind the kitchen door, yelling, "Boo!" Tom picked him up and lifted him high in the air. They all laughed and said goodbye as Coach closed the front door behind them.

On the drive back to campus, Tom asked Woz what he knew about Coach's background. Woz said he'd been a first-team offensive tackle his final two years at Tennessee. He had tried playing for the pros but instead became a college assistant football coach. When his offensive coordinator was selected to be the head coach of Kent State, he brought Coach with him and appointed him as the offensive line coach.

Tom weighed Coach's success—a satisfying job, a woman who loved him, and a great home and family—against the direction of his own life, as he had started doing ever since the discussion about his major with his adviser. It seemed like Coach had it pretty good—living a life Tom would probably like. Maybe Tom should strive for something like it.

———

Tom was studying in their dorm room late one night near the end of the spring semester when Kevin returned from the library and interrupted him. "I've got a date Saturday night. Why don't you ask someone, and we can go out together. I'll drive." Tom had been surprised that Kevin had such an expensive car, a Pontiac GTO. Kevin said it was a high school graduation gift, and the real gift in it was that it worked like a charm for impressing girls.

Tom had settled into a college and football routine that worked for him, and though he'd noticed attractive girls around campus, he hadn't pursued anyone. He still had memories of Cindi, particularly when he saw the Kent State cheerleaders practice on the field, and this often left him with mixed emotions. It had been less than a year since she'd broken up with him, and even though he'd spent a summer drinking, trying to forget about her and his other troubles, he just didn't feel ready to get close to a girl again; the risk of pain was too great. He realized he and Cindi didn't have as much in common as he'd thought and that he'd let himself think that his intense attraction to her sexy looks and body was love.

"Who did you ask?" Tom asked, deflecting Kevin's question.

"A girl in my history class."

"What are you guys going to do?"

"We'll figure it out." Kevin, in the middle of changing his shirt, stopped and looked at Tom. "We're surrounded by beautiful girls, O'Brien. Lots of 'em. Remember, there's more to life than just football and books."

Tom didn't respond. His life *was* about football and books, but over the next several days, Kevin kept bugging him about it, pointing out girls everywhere they went. When Kevin's date, Laura, said that her friend, Becky, would consider going out with Tom, Kevin persuaded Tom to be open to the possibility. He suggested that Tom first give Becky a call to have a coffee or coke before either of them committed to a double date Saturday night.

Tom met Becky at the student union in midafternoon. Crowds of students streamed in and out, and the space was noisy. He couldn't help but compare her to Cindi. She was taller and slender with straight brown hair, not nearly as ready to break into a big smile or bat her eyes as Cindi was. Laura had told Kevin that Becky had attended one of the large high schools in Cleveland, and she seemed to him to have the demeanor of a big-city girl, greeting him with a reserved coolness. Tom was immediately drawn to her. As they settled at a table near the windows, she appeared to be examining him closely, gazing at his height and looking into his eyes with questions. Maybe she'd never gone out with a football player before.

"What are you thinking of studying?" he asked her. She didn't smile, but she wasn't unfriendly either. He liked the shape of her mouth.

"Right now, I'm thinking of journalism. You?" She arched an eyebrow.

"Maybe construction management." At a nearby table, some students laughed and joked, knocking over some books.

Becky kept her attention on Tom. "I heard through Laura that you're on the football team with Kevin but haven't played because you're injured?" News traveled fast. Tom wouldn't necessarily have wanted to start out his first potential date with this detail about his life, but he wasn't put off by Becky's directness.

"I ruptured my Achilles tendon last year," he said.

"Do you think you'll be able to play again?"

"I don't know." He paused. "It's why I'm focusing as much on my studies as on football."

She smiled. "I respect that. Well, you're sure big enough for football. Kevin told Laura you were quite the high school star."

Tom felt his face get hot. "I did well, but then reality hit." He shifted his eyes away from her briefly. "What kind of journalism are you interested in?" he asked.

"Politics. I'm following the protests against the Vietnam War." He thought of some of his late-night conversations with Kevin.

"Are you against the war?" he said.

"Yeah." She grew serious. "Boys from my high school class have been killed there."

Tom nodded. "It doesn't make much sense to me."

Becky studied him for a few moments, then, appearing as if she had made up her mind, gathered her purse. "I better get to class," she said.

"Would you want to go out with Kevin and Laura this Saturday?" he asked her as she stood up.

"I'd like that," she said, smiling. She looked back at him as she walked away.

——

On the night of their double date, Kevin drove his GTO. They picked up Laura at her dorm first, and she immediately said, "Nice car!" She smiled brightly at Kevin, rubbed the passenger seat as she got in, and checked her lipstick in the visor mirror. But Becky's reaction was more muted.

"New car?" she said, though she didn't really ask it as a question. She climbed quietly in the back next to Tom, meeting his eye.

Tom, seated behind Laura, had been breathing in her heavy perfume, but as soon as Becky got in, he found himself leaning toward her, in part to move away from the perfume. Kevin kept talking as they drove, filling any silences. He asked Laura and Becky what they were studying. Tom had been nervous about seeing Becky again—he'd thought about her quite a bit since their last meeting—but the more Kevin bantered, the more comfortable Tom felt sitting next to her. They were both quiet listeners. Becky turned to Tom and smiled as Kevin probed Laura about the class they were taking. Relieved, Tom smiled back.

Kevin proposed seeing a university film series special screening of *The Battle of Algiers* and then eating at the Kent Grill. Tom hadn't heard of that movie, but Becky said she'd been wanting to see it. They filed into their row just as the lights were dimming, with the girls in the middle and Tom next to Becky. He glanced at her in the dark to study her profile—her sharp, serious eyes cutting the sweetness of her softly rounded cheeks and chin and nose, but his attention soon shifted to the movie. It was shot like a documentary in newsreel style and depicted the attempts of a guerilla movement in Algeria to gain independence from the French government, not the typical kind of date film. Tom was shocked by the violence.

At the restaurant after the show they piled into a booth. Kevin wanted to hear their thoughts on the movie.

"It was so similar to what we're doing in Vietnam," Becky said next to Tom, her elbows on the table. She sounded troubled.

"How so?" Tom asked. Up to that point, his thoughts about Vietnam had mostly been limited to the recent protests at Berkeley and to the possibility of being drafted. Honestly, he wasn't really sure why the war was even happening.

"We're acting like a colonizing power, like France—trying to conquer a country that should decide its own fate," Becky said passionately. She leaned forward, and as she did, her arm brushed Tom's.

Kevin leaned forward. "The French did the same to Vietnam in the 1950s, and the Vietnamese drove them out."

"Both sides in the movie were so violent," Laura said next to Kevin, sipping on her glass of water.

"Yeah," Tom said. "I thought so too. It was hard to find the good guys." He understood Laura's reaction, but Becky's emphasis on politics intrigued him. She didn't just have a visceral reaction to the movie but appeared to have thought about it on a whole deeper level. He envied her ability to join Kevin in comparing Algeria to Vietnam. He hadn't made that connection, but he wanted to hear more.

"I think that's a major point of the movie," Kevin said. "It may require violent acts to defeat American and European colonizers."

"Really?" Laura said, turning to him. "I thought we're in Vietnam to help defend the South Vietnamese democracy, not colonize it."

Becky's nostrils flared. "That's the line given by our government," she said. "What we're *really* doing with this war is trying to control Asian governments and resources to benefit our own economy."

Laura just looked at Becky with a thin smile.

Tom realized how much more he had to learn. He was unsettled by what Becky and Kevin were saying but excited to have a deeper dialogue about it than his late-night conversations with Kevin. He'd generally just skated through his high school classes, focused on sports, and studied enough to get decent grades. But now, something in him was shifting. He wanted to be more knowledgeable, to go deeper into ideas that interested him.

The conversation seemed to have struck a chord with Kevin as well. His face was flushed, and he leaned over and put his arm around Laura. "We're not going to solve this tonight, but what a great movie. How about if we go get a beer after we're done eating?" he asked. "We can keep talking."

"Where?" Laura said, her face softening. She moved her body a little closer to Kevin's.

"Some seniors on our football team live off-campus in a house. We're welcome to stop by on Saturday nights. They usually have a keg."

"That sounds good," Laura said.

Tom looked at Becky—she appeared uncertain. "Why don't you drop us off and then go ahead," he said. "We may go for a walk or something." Becky's face relaxed.

After dinner, Kevin dropped Tom and Becky off at the dorm, and Becky suggested they sit on the couch in the lobby. He agreed and told her he wanted to hear more of her thoughts about Vietnam. She smiled up at him, looking amused, and said, "Well, this is an interesting date." Then she started right in describing the Gulf of Tonkin incident, which led to her talking about the US engaging more directly in the Vietnam War. As other students passed them in the lobby, she told Tom about two boys from her high school who had been killed in Vietnam, along with thousands of other US soldiers. The way Becky described it made it feel closer and more personal than what he had seen on the news. She continued to talk, growing increasingly more animated in explaining her disagreement with President Johnson's reasons for expanding the war.

Tom watched her and listened, occasionally asking questions, and the time seemed to fly by. He told her that his former roommate, Sam, had been drafted; she sighed and said she hoped he wouldn't be sent to Vietnam. She believed the US might subdue the Vietnamese temporarily with dominant military forces, just like France did to Algeria, but that it wouldn't be a lasting victory, just as France's victory didn't prevent Algeria's independence. Tom could see her passion, and he wanted to feel that passionately about something too. She spoke articulately, intelligently, and with heart, and he was envious that what she cared about connected to her potential career as a journalist.

She paused and looked into his eyes for several seconds. They'd been talking nonstop for a while. "You're a great listener," she told him. "I'm enjoying this."

"I don't know. I'm just interested in what you have to say."

She cocked her head and smiled. "Well, I doubt if that's typical of most football players."

"Good," he grinned. "I don't want to be seen as a dumb jock."

She laughed and moved next to him. Then she grew serious, lifting his arm and guiding it slowly behind her neck. He drew her closer, and she leaned her head back, resting it on his chest. They sat together in silence. He looked out the lobby windows and watched the entryway, where students were coming and going, while she closed her eyes and breathed deeply.

After several minutes, she lifted her head and looked up at him. "This is pretty nice, Tom O'Brien." She raised her arm and drew his head down. They kissed—a long kiss, gentle and tender.

Then she pulled away. "I need to go," she said.

"Sure." It felt abrupt to him, but he was okay following her lead. They walked to the entryway, and he bent down to kiss her again before she entered the dorm.

On the walk back to his room, Tom thought about how different Becky was from Cindi. He was impressed by Becky, drawn to her independence and her ideas. Maybe he could have a deeper relationship with her than he'd had with Cindi, but he had to proceed carefully. He definitely didn't want to get hurt like that again.

Kevin returned to the dorm soon after Tom. "Hey, big guy, how was your date?" he said. He looked a little buzzed.

"Very nice," Tom nodded. He could still feel Becky next to him.

"Mine, too. That Laura is a partier."

"Good, because you seem to have opposite political views."

"A couple of beers took care of that. And what about Becky? I can see she feels as strongly as I do about Vietnam."

"I think I could learn a lot from her," Tom said. "We'll see what happens."

He thought about his conversation with Becky as he lay in his bed that night, telling himself just to take things lightly with her. But she was still the last person on his mind as he drifted to sleep.

———

Tom called Becky a few days later to see if she wanted to go out with him on the next Saturday night and was surprised when she said she was busy. He assumed that meant she had a date with someone but told himself it didn't matter because he had to study for finals.

"How are you doing?" she asked. Her voice was warm, which encouraged him, so he suggested they study together at the library sometime. "I'd like that," she said, and they made plans for the following week.

Maybe she thought there was something between them, but wanted to remain cautious. Perhaps an arm's-length relationship would be suitable for him, too, assuming this might be what she wanted—particularly if she planned to date others. Maybe he'd also consider dating others, although he didn't really want to after meeting her.

After studying together the following week, they walked through the Commons in the center of the campus. They talked about their plans for summer break, which started the week after finals.

It was a warm night, and other couples sat on the grassy hill. Tom and Becky sat down in the dark and looked up at the stars in the clear night. She pointed out various constellations and related them to stories from mythology. God, she was so smart.

When she stopped and smiled up at him, he gently pushed her back onto the grass, and they lay together, kissing. The night was still, interrupted only by the sound of crickets and an occasional car driving on the campus road. They kissed again at the entrance of her dorm, and Tom, not knowing what else to say after that, told her to have a great summer if they didn't see each other before school was out.

Without missing a beat, she echoed the same. It seemed his assumptions had been correct: She liked being with him, but she didn't seem to be looking for anything more serious. He would take that stance too, he decided, although he wished she'd said she wanted to see him again before they moved out of the dorms for the summer.

Tom finished out his semester, said goodbye to Kevin, Woz, and Coach, and packed up his things to go home. As he and his parents made the drive back to Massillon, he thought about Becky and what he'd learned from her since the night of their first date. He felt different because of her, and when they pulled into town, Massillon seemed a lot smaller to him than it used to.

11

Tom finished his final rep with a burst of speed, pushing the high school blocking sled across the line he had marked with a towel. Even though it wasn't long after sunrise and the summer morning air was still cool, his T-shirt was drenched with sweat. He felt pretty good about the workout, but he was still a long way from reaching the sled weight and the number of reps Coach Peters and Jonesy wanted him to work up to. At least he felt no tenderness in his Achilles tendon.

He toweled himself off and noticed a group of boys entering the practice field. That was just what he'd have been doing two years earlier. The high school rules didn't allow coaches to be present until later in the summer, so really dedicated players would go work out on their own. He recognized one of them, probably going into his senior year. The others were probably sophomores and juniors.

"Hey, O'Brien!" the senior said. "What are you doing here?"

"Hey." He had forgotten the boy's name.

The other boys stared at him, and one whispered, "That's Tom O'Brien." His size and reputation had made such an impact in his hometown, but in college, he'd become so absorbed in his studies that he was less aware of how others saw him and his football player friends.

"How's the team going to be this year?" Tom said, wiping sweat from his forehead with the side of his hand.

"Looking good," the senior said. "We should finish first in the conference, if we can beat Canton." The other boys nodded, seeming to stand taller in an attempt to impress Tom.

"I'm pulling for you guys," Tom said and smiled. "Massillon all the way." He turned to grab his workout bag but then stopped to look back at them. "Keep up with these workouts—that's what gives you an edge and separates Massillon from Canton." He could feel the boys' eyes on him as he left the field.

Tom had always enjoyed finding subtle ways to build teammates up and motivate them through the way he trained and played himself. He thought about how Coach Peters treated him and his teammates in a similar way—no big speeches or harsh words, just someone with experience who helped his players get to the next level.

———

Tom's father actually seemed glad to have him at home for the summer. Although some of the things Tom had said couldn't be undone, the two of them had figured out a way to quietly coexist. Tom could tell his father was pleased to see the way he applied himself to his workouts, even if he still found things to criticize. And if Grandpa was around, his father consistently counteracted every one of Grandpa's encouragements with something Tom should be doing better.

Although he avoided fights with his father, it was a relief to leave the house for his carpentry job each day. Dan had welcomed him back, and the crew was glad to see him. Within the first week, Dan asked if he and Jack wanted to play on their softball team again. Tom had not talked to Jack since their awkward conversation at Thanksgiving. He'd thought of reaching out but hung up the phone each time he started to dial. Jack's lecturing had been really annoying, but it had also hit home. Tom decided to finally call him, using softball as an excuse.

"Jack, it's me. Dan wants us to play on his softball team again."

It was silent on the other end of the line. Then Jack said, "I thought you were pissed off."

"I was, but I can move past it if you can."

"I didn't mean it the way you took it." Jack was silent for a few more seconds. "So . . . you're saying you want to put up with me this summer?"

Tom suddenly felt guilty. He remembered fights he and Jack had over the years—no matter how smug Jack could be, Tom knew his anger could also hurt Jack. "Yeah. I do," Tom said.

"I'll play softball," Jack said. "That would make my summer."

"Good. Practice is tomorrow at five. I'll see you there."

After Dan and the carpenters welcomed them back at the practice, Tom and Jack played catch to warm up. They didn't say anything else about their Thanksgiving argument; they just focused on the familiar rhythm of throwing and catching the ball.

With their friendship renewed, they began hanging out a lot together. There were always gatherings on weekends of their high school friends who had moved into apartments. They enjoyed seeing their friends, but usually only had a couple of beers and then left early. Tom was especially careful not to show any signs of drinking when he came home to his parents' house.

One night, Jack and Tom stopped by the Burger Grill to eat after leaving a party early.

"I gotta say—you're a different animal than you were last summer," Jack said.

"I don't really like to think about it. Last summer was a blur."

"Yeah, I mean, you were taken in by the police . . ." Jack had been picking up some French fries from the basket they were sharing but paused.

Tom grew wary, hoping that Jack wouldn't lecture him again. He made room on the table for the waitress to set down their platters. "I'm trying to be in a different place now. I have a fresh start at Kent State, and I don't want to waste it." Tom cringed a little to hear some of his father in his own words.

Jack carefully chewed his fries. "I've noticed—hardly any beers compared to last summer."

"I need to be in shape for football."

"That's when you're at your best," Jack said. He hesitated again, and Tom wondered what he'd say next. Jack finally lifted his head and looked directly at Tom. "Just don't backslide if you don't have football," he said.

This was better than Jack's ranting at Thanksgiving. "I don't plan to lose football," Tom said, smiling and nodding to some people who walked past their table. "Not if I can help it."

———

When he returned to Kent for the start of football practice, Tom demonstrated his progress from his summer workouts by pushing a heavy sled down the field. Coach Peters and Jonesy said he passed with flying colors. Coach said he could now practice with the other offensive linemen and compete for a starting position.

Tom knew that blocking real people was different than pushing a blocking sled, but he hadn't done it for a while. The first time he participated in a scrimmage, he attempted to clear a path for the running back to run through, but the linebacker quickly filled the space. It was so easy to open a hole for the running back in high school. Either these defensive players were much better than high school players, or his injury had reduced his strength and explosiveness. The more he played, the more he thought it was the latter. The players were better, but so was he. The difference was in his inability to push off as firmly and quickly with his leg.

Tom experienced his biggest challenge when he was opposite Richie, who had, since his play the previous year, been named an all-conference defensive lineman. His size—heavier than Tom—and his speed made him a difficult opponent to block. He filled every hole Tom tried to make for the running backs, stopping them with no gain. He would glare at Tom after each play, with the left side of his mouth twisting down in a perpetual sneer.

Tom had better luck when he blocked Richie on passing plays, which required technique more than explosiveness. During a scrimmage that focused on passing, Tom kept Richie from reaching the quarterback on every pass. He could see Richie becoming more and more agitated. At the end of the final play, Richie tried to get by Tom after Coach Peters had already blown the whistle.

"Get out of my way, O'Brien," Richie said, pushing Tom one way and then the other. He was tough to block, but Tom kept blocking him until the coach blew the whistle again.

"Richie! Save that energy for a real game!" Coach said.

"I just wanted to see how good this Massillon boy is," Richie said, staring Tom down.

"Massillon players know blocking techniques. Tom just showed you classic pass-blocking moves."

"He was holding me!" Richie shouted, moving in as if he was going to give Tom another push. Tom didn't back down.

"Nope. He knows just how far to go with his hands before it's a holding penalty," Coach said. Richie cursed under his breath and glared at Tom for a few more moments before turning away.

Afterward, Tom walked off the field with Woz, who, Tom knew, had his own challenges blocking Richie.

"What's the deal with Richie?" Tom said.

"He likes to show everyone that he's top dog. You surprised him today," Woz said. "But watch yourself—he'll be ready for you next time."

Tom hadn't liked Richie since they'd first met the previous season, but Richie had left him alone because he wasn't a real threat at the time. Now, Richie's contentiousness could potentially be a problem, though he respected Richie's football skills. Woz's words only served to stoke Tom's competitive fires. Richie might be ready for him next time, but he would also be ready for Richie.

———

Kevin suggested they continue rooming together in the dorms in the fall, and Tom agreed. On Kevin's first night back after summer break, he regaled Tom over a pizza about his summer experience as a student worker in a Chicago legal aid office. Kevin's observations of the legal aid clients—primarily Black and Hispanic—opened a new awareness for Tom, revealing a world of poverty, racism, and daily struggles of living that felt more real now than they had before.

"If you're a teenage boy, you could be thrown in prison for stealing a pack of cigarettes," Kevin said. "If you're a single mother who can't afford rent, you could be fined and evicted! If you have a traffic violation, your police record could prevent you from getting a job!" His voice grew louder. He gesticulated wildly with his hands as he spoke, allowing his palm to slam onto the table at one point. A group of students in the next booth looked over.

Tom was beginning to feel as amped up as Kevin. He had never thought much about the issues surrounding race and poverty. They hadn't played much of a role in his existence as a high school football player in Massillon. He found Kevin's knowledge and passion intoxicating, and it was like the night he, Becky, Kevin, and Laura had gone out together. He liked that students, like him, were talking about real problems and things that mattered in the world.

"After my first day, I didn't drive my GTO to work again—I took the bus," Kevin said. "I just couldn't. It was like I was showing off my status with that car."

"I guess we were lucky where we grew up," Tom said.

"Yeah, and it's just a matter of fate. I thought of the Black football players on our team. They're just friends and teammates to us—but now I wonder about their backgrounds—if there's more to their story and experiences than I'm aware of."

"It makes you think about the race riots this summer."

"No kidding! Twenty-six people died in Newark! I mean, that's crazy!"

Their pizza grew cold as they talked. Other tables of students came and went, and still Tom and Kevin stayed until their server, looking annoyed, deposited take-home cartons on their table.

A couple days later, Woz returned to school. He joined Tom and Kevin in the cafeteria for dinner and told them all about his work with a furniture moving company that summer. The foreman had taken one look at his size and hired him on the spot without an interview. He said one of the most interesting parts for him was learning about the company's business practices—pricing, scheduling, accounting, and seeing how everything worked firsthand.

"I had no idea I would be into that," Woz said. "But it was fascinating to learn how the company made a profit."

"Maybe you're going to be the head of Mayflower someday," Kevin joked, leaning back in his chair.

"I don't know about that," Woz said. "But maybe I'm cut out for something in business." He looked earnest and determined.

Tom smiled. Both these guys had undergone transformations over the summer. Kevin was ready to change the world and help the downtrodden, while Woz was thinking he might want to be a successful businessman. It was like their eyes had been opened. Could either of those paths be something he might pursue after graduation? Or was his path something entirely different? He knew only that his priority at the moment was football. Beyond that, he couldn't tell.

—

The 1967 football season began with Tom, Woz, and Kevin spending games on the bench. The conference games were challenging, and the coaches only made a few substitutions. Even though Tom wasn't playing, he was thrilled to be back on the sidelines, watching players go into the game and come out, urged on by their enthusiastic coaches. Each week, the Ohio weather grew colder, often with swirling clouds and, at times, rain. But nothing distracted Tom. He found himself leaning in as he followed the game, his muscles tensed, his mind focused. He was prepared to play whenever he might be called.

In their fourth game against Miami of Ohio on a crisp sunny afternoon, Miami's big linebacker sacked Kent State's senior quarterback, Kovacs, and he hit the ground hard. Jonesy ran out and, after examining him, helped Kovacs off the field. The coaches replaced him with a sophomore quarterback named Patterson who had shown potential as a passer. He completed two passes, exciting the crowd, but then was sacked twice by defensive linemen who broke through their line.

Coach beckoned for Tom and Woz, his eyes wide and serious. "We need more protection for Patterson!" he said. "You guys get in there and show me you can do it!" He clapped them on their backs and sent them in.

Tom's heart raced as he ran onto the field. He was nervous about his Achilles tendon, even though it felt strong and completely healed. Their first play was a half-back plunge, but the defensive linemen quickly closed the hole that Tom and Woz had tried to open. The second play was a passing play. Tom and Woz blocked well, holding the rushers at bay and allowing Patterson to complete a fifteen-yard pass. After another running play, Tom and Woz protected Patterson long enough for him to throw a long pass, giving Kent State a forty-yard gain. Tom cheered wildly and gave high fives to Woz and other teammates.

Miami scored two touchdowns late in the game to take the win, but Coach made a point to find Tom and Woz on the sidelines afterward and compliment them on their pass-blocking. He said they still had work to do on blocking for runs, but they would see more action in passing situations. Tom stared at the coach and nodded, still breathing hard. He hadn't played in a real football game for two years, and he'd missed the thrill of being in the game, the rush of adrenaline coursing through his body. He couldn't control his sense of exhilaration, and as he made his way to the locker room, his mind replayed everything that had occurred after he had entered the game.

Tom showered, dressed, and packed his bag, still unable to believe he'd even gotten to play that day. He went outside to where the team would board the bus to return to the practice facility and meet with the coaches before returning to their dorms. The temperature had dropped and as he pulled his jacket closed and approached the bus, he heard a familiar voice yell, "Tommy!" He turned to see Grandpa standing with his father and Kara outside a gated area.

"Great game, Tom!" they all yelled, even his father. He waved to them, speechless, and felt his eyes water. A lump rose into his throat. He hadn't had anyone cheer for him for such a long time. His father, bundled in a big coat, met his eye and gave him a nod.

Coach stood by the bus door watching Tom as the players boarded. He looked over to Kara and Grandpa waving and shouting for Tom at the gate, then reached out to shake Tom's hand.

"Good first game back, O'Brien. I knew you had it in you."

Tom blinked back some tears and cleared his throat, but no words would come. He shook Coach's hand and boarded the bus.

That night, Jack called from Miami and said he'd been able to listen to the game on the radio. At first, he just boasted about the RedHawks beating the Golden Flashes. Tom rolled his eyes, but let him have his moment. But then Jack said he wanted to hear how Tom felt it went. Tom described the passing plays and Coach's praise. "Your dream is coming true!" Jack said. Tom was silent as he held the telephone receiver in his hand, his heart swelling with pride and gratefulness. It meant a lot to hear this from Jack, who knew better than anyone what he had been through.

———

Kevin had dates every week and continued to tease Tom about his lack of interest in girls. He said Tom had an obsession with football—he called it Tom's monomania. But Tom's experience contrasted with Kevin's, who only played as a defensive back when the game's outcome was known. The coaches gave Kevin experience for the future; they allowed Tom to influence the present. Tom understood the privilege of this and established himself in the coaches' eyes as a valuable member of the offensive line.

It wasn't that he had stopped thinking about girls. He'd thought about Becky quite a bit during the past summer and in the early weeks of his return to campus. But she'd made no move to find out how he was doing either. Kevin hadn't been in touch with Laura since their date last spring, and Tom didn't know which dorm Becky might have moved into this year. In all likelihood, Becky hadn't thought of him at all in a while, so he'd focused on what he needed to—football. Still, once he began playing regularly, he decided to call her.

Tom dialed Becky's number, not knowing what to expect. He wasn't even sure if her number was the same. But she picked up.

"Hi. How's the semester going for you?" he asked.

"Good. Busy," she said, sounding distracted.

"I wondered—are you interested in going out this Saturday?" Tom asked.

Becky said she was busy Friday and Saturday but could see him on Sunday. Tom hesitated, feeling he was competing for her time as before. He'd been hoping for a date with her Saturday night to celebrate the football game he was playing that day, but he supposed he'd have to take what he could get. He said he would pick her up that Sunday afternoon, and after a couple of seconds of silence, they said goodbye.

Tom was unsure how to greet her at her dorm entrance, but she surprised him by turning her lips up for a kiss. She asked him what they should do on such a beautiful fall day, and he suggested walking to Riveredge Park.

Becky took his arm, and they walked from campus toward downtown and the Cuyahoga River, updating each other on what they had done that summer. As she leaned against him, Tom thought that perhaps he'd read too much into things during their phone call. She told him she had enjoyed working as an intern with a neighborhood newspaper at home and, influenced by that experience, had volunteered to be a reporter that fall for the *Daily*, the Kent State student newspaper. When Tom described his summer routine of early workouts before his carpentry job, she laughed. "Why am I not surprised you spent your summer preparing for more football," she said. "I've thought of you when I've read *Daily* reporters' coverage of the games. How's it going?"

"I played a lot of minutes in the last two games. We're not a great team, not many wins, but—"

"But you're enjoying it." She smiled up at him, and he couldn't help but feel enamored by her.

"I am. Maybe you should come watch."

"I don't understand football. It seems so violent to me," Becky said, shrugging. "If I were to watch a sport, I'd choose tennis or gymnastics." They passed some students on bicycles.

"I could watch tennis or gymnastics with you." He realized that he didn't even know when the seasons were for these sports.

She studied something on the horizon. "We could, but sports are just not that important to me."

He laughed. "I guess we're different in that way."

They reached the river and went toward the waterfall near the center of the business district. Tom suggested they walk deeper into the park on the path on the wooded riverbank. They stepped down a stairway and strolled along the river, stopping at observation decks to enjoy the shade and watch the flowing water. Tom was aware of how much he'd missed being near Becky. As they entered the forest, suddenly distant from downtown, it felt like they were in their own private world for a moment. Birds sang in the shaded cool air as they walked along a corridor lined by large trees whose leaves were changing to shades of orange and red. When they came to an opening with a bench on the edge of the shade, they sat down while other couples occasionally passed by.

"Are you still following politics?" Tom asked. It was easy to feel like they had a connection when they talked about issues, and he felt close to her when she engaged with him so passionately.

"More than ever. Vietnam just keeps getting worse."

"Kevin and I talked about the race riots in Newark this summer."

"It's all connected," Becky said. "Our society needs help, whether it's the war or discrimination."

A squirrel clambered down a tree, and birds in the branches increased their volume as if to scold the squirrel for disturbing the peace.

"Have you ever felt discriminated against?" he said.

She looked away from the squirrel and directly into his eyes. "I haven't experienced a man being promoted over me when I'm more qualified, like I know happens. But I feel it in what's expected of me. I'm sure my mom would be happy if I devoted my life to being a mother and housewife, like she has."

"Becoming a journalist doesn't fit that mold," he said.

"Not for me, it doesn't. I went to some women's liberation speeches in Cleveland this summer. I'm thinking of offering to write a column for the *Daily* on women's issues."

"I'd read it," he said.

She laughed, and dimples appeared in her cheeks. "You're a unique football player."

When Tom walked Becky back to her dorm later, he asked her to see him the following Sunday since he had an away game Saturday. She agreed, and he bent down to kiss her goodbye, then walked back to his dorm.

He felt so distant from her at times. He couldn't figure it out. Maybe he was also distant, given his caution after Cindi and his focus on football. Maybe she was feeding off his cues. Still, they seemed to enjoy being together and attracted to the part of the other's life that was quite different from theirs. Was that enough? No, he realized—he wanted more intimacy, and more of their stimulating conversations.

———

On Sunday, Tom asked Woz if he could borrow his car for his date with Becky. He didn't even think of asking to borrow Kevin's GTO, not wanting to come across as that flashy, especially to Becky.

Becky was surprised that Tom had picked her up in a car. As he opened the passenger-side door for her, he saw her notice Woz's football bag in the back seat. She smiled and kissed him on the cheek before getting in. When they pulled away from the curb, Becky asked about his game, and he felt flattered that she wanted to know.

He proposed going to a movie and then trying a new restaurant on the edge of town. Remembering *The Battle of Algiers* and her eagerness to talk about it afterward, he suggested another serious movie, *A Man for All Seasons*. She raised an eyebrow, appeared amused, and said she liked that choice.

Tom found the movie boring initially but grew intrigued when it was clear Thomas More was risking his life. Although he tried to watch it critically and think about the larger issues it was raising, he was also conscious of Becky next to him. She reciprocated when he reached out to hold her hand, but she didn't turn to look at him once. She appeared to be deeply absorbed by the movie.

At dinner, Tom asked what she thought of it.

"I kept thinking of politics today," she said. "How would people in Johnson's cabinet act if they opposed the Vietnam War? What would they be willing to risk if they disagreed with their president, as Thomas More disagreed with his king?"

"Well, they wouldn't have to risk their life like Thomas More," Tom said. "I mean, our presidents don't have people executed."

"It seems like the first moral stand would be to resign," she said, folding her arms. "Maybe the next act would be to speak and write against the war." She paused. "What did you think of the movie?"

"It was good," Tom said. "What struck me, I think, is that it showed a man willing to die for his principles. I don't know if I would have felt that strongly."

She nodded, interested. They continued discussing the movie as the food arrived, analyzing the characters and their motivations. Becky seemed to be in her element as she spoke; she was spirited and enthusiastic about her ideas and ready to debate and argue about his. Tom had never had this kind of conversation on a date before and couldn't even imagine it happening with Cindi, who had often only talked about who was dating whom, and how he was doing in football. Talking this way—wrestling with Becky over different interpretations of a thought-provoking movie—it made him feel alive.

Still, by the time Tom paid the check and they were ready to go, he said, "Enough thinking. It's a nice night. How about if we go to the city park?"

She looked at him and smiled. "Okay."

Tom drove them to a picnic area with a gravel lot near the river. He parked far away from the other car already there and turned to look at her. They both smiled, and he leaned over to kiss her, holding her close. The inside of the car warmed up, and Tom turned to crack a window. They pressed together as much as they could in the front seat of the compact car, moving their hands over each other's bodies. Neither one of them said a word.

Tom felt like he could have stayed there all night, enjoying the pleasure they gave each other, but after an hour or so, he said he'd better get her back to her dorm, since they both had early classes on Monday morning. She readily agreed, as if she'd been thinking the same thing.

He walked her to the front door, his arm around her shoulders, still wanting her body next to his. "When can we see each other again?" he asked.

"I'm going to need to study for midterms," she said matter-of-factly. Her arm was around his waist, but she appeared unbothered about saying she was unavailable.

There it was again—her hesitation—so he adjusted, pulling back from her slightly. "We have an away game again next weekend, a long bus ride, so Saturday won't work for me."

He waited to see if she would suggest anything, but she simply said, "No problem," and smiled. She pulled the door open.

"Let's touch base after my game and your midterms, and we'll figure something out," he said, trying to sound light and noncommittal.

She looked back at him, and they kissed. He walked to the car with a feeling of uncertainty. It had been a great night, and she'd seemed to enjoy herself. Tom was elated when he thought of their conversation at dinner and their time in the car. But what was it she wanted out of their relationship? There seemed to be a limit to how close she was willing to be, like it was fine when they were together, but she had somewhere else to be.

He realized, though, that this didn't change how he felt about her. He wanted more intimacy, a deeper commitment, and he knew he was willing to risk a potential repeat of the pain he'd felt when Cindi had broken up with him.

If it didn't work out, he still had football.

———

While Tom's role in the offensive line grew in importance, as measured by the minutes he played in games, Kevin's role as a defensive back did not. He continued playing on the second or third team, and rarely played in games. He told Tom he didn't know how much longer he would want to play at that level.

"I don't need a scholarship, you know," Kevin said. "I could walk away at any time."

Tom tried to encourage him. "But look at the seniors playing your position. They'll be graduating, and you'll replace them next year."

But Kevin shrugged. "Honestly, I don't know if it's worth waiting. I'm actually having more fun in my classes. Sociology has been way more interesting than sitting on the bench."

Tom couldn't see how any class could be more fun than football, but this piqued his curiosity. "Sociology? Come on. Really?"

"Yeah, like right now, we're reading *Growing Up Absurd* by a guy named Paul Goodman," Kevin said, holding up a book that had been lying open on his bed. "It talks about how our society is dominated by big business and organized systems that are killing our human spirit. Young people like us are rebelling against these systems. We don't need to buy into them."

"Huh. Sounds interesting," Tom said. "I don't have much time between my classes and football, but maybe I'll pick it up one day if you don't mind."

"It's kind of mind blowing." Kevin placed the book on top of his gym bag. "You know, football itself can be seen as a symbol of our sick society. Think about it—it's organized, systematic, and violent, unlike more creative sports like basketball."

"It sounds to me like you're talking yourself into quitting."

"Nah," Kevin said. "I'll give it to the end of the season."

Kevin continued to practice, but Tom could tell his heart wasn't in it. He was also changing, starting with letting his hair grow. It had gotten down to the bottom of his neck when it attracted the attention of Richie during the last week of the season.

"Hey Valenta, what are you? Some kind of California hippie?" Richie said in the locker room after practice. He reached out and pulled at a tuft of Kevin's hair. Tom was getting dressed near Kevin's locker, where Richie and Kevin faced each other.

"What are *you*? Some kind of Neanderthal right-winger?" Kevin said, jerking his head away. "And trust me—California is way ahead of Ohio."

"Ahead at taking drugs and protesting the war. Maybe you should go live in Berkeley."

"I might. The war those Berkeley students are protesting is immoral, you know." Kevin slammed his locker shut.

"Immoral? Shit, no. Those communists deserve to die. You *are* a hippie, Valenta. No wonder you're a third-team has-been."

"Get out of my face," Kevin said. He pushed Richie away.

Richie's face changed from mocking to menacing. Towering over Kevin, he shoved Kevin into the lockers, slamming another locker door shut with a loud crash. Other players stopped what they were doing and turned toward the fight. Kevin, enraged, moved toward Richie, but Tom quickly stepped between them, facing Richie down.

"Are you Valenta's white knight, O'Brien? How close are you guys as roommates?" Richie looked past Tom at Kevin. "Let him try to do whatever he's thinking," he said, sticking out his chin.

"Back off," Tom said quietly. They stared at each other for several seconds.

"Knock it off, you guys!" a voice yelled from across the room. It was the senior quarterback, Kovacs, who was captain of the team.

"Gladly," Richie said, bringing his chest a few inches closer before moving away. "It would've been no contest."

Kevin looked furious. As they walked back to the dorm together, he said, "You don't need to fight my fights."

Tom touched Kevin on the shoulder apologetically. "Sorry—Richie's crazy," he said. "Don't let him bother you."

"He fits in with the right-wing bullies ruining this country," Kevin said.

Back in their room, Kevin picked up the book *Growing Up Absurd*, propped a pillow on his bed, and lay back to read. But he was still scowling, and Tom could tell he was having a hard time concentrating.

Tom grabbed a textbook from his backpack and prepared to study. He thought about the split developing across the country. Becky had compared their current political leaders to Thomas More, a political figure from centuries ago who was willing to die for his beliefs. Were politics in America moving to *those* extremes? And if they were, where did he stand? He knew he favored Kevin and Becky's positions over Richie's, but there was still a lot he didn't know. Instead of studying, he picked up one of Kevin's sociology books and started to thumb through it.

12

Tom and Jack hung out frequently over Christmas break, watching football bowl games at Tom's house, going to parties, and seeing high school friends, though some of those old friendships were not as close as before. It was good seeing everyone, but Tom had more in common with those who had gone away to college, as he and Jack had.

At one party, Tom looked across the living room and was startled to see Cindi in a tight red holiday dress, looking as beautiful as ever. He hadn't thought of her for quite a while, particularly since he'd met Becky. She was surrounded by admiring boys and had just taken a sip of beer when she saw Tom. She left the group and walked over, her eyes on his as she crossed the room.

"You look good, Tommy. How are you?"

"Hi." He didn't know what to say to her. Her lips were a deep red, and she smiled at him.

"I hear you're playing football at Kent State."

"Yeah, my tendon healed enough that I could play." He remembered her in his hospital room after his surgery, leaning over to kiss him, her breasts pressed against him. She stood a few inches closer to him than he thought she needed to.

"How is Ohio State?" he asked, moving back a little.

"It wasn't for me. I switched to Stark College," Cindi said, pouting slightly. He tried to imagine that shade of lipstick on Becky but couldn't.

"Why?"

"I missed Massillon, and I missed Curt," she said, taking a step back. She looked over toward the kitchen, where Tom realized Curt was chugging beer with friends.

"Oh." Though he had ceased to have feelings for Cindi, he was annoyed to know she was still with Curt. "What are your plans after Stark then?" he asked. He took a drink of his beer, trying to show that he wasn't bothered by Curt.

"Curt's going to enlist in the navy. We might get married."

"Congrats . . . I mean . . . if you get married." Tom smiled inwardly, thinking that Becky would never consider getting married at their age. "I wish you guys the best."

Tom spotted Jack, who appeared to be quietly watching them from a distance. "Looks like Jack needs me," Tom lied, pointing across the room. "It was great to see you, Cindi."

"Great to see *you*. I'm glad you're playing again, Tommy," she said too brightly. She reached out to give Tom a hug but, because Tom had already started to move toward Jack, it became an awkward pat. He hugged her from the side, thinking how differently she felt from Becky.

"Did she charm you?" Jack asked as Tom neared him. He was leaning against a doorframe that led to a main hallway. A couple made out by the closet.

"Not anymore. Maybe back in the day, but it wouldn't happen now."

"I don't know. There was a time when you would forget about everything else if Cindi batted those eyelashes and gave you her big smile."

"She's beautiful, but I don't think she's my type anymore. I've moved past that," Tom said, stepping out of the way as a group of guys arrived at the party and entered the room.

"To Becky?" Jack asked, smiling. Tom had told Jack a little about his seemingly on-again/off-again relationship with Becky. "What's she like?"

"Becky's smart, independent, and motivated. She writes for the school paper, she's informed. We talk about things—politics, our government, world affairs, the war . . ."

Jack took a moment to absorb this news. "Is Becky against the war?" he asked.

"Of course. Aren't you?"

"I want it to end," Jack said, "especially before I graduate. I don't want to get drafted or anything." Jack was peering at him through his glasses.

"Me, neither. I think the president should end it right now. I don't see its purpose."

"Well, we're supposed to be stopping communism," Jack said, lowering his beer. "Domino theory. It's what we have to do."

"Becky thinks it's a civil war, and we're making it worse for the Vietnamese, and on top of that it's killing too many of our soldiers."

Jack frowned. "Not sure if I agree with Becky."

"Really? Lots of people are protesting. You don't agree that things have gotten out of hand?" Tom asked.

"There were protests at Miami this fall against Dow Chemical because they manufacture the napalm used in Vietnam. But when you think about it, what's wrong with that? It's a war. It's not going to be pretty—that's the reality. Plus, Dow has good engineering jobs—think of all the people it can employ. It's good for our economy."

This didn't sit right with Tom, but he wasn't confident enough of his information to counter Jack, and he didn't want to get into another one of their arguments. He sensed, though, that their beliefs about the war were headed in opposite directions.

He also realized how far he'd come since he dated Cindi. He glanced at her, once again talking with the group of admiring boys, this time by the couch. It had been almost two years since they'd broken up, and they were living in different worlds.

—

Tom, his father, and Grandpa watched a lot of football together over Christmas break, the highlight being the Cleveland Browns conference championship game. The Browns lost, but Tom and his family were proud of their winning season and reaching the playoffs. It seemed to Tom, as Grandpa refilled his glass with Irish whiskey and Tom's father sat quietly in his armchair, that the family was back in equilibrium for the most part, like when he was doing well in high school football. Grandpa talked to Tom about the Kent State football team, wanting to know the team's prospects for the following fall, and he chatted with Tom about his performance in games. Tom's father listened to every word, but he kept his distance, sullen and reserved as he always was when Grandpa and Tom seemed close.

The equilibrium was disturbed, however, by tension from Kara. One Sunday afternoon, when she and their mother were washing the dishes after dinner, Kara clunked cups around in the sink when Tom entered with some plates.

"Stark is close to home," their mother said to Kara. "A lot of girls around here attend Stark." With Kara in her final year of high school, the family had talked about her plans for the future while they were eating, and their mother had said she thought Kara should pick a program at Stark College and get a two-year associate degree.

"It's a good choice for you," Tom's father said from the other room.

Kara scrubbed a fork furiously. "My grades right now are pretty good," she mumbled, "better than what some other kids have who are applying to other schools."

"You'd do well at Stark," their mother said, handing her a pan.

Tom could see that Kara had more to say, but instead, she shoved the pan beneath the faucet, and it splattered water everywhere.

When, later, Tom and Kara went shopping in town for a gift for their mother, whose birthday was coming up in the new year, he tried to see if he could get to the bottom of it.

"Only one semester left of high school," Tom said, next to a rack of scarves. Kara was looking through them to find a color their mother might like.

"I can't wait to be on my own," she said without looking up.

"I remember those days. But I'd say you're better off than I was at that time," Tom said with a smile, trying to soften her up. She didn't react. "Do you think you'd move out and get your own place if you went to Stark?"

Kara hesitated, her face becoming serious. "I haven't said this to Mom and Dad, but I want to go to Ohio State."

Kara? A Buckeye? Tom was surprised, but the more he looked at Kara standing resolutely next to those scarves, the more he liked the idea. She was capable and smart, and he could envision her enjoying school at a larger university. "I could see you there," he said.

"There's more," she said. Tom straightened up and faced her. Her eyes were glistening.

"I want to play field hockey at Ohio State," she said.

"That would be great. What kind of program do they have?"

"Peggy, our top scorer, visited two weeks ago and talked to the club coach. They want her to play for them."

"You could too."

"Yeah, but here's what she found out. The coach told Peggy that the Big Ten is going to make field hockey an NCAA sport, with scholarships and everything. And . . . I don't know how she heard of me, but she wants me to play for them too!"

"What? You have a chance for a scholarship?" Tom was amazed. Kara had been noticed by the OSU coach, and she might have a chance to go to Ohio State and play at the NCAA level! This was, in so many ways, Tom's dream—he was envious and yet thrilled for his sister.

Kara put down the lavender scarf she was holding. "I have the application done. I filled it out two months ago, but I haven't told Mom and Dad. You heard them—they want me to go to Stark. I would need their support to go to Ohio State."

Tom thought of the way Kara had encouraged him when he was stuck, suggesting he call the Kent State football coach. "I'll talk to them. We can't waste this opportunity. Would that be alright?"

Her eyes widened. "Yes!" She beamed gratefully, knocking some scarves to the side as she lunged forward to hug Tom.

Tom hugged her back, smiling, then helped her put the scarves back into a stack. "All right. Let's corner them when we get back."

As soon as they returned, Tom approached his parents in the family room, where they were watching TV with Grandpa. He went to the TV to lower the volume while Kara stood slightly behind him, as she had often done when they were growing up. Tom's father, who had been kneeling to add logs to the fire, turned to look at Tom questioningly, as if expecting bad news from him.

"What's this about?" his father asked.

Grandpa set his whiskey glass down on the armrest of his chair. "Everything okay, Tommy?"

"You know how you guys have always wanted an O'Brien at Ohio State? Well, Kara has an opportunity," Tom said. Tom's father stood up quickly. Tom put his arm around Kara and moved her forward, so she was next to him.

"I've been invited by the OSU coach to play for her field hockey team," Kara said.

The family looked startled. "She'd be fantastic," Tom said, his arm still around Kara's shoulders. Kara's body was tense. "Tell them more," Tom said to Kara.

Kara filled them in, her face defiant but her voice thick with emotion. She told them about her teammate Peggy being invited and about the Big

Ten's plan to make field hockey an NCAA sport. When Kara mentioned the NCAA, Tom's father sat down next to their mother, looking from Tom to Kara and back to Tom again.

Their mother took some time to grasp the possibility and its meaning. "Columbus is so far away," she said after a short silence. Kara sighed impatiently.

Tom decided to try to facilitate. "What if she got a scholarship to attend? Would you be okay with it then?" Their father nodded slowly, but he could see their mother still had her doubts. "I don't go back to school for another two weeks. How about I drive Kara to Columbus, so she can meet the coach, and after that, you guys can decide?"

To his surprise, their father said, "That sounds reasonable," and their mother sniffled and said yes. Tom heard Kara quietly gasp next to him, but she otherwise kept her composure until, shortly after, she bounded up the stairs.

Grandpa smiled at Tom from his armchair, raised his glass, and gave him a silent toast.

The following day, while Kara called Ohio State to make an appointment during Christmas break with the club coach, Tom found himself in his room, shuffling through the stack of scholarship withdrawal letters he'd stored away in his desk. He didn't know why he'd kept them exactly, since it still pained him a little to see them, but it struck him now that each letter represented an opportunity he'd had before his injury. If the circumstances had been different, or he'd gone anywhere else other than Kent, would be the same person today? He would never have met Coach Peters, Kevin, or Woz . . . or Becky, for that matter.

Tom looked up at his old Ohio State poster, still on his wall. He'd never formally been offered a place on the team at OSU but would have gone if given the chance. He didn't regret that he was at Kent State, but life felt uncertain. He was neither a starting player nor the best student at Kent. He didn't know as much about politics and the world as Kevin. He didn't know how much Becky really cared for him.

Maybe it was seeing the letters of rejection, but Tom's thoughts made him feel uneasy about his future. The only thing he was sure of was that Kara had a chance to pursue a path she was excited about, so he wanted to do everything he could to help her achieve her goal.

When Tom and Kara made the two-hour drive to Columbus during the week after New Year's Day, he offered Kara bits of advice about college, choosing classes, and talking with coaches. But as they entered the city and drove toward the massive campus, Tom studied the familiar academic buildings in the distance and saw once again the stadium he'd longed to play in.

Tom dropped Kara off at the athletic training facility. He wanted her to do this independently, but he also didn't want to run into Buckeye football players. As she got out of the car, however, he saw three large students about his size wearing letter jackets. They appeared to be Buckeye linemen. He sat behind the wheel, envisioning what it would have been like to play for a winning program like Ohio State's, where there would be a chance to go to the Rose Bowl every year. Instead, he was at Kent State, playing for a team that had trouble winning more games than it lost. The thought depressed him.

Tom parked and decided to walk around. There were few students on campus that day, but he found himself trying to blend in, as if he were one of them and belonged there. As he walked, he realized his dream of wearing one of those OSU letter jackets was long behind him. He rounded the bend, saw the training facility again, and thought about the irony of fate—how what had been planned for him was now happening for Kara. He was proud of her and knew she needed his support, but he was also stuck on how unfair life was.

Tom got back in the car and waited. When later, the training facility door opened and Kara emerged with a spring in her step and a huge grin playing on her face, he felt selfish. She waved and broke into a run. He remembered the first field hockey game he had watched her play, and how he'd participated vicariously in her every move. That's how he needed to approach this, he told himself—to celebrate her success and not make it about himself.

Kara chattered nonstop on their drive home.

"I guess the coach noticed me at the state tournament last year when she was scouting Peggy. I had no idea college scouts were even watching us!" she said.

"You made an impression," Tom said, changing lanes.

"Yeah, and she told me she wants me on her team!" Kara sat up higher in her seat. "Can you *believe* it?"

"You deserve this, Kara," Tom said. "When did she say field hockey would become an NCAA sport?"

"She wasn't sure, but apparently the process is already in motion—they expect scholarships *next year.*"

"Just in time for you."

They talked about how best to share the information with their parents. When they pulled into Massillon, Tom surprised Kara by stopping by their grandfather's house before going home. Grandpa was flabbergasted that Kara might get a scholarship from Ohio State. He gave her a long hug, and she began to cry, bringing tears to his and Tom's eyes as well. Kara was following in the footsteps of athletes in her family.

Tom realized that when he could look past himself, her win was his win too. And despite all the mixed feelings he'd had in recent days, this gave him a deep sense of satisfaction. *Something* was happening right, and he was glad for the part he'd been able to play in helping it along.

That evening, he received a surprise call from Coach Peters, who informed him that the other coaches had selected Tom to receive a full scholarship for the coming year. Tom thanked him and hung up in a daze. It had been a day of significance for him . . . and for all the O'Briens.

———

After the Christmas break, Tom was still unpacking his clothes in the dorm room when Kevin burst in with his bags. He looked different, and Tom realized he had started growing a mustache and beard.

"What a great break! Music, movies, lectures. There's always so much to do in Chicago."

"You mean you didn't think about football?" Tom asked with a smile.

Kevin dropped his bags on the floor by his bed. "I'm so glad I quit football. I've decided I'm going to study more—I want to learn how to improve our society."

"Good for you. I think *my* semester will be more about football than ever. The coach called me over break and offered me a scholarship for the coming year."

"What? Congratulations!" Kevin clapped Tom on the back. "I know that's what you wanted. Looks like we both have reasons to celebrate."

They met Woz at the cafeteria for dinner that evening, and afterward, decided to all go see *The Graduate* together. Tom enjoyed reconnecting with his two closest college friends again but was struck, as he always was, at how different they were from one another. They were both great guys who seemed to be after completely different things in life. When the three of them returned to their dorm and sat in the lounge to hang out, they started talking about the movie.

"I felt like I could relate to Ben," Kevin said, putting his feet up on a coffee table and watching some of the other returning students go by.

"Really? The whole thing seemed depressing to me," Woz said. "I mean, the movie ended without us knowing what Ben was going to do with his life."

"But that's the point," Kevin said. "He *doesn't* know what to do—it's an empty world."

Tom wasn't sure what he felt about the movie. He didn't mind that it didn't have a conventional resolution, but it left him feeling unsettled. He was troubled for Ben who, in many ways, represented Tom and his friends and what they thought their lives should be about after Kent State. "The business-man was only going to give Ben that one word for advice," Tom said. "Plastics. What do you do with that?"

"Plastics! That blew me away. Incredible," Kevin said, shaking his head.

Woz looked from Kevin to Tom. "But there's nothing wrong with plas-tics," Woz said. "It's a legitimate business—a future he could build on."

"Come on." Kevin sat up. "It showed our society's values—money, busi-ness, and cheap products. Would you want to spend your life getting rich from plastics, basing your life on something so meaningless?"

"Well, I could counter that people need plastics, and money and business are the way the world works," Woz said, looking annoyed. "Why not make a career of providing what people need and want?"

Kevin and Woz both had good points, Tom thought. It was easy to mock the businessman, who cared only about money and possessions. But as he pondered the movie and continued to debate its message with his friends, what stayed with Tom was Ben's uncertainty about what to do with his life. Tom didn't know what he wanted to do either, having only vague thoughts about managing con-struction projects. He was glad he didn't have to decide yet.

———

Although Tom was expected to work out regularly with the football team in the off-season, he had more time to devote to his courses that spring. He decided he should sign up for an introductory construction management course; it seemed a practical thing to do, though he kept hearing the word "plastics" in his head. He found the course useful but was more intrigued by a sociology course on modern society that Kevin convinced him to take that semester. Kevin especially recommended the course reading, *The Sane Society*, by Erich Fromm. He said that it "proved how sick modern capitalism was" and that it "presented forms of communal living." He emphasized the word *communal* and shook his head dreamily.

Fromm's book made Tom think. As he lay on his bed reading, he pondered the idea of an alternative society where people could give their lives and energy to something meaningful—society that united, rather than separated, people from their fellow human beings. Tom thought of his father and grandfather giving their lives to the steel business—and the way their dissatisfaction with their jobs seemed to drive Grandpa to drink or Tom's father to be overly critical.

As Kevin's enthusiasm for his studies increased, the distance between Kevin and Woz only grew. Woz began leaving the cafeteria table early if Kevin started to "preach," as Woz called it. While Kevin continued to talk, Tom would watch Woz grumpily trudge with his tray to the other side of the cafeteria and loudly drop his utensils into a bin of dirty dishes.

But when Tom and Woz were alone, Tom was less guarded, and had more of a chance to ask him about his classes without Kevin interrupting. Woz really seemed to be enjoying his spring classes in finance and marketing, and there were a lot of parallels with his own classes in construction management.

"What I'm talking about is success in the real world, not an ideal world that Kevin's trying to pursue," Woz told Tom one evening as he cut a bite from his pork chop. "Kevin doesn't get that we're not that far apart; I don't want a corrupt society or meaningless way of living either. I just think there's a different way to approach life."

It seemed so reasonable to hear Woz talk about it like that. But Tom continued to see himself as somewhere in the middle between his two friends. Things just didn't seem so black and white for Tom, and he worried that no amount of studying or reading would help him figure it out.

———

Tom had been anxious to see Becky when he returned to campus after the break. He'd missed her, especially after seeing Cindi in Massillon, but as before, neither of them contacted the other right away. Tom knew it was easier to schedule studying together rather than compete for Becky's time on weekends, so he suggested this when he finally gave in and called.

They got together at the library on a Wednesday, and Tom tried to concentrate on the paper he was writing for sociology. Instead, he spent most of the time thinking about Becky's nearness. She furrowed her brow and chewed on a pen as she read her book, but when she noticed Tom watching her, she smiled, and her dimples appeared. He wanted to pull her close. After another half hour of not writing more than a paragraph, Tom said he could use some fresh air and asked if she wanted to take a walk. She shrugged, dog-eared the page she was on, and closed her book.

It had gotten dark outside, which made Tom feel he was alone with her. Walking in step with Becky, he put his arm around her, and she rested her head against his chest. They were bundled up comfortably in jackets, and she wore a knit cap, which he rested his cheek against as he hugged her close to keep her warm. They walked past several academic buildings and dorms without saying very much.

When they arrived by a grassy area off the main path, they sat down on one of several benches, and he leaned toward her to give her a small kiss. She cupped his face in her mittened hands and extended his kiss with a deep, long one in return. Her nose was cold, but her lips were warm.

"Why are you interested in me, O'Brien?" she asked, pulling away after a few moments and pretending to look at him suspiciously.

He was honest. "I like the way you think," he answered. "You're not like any other girl I've met."

She brought his face down closer to hers. "I like the way you think too. You're not like any other football player I've met." She smiled and kissed him again.

"Wait a minute. How many football players do you actually know?" he asked softly, his lips still touching hers.

"Not many," she whispered. "They're not usually my type."

"So I'm the exception?" he smiled. Becky didn't answer but moved closer on the bench and rested her head against his chest. They sat quietly for a few moments, but Tom felt uneasy about her comment. He filled the silence by talking about his break, mentioning his sister's opportunity at Ohio State and the conversation he'd had with Jack at the holiday party back home.

Becky didn't have much to say about field hockey, but she picked up her head to look at Tom when she heard about the protests in Miami. Tom knew Becky had attended several women's liberation and antiwar meetings in Cleveland during her break, and he tried to picture her at one of these.

"What was it like at those antiwar meetings you went to?" he asked. Her passionate opposition to the war had only intensified. She discussed the fundamental issues and told Tom how important the fall election was—that President Johnson had to be replaced, or thousands of American soldiers would continue to die. This made Tom immediately think of Sam. Tom wondered if Sam had been sent to Vietnam; he realized he should have kept in better touch with his friend.

As Becky talked, Tom was struck by how informed, active, fearless, and exciting she was. He wished it wasn't as cold as it was that evening, but he could see her nose getting red after a while. He walked her back to her dorm, kissed her at the door, and thought of their conversation the rest of the evening, even as he stared at the one paragraph on his still-unwritten paper.

In the coming weeks and months, Tom continued to invite Becky to study at the library, hoping for a good excuse to see her that still allowed him to get work done for his classes. She was sometimes too busy, which would leave Tom feeling discouraged, but then at other times, he and Becky would stroll past their bench near the grassy area after a study session and wind up making out there for a while. It was confusing, but he never questioned it when her lips were on his or when their bodies pressed together in Woz's car on the occasional weekend date.

On a warmer night in April, they were kissing on their bench when they heard the voices of some other students getting close. The students spread out some blankets and settled on another part of the grassy area, talking among themselves in the dark. Tom and Becky sat back and gazed at some of the city lights off in the distance. The students' voices got louder as they talked about the war.

"Have you noticed the number of students picketing campus buildings?"

Becky asked. Tom had seen several students with signs to stop the war, some of them heatedly debating with other students who were going in and out of buildings. He knew Becky had also begun following protests at other universities. He nodded, and she told him about the pushback protesters were receiving from campus security officers and city police. Maybe he and Becky were energized by the voices of the students in the group next to them, but they discussed the antiwar movement in depth that night in a way Tom had never heard. The more she filled him in, the more he connected her views with what he'd been reading and learning that semester.

"Hey," Becky said, sitting up. "Why don't you come with me to the demonstration on Friday?"

Tom sat up too. "What is it against?" he asked.

"We're going to picket the placement center where corporations recruit students," she said. "A lot of them are under contract to the US military."

Tom hesitated, remembering Jack's disapproval of protests against Dow at Miami.

"We need to show those students that they'd be helping advance an immoral war that's killing American soldiers," she said. Her voice had grown louder and the other group seemed to be listening.

Tom nodded. "Yeah, I'll come," he said. His heart was beating fast. This felt right.

———

On Friday, Tom dressed in jeans and a T-shirt and skipped the construction management class he had that morning. He met Becky outside the student union. She squeezed his hand and said, "This is the stuff that matters." They joined with other demonstrating students at the campus building housing the placement center. There was an exciting energy in the air. Several students said hi to Tom or gave him a nod. Picking up signs—Tom's said "Bring Our Troops Home"—he and Becky began marching back and forth in front of the building with about thirty other students, chanting, "Stop the war in Vietnam." Becky raised and waved her sign as she and all the other protesters passionately chanted. Their voices were clear, their gazes direct.

Tom skipped the rest of his classes that day, chanting and marching for hours, talking intermittently with protesters, and listening to Becky's arguments when students from campus came to debate them. Four campus police officers took position about fifty feet away to establish a presence, and some of the protesters joked that it was good to have a big football player like Tom there to protect them. Kevin, arriving on the scene after an exam, raised his fist in the air when he saw Tom, and joined their marching. By the end of the afternoon, Tom firmly believed there was no reason for the US to be in Vietnam. Something in him had stirred in a way it never had before.

———

When the spring temperatures rose even more, the green foliage and blossoming flowers led Tom and Becky back to their favorite places, the Riveredge Park and the grassy knoll on the Commons. She would hold his arm as they walked in the park, or they would kiss on a blanket on the Commons after daylight had dimmed. Becky was so sexy—especially when she started wearing shorts and sleeveless T-shirts in the warm weather. He still borrowed Woz's car when he could, and they would park by the river, becoming more and more physical as they made out that spring. One evening, after they had tugged at each other's clothes a while and were both flushed and excited, she told him it might be nice to find a bed somewhere.

"Like a hotel room?" he said, his heart beating even faster.

"That sounds good to me," she said. She moved to give him another long kiss, her lips warm and soft, her hand on his neck. "How about tomorrow night?"

Still aroused, he drove her back to her dorm, while imagining being in bed with her. He couldn't help smiling at her in the passenger seat, and she laughed, her dimples showing. He loved her dimples, and he reached over to hold her hand. "What are you smiling about?" she wanted to know. He didn't answer; he just let his smile grow.

He made reservations for the next night at an older hotel downtown, just a little over a mile's walk from campus. Becky stood outside while Tom checked in. A heavy-set woman took his money and gave him a room key. She had a smirk on her face, and he thought she was going to ask him his age or make a sarcastic comment, but she just turned away.

When they entered the small room, Becky laughed. "Nothing more than the basics," she said. But it didn't matter; all they wanted was the bed. Tom took her in his arms, and he felt her relax as he kissed her. She kissed him back passionately, her mouth parting slightly. He fumbled with her shirt, and she unbuttoned his, and soon they were naked. Her skin was so smooth as he pressed against her and ran his hands over her hips. Their lips moved to each other's necks and chests. They laughed when they saw that each of them had brought a condom. Becky surprised Tom by rolling on top of him. She began slowly, controlling the tempo to match her desire. Tom lay back, hands on her moving hips, his desire climbing until they were overcome with intensity.

They made love again in the morning and then showered together. Tom joked that they needed a big breakfast after that night. Becky hesitated, almost imperceptibly, then agreed. That moment stayed with Tom as they ate breakfast at a café, walked to her dorm, and kissed each other goodbye. Her uncertainty puzzled him, but as he walked back to his dorm, he knew something bigger was happening. He wasn't only becoming politically active—he was falling in love.

13

When Tom arrived at the construction site in Massillon for the first day of his summer job, Dan and the crew reacted to his long hair with good-natured teasing. Tom had grown it well over his ears and combed it back, with a part almost in the center. He smiled at them, knowing he'd get their attention. This was his third summer working for Dan, and the crew all valued how easily Tom readapted each summer, and how instinctively he moved to help where help was needed. He suspected that many of them probably didn't agree with his feelings about Vietnam, but they respected him, and neither he nor they brought it up.

The reaction to his hair at home was less accepting. His father just looked at him, showing his displeasure without speaking. At Kara's high school graduation, the family posed for a photo with her, but Tom noticed his father staring at his hair just as the picture was taken. It didn't help that Kara, who had been accepted by Ohio State and talked incessantly about leaving Massillon, announced that she loved Tom's hair, which made his father even more displeased. She and Tom went to the high school every morning at sunrise to work out together, and she thought it was incredibly funny that they both needed to pull their hair back into a ponytail. As usual, Tom's mother was caught in the middle, at first trying to follow her husband's lead but then becoming ambivalent because criticizing her children was not in her blood.

Grandpa, on the other hand, was amused and curious. He told Tom he was okay with the hippies and their long hair and bell bottoms, as long as they supported the workers and the employee unions. Grandpa didn't want Tom to fight in Vietnam, but he thought it was unfair that college kids got out of it. Grandpa knew that several younger workers at the steel plant had been drafted. Although Tom had expected disapproval of his hair and views from his father, he didn't know how Grandpa would react. As usual, he valued

Grandpa's perspective. He hadn't thought about the fairness of the draft and how it favored the college-educated.

Jack couldn't seem to take his eyes off Tom's hair. Tom caught him studying it with a look of disapproval while he talked about his summer internship for an engineering firm in Cleveland. "You're matching your looks to your beliefs," Jack finally said, shaking his head. Tom was put off by this. Jack hadn't bothered to ask him how school was going, let alone about his decision to grow out his hair.

"I guess I am," Tom said curtly.

"Have you been to any protests?"

"Yeah—in April."

Jack sighed. "I don't like the war," he said. "But I'm not ready to protest. They just need to finish it."

"What does that mean? We should stop it now before more people are killed." Tom had begun getting impatient with people who didn't see the obvious solution.

"Yeah, maybe," Jack said. He started to say something else, but then left it at that, as if he knew he and Tom would not arrive at an understanding. They both sat quietly on the couch in Tom's basement, staring at the TV. Tom pushed his hair behind his ear. After another twenty minutes, Jack said he needed to meet his brother and got up to go.

With Jack's internship in Cleveland about an hour commute each way, Tom and Jack only saw each other on occasional weekends that summer. Jack was unable to play softball with Dan's crew, so Tom felt like he had even less to talk with Jack about when they got together. They avoided the topic of the war entirely.

———

Tom spent much of his spare time over the summer break learning about the Vietnam War, racial issues, and women's liberation. He read his father's *Time* magazines every week and watched the national news, noting the growing number of protests and the political debates between the left and right wings of Democrats and Republicans.

The more he learned, the more he believed in the importance of having his generation's voice be heard on the political decisions affecting them.

He tried to talk to his father one evening after a news report on Vietnam, hoping some sort of conversation might break through the usual awkward silence between them. They never truly talked about anything other than sports, but to Tom, what was happening in the world was too important not to discuss.

"Do you think the war is for a good cause?" he asked, angling himself on the couch to see his father better.

"I believe the military should follow the orders from the president," his father said, without looking at Tom.

"Yeah, but—I don't see the reason for those orders."

Tom saw his father's jawline tighten. "We're trying to stop communism in Asia."

"What do you think of the protests?" Tom said.

It was quiet. The sound of the dishes in the kitchen had stopped as well. His father crossed his arms. "Some have been violent. Several states have their National Guard on alert," he said.

"Does that include Ohio and your company?"

"Yes, it does," his father said, turning to face Tom. "I hope you're not protesting."

Tom stayed silent, feeling that they were approaching conflict. He pretended to be absorbed by the next news story, until his father turned his attention back to the TV. Tom wanted to discuss the war, but there was no need to provoke his father.

That night, Tom called Becky, hoping she might invite him to come see her in Cleveland.

"I almost got into a fight with my father trying to talk about the war," he told her.

"You did?" She sounded distracted.

"He's in favor of it."

"So are my parents, but I just keep trying to educate them," she said. Her voice seemed closer to the phone, louder but muffled, as if she was holding the receiver between her ear and shoulder because her hands were busy.

"That may not be possible with my father," he said. "How have you been, anyway? I keep thinking about our hotel visit."

"I'm fine," she said. She didn't say anything about their night at the hotel, ask him how he was doing, or indicate she'd otherwise even been thinking about him. He regretted calling her.

"Have you been in any protests in Cleveland?" he asked, trying to bring the conversation back around to politics.

"Last week outside the federal court building, a group of us got—" Someone at Becky's home picked up another phone and started dialing. Tom listened to the rotary dial. "I'm on the phone," Becky said to the person, sounding annoyed.

"I need it," a male voice said and hung up. Becky sighed.

"I have to go. My brother." She said a quick goodbye, but not before her brother picked up the phone and started dialing again.

Tom stood at his window, looking at the neighborhood for several seconds. He wasn't sure if he should call Becky again, or if she even wanted him to. Had she regretted sleeping with him? He wouldn't see her or Kevin or Woz again until the fall, and Jack wasn't around. The summer suddenly felt very long. He had no one to talk to about the issues he was struggling with. He wasn't sure if he'd ever felt so alone.

———

One Sunday at the end of dinner, Tom's father put down his fork, quietly turned to Tom, and told him a new employee had started at his workplace. Tom didn't see what this had to do with him, but his father cleared his throat and said it was Sam, who was now a Vietnam veteran.

Sam wasn't in Vietnam! Tom's eyes widened in excitement, but he could see that his father's face was somber. "Just to alert you," he said, "Sam lost his arm in the war."

Blood rushed to Tom's head and he straightened up in his chair. Sam—easygoing, smiling Sam, who had played football with Tom—only had one arm left? Tom tried to control his emotions. "I'm glad he didn't lose his life," he said, with a tightness in his throat.

His father nodded and looked down. "He asked about you," he said. "You should give him a call."

———

When Sam answered the door to his small studio apartment the next evening, Tom expected to see the boy he remembered—high energy, blond hair combed down on his forehead, built like a linebacker, but with one of his sleeves empty where his arm used to be. But Sam's long hair was one length, pulled back into a ponytail. His body was much thinner, and his left arm extended a few inches down from his shoulder, ending in a scarred stub that Tom could see inside his T-shirt sleeve. Tom tried not to stare. He didn't want to make Sam feel any worse, but he felt sick to find his friend like this.

The small apartment was nearly empty, with a mattress on the floor in the corner, a kitchen table, a couch, and a small TV, with a large stereo system and speakers on one wall. A couple of dirty plates and a fork were on the floor next to a speaker, and on one of the plates was a pile of already-smoked joints.

Sam welcomed Tom in, but it was without the energy or enthusiasm Tom remembered. He looked wary and hesitant, and his skin was sallow. Tom felt he needed to compensate for Sam's beaten-down demeanor.

"Sammy, good to see you," Tom said, clapping Sam on the back, but his hand brushed the left sleeve of Sam's T-shirt and he froze for a split second.

"You, too." Sam's eyes were curious but distant. His lips were chapped.

"So, you didn't want to go back to living in our old apartment?" Tom asked, stepping just inside the door.

Sam smiled. "I thought getting arrested once there was enough."

Tom laughed uneasily. "Those were the days, weren't they?"

Sam grew quiet. "It's a world I hardly remember." Tom looked at Sam, nodding his head. "Your father said you're playing football at Kent State," Sam said. "Congratulations." He led the way to the dirty kitchen table. "What's it like to play again?"

Tom sat down, and the folding chair squeaked as he put his weight on it. Sam seated himself across from Tom, the bottom of his T-shirt sleeve hanging over the table. Tom told Sam about his call to Kent State and his training, which had gotten him back in shape to play several games last fall.

"I'm not as fast as I used to be in high school, and we haven't won a lot of games," Tom said, feeling guilty that his path had been so different from Sam's. He imagined what Sam had gone through, what had made his friend now look so haunted.

"You look good," Sam said. "The last time I saw you, you were starting to get a beer belly."

"I'm lucky to be playing football again." Tom stopped, afraid to say more. He did not want to boast about his good luck to a friend who had lost his arm fighting in a senseless war.

"I'm lucky to be alive," Sam said, looking down at his right hand on the table. "Vietnam was . . . worse than people described. It was hell." He pressed his cracked lips together, as if to hold in his emotions.

"I can't tell you how sorry I am about your arm," Tom said. "Or what you must have gone through."

"I was stupid—walked right into a booby trap. But at least it got me out of there."

Tom wanted to ask more, but Sam looked out the window, seeming unwilling to talk about the war.

"I might look into using the GI Bill for college," Sam said. "How do you like being a student again?"

Tom swallowed and told Sam about the Kent State campus, living in the dorm, and practicing at the athletic training facility. He described his classes, mentioning how he liked learning about societal issues. He was about to bring up some of the protests that had been happening on campus when he paused. Tom wondered about Sam's position on the war. He thought Sam was probably against it since he called it hell. But if Sam felt the war was for a good cause and had given his arm for it, Tom didn't want to question that.

"If there are protests against this damn war on your campus, tell me, and I'll drive over to participate," Sam said. Tom was relieved.

"I was in one this spring against military recruiters."

"Good for you, O'Brien. The war disgusts me—it's a waste in so many ways." To Tom, there was no trace of the light-hearted, uncomplicated friend he'd known a few summers ago. "I'm a member of Vietnam Veterans Against the War," Sam told him.

"That's great," Tom said, and they fell silent.

Sam sat up, seeming to snap out of his gloomy mood. "I haven't even offered you anything," he said, looking around his kitchen and toward the fridge. "I don't have much right now." His eyes went to a kitchen drawer. "You want to smoke some dope?" he asked.

Tom knew people at Kent State who smoked marijuana, especially at the house where the older football players lived. He suspected this included Kevin, although they hadn't talked about it. He hadn't tried it himself, but he was curious.

"I couldn't have gotten through Vietnam without it," Sam said. "It helps me now with the pain in my arm and keeps me relaxed."

"This is my first time."

Sam went to the kitchen drawer and chose a joint. He put a Doors album on his turntable and then lit the joint, showing Tom how to inhale and hold the smoke before exhaling. Tom took the joint from Sam's fingers and held it to his lips. He coughed at first, but, after a few attempts, was able to follow Sam's lead. He didn't notice any effects until suddenly Jim Morrison's voice singing "Light My Fire" sounded like it was inside his head. Tom swayed to the beat, and Sam began laughing, looking relaxed for the first time since Tom had arrived, which made Tom laugh, too.

"My best investment of army pay has been this stereo system," Sam said, patting it with his one hand.

"I can see why," Tom said, his smile feeling like it stretched across his face from ear to ear. He continued swaying to the song.

They listened to the Doors and other albums for at least an hour. Sam got a box of Oreos from his cupboard, and Tom said he'd never had cookies that tasted so amazing. When he later said goodbye, they hugged at the door, smiling. Tom walked to his car and saw that the streetlights gave off a sparkle against the dark sky he'd never noticed before. He became calm as he stared at its beauty. No wonder people smoked dope.

———

Tom spent the rest of the summer focused on saving money and staying in shape, occasionally seeing Jack and Sam on weekends, although usually not together. Sam invited Tom to come with him to a concert in Cleveland featuring local bands, and Tom suggested inviting Jack and Becky, too. Tom's call with Becky, however, was brief. She told him she was busy but looked forward to seeing him in a few weeks at school. He hung up, feeling deflated. She was too busy to even meet up with him in Cleveland?

Sam offered his car if Tom would drive; Sam could navigate short distances with one arm, but he said he'd prefer that Tom drive it into Cleveland. When they picked up Jack on the day of the concert, he looked into the open passenger window and said, "Is that Sam?"

"Yours truly," Sam said, smiling at Jack's question.

"I didn't recognize you," Jack said, glancing down at Sam's left sleeve. "You've freaked out with that long hair." Tom and Sam exchanged a look as Jack got in the back seat. "Pretty soon, your hair is going to be as long as Sam's," Jack said. I'm riding with a couple of hippies." Jack seemed uncomfortable. He took his glasses off and cleaned them.

"You're privileged," Tom said, looking at Jack in the rearview mirror as they pulled out of the driveway. He wondered if Jack knew how dumb he sounded.

The three of them spent the hour-long drive catching up. Jack asked Sam how he'd lost his arm in Vietnam. The windows were down, and Jack practically yelled his question. Tom winced, but Sam seemed to welcome the directness of Jack's question.

Sam rolled up his window, which made his hair fly around less. He described how his platoon squad had been sent on patrol to probe the North Vietnamese lines and had run into an ambush. Fortunately, he said, the squad's point person had detected the North Vietnamese soldiers, and they all hit the ground before the enemy opened fire with a machine gun. It was deafening, and they were lucky no one was shot, but their leader—a fool, in Sam's eyes—ordered his squad to pursue the Vietnamese. Sam described how they reached a campsite where coals in the fire still smoldered. They made a careful search of the surrounding jungle but didn't see any sign of the enemy.

When Sam returned to the campsite, he noticed a pistol in a holster under a leafy bush. He reached for it without thinking, and it set off a booby trap bomb that blew his arm off. He later learned later that he'd gone into shock, but the medics managed to stop the bleeding and stabilize him until a helicopter picked him up. The army transferred him from one miserable hospital to another until finally sending him home with an honorable discharge.

Tom stared ahead at the road, his heart beating rapidly, as he tried to put himself in Sam's place. What risk, what danger Sam had experienced. What if he had run into a Vietnamese soldier in the jungle? Tom often saw the opposing football team as his enemy, but they weren't trying to kill him. He couldn't imagine the fear he would have felt in that jungle. It made the hairs on his arms stand up.

As he drove, he thought of his father's words about mission and purpose—words from his father's own army experience. When Sam's squad leader ordered him to chase the North Vietnamese soldiers through the dense jungle, what mission was Sam on? Those soldiers were defending their country. Why was the United States—the most powerful nation in the world—attacking this small country thousands of miles from its borders?

"Hey, slow down," Jack said. Tom realized he had sped up, maybe imagining he was fleeing the North Vietnamese.

"What do you think our chance is of winning this war?" Jack asked Sam, leaning forward in his seat.

"We can't win it," Sam said. "Every time we gain ground, the Vietnamese disappear into the jungle, only to attack us somewhere else. They know their country, and we don't. They already wore down the French, and the French left. We'll leave, too."

"Well, I keep waiting for our firepower to take control, so South Vietnam can hold its own with the North. Then we could come home," Jack said.

"It'll never happen," Sam said.

Sam's experience and perspective on the war disturbed Tom. What Sam was saying essentially meant he'd lost his arm for nothing, and thousands of soldiers had died for no reason. The war was wrong—so wrong—and Jack was naïve.

"I hope something is resolved before we graduate," Jack said. "I don't want to be drafted and end up in the jungle, like you did."

Tom felt angry and impatient. "That's why we have to protest," he said. "Our politicians need to end it, or our soldiers—young guys, our friends—will be there forever."

"I'm willing to give our soldiers more time if it achieves what we need," Jack said.

Sam rolled his window down and held his hair back with his right hand, with his elbow outside. He stared out at the highway, silent.

———

The concert was being held outdoors, and they found a parking spot in a nearby lot when they arrived. Sam suggested they share a joint before the music started.

"We can do it right here in the car," he said. "No one will see us."

"Whoa—really?" Jack said, frowning.

"Yeah, it'll be fine," Sam said, pulling out a joint and his lighter.

Jack opened his door. "I'll go wait for you guys at the gate," he said, looking Tom in the eye before he got out and slammed the door.

Sam lit a joint. He and Tom shared it in the front seat, passing it back and forth at knee level and watching to ensure they weren't seen. When they finished, they walked to the gate to join Jack. The breeze was soft and warm and the sky was perfectly clear. Tom was mesmerized by the stars. In their seats, they could smell whiffs of marijuana coming from behind them. "See, we're not the only ones," Sam said.

When Sam went to the concession stand to get a drink, Jack turned to Tom.

"You've changed." He shook his head. "A long-haired pot smoker?"

Tom felt mellow from smoking the joint, and he wasn't about to get into an argument with Jack. He preferred to simply relax in the warm evening, and he started to sway to the beat of the music. Jack scowled at him.

"You should try it," Tom said after a while.

"You look ridiculous," Jack told him as Sam returned. He sat back and put his feet up on the back of the empty seat in front of him, looking sullen.

On the drive back, Sam turned the radio to a rock station, and cranked up the volume, making it impossible for anyone in the car to have a conversation. He and Tom rocked their heads to the music. They dropped Jack off, and Sam turned down the radio.

"I think we freaked Jack out," he said, smiling.

"It's good for him,' Tom said. "The guy has always been so opinionated; he needs to be freaked out now and then." They were hungry, so they went to the truck stop café.

Tom thought he might hear from Jack before he returned to Kent in August. But they didn't contact each other, which, Tom realized, was fine with him.

14

Tom unpacked his bags in his dorm room, glad to be alone in what felt like his home base. He looked forward to going to football practice every day—he relished having that sole focus before classes began, away from family and friends in Massillon. Now that he was on a full athletic scholarship, he wanted to dedicate himself to improving his performance on the field that fall.

He had the dorm room to himself since Kevin, no longer on the football team, did not need to return to school early. It was good to see Woz, who stopped by Tom's room that afternoon. He made fun of Tom's long hair but without the judgmental tone that Jack had used. He told Tom about his summer job with the same moving company, but this summer, he had been asked to help with the scheduling and routing instead of the heavy lifting. Woz said he loved the work, especially when he realized he could apply actual techniques he'd learned from his business courses. This made Tom, who was still not all that confident about his career plans, feel envious. Still, he was grateful to see his friend again. Woz seemed a lot more relaxed without Kevin there.

Tom worked hard in pre-season practice, running faster wind sprints and lifting heavier weights than he had in the spring. Coach Peters laughed at Tom's hair and a couple of other linemen who had let their hair grow.

"I don't care what you guys look like or what your politics are, as long as our offensive line dominates the other team," Coach said. Coach's positive encouragement was much more motivating than his father's pressure and criticism. Often, when Tom stopped to look at where he was—on that training field and with those teammates—he couldn't think of anything else he'd rather be doing, or any coach he'd rather be learning from. Playing for Kent State hadn't originally been in his plans, but it tapped into something he needed and wanted. He hoped he wouldn't let Coach down that season. And he hoped he could stay free from any injuries.

——

Although football was his priority, Tom continued to stay current on political events, frequently going to the university library to read its newspapers. One of his favorites, the *Chicago Tribune*, ran a series of articles about the upcoming 1968 Democratic National Convention. Through it, Tom learned about demonstrations that were planned to persuade the delegates to adopt an antiwar platform. In one piece, Tom read that the mayor of Chicago had asked for the Illinois National Guard to support the Chicago police in case riots broke out. It made him think about his father's role in the Guard; he couldn't imagine his father in the middle of a riot scene and was relieved his father was in the Ohio Guard.

Sensing that tensions were rising in Chicago and elsewhere, Tom started going down to the large TV in his dorm lounge every evening to watch the news. On the weekend before the convention, they showed footage of National Guard troops standing by, prepared as if for war, with the police lining Chicago's Michigan Avenue, wearing white riot helmets and armed with guns and batons. Protesters taunted the officers, holding signs against the war and picketing the Hilton Hotel where Democrat delegates were staying. The police pushed the protesters back into Grant Park, arresting those who resisted. The violence was alarming. It seemed like it wouldn't take much to set off a powder keg.

The Democrats' votes for their presidential nominee and party platform were scheduled for Wednesday, when the largest demonstration was planned. Tom especially wanted to see these demonstrations and hear the outcomes of the votes. As soon as he returned from football practice that afternoon, he gathered with other students in front of the lounge TV.

The live broadcast showed large throngs of protesters in the streets, often cutting to footage of delegates from the floor of the convention, where Tom learned the antiwar nominees and platform had been voted down. Leaning forward in his chair, Tom studied the frustrated protesters. He was amazed by their number and willingness to confront the police and soldiers trying to control them. He watched as surges of protester movements increased and the crowd noise grew.

Then suddenly, a chaotic scene unfolded. Tom watched in horror as the Chicago police charged the crowd in Grant Park, clubbing and arresting protesters indiscriminately, presumably because a protester had lowered an American flag. Protesters who had been marching near the Hilton turned and ran—many of whom seemed like college students similar to Tom and those with him in the lounge. Police chased them with raised batons, and protesters and bystanders alike were screaming, running, and getting knocked down by the police. When protesters fell, police stood over them, beating them as they raised their arms to protect themselves, and then police dragged them to the police vans that had been gathered to take protesters to jail. Tom saw one policeman hold his baton horizontally and swing the end of the club into the stomach and chest of a young man no older than himself. The young man crumpled to the ground and was dragged and shoved by police into a van.

Tom stood up. Other students in the lounge stood with him, yelling, "Did you see that?" He stared at the TV in disbelief as cameras filmed the mayhem for several minutes. In response to the police brutality, protesters chanted repeatedly, "The whole world is watching!" Tom wondered if Becky was watching from Cleveland, his family from Massillon, and his friends from wherever they were, all witnesses to the violence. He stayed glued to the TV well into the evening, forgetting to eat dinner.

Later that night, after returning to his room, he lay on his bed silently and stared at the ceiling for a long time. The police had attacked US citizens with the backing of the National Guard. If it could happen in Chicago, it could happen in other places. Seeing his workout bag on the floor, Tom thought of football. He always enjoyed physical challenges, doing whatever he could to prevent defenders from tackling the quarterback or running backs. It could become violent, and Tom had seen severe injuries on the field like his own. But there were rules to govern football violence, and penalties if they weren't followed.

The riots in Chicago followed no rules. Police who were supposed to be protectors of the public—like he was of quarterbacks—had lost control, purposely injuring innocent people. Tom went to bed, overwhelmed. He was upset as much by his country's police brutality as he was by its role in the Vietnam War. He had seen race riots on TV, but nothing like the Chicago riots. He couldn't believe what his country was capable of.

———

When Tom went to football practice the next day, he was still upset. Most of the players had heard or seen footage of the riots. Woz, walking out to the field with Tom, said, "Unbelievable," although not with Tom's passion or outrage. Tom took his anger out on the practice team, blocking the third-team defensive tackle so fiercely that Coach stopped him, reminding him to focus on the new running play they were trying. After practice, Tom had just finished getting dressed when a noisy argument erupted in the locker room, with Richie roaring that the protesters got everything they deserved. One of the coaches came out of the office and yelled at them: "Remember, you're here to play football!"

Two days after the riots—the Friday before Labor Day weekend—Tom walked into his dorm room and was surprised to find Kevin there. He hadn't expected him back at school until Monday, the day before classes would begin. Kevin had a large bandage on his forehead and bruises on his cheekbones. Tom guessed immediately what had happened.

"You were at the Chicago riots."

Kevin slammed his closet door. "Yeah. I was. Those bastard pigs did this to me!"

"I watched it. I couldn't believe what happened," Tom said. Kevin appeared to have some pain in his shoulder or back, and he also had bruises on his arm. Tom went to Kevin's side of the room and helped him move a box of books onto the desk.

"My friends and I went to Grant Park—all we planned to do was carry some signs," he said. "Instead, police attacked us, and the Guard tear-gassed us."

"Were you arrested?'

"No. We got caught, and they started beating us. The police tried to drag us to a van, but we got away." He shoved the box to the far side of the desk and pulled out some other books from his bag. "Not before I punched a cop in the face!"

There was a fresh cut on one of Kevin's knuckles. "I'm glad you're okay and it wasn't any worse."

Kevin raised his head, his jaw clenched. "Oh, it couldn't get much worse. I'm going to join SDS and start resisting this bullshit."

———

Tom's mother wanted him to come home on Labor Day weekend before they drove Kara to Columbus for college. She shook her head at his hair but then pulled him into a warm hug. Kara, excited to begin life at Ohio State, chattered and giggled with him more than usual. But things with his father seemed tense, as they had since Tom questioned the role of the US in Vietnam; they hadn't exchanged too many more words since then. Tom resented the way his father averted his eyes rather than looking at Tom directly, as if not wanting to recognize Tom's views. But Tom wasn't a child anymore—as his father often made him feel—and he didn't want to sit idly by while injustice was happening. He wondered what his father's position was on the National Guard's behavior in Chicago.

Though the images of the riots were very much in Tom's mind, he managed to avoid any discussion about them until they picked up Grandpa for church on Sunday. Tom noticed that Grandpa moved slower than he had that summer, but his eyes sparkled when he saw Tom.

"Crazy what happened in the news," he said to Tom in the back seat of the car, but then his father gave Grandpa a stern look in the rearview mirror. Grandpa fell silent and reached over to pat Tom's hand on one side and Kara's on the other. Tom thought he seemed tired. He put his hand over Grandpa's, observing the great number of liver spots on it and how thin the skin felt.

Their Sunday dinner conversation centered on Kara's future at Ohio State. It was after dinner when the Chicago riots came up again. Tom, his father, and Grandpa had decided to settle in front of the TV to watch a baseball game. Grandpa leaned back in his chair with a glass of whiskey, and Tom's father searched the TV to find the game of the week. He happened to land on a channel showing footage of the riots.

"That sure was a mess," Grandpa said, taking a big drink.

Tom's father paused, then turned away from the TV to face Grandpa and Tom. "What those protesters did was disgusting," he said.

Tom felt the hairs on his arm rise. "The *protesters?* It was the police who started the riots," Tom said, taking his feet off the coffee table. He could have also named the National Guard but stayed away from it.

"The protesters brought it on themselves," his father said. Had his father not seen what happened?

"Did you even watch it?" Tom asked incredulously. "The police were out of control, beating kids like me with clubs!"

Tom's father stood up, blocking the view of the TV. "Those weren't kids like you! Anyone could see that most were radicals who went there to incite violence."

"That's not true!" Tom said, standing up and facing his father. "My roommate was there and got clubbed on his head."

"That's not surprising—he shouldn't have been there in the first place."

Tom's blood was boiling. He raised a finger at his father and opened his mouth to say something else, but Grandpa jumped in. "It's like the attacks on ironworkers in the steel strike that happened in my early days at the foundry." Tom and his father stared at Grandpa. "There were bad apples on both sides," Grandpa said.

Tom could see that his father didn't want to hear it. "Those protesters tried to disrupt the democratic process," he said. His mother and Kara appeared in the doorway, their eyes wide but expectant.

"What are you talking about?" Tom practically yelled. "They carried some signs and got clubbed for it! They were trying to change America for the better!"

Tom seethed and knocked into the coffee table as he stormed upstairs to his room. He heard angry voices downstairs but with the door closed, couldn't make out what his family was saying, until his father raised his voice loud enough to declare, "I didn't raise my son to be anti-American!" Later that afternoon, his father, staring straight ahead at the road, silently dropped him off at the bus terminal to return to Kent. Tom didn't say goodbye.

———

Kent State lost more football games than it won in its 1968 season, but Tom had an incredible year. Coach Peters had elevated Tom and Woz to the first team to replace departing seniors, and Tom responded with a dedication that matched his high school years. He continued to excel at pass-blocking and grew more effective in opening holes for running backs, thanks to his strengthened tendon, although it still didn't feel as invincible as it once had. Or maybe *he*—even playing as best he could—didn't feel as invincible as he once had.

It was evident that Coach considered Tom the best offensive lineman on the team. Coach often tested him by having him go head-to-head against Richie in practice; Richie, in his senior year, was likely to be drafted by the pros. He usually went out of his way to challenge Tom, both on and off the field. Their dislike of each other had not diminished, and Tom found him needlessly aggressive. Tom's hair had grown long enough to flow out under his helmet, and Richie started calling him "Goldilocks."

"You seemed a bit slow today, Goldilocks," Richie said.

Tom looked up from toweling himself off after his shower. "Really? You never reached the quarterback once when I was blocking you."

"I was holding back. I didn't want to mess up your girlie looks for your protests."

Tom didn't say anything but noticed other players paying attention, particularly those with longer hair. One said, "Shut up, Richie." Richie's allies were also observing this exchange, and one of them, throwing his towel onto a bench, said, "O'Brien should join the Viet Cong."

Tom put on his clothes. He didn't fear Richie, but this battle made no sense. Tom's perceived lack of interest ended the tension, but he knew there were two camps on the team. And the camp he was in—the players with longer hair against the war—numbered fewer than the players in Richie's group who supported the war. He held his ground when Richie challenged him, which he could see infuriated Richie and his friends.

———

Football consumed a great deal of Tom's attention, but he always took time to get Kevin's updates on campus activities against the war. True to his word, Kevin had joined Students for a Democratic Society after the Chicago riots, becoming more and more vocal for student mobilization against the war. He also grew his thick hair down to his shoulders and wore a full beard and mustache. His first SDS action was to support a sit-in organized by the campus Black Student Organization to protest police recruiters on the Kent State campus.

Tom also followed campus politics through Becky when he could. He wondered about their relationship, even though he felt he had been more connected with her on both a physical and intellectual level than with any other girl he'd ever known. Becky had become a columnist for the *Daily* that fall, writing on women's issues. The priority she placed on that, combined with Tom's focus on football, gave them little time to see each other, although Tom wasn't sure she wanted to see him as much as he wanted to see her.

Becky called him one night, surprising him by asking if they could get together on the coming Saturday.

"Yeah, of course. What would you like to do?" Tom asked.

She was quiet for a few seconds. "How about if we visit our favorite hotel?"

Tom sat up straight in his desk chair, instantly alert. "Sure, I'll make the reservation," he said, becoming aroused as he thought of her body next to his again. But after hanging up, a part of him wondered if he was being used somehow—if she cared more about having sex with him than she cared about him. Still, he didn't want to pass up the chance to be with her.

And he was thrilled that he hadn't. He felt so close to her that night—a night full of passion, holding each other, dozing, and then passion again. But in the morning, as he looked at her lying there with her eyes closed, he was wary about what to expect next.

"I think I'm maybe just a sexual outlet for you," Tom said at breakfast.

She laughed, as she stirred her coffee. "That would be a good switch—isn't it usually horny football players who chase women?" She took a sip from her mug.

"But you don't have much time to do anything else with me." He saw Becky's face become serious.

"Tom, I thought you were joking. I care about you a lot—you're not just . . . a body," she said, setting her mug down. "But writing my column is more work than I thought, and I want to take the time to do it right. It's important to me." She reached across the table and took his hand in hers.

He could understand that. "I know I'm pretty busy, too—football doesn't really leave a lot of free time." She nodded. He wanted to feel better, and he did—a little—but he wondered if she was also saying that her column was more important than everything else in her life, including him.

When they kissed goodbye, neither of them said anything about when they would see each other again, though Tom wanted to. Tom lay on his bed in his dorm room for the rest of the day, tired from lack of sleep but not at all sleepy. He tried to read but often closed his eyes, feeling depressed and unsure about Becky's feelings toward him. The fact was that despite how busy he was, he thought about and made time for her because she was important to him—he didn't feel that she did the same for him.

Tom was glad to get to football practice on Monday, where he could put his feelings aside and focus on blocking Richie in several fierce contests. Coach Peters had to break them apart at one point.

———

Tom's uncertainty about Becky seemed to match his growing uncertainty about his courses and future path. His adviser complimented him on his grades, which were higher than the grades of most student-athletes. At his adviser's encouragement and influenced by Woz's business major, Tom decided to declare his major in construction management. But he could tell he didn't have the same kind of enthusiasm that Woz did. Sure, he could picture himself in a professional job in construction, with foremen like Dan working for him. It would be a job his parents would be proud of. But he couldn't escape his uncertainties about the American capitalist system, which he believed had worn down his father and grandfather.

As Tom walked to class one day, ideas he'd been introduced to in Fromm's *The Sane Society* again came to mind. Did he want to be part of some corporate construction company that primarily focused on profits? How would that help address issues like poverty and racism?

Whenever Tom had doubts for the remainder of the semester—whether they were over his major or over Becky—he focused on football. Concentrating on the sport helped him temporarily forget about everything else. He worked out his frustrations on Richie and spent extra time helping younger, less seasoned players develop their skills. He was rewarded by the respect he earned from the team, even by some of Richie's friends.

15

The football season came to a close with another loss. The team's record was average, but Tom's confidence in his performance had grown steadily throughout the season. Coach seemed proud of his offensive line, and although he didn't say anything, Tom could tell he was frustrated with Kovacs's inaccurate passing and the team's lackluster defense.

Tom's mother called him during finals week to ask how his studying was going, which was strange, since she rarely called in the morning. After he told her his final schedule and assured her he was eating enough each day, she grew quiet.

"What's wrong?" he asked.

"Tommy, Grandpa had a stroke yesterday," she said. "He fell in his house and—"

"What?" Tom interrupted. "Why didn't you guys call me yesterday? You could have at least—"

"—your father happened to stop by that day and found him. He's okay right now. The doctors stabilized him, but his right side is partially paralyzed. He'll need physical therapy." Tom's heart thumped, and his eyes stung with tears. He knew his grandpa's health was not the best—and hadn't been for a while—but this was a shock. His grandpa could have died, and no one would have known.

"I'm coming home. I'll check the bus schedule right now and be there as soon as I can."

"No, your father says that isn't a good idea. Grandpa is okay at the moment—as stable as he can be—and there's nothing you can do. We think it's better if you stay and finish your finals, then just come home for Christmas break next week. Grandpa—"

"But—"

"Grandpa will have been moved into a nursing home by then, and he'll probably be even better by next week when you see him."

"No! I'm coming today," Tom informed her.

"He wouldn't want you to see him like this," she said quietly. Tom paused. He could hear his father's voice in the background. "Your father insists that this is best and says it's not up for debate," she said.

Tom glared at the textbook on the desk in front of him. Was this just because his father was jealous over his relationship with Grandpa? Or was his mother right—that Grandpa wouldn't want to be seen in the shape he was in? Tom certainly didn't want to upset Grandpa if he wasn't ready to be seen. He gritted his teeth.

His mother went right on talking. Grandpa would probably need to live at the nursing home even after his therapy was done. They would take good care of Grandpa in his week of transition to the nursing home. Tom, overwhelmed, didn't say anything more. The lump in his throat was too tight.

Tom finished finals week the best he could, but he was in a daze. During one of his construction management exams, he realized he'd just been staring blankly at the first problem for nearly twenty minutes. He went home immediately after his last exam, getting a ride with a friend. He breezed into the house to get the car keys, gave a quick greeting to his mother and father, and then went straight to Grandpa's small apartment at the nursing home, where he found Grandpa propped up on his bed. Grandpa smiled and shook Tom's hand with his left hand while his right arm stayed at his side. The creases in Grandpa's face and neck had deepened, and his eyes were sunken and dark underneath. The right side of his mouth drooped.

"Tommy, I need a drink," he said, his voice hoarse but friendly. Because his mouth drooped, Tom had to listen closely to understand him.

"Do you have a bottle here, Grandpa?" Tom's heart ached.

"No. Your parents didn't think I should have any whiskey for a while."

Tom nodded. "I'll sneak your bottle from Dad's collection and bring it to you later," he said. Grandpa leaned his head back against a pillow, and Tom surveyed the small apartment. The shared bathroom was opposite the entry, with Grandpa's room on the right and his roommate's on the left, both with curtains drawn. In addition to Grandpa's single bed, he had a small closet, a reclining easy chair, a dresser of drawers, and a TV on a TV stand. Pictures of

Grandpa's family were on the dresser, including Tom's and Kara's high school graduation pictures. Tom could hear the frail, muffled voices of other residents through the walls and the shifting of sheets from Grandpa's roommate on the other side of the curtain. How hard it must have been for Grandpa to suddenly have to give up his house to live in a place like this and depend on nursing aides to care for him.

One of the nursing aides entered and gazed up at Tom, who towered over everything in the tight space. They were preparing to help Grandpa use the restroom and then take him to supper.

Tom told Grandpa he'd be back after supper, and he wouldn't forget what Grandpa had asked for.

———

Over the break, Tom spent time with Grandpa, talked with Kara—who had survived her first semester at Ohio State—and went to see Sam on a couple of evenings. Sam had tried classes at Stark College but dropped out. He continued to work at the steel plant to save money, telling Tom he was thinking he might soon leave Massillon to join a friend who lived on a communal farm outside of Columbus. As he and Sam smoked dope and listened to music at Sam's apartment, Tom asked about the communal farm. He'd heard plenty from Kevin in the last semester about alternative lifestyles and communities that centered on peace and love instead of material success. He told Sam that maybe he'd visit him there.

Tom also tried to contact Jack at the beginning of the break, even though the last time they got together Jack had acted like an ass and criticized him for smoking dope. He learned that Jack was vacationing in Mexico with his college friends. Tom didn't feel sorry that he couldn't see Jack while he was home. They had grown apart and clearly seemed to be heading in different directions.

Besides watching bowl games with Grandpa, Tom spent time in his room at home, mostly with the door closed. He got caught up with *Time* magazine, especially in reading news of the Vietnam War. The success of North Vietnam's Tet Offensive and the increasing number of deaths of American soldiers was upsetting enough, but to know that President Johnson was still sending even more US troops in the final days of his administration forced Tom to contend with reality on a more personal level.

He set the magazine he'd been reading down on his bed and thought more about his future. His student deferment wouldn't last forever, but would the war still be going on in two years when he graduated? If so, he would have to make hard decisions: let himself be drafted, enlist in a service such as the navy to avoid dangerous army patrols, or join the National Guard. Or would he consider something drastic, like moving to Canada?—although he didn't consider himself a conscientious objector.

He'd hoped Richard Nixon, taking office in January to succeed Johnson as president, would end the war before he graduated, but he was not optimistic when he read about Nixon's speeches on "peace with honor." His short-term path was clear: play football and make progress in his college studies. Beyond that, his future, especially in these tumultuous times, remained uncertain. What did he want for a job after graduating? Where was his relationship with Becky headed? Would he escape from being drafted? And would he be able to find a place for himself—a role in society—that didn't put him in conflict with his morals?

———

On Christmas morning, the family finished opening gifts, Kara and their mother went to the kitchen to get coffee, and Tom picked up wrapping paper from the floor. Unprompted—maybe because it was Christmas Day or because Tom had been smart to avoid any arguments—Tom's father said his performance in the games that he and Grandpa attended had improved from the previous year.

Those words surprised Tom. Up to that point in the break, any conversations involving Tom and his father had been initiated by Tom's mother, usually football related, perhaps to keep the topic off his hair, which now touched his shoulders. This praise briefly made him feel like a boy in a Pop Warner game, with his father always present and encouraging. He turned to look at his father sitting on the couch, but his father just kept thumbing through a book he'd received, seeming to have no interest in saying anything more.

Tom took a risk. "Do you think I improved more than I did in my second year of Pop Warner?"

"Yes, I'd say that," his father answered, but he still didn't look at Tom until Kara and Tom's mom returned with coffee for everyone. Then, his father briefly met Tom's eye before turning away.

A little later, at the request of Tom's mother, he and his father picked up Grandpa for their Christmas dinner. Kara came out to the driveway to give Grandpa a long hug. "Look at my two grandchildren! College students!" Grandpa said. Tom smiled as he and his father carried Grandpa up the porch stairs in his wheelchair; Grandpa could always liven up any situation. "I think it's time for happy hour," Grandpa said. His therapy had improved the droop on the right side of his mouth, and he was a bit easier to understand.

Inside, Tom's father went to the cupboard and brought out the Irish whiskey.

"Wait a minute. Tom's about to turn twenty-one, right?" Grandpa said as he was rolled closer to the warmth of the fireplace. "I think he deserves a drink this year to celebrate his football season."

Tom's father started to shake his head, perhaps remembering Tom's drunken state on the night he mowed into the mailbox, or at the police station when he'd been picked up for underage drinking.

"You sure had one hell of a season, Tommy. We couldn't be prouder of how far you've come after everything that happened," Grandpa said. He choked up on his words.

Tom's father looked first at Grandpa and then at Tom. He nodded. "Let's do that."

Tom's eyes widened as he looked at his father.

"Kara, get a coke and glasses and ask your mother to join us," Tom's father said. He poured Tom, Grandpa, and himself glasses of whiskey. Tom's glass only contained a quarter inch of whiskey, but it was something.

"Let's toast to our college students and their successful football and field hockey seasons," their father said, raising his glass.

"Here, here," Grandpa said.

Tom was careful to only sip his whiskey in the presence of his father, rather than down the glass. A warmth rose from his stomach into his chest, though he didn't think it was necessarily only from the alcohol. These good feelings would not have happened without Grandpa, even though his father had surprised him.

———

There were bowl games on TV the day after Christmas, and Tom went to watch them with Grandpa. His father had to work that day on year-end inventory, so it was just the two of them in Grandpa's small room at the nursing home. Grandpa, of course, wanted a glass of whiskey when Tom arrived. Tom joined him, and they settled into their chairs in front of Grandpa's small TV.

"How are things going for you really?" Grandpa asked after taking a sip of his drink and analyzing a screen pass touchdown.

Tom had had a few sips and was warm and comfortable in the chair by his grandpa. "To be honest, sometimes I don't know where I'm going. At all."

"Join the club," Grandpa said. "A lot of us have lived life wondering the same thing, and there's nothing wrong with taking time to figure it out."

"I don't know what I'll do if this war is still going on when I graduate. If I don't figure things out, I'll probably get drafted."

"It's a tough call," Grandpa said, shifting in his seat.

"I don't know why we're still in Vietnam," Tom said. "We have enough problems at home to deal with. It's a mess." Someone coughed in a room down the hall.

Grandpa looked at Tom and nodded, his eyes alert. "All the overreaction to your protests reminds me of the 1920s when businesses and the government shut down our unions."

"What did you do?"

"We couldn't do much, other than just keep working. But my outlet, as you know, was sports—playing sandlot baseball, watching football."

"I don't know where I'd be without sports," Tom said, setting his glass down. "I want to have the same type of commitment to a job that I've always had for football, but I don't know what job that would be. I feel stuck or lost when I'm not on a football field or doing something with sports—it's so clear and easy there to see how I fit and what I can contribute."

Grandpa poured himself another drink and looked at Tom. "It may not be possible to have that type of commitment in a job, Tommy. I don't know what's more meaningful than an athlete striving to be his best. I don't see heads of corporations or government being more satisfied than athletes who do well after years of hard work."

"Yeah, I don't buy into American success stories," Tom said.

"Me neither," Grandpa said, his voice louder. "Is what CEOs do more meaningful or important than helping children grow through sports, where they learn to work hard and deal with winning and losing and figure out the best way to play a game?"

Tom smiled. Grandpa was becoming increasingly more drunk, but even with his speech, he made more sense than Tom had ever heard. "That's what you've done for me," he said.

"You're damn right," Grandpa said, smiling back. "And I tell you what—you've experienced more in life so far than many grown men in their careers. You know the highs and the lows better than they do."

The crowd in the stadium roared, and Grandpa's eyes shifted to the TV. "Look at that touchdown!" he said.

The players on TV jumped up and down, celebrating their score. Tom knew and loved that feeling. He also knew his grandpa had always been in the stands at Tom's games when he could—jumping and cheering for him. He'd never heard his grandfather talk about life like he did today. Tom had needed this conversation and his grandpa's perspective, but when he turned to thank him, Grandpa had dozed off.

Tom continued to watch the game while Grandpa snored lightly next to him. When the offensive linemen failed to block defensive players, Tom thought of the drills Coach would have those linemen do to avoid that broken play. Tom himself had done countless drills over the years to figure out where a play had gone wrong in a game and find a way to prevent it in the future. It occurred to him that starting with his big injury in high school, his life had become a broken play of sorts, and he was still looking for a way to do the next play better.

16

During the 1969 spring semester, Tom concentrated on his studies, plodding through his courses on the basics of construction management. He could see how the project management tools he was learning could be applied to the work Dan and his crew did. But the course he found himself enjoying the most was an elective on comparative economics, taught by a young professor who wore his hair as long as Tom did.

The instructor, sitting cross-legged on a table at the front of the room, lectured passionately on the benefits of economic systems that were alternatives to capitalism. He spoke of the economic disparities and environmental destruction caused by capitalism, and Tom, connecting much of what he was learning in the course to Fromm's *The Sane Society* and other books, took pages of notes each class period. More and more, he felt like his eyes were being opened to the flaws in American society.

He kept track of antiwar politics through Kevin's participation in Students for a Democratic Society activities. "We want to be the Berkeley of the Midwest," Kevin told him after he returned to their dorm room from a meeting one night. He sometimes paced back and forth between Tom's side of the room and his desk when he got back from SDS events, recounting what had happened, gesturing as he spoke, and once even slamming his fist on his desk. "You should come to our meetings, O'Brien. We're going to ramp up protests against the war."

Other SDS chapters around the country were staging demonstrations against the war, and Tom agreed that the Kent State SDS chapter should be a leader in antiwar protests. Increasingly, Kevin shared his views on the war with almost anyone, including students who stopped by their dorm room or who sat at tables in the cafeteria. Tom occasionally chimed in on these conversations, but he could also see the way some students began to cast side-long glances at Kevin.

When Tom turned twenty-one in February, Woz and Kevin took him to a campus bar for some beers to celebrate his legal right to drink. After two beers, Kevin could not avoid expressing his feeling about Vietnam. Tom knew how much Woz disliked Kevin's preaching, so he tried to change subjects to no avail.

"All I'm saying is universities need to represent a moral position that counters Nixon's lies," Kevin said, accidentally bumping Woz's glass with his elbow.

"Well, what I want from the university is an education that helps me get a good job," Woz said, leaning away from Kevin.

"We can have both," Kevin said. "But not if university administrators keep us from voicing our concerns."

"They're keeping radical students under control, so those students don't disrupt our classes or cause our university activities to be cancelled," Woz said. His eyes lingered on Kevin with the words "radical students."

Tom interrupted, holding up his fingers to the server. "Another round?" he asked his friends.

Kevin, looking flabbergasted, turned to Tom. "So, where are *you* in this debate?" he asked. Woz turned in his seat to look at Tom.

"I'm okay with protests," Tom said, sliding his glass through a ring of condensation on the table. "I think this country is heading in the wrong direction."

Kevin nodded. "You'll get your chance to protest with the plans we're making for this spring," he said.

Woz looked at both of them, shaking his head. "We have the greatest country in the world," he said, sitting higher. "Sure, some things can be improved, but I think Nixon will get us out of Vietnam."

Kevin's jaw dropped. "Come on, really, Woz? You're so full of shit. We're headed toward fascism. Open your eyes!"

Woz's face turned red. "I better go study," he said. "Happy birthday, O'Brien." He stood up abruptly, knocking the pendant light over the table with his head. He dropped some money on the table near his napkin and left.

"I just don't understand how Woz can't see what's going on," Kevin said, putting his feet up on Woz's chair.

"I disagree with him, too," Tom said. "But take it easy—he's my friend." He reached his arm up to steady the swaying light as their beers arrived.

"Friendships don't last when politics get serious," Kevin said, sliding the extra beer that would have been Woz's toward him.

Tom believed he could continue being friends with Kevin and Woz. But, as with the football team, there were two camps. Tom spent time that semester with either Kevin and his friends, or Woz and his friends. Few people attempted to cross the boundary as he did. It was easy to enjoy being with Woz and his friends, many of them fellow football players. But Tom found Kevin and his friends more stimulating in their commitment to a cause he'd come to believe in.

———

Kevin persuaded Tom to attend an SDS meeting with him one Saturday night at an off-campus house where three SDS leaders lived. There was a Cream album playing loudly when they walked in, and the ten or so people who had gathered were passing around a couple of joints. Tom was reminded of his time with Sam in Massillon. But these guys were different from Sam, majoring in liberal arts and not ready to drop out of college.

Tom sat on a pillow on the floor, mellowed by the pot, but fascinated by the conversation. The group had been keeping close track of what was happening at other universities, and Kevin pushed them to define their next steps for making their voices heard. One student with long red hair and thick-rimmed glasses nodded, blowing out a puff of smoke. The group agreed that they needed a spring event to help Kent State contribute to the nationwide movement against the war and decided they would aim for early April.

Tom attended the next few meetings, more as a listener than a proponent in any of the planning, but Kevin confronted him one evening in front of the others.

"Did you see your girlfriend's article in the *Daily* this week?" Kevin said, turning to him suddenly. The other members looked at Tom.

"No, I didn't," Tom said. "And Becky's not my girlfriend." He hadn't seen Becky that semester nearly as much as he'd wished, and though he told Becky he was busy with his studies and new activities, he couldn't help but feel somewhat rejected by her. It was annoying that Kevin had brought her up in front of the group, but he supposed Kevin didn't know anything about their status or the mixed signals she'd been giving.

"She wrote that SDS is a sexist organization, ignoring women's issues, which she says are as important as the war and racial issues," Kevin said to the whole group, pulling out an issue of the *Daily* from beneath a stack of magazines.

"Well," Tom said, looking around. "I don't see any women at your meetings."

Kevin seemed amused for a second. "Maybe we need to do some work. But look," he said, becoming serious again, "we don't need to be blindsided by a group we should be allies with."

"Listening to them might be a good start," Tom said. The red-haired student nodded, as did most of the other guys.

"Okay, you're right," Kevin said. "So how about it? It might help if you talked to her."

Tom thought it would make a good excuse to call Becky—he took her article.

———

Tom met Becky for coffee the following week when she had a break between classes. She was twelve minutes late and gave him a slight wave as she stepped into the coffee line. When she came to sit down in the booth with her mug, she appeared wary, choosing the seat opposite Tom. He imagined that was because she expected him to talk about their relationship, which made him feel hurt. But he tried to control his emotions.

She seemed relieved when she found that he wanted to talk about her column on SDS. "I thought it would get Kevin's attention," she said, lifting her mug to her lips. A bit of steam rose up out of her coffee, and her eyes looked tired. Tom knew she'd been working long hours for the paper, but from one of his few visits to the small *Daily* office, he also knew she was happy and seemed in her element in there.

"Kevin felt blindsided by the article," Tom said. He wondered if he should have kissed her as she sat down—just a peck to keep things casual but to let her know he cared. Maybe that was too much pressure for her.

"That doesn't bother me," she said, putting her elbows on the table. "Women often feel like second-class citizens in the antiwar movement."

"What can SDS do differently?" Tom asked. "I didn't disagree with your piece. It made me think."

She leaned forward in the booth. "There's a women's liberation organization on campus. SDS should involve them."

"Can you help get them together?"

"No," she said matter-of-factly. "I'm a journalist, not an activist."

He was unsure of what to say to that and tried to change the conversation to find out how she was doing. But when he did, her eyes grew wary again. He felt dumb and vulnerable and quickly ended the conversation with a business-like goodbye. "Thanks for meeting with me," he said. "I'll relay what you said to the group."

Becky stood up when he did, then kissed him, maybe conscious of his sensitivity. Her lips were warm and dry. She offered him a smile.

As Tom walked away afterward, he clenched his jaw. He and Becky hadn't been intimate since before Christmas. He'd felt so close to her that night, and she'd told him she cared for him. Why did it feel like they were going backward? He tried putting his feelings aside so he could focus on what he needed to do for his next class.

———

Kevin and his fellow SDS members attempted to enter the university's administration building on April 1, 1969, with a list of demands related to stopping the war. Tom chose going to class over participating in this demonstration and learned afterward that Kevin and other SDS members had made it as far as the elevators before they were stopped by the police, with Kevin and a few others having to be dragged out after sitting down and refusing to move.

On April 16, Tom decided to join supporters of the students who were subject to a disciplinary hearing because of their actions on April 1. As the supporters stood outside the administration building, they were met by students opposed to SDS. Fighting broke out, with students shoving and punching one another, and the Ohio State Highway Patrol arrived to arrest fifty-eight people. Watching the fights from a distance, Tom was tempted to help the protesters, thinking his size could help end the conflict with the students opposed to SDS. But as a football player on scholarship, he knew his coaches would not want him to get arrested, so he stayed in the back of the crowd.

Although Tom had chosen not to get involved, this protest raised the stakes for him. It was not just a small group of students carrying signs and being watched by campus police that day. He witnessed the divisions among a large, angry group of students, their strong feelings that led to shouting and physical confrontations, and the forcefulness of the State Patrol as they made arrests. TV crews came out, and the national news it generated the next day—bringing attention to an unjust war—validated his decision to participate in the protest and motivated him to look for other opportunities.

Tom closed the semester with a successful finals week and good grades. He talked to his adviser about the timing of his graduation, having started college a semester later than Kevin and Woz. Tom was told he could try to catch up with them by using summer courses over the next two summers, or he could graduate at the end of the fall semester in 1970. He leaned toward taking classes in the fall of 1970, extending his student deferment and allowing him to play another football season. But he signed up for two courses in the upcoming summer session to keep his options open.

Kevin suggested they live together that summer in the off-campus house rented by older football players; a couple of those students were graduating. Tom agreed.

The warm summer weather brought the foliage and flowers on campus to peak bloom. The instructors taught at a more relaxed pace, and the smaller summer classes stimulated Tom's learning. Kevin invited some girls who had attended the April protests to their house and immediately fell in love with one of them. One of the other girls, her long straight hair held in place with a leather headband, cuddled up to Tom. He thought briefly of Becky as he placed his arm around the girl, but he hadn't seen her for weeks. He tried to shake off the slight pang in his chest and turn his attention back to the girl. He laughed and enjoyed the evening with her, without feeling pressure to see her again or make the moment any more than it was. It felt like a step forward for him.

In August, Kevin and his girlfriend made the pilgrimage to a farm in upstate New York for the Woodstock Festival. Kevin had begged Tom to come with them, but football practice made it impossible. Kevin and his girlfriend came back ecstatic over their experience. He said it changed his life—proof that their generation could live in peace and love in a population of 400,000. Kevin described taking LSD for the first time, making incredible friends, and he and his girlfriend taking off their clothes to swim with a crowd of naked people. Tom wished he had gone.

———

Tom's relaxed life ended with the start of football practice. The confidence he felt from the previous season carried over, and he had high expectations for himself the coming season. Coach Peters did as well, meeting Tom's eye as he told his players he thought they could probably be the best offensive line he had ever coached. Maybe because of that, he seemed tougher than usual, starting them with challenging strength and endurance drills to get them back in shape. Even Tom, who had kept himself fit during the summer, was wiped out by the end of practice. He noticed that Coach was more anxious and edgy in general. Tom assumed it was due to Coach's high expectations for their line, but it was unusual—he had never seen Coach act that way.

The coaches scheduled their fall scrimmage three weeks before their first game. The players had practiced several live situations but hadn't been all together in a game environment. The coaches split the players into two teams equal in experience and skills. When Tom discovered he would be playing across the line from Richie, he looked at Coach. "It will be good for both of you," Coach said, crossing his arms. Tom wasn't sure, thinking he would rather save himself for a real game. But when Richie sneered, "Hey, look— I get Goldilocks," Tom's adrenaline rushed. His first block moved Richie a couple of yards backward, allowing the running back to gain seven yards. Two plays later, however, Richie stuffed Tom backward and tackled the running back at the line of scrimmage. They competed intensely for the entire game, so much so that Tom could feel both teams watching them closely. After the scrimmage, Coach took Tom aside.

"That's the best I've seen you play," Coach said. "I don't think Richie has ever been tested like that." Tom nodded and tried to appear as if he wasn't still trying to catch his breath. Coach took a hold of Tom's helmet. "If you can play at that level this season, O'Brien, I think you'll get the attention of the pros."

Tom looked Coach in the eye and thanked him, his heart skipping a beat, and headed to the locker room with Woz, who was limping slightly from a sprained ankle. "You showed Richie," Woz said, sweat running down the sides of his face and neck. "He had to give everything he had to handle you."

Tom was in a daze, unsure of how to process what Coach had said. His Achilles injury and the long recovery process had caused him to lose faith in his ability to play in the pros one day, but Coach's words had reignited his old ambition. Tom knew he shouldn't have any expectations, but he couldn't stop thinking about the possibility of playing in the NFL with the best football players in the world. What if he could still realize his dream?

The night before his first football game of the season, his mother called to say that his father and grandfather wouldn't be attending. Grandpa had a bad cold—nothing to worry about; they would be there the following week for the first conference game. That was fine with Tom. He would have valued their presence and support, but he felt organized and ready for the fall semester—for his studies as well as football.

The morning of the game, Tom arrived at the locker room early. He didn't want to be rushed. He put his uniform on slowly, stopping to do leg stretches before putting on his pads. Woz had arrived early, also. Jonesy was taping his ankle and re-taping it after testing it for tightness. When his ankle was ready, Woz walked to Tom's locker.

"Strange thing this morning with Coach," Woz said.

"What?"

"When I got here, he was coming out of his office in his sweats with a towel, heading toward the shower. I think he might have slept in his office all night."

"Why would he do that?" Tom asked, looking toward Coach's office.

"Maybe he's anxious about the game and wanted to be alone."

"Huh," Tom said. "I don't know." Coach's door was slightly ajar, and there was a takeout container on the desk with a fork handle sticking out of it. "Maybe we'll find out later." Tom finished getting dressed, then went out to the field early to focus on the upcoming game. He gazed at the end zones, the stadium seats, the lights. What would it be like to play in an NFL game?

After the two teams warmed up, the players went to the sidelines while the captains called the coin toss. Kent State chose to receive the ball on the kick-off. Their half-back returned the kick to the forty-yard line, and Tom felt a surge of adrenaline as he ran onto the field with the other offensive players. The coaches surprised their opponents by calling a pass on their first play, even though Kovacs wasn't known for accuracy. Tom readied himself. He was in great shape, he felt mentally strong, and he wanted to prove to everyone what caliber of play he was capable of.

When the quarterback dropped back to pass, he drifted to the right, and Tom blocked his defensive lineman in that direction. The quarterback, not seeing an open receiver, started to scramble. He yelled, "I'm going left!" deciding to run instead of pass. Tom responded immediately, planting his right foot and beginning a sharp cut to his left to get in front of the quarterback. Just as he pushed off, a searing pain shot through his right leg and he fell to the ground. His body writhed on the grass, but his mind was alert, and a million questions rushed through his head, including the one he feared the most—had he ruptured his Achilles again? The stadium grew quiet.

<h1 style="text-align:center">17</h1>

As Tom lay on the field waiting for Jonesy, his eyes brimming with angry tears, he wondered if his football days were over for good this time. It was like a repeat of a nightmare. Tom struggled to look at his leg, doing his best to crane his neck without moving. His teammates hovered nearby but moved back when Jonesy ran up with Coach.

Jonesy knelt next to him, confirming the pain in his right calf, and motioned for Woz and another lineman to help carry Tom off the field. Tom looked toward the stands, glad that his father and Grandpa had not come. The spectators broke into applause for Tom.

On the sidelines, Tom caught sight of Richie, who didn't have the same arrogant expression on his face he usually did. Woz and the lineman lay Tom down as directed. Jonesy removed Tom's shoe and slowly moved his foot in different directions. He winced, and blood rushed to his head.

"I know this hurts," Jonesy said, leaning over him. "But I don't think you ruptured your Achilles again. We'll have the docs look at it after the game, but I think you should be able to play again." Tom didn't answer. He stared blankly at Jonesy for a few seconds until Jonesy said, "Did you hear me, O'Brien? You should be able to play again."

Still, Tom had nothing to say. He just kept staring as Jonesy elevated his leg and went to confer with Coach Peters, who looked Tom's way and gave him a thumbs-up. Despite the throbbing in his leg, he did his best to watch the game from where he lay, but in his head, he was replaying all the events of his last year of high school and the summer that followed. Woz came to kneel next to him whenever he could, shifting his weight because of the tightness in his ankle. Woz's presence was the only thing that kept him from descending to a darker place.

Following the game, Jonesy went with Tom to the hospital, where they met the sports doctor. After taking an X-ray and examining his foot, ankle, and calf, the doctor confirmed that Tom's Achilles was not ruptured. He had a Grade 1 Achilles tear, which would require a cast and crutches for six weeks, and then a walking cast until he felt comfortable without it. The doctor anticipated that he would walk without a cast by Christmas. When Tom heard this, his mouth went dry. "What about football?" he asked. "I have another year next fall." Tom thought of his father.

"It will take extensive physical therapy and strengthening exercises, but you should be able to play again," the doctor assured him.

Jonesy, standing by Tom's leg, smiled at him. "Coach Peters will be thrilled to hear that." Tom nodded, but he didn't feel thrilled himself—he just knew that something had been taken away from him.

That night, Tom called his parents to tell them about his injury. His mother sobbed quietly, and his father was silent. Later that week, he received a card from Kara expressing her sympathy and encouragement; she looked forward to seeing him at Thanksgiving.

———

Tom lay on the couch for hours with his leg elevated after Kevin brought him home. He tried to watch TV but couldn't follow the programs. He wasn't motivated to do anything, least of all eat the pizza Woz had dropped off. The reality set in—he would miss the rest of the season, a season that had been full of promise. Coach had told him he might be a potential pro draft choice. Tom grimaced, thinking how far away he was from that now.

As the days went on, he responded to Kevin's attempts at conversation with either silence or one-syllable replies. He slept very little and simply stared at the books Kevin left for him on the coffee table. It took him five days to decide that he needed to get his act together. He was falling behind in his classes and would need to struggle to catch up on his reading assignments.

Kevin offered to take him to his classes in his new car—a Volkswagen Beetle that he had paid a psychedelic artist to paint in Day-Glo colors. Since most of Tom's courses that semester were on construction management in one engineering building, he didn't have to move from building to building to change classes, which made it easy for him with his cast. He squeezed his large frame into the front seat, with his crutches sticking out the window, and had Kevin drop him off early and pick him up at the end of each day.

But sitting on benches between classes soon bored him, as did the topics of his classes. He thought about the courses he enjoyed the most, which weren't his construction management courses. They were his courses on economics, society, and politics. He made an excuse one day to ditch a construction management course, blaming the difficulty of hobbling around on crutches. But then he skipped another and another after that, until he was hardly going to any at all, just trying to keep up with the assignments at his house.

———

The week after he received his cast, Coach Peters asked Tom how he was doing. "I'm sorry you injured yourself after such a good fall practice," he said.

"Me, too," Tom said. A pair of shoes and some wadded-up sweats were sticking out from underneath Coach's desk.

"You unfortunately know better than most players that injuries happen in football," Coach said. He had dark circles under his eyes.

"I guess I thought I'd had my share," Tom said, sounding more glum than he'd intended.

"Yes, but you've also had experience in how to deal with them," Coach said, looking at Tom pointedly. "Your fate isn't sealed, O'Brien. Jonesy will work with you this spring as he did before, and you'll be ready to go next fall. Just keep working."

Tom could only nod, thinking what a long path it would be to get back.

"I want you to come to our meetings at practice and our games as much as you can," Coach said. "We still need you—our younger players look up to you and value your advice."

Tom agreed he could do that. He sat in a wheelchair on the sidelines during the next home game, wrapped in a blanket and cheering the team on. Coach seemed pleased to have him there, but when they lost yet another game, Coach's anger seemed more directed at himself than at any player.

———

One afternoon when Tom lay on the couch, Becky surprised him with a phone call. She said she learned from the *Daily* sportswriters about Tom's injury and suggested they get together. She picked Tom up in a used car that had recently been given to her by her parents. Tom stowed his crutches in the back seat and hopped to the door to sit down.

"Quite a change from the last time I saw you," she said, smiling from behind the wheel. She leaned over to kiss him.

"Yeah, I'm kind of helpless," he joked. He didn't detect any of her usual wariness or distance. He was still amazed that she had called.

As they drove, she asked him about his classes, and he admitted he'd been skipping most of the courses for his major. He told her about his plan for getting his courses done for graduation but realized, as he talked, that he sounded bored and unmotivated. Even as she looked at the road, she raised an eyebrow.

"You need some intellectual stimulation," she said. "I could give you a reading list of books on women's rights." She was unlike other girls Tom knew in that she was dead serious when she said this.

He smiled. "Sure."

They had dinner together, then Becky surprised him by driving to the picnic area near the river and parking in the gravel lot. It was a dark weekday evening, and they were alone. They moved to kiss each other, and she laughed at how the cast on his leg limited his movement. He loved hearing her laughter again and wondered how long this change would last. She suggested they study together that week when she dropped him off at the house. They began seeing each other at least twice a week, and she even came to spend the night at his house a few times.

———

During Thanksgiving break, Tom's mother hovered over him, offering him snacks, drinks, pillows, or news magazines. Both she and his father seemed to be watching him for signs that he might fall apart, as he guessed they felt he did after his Achilles rupture in high school.

"I know how much football means to you," she said one afternoon when she brought him and Kara slices of pie. "I'm just so glad you'll be able to play again in the fall." He knew she hoped his injury would not cause him to drop out of school, which would mean he wouldn't earn a degree and would be vulnerable to the draft. Next to him on the couch, Kara leaned against him, as if to give him an undetectable hug.

His father was relieved to hear that Tom could play football again and would get to keep his scholarship, but he seemed to have doubts, maybe unsure if Tom could repeat what he had done to prepare to play for Kent State. Tom remembered his father's encouragement after his first injury in high school when he had said, "Don't worry—we'll get this fixed." Now his father was silent.

Tom still had spells of depression over the loss of the football season, and he often spent time on his bed with his eyes closed, thinking of what it would have been like if he'd been able to play as he'd intended. Thankfully, he no longer needed his walking cast. Although he limped, it was easy to drive to visit Grandpa in the nursing home, sometimes talking and watching TV for hours. On his first visit, he was alarmed by how much Grandpa had deteriorated. Physical therapy after his stroke had only slightly improved the paralysis on his right side. He rarely used his walker anymore, spending most of his waking time in a wheelchair. Grandpa complained about back pain that went down his leg, and he took painkillers, which the doctor didn't want to be mixed with alcohol. Without his whiskey, Grandpa was a quieter man. But his eyes lit up when Tom arrived, and he reached out his left hand to grip Tom's.

"How are you handling your injury?" Grandpa asked over the sound of the TV.

"I'm so pissed off and bummed out. My coach had said I could have had a chance at the pros, the way I was playing. And then . . . this again." Tom gestured at his leg.

"I don't doubt it one bit. Injuries are the only thing that have held you back."

"I guess I've had a pretty good run," Tom said. He sat down next to Grandpa's wheelchair.

"You're damn right, you have."

Tom could see Grandpa fumbling with his blanket, and he reached over to help pull the blanket up higher on him. "I'll see if I can play again next year. As soon as the doctor gives me the green light, I'll start training again."

"That-a-boy. You're going to get knocked down in life—you can't help it," Grandpa said. "If it isn't injuries, it would be something else. Getting back up is what counts." Tom moved closer to Grandpa, sharing an armrest with him. He could always count on him for support.

———

Tom was grateful to see Becky when he returned from Thanksgiving break. Without the daily football routine, he'd been feeling purposeless, and she inspired him to study. They went to the library together every week, and she gave him books she thought he should read. One evening when they grabbed some coffee after studying, she asked him if he'd finished the last book she'd passed along to him, Betty Friedan's *The Feminine Mystique*.

"I did. Betty Friedan seems pretty down on men," he said.

Becky stopped stirring her coffee and looked at him. "It's not so much being down on individual men," she said. "It's the American culture and the expectations that hurt us."

"I don't know. I kept thinking of you when I was reading. I see her influence on you—you're your own person."

Becky seemed pleased. "I'm glad you see that. I believe her when she says women want something more than a husband, children, and a home."

"And what you still want is to be a journalist?"

"That's right."

More than anything else? he wondered. He was envious of her singularity of purpose at the same time he realized this seemed to leave less room for him in her life. But out loud, he simply said, "I'm jealous. I have no idea what I want."

She paused, looking at him. "Tom," she said, lowering her coffee, "I know how much football means to you, but your injury may be good for you."

He was a little taken aback. "How so?"

"You're more vulnerable, and I like that in you. It also might help you see beyond football, making your future clearer to you."

He nodded, but his thoughts were swirling. *My future to do what?* He couldn't see himself managing projects for a construction company in the dog-eat-dog world of modern capitalism, nor could he see himself working for a corporation, like his father and Grandpa.

Tom let his coffee grow cold.

———

On the first of December, several friends from the football team gathered at Tom and Kevin's house to watch the 1969 lottery drawing for the military draft. The Selective Service was conducting the drawing that night for men born between 1944 and 1950, a new approach intended to address inequities caused by the draft deferment system for college students. About fifteen football players sat or stood in the living room, squeezing in around the TV. They all knew that the lottery results could significantly impact their lives; several of them might end up being drafted to fight in Vietnam after they graduated. Tom was quiet, ready to accept whatever happened, whereas Kevin was defiant, saying no matter what his number was, he wouldn't go to war for a country as corrupt as the US was.

When their friends arrived at the house, they joked over who would be lucky and unlucky. They griped about football practice that day and about their final exams. But as the TV announcers described the drawing process for the lottery, they all became quiet. Tom could tell that everyone felt as jittery as he did.

Every date was drawn one at a time from a glass jar. If a student's birthday was on the first date picked, he would be assigned the lottery number one. Students with birthdays on the second date drawn would be given the lottery number two, and so on. The Selective Service projected that men with numbers up to 195 would probably be drafted.

The room was silent as dates were drawn for the first four numbers. One of their friends groaned when the fifth date, October 18, his birthdate, was picked. His low lottery number of five was sure to be included in the next year's draft. When birthdates of others were drawn, some with numbers well below 195 cursed loudly, a couple storming angrily out of the house. Tom looked at Kevin wide-eyed after the door slammed, more aware of what was at stake. As the drawings moved near the number 150, the people not drawn yet grew hopeful that the lottery might reach 195 before their birthdate was drawn.

Tom's birthdate was drawn for number 189. Woz's number was 215, and Kevin's 303. When Kevin's number was chosen, he yelled, "All right!" and stood up, pumping his arms. Tom kept thinking about his situation, given how close his number was to the projected cutoff. Would his draft board reach 189, resulting in him being drafted? If it were likely, should he explore enlisting in the navy or joining the National Guard, to avoid the risk of fighting in the Vietnamese jungle? Or consider moving to Canada?

When the lottery was over, the room was more subdued than before—everyone seemed ready to be alone. Those with high numbers didn't want to celebrate around those with low numbers, and those with low numbers wanted to start figuring out what they would do. Those in the middle tried to consider the implications of getting drafted or not. Tom sat on the couch, unable to stop thinking about this new uncertainty in his life.

—

The remaining weeks of the semester felt like torture. Tom needed to finish two papers and study for four final exams, but he couldn't focus. He alternated between smoking pot with Kevin and studying with Becky. Kevin didn't seem to have trouble learning while he was high, probably because he actually liked his courses—a combination of history, philosophy, and religious studies.

Tom's interest in Kevin's courses spurred him to select liberal arts electives for the spring semester. When Tom entered his adviser's office, he was met with a look of concern. Tom thought it might be because of his long hair—a rare sight in an engineering building—but it became clear that his adviser was worried about Tom's performance in his courses, based on what he had heard from his colleagues who taught them. Tom fidgeted in his chair, embarrassed; he hadn't thought his adviser would know about his challenges, but he was even aware of Tom's football injury and expressed his sympathy. Tom couldn't wait to leave his adviser's office and by the time they were done talking, he couldn't wait to leave construction management.

Tom's attempts to work on his papers seemed to frustrate Becky. She finally pushed his arm aside and helped by editing the introductions and the conclusions, saying the entire time that she shouldn't be doing it. One evening, Tom showed up at the library high, and Becky vented her irritation at him. He found her anger entertaining and smiled as she completed her tirade. She was silent when she drove him home but still allowed him to kiss her when she dropped him off.

Tom turned his papers in and then became anxious about his finals. He pulled an all-nighter to review his textbooks, drifting in and out of sleep and lingering too long on pages in a daze. He felt unprepared, having not found the energy to take notes for most of the semester, as he had in the past. He did the best he could, but his studying and the exams went by in a blur. When his instructors posted the grades at the end of the week, Tom received all Cs and Ds—the poorest he had ever performed as a student.

"I hope you've bottomed out," Becky said when she heard how he did.

When Becky left on Friday for Christmas break for her home in Cleveland, they hugged each other goodbye. Tom waved as she pulled away from the curb, though she seemed to be adjusting her rearview mirror at the time. As he watched her car grow smaller in the distance, he thought of the way she'd supported him that semester when he was struggling with his injury, the loss of football, and the threat of the lottery. Maybe their relationship was reaching a new level. He felt a swell of love for her.

Tom's parents planned to pick him up for Christmas break on Sunday. Saturday was a beautiful winter day, and Tom and Kevin took a walk in the sunshine after smoking a joint. The four inches of fresh snow covering the ground were melting in the 40-degree weather, and the intense sun and whiteness of the snow dazzled Tom. When they returned to their house, the phone rang, and Tom answered it.

"Tom." It was his father.

"Yeah."

"I have bad news. Grandpa died this morning."

18

Tom was in a daze. Kevin threw some items in a bag for Tom to take home and exchanged a worried look with Tom's parents when they arrived to drive him back to Massillon for Christmas break. Tom's mother spent almost the entire drive turned halfway around in her seat, casting anxious glances at Tom and looking to Tom's father for help. But Tom didn't say a word. He rested his temple against the window, appearing to stare outside but seeing nothing.

When they pulled into town and drove past Grandpa's nursing home, Tom's eyes went to Grandpa's window. The curtains were drawn. He felt his throat tighten, and his heart seemed to split in two.

Tom didn't eat much of anything that night. With his eyes red-rimmed, he learned that Kara had gotten home two days before Grandpa died. She'd been the one to answer the call from the nursing home with the news that Grandpa had passed away. When she ran to find their father, she cried so hard that he had to ask her to repeat herself. Tom looked at his father now, sitting next to Grandpa's chair. He couldn't see the chair without feeling an intense loneliness set in.

Tom went upstairs to get away. He had never had to be in the world without his grandpa before, and he didn't know how to do it.

———

Tom's parents planned Grandpa's funeral for the week after Christmas—including an Irish wake at their house on Tuesday evening. The funeral-home director and his assistant brought Grandpa's casket to their house for the wake. Tom stood at a distance next to Kara, watching the gathering unfold, unsure of what to do. He had never attended an Irish wake before. He felt he should go to Grandpa, but he hung back, not wanting to dishonor Grandpa's memory by doing something out of turn.

"I can't believe he's gone," Kara said, her voice shaking.

Their mother motioned for them to come with her and their father to view Grandpa's body. This was the first time Tom would see a dead person, and he grew anxious as they neared the casket. Grandpa wore his church suit, and his wedding band was visible on his folded hands. But it was not Grandpa. Tom recognized his face, yet it was without the mischievous, light-hearted expression he often had; Grandpa's life and spirit were gone. Tom ached, wishing just one more time to hear Grandpa call him "Tommy boy."

Tom's relatives were clearly taken aback by Tom's long hair. It was good to see them again, but he kept a distance, wanting to be alone. He watched as family and friends viewed Grandpa's body in the casket, often with sadness and occasionally tears. He thanked them when they offered their condolences. He stood stiffly in his suit, feeling uncomfortable. Time moved slowly.

The guests served themselves drinks and snacks and told stories about Grandpa's life. Tom's mother introduced him to an older man—small and hunched over, his face lined with wrinkles—who had worked with Grandpa in the foundry. But before Tom could talk with him, Tom's father interrupted them and told Tom he had some guests. Confused, Tom went to the entryway and found Kevin, Woz, and most surprisingly, Jack. They all wore suits.

"I can't believe it," Tom said, becoming emotional. "I didn't know you all were coming."

Jack looked choked up. "Your father called to tell me your grandpa had died. He said he hoped your friends could come to the funeral and gave me the phone number of the house where you and Kevin live."

Kevin reached out and put his hand on Tom's shoulder. "We know how much your grandpa meant to you. Woz and I drove up this morning and met Jack."

"We didn't want you to do this alone," Woz said, stepping forward to hug Tom and slightly bumping the hall table.

Holding back tears, Tom invited them into the room with Grandpa's casket. Many of the guests looked at them, especially at Kevin, with his full beard and hair down to his shoulders, and Woz, whose massive presence filled the room. Tom walked his friends to the casket, and they were quiet, honoring Grandpa with their silence.

When they'd paid their respects, Tom's father told them to help themselves to food and drinks. He gave Jack a nod. Tom introduced his friends to his relatives, who each stopped their conversations to look with curiosity at Tom's friends.

Tom's mood was changing. Kara stood behind his cousin, watching them with interest.

"Kara, come here. I'll introduce you."

She walked over to them, smiling, and they stopped talking.

"This is my sister, the starting sweeper for the Ohio State field hockey team."

"That's impressive," Woz said. "I always wanted to learn more about that sport."

Kara smiled at him. "Well, I can say I probably wouldn't be playing had it not been for Tom's and Grandpa's encouragement," she said. Her eyes lingered on Woz's, and Tom looked back and forth from his sister to his friend. Woz was blushing.

The group stood with small plates of food in their hands. As they ate, Tom told them about almost freezing his fingers when he was four, playing catch with the new football Grandpa had given him on Christmas Day. Jack remembered how much Grandpa hated the Steelers whenever they played the Browns, which caused Woz to raise his eyebrows.

"Since he was your grandpa, I'll forgive him for that," he said, telling Kara he was from Pennsylvania. She reacted with a hearty laugh.

Tom felt a hand on his shoulder and turned around to see the older man who'd worked in the foundry with Grandpa.

"Your grandpa talked about you all the time. You should know he was always really proud of you," the man said.

Tom looked at the man, and then his eyes looked toward Grandpa in his casket. "Thank you," he said, feeling a lump in his throat. "I don't think I've ever had a bigger fan."

The man smiled. "Maybe not, but this town thinks you're something special." Tom's father passed into view. "Your grandpa told me his grandson had it all."

Tom lowered his head. "I don't know about that." Someone near them coughed.

"Your grandpa mentioned your injuries to some of us," the old man said, studying Tom closely. "Things like that happen." Tom nodded. "They might happen again—you never know." The man crinkled his eyes and continued staring at Tom for several long seconds. Tom met his gaze, his heart beating rapidly. The man then nodded and patted Tom on the shoulder. Tom stood frozen. He felt he'd just been given a message from Grandpa.

Tom's father tapped a spoon on a glass and stood next to Grandpa's chair. "I'd like you all to join me in a toast to my dad's life." He raised his glass and recited the Irish Blessing, his voice breaking at the end. Tom's mother moved in and held his arm.

Tom looked around the room full of Grandpa's family and friends. He couldn't think of a better way to celebrate Grandpa's life. Tom could feel Grandpa everywhere—in everyone's eyes, in everyone's laughs. He felt so grateful to be his grandson.

———

By ten o'clock that night, everyone had left except Tom's friends. Tom invited them to the basement, so they could relax on the couch. Tom called for Woz a couple of times, but he didn't seem ready to end his conversation with Kara, standing near her by the kitchen table. Tom imagined Kara might want to be invited, but after the emotional day, he craved a guy's-only gathering, something that felt easy and familiar.

Downstairs they settled into the old couch and some easy chairs, Woz finally joining them. He filled the stairwell as he descended, more with his broad smile than his size.

"I think your sister is casting an Irish spell over Woz," Kevin said, taking a drink of whiskey. He had taken off his suit jacket and was loosening his tie.

"What? She was telling me about field hockey. It was interesting," Woz said. He used a defensive tone, but he couldn't wipe the smile off his face. "You know," he said to Tom, "her sweeper position sounds to me a lot like a middle linebacker."

"Not many strikers get by her—she's strong and fast," Tom said.

"I can tell," Woz said. He sat on the edge of the couch, as if still going over his conversation with Kara. He didn't seem to be aware that he could relax and take off his jacket.

"What you can tell is that she's fun, unlike quiet Tom," Kevin said. "And what *she* can tell is that you're interested in her. No subtlety whatsoever."

Tom and Jack laughed as Woz looked at them, seemingly tongue-tied. Jack helped him out by changing the subject. He talked about school, finals, and graduation at Miami. Then he asked, "How did you guys do in the lottery?"

Woz seemed eager to prove he wasn't smitten. "Kevin and I made out well with high numbers," he said, "but Tom is in the middle."

"You guys are lucky. I got twelve."

"Twelve? What are you going to do?" Tom asked, sitting up.

"I don't know. I sure don't want to go to Vietnam," Jack said. He looked toward the top of the basement stairs. "I'm thinking of joining the National Guard. But the downside of that is it's a six-year commitment."

"Too bad," Kevin said. "If I had a low number, I'd think about moving to Canada."

A look of annoyance passed over Jack's face. "I don't think I could declare myself a conscientious objector just to avoid the war," Jack said.

"I could," Kevin said, his voice louder. "War is evil, especially this one!"

"Uh-oh," Woz said. "This might be the start of a sermon."

Jack frowned and shook his head, peering closely at Kevin through his glasses.

Tom got up to pass the tray of snacks his mother had given them. He didn't want the two to argue; he just wanted to sit back and enjoy his friends. "Do the engineering consultants still want you to work for them?" he asked Jack, trying to change the subject.

Jack seemed to catch on. He took some chips. "They say they'll give me an offer to start work after I graduate this spring."

Woz sat up and looked at Jack. "Tell me about it."

Jack described the air conditioning and heating systems he worked on as a mechanical engineering intern. Woz asked him questions about clients and projects, and Jack seemed pleased to be able to talk about his experience. Kevin looked at Tom and mouthed, "Boring," while munching on some pretzels.

"At least you're not designing missile systems," Kevin said after a few minutes. "But either way, I can't see helping *any* large corporation become more powerful in a capitalist economy. Capitalism doesn't work."

Jack fell silent, looking surprised by Kevin's judgment. But Woz, who already had plenty of experience with Kevin in the cafeteria, was ready to confront Kevin. "Your hippie philosophy would have us all living in communes and tending organic gardens," Woz said. His nostrils flared. Kevin's face became flushed. Tom realized he was not going to be able to stop their debate.

"Believe it or not, there are economic systems that don't rely on exploiting people and resources," Kevin said. "We should be working toward a better society that eliminates poverty and racism and doesn't depend on profits from military conflicts."

"Here we go again," Woz said. He rolled his eyes and looked at Jack.

Even though Jack and Woz had only met that morning, they seemed to be in sync with their career plans and view of their futures. But given all that Tom had read and seen in his time at Kent, he related more to Kevin. When Jack and Woz talked about how they were going to pursue business careers, he felt like these paths would only add to the problems in society.

"So, what about you?" Jack said to Tom. "What are you going to do? How are you handling your latest injury?"

Tom looked down at his leg. "I miss football. My coach and trainer think I can play next fall, so I'll go through physical therapy and exercises this spring, just like I did a while back." Jack caught his eye; he knew how that had gone last time. "But it's a long haul," Tom continued. "In the meantime, I'm not sure *what* I'm doing. I almost flunked my finals, I don't know about my major, and I could be drafted . . ." His voice drifted off.

Jack's expression softened. "I know these aren't easy times," he said. "Losing football—again—and now your grandpa."

Tom sighed, wishing he was on a football field, where everything seemed so clear, where he enjoyed both the games and the practices. He missed Coach's guidance and mentorship, and now he missed Grandpa's encouragement and support.

"Let's end the night with one last drink," he said. His friends nodded and sat forward. Tom poured a shot of whiskey into his glass and passed the bottle to the others. They raised their glasses in a final toast to Grandpa. Tom looked at his three close friends and wondered what he would do without them.

———

Tom was one of the pallbearers at the funeral. The priest led the Catholic funeral rites at the church and the burial site. Tom's coat wasn't enough protection against a cold winter wind during the burial, but he welcomed the discomfort because it took his mind off his grief. Like everyone else, he was glad to go back to the church for lunch afterward to warm up.

After lunch, Tom and his friends met in the parking lot. The crowd was dwindling. Once again, Woz had to be pulled away from Kara. Tom shook hands with each of his friends, immensely grateful that they'd come. Kevin grasped Tom's shoulder and pulled him close when they shook hands. Woz barely fit into Kevin's Day-Glo Bug, and everyone smiled. He looked embarrassed that Kara had watched his struggle to squeeze in the front seat. "I can't believe I'm riding in this," he said before closing the door.

Tom realized that none of his friends would have been there without his father contacting them. He had never thought that his father knew how important his three friends were to him.

———

Tom's Christmas break was mainly one of solitude. He no longer had Grandpa to watch bowl games with. He sat with his father for a couple of them, but the silence was too awkward, and Grandpa's absence too painful.

In the kitchen one afternoon, his mother said that she hoped he would soon figure out his career plans, as Jack and Woz had. She was careful in the way she spoke about Kevin though, probably afraid her son might somehow follow in his anti-establishment footsteps. As quickly as he could, Tom took the sandwich he'd made and went back up to his room.

Without Grandpa around over the break, Tom felt alone. He called Becky a few times. They talked for half an hour the first time, and she sounded genuinely sorry about the loss of his grandfather, but all the other calls were short because she had family in town. She never called him back on her own accord. Why wasn't she there for him?

The only person who could draw him out of his solitude was Kara. One evening, she asked Tom about Woz, who she said should be called "Ron." She had already written him a letter and had just received one in return.

"What do you think about inviting Ron back to visit over spring break?" she asked, biting her lip a little.

"I think he's one of my best friends, and he'd love it, though from what I can tell, he's not going to be that interested in hanging out with *me*." Tom smiled. Kara practically bounded out of the room, thanking Tom twice as she left. He found her composing another letter to Woz shortly after.

Otherwise, Tom spent most of the break in his bedroom, thinking about Grandpa, worrying about what came next, and trying to shake off his feelings of emptiness and aimlessness. He read a lot, catching up with his backlog of news magazines, particularly following reports about campus protests and counterculture trends.

But it was a book Kevin loaned him—Tom Wolfe's *The Electric Kool-Aid Acid Test*—that made him sit up one day. The stories about Ken Kesey and the Merry Pranksters showed him alternatives to living a traditional lifestyle. With so much wrong in the world, Tom didn't feel hopeful that a traditional lifestyle—whatever that meant—held much for him. He dog-eared several pages in the book, curious about the idea of using LSD to transcend the mundane world and Kesey's desire to create a new religion. Maybe he would visit California one day to see how people like this lived.

19

Tom walked up and down the aisles in the Kent State bookstore, locating the textbooks for his 1970 spring semester courses. Unlike previous semesters, when most of his books were in the business and engineering sections, he was surrounded by books for liberal arts courses. He was glad he decided to push his remaining construction management courses to either summer school or the fall. He didn't know if he had the patience for classes like those he had almost failed last semester.

He bought an anthology, *The American Tradition in Literature*, for an English class; *Capital* by Karl Marx and *The Other America* by Michael Harrington for an economics class; and *The Making of a Counter Culture* by Theodore Roszak and a packet of articles for a philosophy course. He also perused others. His interest grew as he read the inside flaps of book covers, and he finally sat down in an easy chair meant for people browsing. He sat there for over an hour, leafing through books for other liberal arts. The idea of gaining knowledge that might guide him was exciting; he was eager to learn from writers and thinkers. His break from football, no matter how frustrating, was giving him time to explore his academic interests.

When he got home, Kevin was sitting on the porch smoking a joint. "Let's see what you got," Kevin said, reaching for Tom's bag of books. Kevin had chosen to major in philosophy with a minor in religious studies, and the only plan he had after graduation was to travel, maybe backpacking around Europe, staying in hostels, using a graduation gift he expected from his father. Kevin looked at each of Tom's books. "We're taking the same philosophy class!" he shouted, holding up Tom's Culture and Identity textbook. He was eager to read Roszak's book on the counterculture.

"You're going to start a new life," Kevin said, leaning back in a weathered patio chair. "Once you start these classes, you'll wonder whether football is worth it."

Tom gathered his books, eager to go inside and start reading already. "I think I can do both," he said.

"We'll see." Kevin pulled his hair back into a low ponytail. "You know, without football, you'll also have more time for Becky. I ran into her this morning."

Tom looked up from his books. He had been wondering if she would want to see him as often as she had in the fall. "What did she have to say?"

"She wanted to hear about your grandpa's funeral. She's going to call you."

Tom nodded, thinking about where his relationship with Becky might go this semester. He could see Kevin studying him, maybe trying to figure it out as well.

"I read your book, *The Electric Kool-Aid Acid Test*," Tom said quickly.

"Yeah? Did it make you want to try some acid?"

Tom smiled and shrugged. He'd been thinking about it ever since finishing the book. He knew not everyone had positive experiences with it, but he was willing to risk it.

"Right on," Kevin said. "If you're really in, how about I talk to my friend, Lucas, and see if we can trip with him when it gets warmer?"

Tom said he was in. He was sowing wild oats, like Grandpa said people should when they're young.

———

"I'm sorry your grandfather's gone," Becky said as they walked into the student union. Students streamed past them. "Are you doing okay?" She took his hand briefly, then let it go.

"I guess," he said, his hand still extended.

"It had to be hard, especially after you struggled through finals like that." She directed them to a bench along the wall.

"I'm better now," he said. He wasn't sure how to take her comment; she knew some of the doubts and questions he had about his future, and besides, people got Cs and Ds sometimes. "I'm excited about the liberal arts courses I'm taking this semester," he said. "Especially *The Making of a Counter Culture*."

She sat at an angle on the bench, so she could face him better. "You're looking more like a hippie than ever with your beard," she said, reaching up to touch it. He had started growing it after Christmas break, about two weeks earlier.

"Do you like it?" he asked.

"I don't know. I suppose it depends on what kind of statement you're making."

He asked her what she had been doing. She described her work to help organize Vietnam Moratorium demonstrations involving churches and community groups in the spring, so the Moratorium would be about more than just university student protests. Tom watched her as she spoke, always impressed by her passion and confidence.

"That's admirable," he said. "But I think our whole culture needs to change, like the groups in California *The Electric Kool-Aid Acid Test* talks about."

Becky made a face. "Isn't that book all about drugs?"

"Some people think drugs can produce a new consciousness—the kind of thing that will change society."

She paused, frowning at him. "Are you thinking about taking acid on top of smoking dope, Tom?"

The student union was loud around them. "I might try tripping," he said.

She seemed to choose her words carefully. "I don't know if I could do that—it's dangerous sometimes. I'd personally rather try to change society by influencing the politics." She sat back, her knees facing away from him.

———

Coach wanted to meet with Tom early in the semester to discuss his spring therapy program to strengthen his leg.

"I'm sorry I didn't have time to see you at the end of the season," he said. "We've been under the gun." He riffled through one of the stacks of papers on his desk. His whistle fell to the floor.

"No problem, Coach. I was dealing with some things and was busy too." Normally, Coach would probably have paused to ask more, but he didn't today. He seemed disheveled; his shirt was wrinkled, his hair uncombed.

"I'd like you to meet with Jonesy next week so he can go over your exercise program this spring." Coach located the paper he'd been looking for, and Tom could see it had a few coffee or food stains on it.

"Okay, I'd like that."

Coach looked at Tom. "We really missed you in our remaining games, although I don't know if we would have won any more, even if you'd played."

For some reason, Tom sensed that Coach needed to be comforted. He searched for what to say. "I'm sure the guys tried their best."

"Well, it's not going to save us." Coach rubbed his forehead with his hand, his eyes closed. "Look, Tom. Don't tell anyone, but my guess is that some of us are going to be fired." Coach had an expression of resignation and anger.

Tom was stunned. "That's crazy!" he said.

Coach stood up, walked to the window, and then looked back at Tom. "It's not my only problem. I'll tell you this because you've met my family. Jill and I are separated—it's not going well." His shoulders were slumped.

Tom was speechless. Coach was a model he had aspired to follow—a man who loved his job, team, and purpose, living a good life with a woman to love and support him. He couldn't imagine Coach not being able to make his marriage work given his patience and kindness. But maybe he had challenges with Jill like Tom had with Becky.

"Well, life goes on," Coach said, clearing his throat a little. He picked up his whistle and came over to clap Tom on the back. "I've really enjoyed working with you, and I hope we'll continue to be able to."

"Me, too," Tom said. "I'm sorry, Coach." Tom hesitated, not knowing what else to say. He walked out of the office, glancing back at Coach's door, still not believing what he'd heard.

———

A few weeks later, Tom heard that Coach Peters and all the other assistant coaches had been fired. He also heard that Coach's wife had filed for divorce. Tom felt sorry for little Jimmy.

Tom happened to be doing therapy exercises with Jonesy on the day Coach was cleaning out his office. He was glad for the chance to say goodbye, but it was hard to express what he was feeling. "Thanks for believing in me," he said finally. "It means more than I can describe." His eyes damp, Coach silently nodded and gave Tom a brief hug. As Tom walked away, he thought of Grandpa, who told him to get up when knocked down. What if you got up like Coach, just to get knocked down again?

——

Tom's spring classes were unlike any learning he'd experienced before. He was drawn to the transcendentalists in his American literature course—especially Emerson and Thoreau—writing down quotes, such as Emerson's "A foolish consistency is the hobgoblin of little minds," and Thoreau's "Simplicity, simplicity, simplicity!" He read excerpts from *Walden*, fascinated by Thoreau's move to a small cabin on Walden Pond to rid himself of material possessions and unnecessary socializing.

None of Tom's readings that spring, however, had the impact of Roszak's *The Making of a Counter Culture*. Tom came to believe that his life experiences and reading of previous books had prepared him for this book. He dug into it, hoping it would give him answers to his questions about what to do with his life. Kevin felt the same, and they worked on assignments together, compared papers they wrote, and enjoyed discussions in class about the technocracy that dominated industrial capitalism. On their midterm exam, they were asked to describe counterculture elements—joy, art, and ritual—that resisted the technocracy, leading to a more humane society. Tom began to see a purpose he might pursue—helping to create a new culture.

——

The spring days grew warmer. Kevin, one afternoon, reminded Tom of what they had learned from Roszak about the value of psychedelic experiences in a new culture. He said it was time to pick a beautiful day for an LSD trip. Tom agreed, and Kevin contacted Lucas.

Tom had met Lucas some time ago when he, Kevin, and others were all stoned at a party. Lucas, probably two or three years older than Tom and Kevin, was short and pudgy. He wore a bushy Fu Manchu mustache and an Afro hairstyle. He shook Tom's hand, but didn't meet his eye, instead looking at Kevin and asking if he had a joint.

When Lucas arrived on the chosen Saturday morning, he said the acid tabs were fifteen dollars each, more than Tom had expected, and suggested they go to a picnic area near the river for their trip. The crisp spring morning warmed quickly by the time they reached the park. Tom looked at the LSD tab in his hand with a mixture of curiosity, eagerness, and uncertainty.

They dropped the tabs on their tongues and started wandering through the park. After about twenty minutes, Tom realized each branch and leaf of the tall oaks lining the trail was growing and shrinking as he passed. Everything pulsated with vivid colors, and the gurgling of the sun-kissed Cuyahoga was like a symphony in his head. He smiled, fascinated by the effects. Kevin laughed and asked in a distant voice whether Tom saw the trees growing as they walked by them.

Tom came to a small oak and stopped to examine the leaves. He brought one close to his face. Even the veins in the leaf seemed to pulsate, and he was shocked when a ladybug crawled from the underside of the leaf, stopping to stare at him. Suddenly anxious, he let go of the leaf and stepped back, then turned to walk toward the river. Kevin continued to laugh, waving his arms as he walked.

Tom sat down on the bench at the side of the river, and Kevin and Lucas joined him. They stared intently at the water flowing by, noticing small whirlpools and changing colors. Kevin turned to look up the river and jumped up, seeming afraid. He pointed and yelled, "Look at that!" It was a large branch floating toward them. Lucas laughed as the branch swept by, but Kevin's eyes were huge, which made Tom nervous.

"C'mon," Lucas said. "Let's get away from the river."

"Okay. That freaked me out," Kevin said, his eyes still huge.

Tom was getting used to the strange sound of Kevin's voice. "Me, too."

They got up and walked on the river trail, where large trees formed a canopy. When they reached a clearing, Kevin suggested they lie down on the grass. Tom closed his eyes and lost track of the passing of time. When the sun slipped out from behind a cloud, warm, moving lights and silent explosions of gold and yellow patterns lit up his eyelids. He told Kevin to close his eyes and watch the colors. "Incredible," Kevin said. They lay there for what seemed like hours. Tom's heart slowed, and his forehead relaxed. He felt at peace, part of a truly beautiful world, and he thought of his and Kevin's goal to live an alternative life. He felt a closeness to Kevin that he would never forget.

20

Tom and Woz were often at the gym together, with Tom doing therapy on his leg under Jonesy's guidance and Woz working out in the weight room. Woz had completed his college football career and would graduate in June. He told Tom that he had no illusions about playing professional football and was eager to find a job, but he also wanted to keep in shape, following spring practice rituals he had been doing for years. The new coaching staff had not yet arrived, so other team members followed drills directed by the trainers.

Woz suggested they get together at the Kent Grill for some beers and burgers on Saturday night to celebrate the completion of midterm exams. Tom asked if Kevin could come, too. Woz groaned but said, "Sure."

On Friday, Tom checked the posting of his midterm grades outside his instructors' offices and was pleased that he'd gotten As and Bs this time around. What he'd learned from these courses was helping him define a purpose different from construction management. He continued to think about helping create a new culture, one based on creativity, community, peace, and love. He didn't yet know what this meant in terms of making a living after graduation. But he knew it should be done with friends who also wanted to create a new culture.

Kevin agreed to go out with Tom and Woz, joking that maybe he and Tom could beat some enlightened thinking into Woz's thick skull. "Be cool," Tom said. "This is just a get-together between old friends."

Woz was in a booth when they arrived, a pitcher of beer and three glasses in front of him. The bar was filling up quickly with loud college students celebrating the end of midterms.

"How's the hippie?" Woz asked Kevin.

"I'm wonderful," Kevin said as he slid into his seat.

"I see you have O'Brien copying your Jesus look."

"Yup," Kevin said, filling his glass with beer. "We're going to save the world."

"God forbid."

Tom poured a couple of glasses of beer and slid one over to Woz. Woz looked the same as he always had, his curly hair and sideburns perhaps a little longer than they were during football season.

Woz took a sip of beer, then looked at Tom. "I was hoping to get your thoughts on something," he said. "Your sister has invited me to visit her in Massillon over spring break."

Tom smiled at Woz, saying that would be great. Woz described how Kara wanted Tom's support in case her parents had concerns about Woz's visit, and Tom assured him there would be no problem. His mother would fix Woz up in the basement with their fold-out couch.

Woz breathed a sigh of relief and said he'd visited Kara in Columbus two weeks ago. Things were developing so quickly for Woz and Kara, compared to his uncertain years-long relationship with Becky.

Kevin laughed at Woz's news, warning Tom to keep Woz away from his sister in case her pretty smile might make him lose control. Woz directed a steely gaze at Kevin, then turned away from him.

"More beer?" Tom asked. He emptied the pitcher into his friends' glasses, then waved down the server for another. "You guys only have half a semester left before graduation. What are your plans?" he asked, looking only at Woz.

"I've had some interviews through the placement office," Woz said.

"Yeah? What kind?"

"Financial positions—at some companies in Cleveland and Chicago."

Kevin sat forward. "Do you think you could actually do that?" he asked, his brow furrowed. Tom thought he probably shouldn't have invited Kevin.

"Some of those positions seem boring," Woz said, "but I'm kind of excited about the ones with accounting and consulting firms. I'm waiting to hear from Arthur Andersen."

"Why them?" Tom asked.

"Well, to be honest, your buddy Jack got me thinking about it at your grandpa's funeral, when he started talking about the engineering consulting company he works for. He said he likes working for clients on a variety of assignments. That appeals to me, too."

Kevin tilted his head and closed his eyes tightly, the furrows in his forehead leading down to the wrinkles around his eyes. He started to say something, but the raucous noise of drunken students across the aisle forced him to wait. He finally said, "I can't believe you're thinking of working for corporate America."

"Well, forgive me, your highness," Woz said, growing serious.

"You're going to be one of the experts who helps the technocracy become even more powerful," Kevin said.

Woz looked indignant. "I have no idea what the hell you're even talking about."

Kevin turned to Tom. "You're his good friend. Why don't you tell him what a mistake he's making."

Tom shifted in his seat. He didn't like being in the middle of an argument between his friends. And besides, he was buzzed. Before he could think of a fitting response, he topped off their glasses, hoping he could somehow lower the intensity of the conflict.

"Tell him about our acid trip last weekend—about feeling part of the universe," Kevin said.

Woz stared at Tom. "You took acid, O'Brien?"

"Yeah," Tom said, irritated that Kevin had moved the confrontation in that direction.

"It's one thing to smoke a joint now and then and follow Kevin's hare-brained ideas," Woz said. "But to take hard drugs to have some mystical experience is insane."

Tom was offended. "I'm not going to judge *your* choices," he said. "But yeah, I agree with Kevin that our society needs to change and that drugs might make us more aware."

Woz continued to focus on Tom. "Are you going to get a job? Or are the two of you going to drop out and join a commune?"

"I don't know what I'm going to do, but I've thought about living in a community that believes in change," Tom said. He wished he'd drunk less beer. "I've even thought of you, Woz—how you could use your financial skills to help change society."

"I'm honored, but that's not for me," Woz said. He looked done with his drink, even though his glass was still full.

Kevin rolled his eyes. "Is that predictable or what?" he said to Tom with a look of disdain at Woz.

"Look, asshole," Woz said, standing up. "I don't need any more of your crap. We can each live the life we want. I need to go."

Tom was surprised how quickly it had come to this, and he felt guilty for bringing them together. Woz fumbled for his wallet.

"I got it," Tom said. He tried to smile at Woz. "Good luck with your interviews."

"Thanks. I'll see you in Massillon."

When Woz left, Tom turned to Kevin with a look of frustration. "That's the last time I'm bringing you two together," he said.

Kevin smirked. "Fine. I don't need a corporate accountant in my life."

Tom was silent. He and Kevin agreed philosophically, but he wasn't going to abandon his close friendship with Woz.

———

Although Tom had turned inward that spring—exploring new ideas and testing new beliefs—he still paid attention to the war. Protests continued to increase, since Nixon's policies seemed essentially the same as Johnson's. As Becky had said, the Vietnam Moratorium marches highlighted the increasing unrest—through the involvement of broader slices of American citizens rather than just college students.

When Tom read in the *Daily* about an upcoming Moratorium event at Kent State, he wanted to talk to Becky about it. He also wanted to see if they could get back to the relationship they'd had in the fall. After their awkward conversation about his new courses and drugs, they had seen very little of each other. When Tom tried to schedule a date with her, she often told him that she had a tight deadline to meet for the *Daily*, but when he told her he wanted to talk about the Moratorium, she offered to meet him at the Commons.

They greeted each other with a kiss as always, but Becky barely brushed his lips with hers. It was a warm spring afternoon, and they sat down on a bench facing the grassy hill. He thought of bringing up their relationship right then but, afraid of what she might say, asked her instead if she was helping organize the Moratorium events mentioned in the *Daily*.

"Not this time," she said. "I'm not as active as I was in the past because I've been named the *Daily's* lead political reporter. I'll be covering it instead of participating in it."

"What? Congratulations," he said, reaching forward to hug her. "You're on your way to becoming a journalist."

She smiled but hugged him back more stiffly than usual. "I hope so. I'm going to try to set up some job interviews over spring break." Tom was hit with another wave of jealousy over her confidence about what she wanted.

"How about you?" she asked, turning her eyes back to him. "Are you still planning to finish your construction courses this summer?"

She had caught him off guard. His courses on society and culture had pushed those summer plans out of his mind. He nodded. "Right now I'm focused on my liberal arts courses," he said.

"I read a review of that book you like so much," she said. "*The Making of a Counter Culture?* The reviewer was not impressed. He called it an anti-reason book with an irrational cure."

Tom nodded. "Well, thanks for looking into it," he said, his disappointment obvious in his voice.

"Look," she said. "I believe society needs to change too, but not through drugs and communes."

Tom didn't know what to say. She stopped talking and looked out on the Commons in a way that began to make him feel uneasy. She finally turned to him. "Did you trip on acid?"

"Yeah. It was incredible."

She looked at him for a long time, and his palms started to sweat. "You didn't freak out?" she asked.

"No, it was completely peaceful. The colors were so intense. I wish you'd been with me."

Becky gazed back out on the Commons, seeming to be deep in thought. She closed her eyes and pursed her lips together. After what seemed like an eternity, she turned to look at him, her bottom lip quivering.

"I don't know where you're headed, Tom."

"What do you mean?'

Becky looked up at the clouds drifting over them, seeming to choose her words carefully. "You seem different from the person I met three years ago.

Your dedication to football was impressive, and things were good with us after your injury. I felt close to you then. But I don't know who you are now."

Tom's mouth went dry. Instead of getting back together as he had wanted, they seemed to be separating.

"I was hoping we could start seeing each other again," he said. She closed her eyes again and slowly exhaled. When she opened her eyes again, she looked at him with a combination of pain and grim resolve. "I would need us to have a common vision of where we're going."

He stared at the ground, trying to collect himself, then looked back at Becky. "Wait—are you saying we're breaking up?"

She continued to watch him closely. Her eyes grew wet. "I thought a lot about us over the holidays. You're a wonderful person, Tom, and I like you a lot. But we're going in different directions. I just don't see how we make sense."

Tom felt his own tears coming. "But you've meant so much to me," he said. He was embarrassed that some students passing by were watching him.

"And you to me. But people grow . . . or figure out how they're going to grow."

Tom wanted to leave. He couldn't believe this was happening. But it was Becky who stood first. She looked at him with a half-smile, her dimples appearing.

"You're a good man, Tom. Take care of yourself." She bent down and drew his head to her. He let her kiss him, and then she turned and walked away, looking back once.

Tom walked in the opposite direction. He needed to go the way Becky had gone, but instead, he trekked across campus, his mind turning to memories of Cindi telling him their relationship was over, before he eventually circled around and went home. Why couldn't he keep the love and support from a woman he loved? He thought of Coach, who seemed to have succeeded in purpose and love, and then had them both fall apart. And he thought of Grandpa, no longer available for advice. Tom felt alone and abandoned. Was this the story of his life—losing people he loved?

21

On a Saturday morning in early April, Tom and Woz drove to Massillon together for their spring break. Drops of rain hit their windshield as they began the drive, but they saw glimpses of the sun as the temperature rose. They hadn't spoken much since the argument with Kevin at the bar. Tom, in the passenger seat, kept his eyes on the road ahead and tried to keep a conversation going. Otherwise, the interior of the car reminded him of all the times he had spent with Becky in Woz's car, which made his heart heavy.

"Are you excited to see Kara?" Tom asked, turning up the music a little.

"Is the pope Catholic?" Woz smiled, drumming his fingers on the steering wheel.

Tom guessed that neither Woz nor Kara had ever been in a longer-term relationship. "You're about to graduate, and Kara has two years left. How's that going to work?" he said. Had he sounded envious?

"We've talked about it," Woz said. "I think I'll take the job offer from Arthur Andersen in Chicago. If I prove myself after a year, they offer flexibility in assignments. I could move to their office in Columbus or be assigned audits in that region."

Woz really had it thought out. "I'm impressed—you two are serious."

"Yeah," Woz said, as if it should be obvious.

Tom's mother greeted him with a hug, and then surprised Tom by hugging Woz as well, her tiny body almost disappearing inside his large arms. Kara, who had found a ride home from Columbus the day before, moved to Woz quickly and stood on her toes to kiss him. She turned and said to everyone, "This is Ron, not Woz." Tom's father shook Woz's hand and welcomed him in. Although smaller in stature, his erect posture and quiet demeanor matched the impact of Woz's size. Tom smiled to himself when Woz said, "Thank you, sir." His father finally turned to Tom and shook his hand perfunctorily, seeming to keep his distance from his long-haired son.

Kara and Woz created a new energy in the house. Kara planned to give Woz a tour of Massillon after lunch, and Tom's mother told them about the meals she was preparing—steaks that night and a pot roast after church on Sunday. She mentioned to Tom that they would welcome Jack if he were in town, and Kara nodded. Tom guessed this was Kara's idea, since Woz and Jack had hit it off so well at Grandpa's funeral.

Kara and Woz left pretty quickly for their tour, and the house became silent as soon as the front door closed. Tom's mother waved to them through the family room window, then turned around and tried to fill the void.

"Who would Woz—I mean, Ron—work for if he accepts the offer?" she asked.

"He told me Arthur Andersen, an accounting firm in Chicago." Tom stood in the entryway between his parents.

"He'll audit companies?" his father asked, his tone surprisingly pleasant.

"I think so." Tom was surprised to see his father's interest. He guessed it was either because of his father's own experience with audits or his interest in the career of a potential son-in-law.

"Better to be the auditor than the one getting audited," his father said to Tom's mother. She nodded her head approvingly.

Tom's mother turned to Tom. "I'm sure you'll get a good job offer after you graduate this summer too."

Tom paused. Was this a loaded question? "I hope so," he said, moving to take his bag upstairs. He noticed his father looking at him with a curious expression.

"It will be good to see you clean-shaven and with a haircut again, like Ron," his mother said. He fumbled more than he needed to in picking up his bag.

"I'm going to do some reading," he said, gathering magazines from the rack by the couch and climbing the stairs.

———

Tom stayed in his room all afternoon while Kara and Woz were out. Sitting with his arms crossed, he stared at his old football trophies, the books on his desk, and the magazines on his bed, frozen with thoughts about his future. He wondered what Becky was doing over the break and whether she was thinking of him, but then quickly shook his head at that impossibility. About the only thing that brought him out of his funk lately was reading; it helped take his mind off the instability of his life.

Sighing, he picked up a news magazine and started to thumb through it. As usual, he paid particular attention to the reports on Vietnam. He'd begun monitoring the deployment of US soldiers in Vietnam, hoping the government would decrease the number of men drafted, so it wouldn't reach his lottery number. But nothing had changed in the draft, and he felt he was still in limbo. If he planned to graduate after the fall football season, he would have to complete the required number of construction management credits for his major. He dreaded those courses; they just didn't feel relevant or important to him anymore. But he wanted to play football, and he wanted to keep his student deferment. Tom felt caught between two terrible realities—one a physical war in Vietnam and the other an internal war with himself.

He put the magazines aside and picked up the American literature textbook he'd brought home to study. He reread Emerson's essay, "Self-Reliance," highlighting, with a marker he found on his desk, lines about the need to be a nonconformist. He flipped to Thoreau's *Walden*, rereading excerpts from it and highlighting lines about the mass of men leading lives of quiet desperation. That afternoon, Thoreau's writing about the natural environment surrounding Walden Pond moved Tom in a way it hadn't before—he took in the description of the pleasant hillside covered with pine woods and hickory trees, the thawing of the earth on spring days, the songs by the larks and peewees, and the snake in the water that Thoreau watched for more than a quarter of an hour. Tom recalled walking through the woods during his LSD trip—the lush canopy of trees, the leaf that pulsed in his hand, and the steady gurgling of the river. He pledged to himself that he would try to live surrounded by the beauty of nature, wherever he might end up.

After a while, he heard Kara and Woz come home and went downstairs to greet them. His mother teased him for staying cooped up in his room, antisocial until his friend and sister got home. She told the three of them to go to the patio, where Tom's father was preparing charcoal to grill the steaks.

They sat at the patio table with Tom's father, waiting for the coals to burn down. Tom's father asked Woz about his job offer. Woz came to attention in his chair, well-prepared for that question. He described the auditing role he would be assigned, and Tom's father seemed impressed. His approval of Woz's plans was a visible contrast to his disapproval of Tom's. Their conversation continued as if Tom were not present.

"How about the draft?" his father asked Woz, surprising Tom at his leap into sensitive territory. But Woz again was prepared.

"I'm lucky to have a high lottery number, so I don't think they'll reach me, especially since the war seems to be winding down," Woz said.

"I think you're right," Tom's father said. "The president's plan is working—more responsibility is being turned over to the South Vietnamese." Tom's head jerked up.

"I hope so," Kara said, reaching over to hold Woz's hand.

Tom couldn't stay silent. "That's overly optimistic. You guys understand that Nixon has killed over 10,000 US soldiers since he took office, right?"

Woz's face became still. "It's going to take time," he said.

"Too much time," Tom said, leaning forward in his seat. Kara caught Tom's eye and, almost imperceptibly, shook her head.

Woz seemed to carefully weigh his reply before speaking. "It's a tough situation," he said. "No one thought the war would last this long."

"It's a situation that should have never started," Tom said. "This war is immoral—our soldiers have killed women and children!" He felt his heart beating faster.

"Really?" Kara asked, looking up at Woz. Tom sensed that she wanted to come to Woz's defense, but she didn't know the facts. Woz, seeming to grow ever more cautious, was silent.

"Yeah, the My Lai Massacre," Tom said to his sister. "The soldier in command has been charged with murder."

Tom looked at them, shaking his head. He couldn't believe that Woz and his father didn't get it. It was so clear to him: the war was a mistake that needed to end quickly. He and Woz should never have been put at risk of being drafted and sent to a meaningless conflict where they might die.

Woz cleared his throat, appearing to feel the need to protect Kara. "Terrible things happen in war," he said.

"Yes, they do," Tom's father said. Smoke rose from the grill.

Woz looked like he wanted to get out of the conversation. He turned to Tom. "So, what are you going to do about the draft?"

Tom realized that Woz had moved from defense to offense.

"My number is 189. We'll see where things are after fall football season." His father looked up—Tom had not told him he was confirmed to play.

"What if you get drafted then?" Woz said. "Jack told me he might join the National Guard."

Tom could tell that this news also got his father's attention. He'd likely welcome Jack to the Guard, which annoyed Tom greatly. Jack—practically the other son—was the one who hadn't disappointed his father.

"I might go to Canada," Tom said. His thinking about that possibility had increased that afternoon when he had read that the demand by the draft had not declined.

They all turned to him, seemingly shocked by this news.

"But that means you might not be able to come back without being arrested," Woz said. His face had softened.

"Their society seems a lot healthier than ours," Tom said.

His father stood up suddenly, the legs on his chair scraping against the cement patio. He went inside, presumably to get the steaks. They heard a clattering of platters or something else in the kitchen.

Kara turned to Woz and Tom. "Geez, you guys—let's talk about something else."

"I agree," Woz said. He still looked surprised at what Tom had said.

Tom was silent. His father eventually returned from the kitchen to put the steaks on, but he didn't meet Tom's eye. Woz changed the subject to football, claiming the Pittsburgh Steelers would be a good test for the Browns that fall. Tom's father chuckled, setting down the metal tongs he was holding. He reminded Woz of the poor record Pittsburgh had had in the previous season and began a conversation with Woz and Kara about the Browns and Steelers rivalry.

Tom felt like an outsider for the rest of the day. No one asked him to say anything more about his idea of going to Canada. His father's reaction seemed devoid of sympathy, curiosity, or even care.

———

After breakfast the following morning, they all prepared for church. Woz surprised Tom when he came up the basement stairs, wearing a gray suit and tie. Kara squealed, "Look at this handsome man!" Tom hadn't been to church for months, but he decided to go, since Woz was. But he wasn't going to wear a tie.

Tom's mother beamed as the usher took them to their seats. He guessed she liked seeing her daughter being accompanied down the aisle by two giant football players. Tom was glad that Woz was there, attracting attention as Kara's boyfriend and drawing attention away from himself. He participated in the mass, but his mind was elsewhere.

Jack arrived soon after they returned from church. Tom had called him as his mother suggested, and Jack happily accepted the invitation. Their dinner conversation, driven by Tom's father, centered on updates from Jack about his life plans. He had taken the job offer from the engineering consulting company in Cleveland, where he'd worked the past two summers. He had also decided to join the National Guard, instead of waiting to be drafted.

"Any advice?" Jack asked Tom's father. Tom snorted to himself, but Jack appeared to hear it, glancing at Tom for a quick moment.

"Just get through basic training and then we can talk," Tom's father said.

Jack seemed to absorb his father's words like a sponge, as Tom had seen him do since grade school, and his father looked just as approving of Jack as he'd always been. Tom felt that Woz had now joined Jack, both of them acting like sons to his father, who cared more about them than his own son.

Tom missed Grandpa.

After dinner, Tom, Woz, and Jack went down to the basement while Kara gave their mother a hand with the dishes. They sat in the same places they had after Grandpa's funeral. Jack seemed in a good mood from the attention he'd received from Tom's father, and he asked about Tom's and Woz's plans. "It's your turn," he said.

"I think Woz's plans are strongly influenced by my little sister," Tom said, opening a can of beer. "Tell him, Woz."

Woz acted slightly embarrassed, but he described his goal to have Arthur Andersen transfer him to Columbus after a year in Chicago and live there while Kara finished school.

"I've got a romance going, too," Jack said. "Her name is Lynette. I almost brought her home to meet my mother during the break, but we decided to wait until graduation when the parents can meet each other. What about you?" Jack asked Tom.

"What about me?" Tom said.

"Any romance in your life?"

Tom took a swig of his beer. "I still see Becky, but nothing serious like the two of you." He didn't feel like telling them that their relationship seemed to be over.

"How's football?" Jack asked, opening his own beer. "Is your leg going to be strong enough to play in the fall? And will you graduate then?"

Tom regretted inviting Jack. "Yeah, I've started therapy, and it's feeling pretty good," he said. "My plan is to graduate after the fall semester."

"What would you do if you got drafted after you graduate?"

Tom grew quiet, not wanting to repeat the same awkward discussion with Woz and his father from the day before. He could hear footsteps in the kitchen above, and the sound of water running through the pipes in the ceiling of the basement.

"He might go to Canada," Woz said. Tom frowned, not expecting Woz to be so direct.

"What?" Jack said, flipping his head quickly back to Tom. "Are you kidding?"

Tom now regretted coming home for spring break with Woz.

"So then . . . what are your plans after graduation if you don't get drafted?" Jack asked slowly.

Tom felt there was no winning and decided to give up. "I'm not sure yet," he answered flatly. "Kevin and I have talked about doing something to improve society."

"What the hell does that mean?" Jack's voice grew louder. "Does it include being on a continuous high?"

"He's taken acid," Woz said. Tom glared at him, while Kara came down the steps.

"You guys seem so serious," she said, her smile fading.

Jack didn't let Kara's entry stop him. He stared at Tom. "So, it sounds like you plan to live in a commune in Canada and be enlightened by drugs. Is that it?"

"What?" Kara said.

Tom stared back at Jack. "I'm not interested in corporate America." He clenched his jaw as he looked at each of them. Who did they think they were, ridiculing his beliefs?

Woz, catching Kara's eye, said to Tom, "Look, I didn't mean to get you upset."

But Jack wasn't ready to let go. "You've been great at everything you've done, O'Brien. I've always envied you. Now you seem to want to live in some la-la land."

Tom stood up. "I need to get out of here." Woz called after him as he stomped up the stairs, but he didn't turn around. He grabbed his jacket and went outside and walked around the block. He kept walking for a long time. Why couldn't his family and friends support him? They were concerned for him, sure, but being with them was not helpful. He needed their understanding, and all he was getting was judgment and criticism.

When he returned, Jack's car was gone. Tom went straight to his bedroom and packed his bag. The following day, much to his mother's disappointment, he announced he was taking the bus back to Kent. "I need to get a head start on studying," he said. Kara and Woz tried talking to him, but he just shook his head at them and stayed in his bedroom reading until it was time to leave.

22

The new offensive line coach arrived soon after spring break. In his first meeting with the offensive linemen, Coach Moretti, a short bull-necked former lineman who had played for Colorado, outlined his plans for spring practices, including the spring game in late April. Following the meeting, Tom approached Coach Moretti and updated him about the condition of his tendon. The coach checked his clipboard, studied Tom for a moment, and said to keep working hard on his therapy. But as Tom watched Coach Moretti interact with the other players, he got the sense that the coach was focused on the younger linemen. He imagined he was viewed as a senior with his second Achilles tendon injury, someone who probably had little chance of playing in the fall. He was relieved when, in the workout room later, Jonesy told him he was making good progress. He worked harder that day to strengthen his leg.

Since the break in Massillon, Tom had concentrated on football and classwork. When he saw Woz in the gym, he greeted him as a friend, but he turned down Woz's invitation to have a beer, saying he had to study. His friendship with Kevin only seemed to deepen, though. They grew even closer after Nixon accelerated US attacks in Vietnam—aligned in their outrage.

Tom's professors increasingly used the war as a case study of a democracy in trouble. They spurred debates among the students over what should be done.

"Do you think Nixon and Kissinger are violating the moral codes that are the basis of our country?" a professor asked one morning.

"I think they're doing what they need to do to end the war," a girl said from somewhere behind Tom. "It's the destruction by demonstrators that is violating our codes of democratic behavior."

"What?" Tom shouted, turning in his seat. He was in the second row, and all eyes were on him. "Nixon is bombing innocent civilians in a small country that we should let resolve its own differences. We need to demonstrate to educate the American public. The real destruction is Nixon's carpet bombing. It's wrong!"

The girl tried to respond, but she was interrupted by other students who were as passionate as Tom. The professor tried to bring order back to the class.

As the weeks went on, the atmosphere on campus grew more tense, and Tom was continuously disquieted by what he saw happening with the war and the country's destructive culture. Glad to have football to turn to, he threw himself into practices and workouts.

His dedication paid off during the spring game. Coach Moretti, at Jonesy's request, was careful not to play him too many minutes, but he enthusiastically cheered him on whenever he was in. After the game, Coach Moretti said he'd earned his position on the first team that would resume practices in late summer. Would Coach Moretti feel he had a shot at the pros after college?

Tom rode home with three teammates who were dropping him off, bobbing his head to "Whole Lotta Love" by Led Zeppelin. Playing football elevated his mood, as it always had. Finding out that he was back on the first team, in light of all the chaos and uncertainty in the world, offered Tom a sense of hope that day. Football gave his life order, and he couldn't wait for the fall football season to arrive.

———

On April 30, 1970, President Nixon announced the expansion of the Vietnam War into Cambodia. Tom had been doing sit-ups near the couch and thinking about football when Kevin burst through the front door after a student antiwar meeting, swearing at Nixon. Tom immediately flipped on the TV to find a news station. "What a moron!" Kevin yelled during the president's press conference. Afterward, he finally calmed some and sat on the floor near Tom. "We're taking part in a nationwide strike tomorrow," he said.

"I'll be there," Tom said.

Tom and Kevin joined about 500 students on the Commons for the May 1 strike, conducting a walkout from classes as part of the demonstration. Standing in the throng of students and some faculty, Tom looked out over their heads at the student leaders. Three of them took turns standing on top of a bench and, through bullhorns, spoke heatedly about Nixon's betrayal—that instead of ending the war, he was expanding it.

"Peace now! Stop the bombing!" Tom chanted with other students. The more they chanted, the more Tom felt part of the emotions and electricity of the crowd. Students walking to class joined in, raising their fists in the air, and the crowd quickly grew. Some girls sat on the shoulders of their boyfriends. Kevin got his hands on a bullhorn and chanted from on top of a bench. They occupied the Commons for hours.

There was another rally planned for Monday, May 4, and the organizers told everyone it was imperative they attend. Tom, still on a rush of adrenaline, passionately echoed their sentiments to all those around him.

He spent that evening at the library trying to study for a test, but he had a hard time concentrating. Kevin had gone to meet friends at a bar downtown. "Something could happen," he'd said. When Tom came out of the library around midnight, several students were walking briskly toward downtown.

"What's going on?" he asked, catching up to them in a trot.

"There are protests downtown!!" said one of them, tucking his hair behind his ear and picking up the pace. Tom followed.

Approaching downtown, they heard chanting, breaking glass, and loud ringing alarms. A bonfire was burning in the street and there were sirens all around. Tom was sure Kevin would be in the middle of the action, and he debated whether he should go closer and join the crowd that had already gathered. Edging toward the bonfire, Tom began to chant. Police, with their bullhorns, ordered the crowd to disperse, but the crowd refused to budge. A line of officers stepped forward, the orange glow of the fire illuminating their helmets. They shot tear gas canisters, and as a thick white smoke began to rise, the people closest to the bonfire responded by throwing beer bottles and empty canisters at the police. Tom's nose began to burn and his eyes began to tear, so he quickly moved away from the action to avoid the drifting tear gas. Not wanting to be part of the violence, he stepped back into the shadows and started to head for home, continuously looking back at the scene as he left.

———

Tom had just finished unloading his backpack when Kevin arrived home, his shirt drenched with beer.

"We showed them!" he said. "Now the city knows how we feel about Nixon and the war. Where were you, O'Brien?"

"I was there with you guys around midnight—right when the police sprayed tear gas."

"That's great—we need to show our numbers. We could have used you to help throwing those canisters back at the police." He was pacing the family room, speaking loudly.

Tom was silent. He felt more strongly than ever about the need to protest, but he wasn't ready to break windows, throw rocks and canisters, and risk getting arrested. He also worried about how Coach Moretti might feel about his players defying the police. Tom didn't sleep until almost four in the morning, when he finally fell into fitful, violent dreams filled with smoke and flames and angry voices.

Kevin got up early Saturday morning to meet with student leaders, waking Tom as he tramped down the hallway. He returned with the news that the city feared radical revolutionaries had infiltrated Kent to destroy the city. The mayor had spoken at a press conference and stated that outsiders might be planning to blow up businesses and spike the water with LSD.

Tom, who had been eating cereal out of a box in the kitchen, let a cabinet door slam. "Outsiders? Don't they understand these are just upset students?" he asked.

"No, they think the city is going to be attacked by armed revolutionaries," Kevin said. "They're actually thinking of asking the governor to send the National Guard." Tom was alarmed, immediately thinking about his father. He couldn't picture his father in a uniform, leading troops in confrontations with rioting students. The thought of it made him feel ill.

———

On Monday, May 4, Tom and Kevin went with other students to the Commons for the big rally scheduled at noon, chanting from the moment they arrived. The governor had compared demonstrators to communists, brown shirts, and vigilantes, and Tom was more determined than ever to prove him wrong. University officials were already gathered, handing out leaflets saying the event was canceled, but everyone ignored them. Hordes of people—not all of them students—continued to arrive, gathering on and around the

Commons. Near the start of the rally, Kevin told Tom that the leaders had estimated over 2,000 people were in attendance.

A curly-haired student with thick sideburns and horn-rimmed glasses was addressing the crowd when the National Guard, already on campus, showed up with weapons. A military jeep approached, forcing some of the crowd to move back as it drove across the Commons. Through a bullhorn, the driver ordered protesters to disperse or face arrest. Some of the crowd responded by throwing rocks at the jeep. The driver drove away, joining the assembled Guardsmen.

From where he stood, Tom saw the Guardsmen form lines and then move forward toward the protesters. Putting on gas masks, they shot tear gas canisters toward the crowd, but the wind made the gas ineffective, and students lobbed the canisters back. The Guard began to march across the Commons with bayonets fixed on their rifles. Using bullhorns, they demanded that the crowd disperse through a parking lot. As the lines of Guardsmen moved toward Tom and Kevin, Tom grew anxious. The crowd was growing panicked. Emotions were high.

"Let's move to the parking lot like they want! This is dangerous!" Tom yelled to Kevin through the noise.

"No! They need to be stopped!" Kevin shouted.

As the Guard advanced, Tom made his way slowly toward the parking lot, but Kevin and a small group of students confronted the soldiers, throwing rocks and canisters and shouting at them. Tom walked but paused when he saw a young woman with a notebook trying to talk to a Guard soldier a short distance away. His heart leaped: it was Becky! In that same instant, the soldier angrily grabbed Becky's arm, looking like he was going to take her to a nearby van to be arrested. Tom began to push against the crowd, running toward Becky as she resisted the soldier. People were moving in all directions.

Before Tom reached Becky, the soldier let her go and moved to join several soldiers who were kneeling on the Commons and pointing their rifles at the students in the parking lot, about 300 feet away. Shots rang out just as he got close to her. Surely they were blanks? He jerked his head around and saw two students fall. It didn't seem possible that soldiers would fire live ammunition at unarmed students, but through the chaos, students in the parking lot were yelling, "They're shooting us!" Tom's heart leaped into his throat. He quickly put his arm around Becky, dove to the ground, and covered her body with his.

"We need to get out of here!" he yelled into her hair. People were screaming and running past them.

"I can't believe this!" Becky shouted. "What's happening?"

They both turned toward shouts from the students who had been throwing rocks, and saw soldiers advancing on them, shooting more tear gas canisters. One of the canisters landed near Tom and Becky and exploded, immediately sending a thick cloud of gas into the space around them. Within seconds, Tom felt his eyes and skin start to sting unbearably, and he began to cough and sneeze, feeling like he was suffocating. He pulled Becky up, and they began running, falling into step with others who were also trying to escape the gas.

Tom's eyes were streaming tears, and he had to close them, running blind, while he held tightly on to Becky. Someone screamed and fell near them, and Tom felt his right foot come down on an object, his ankle rolling violently to the side. He yelled in pain, falling and almost pulling Becky down with him. He saw that his foot had landed on an empty tear gas canister, and he grabbed his ankle, trying to ease the pain. Becky knelt beside him. They continued coughing until the wind gradually took the gas away.

Ambulances were arriving at the parking lot, their sirens wailing. Eventually, Tom, still splayed on the ground and grabbing his ankle, watched as students dispersed, the Guard began to withdraw, and emergency crews from the ambulances ran to deal with the bodies on the ground and the other wounded students near the parking lot.

"They shot students!" Becky said, her voice thick with emotion. "That could have been us." She appeared dazed but furious.

Tom turned his attention to her. "What were you saying to the soldier?" he asked.

She watched the activity on the parking lot. "I told him I wanted to interview their commander." Tom was amazed. Even in the midst of all the chaos, Becky was seeking the truth and trying to tell the story.

"You need to write this—tell people what you saw today. Go somewhere safe, so you can get this story out. I'll be okay. I'll get help."

"No, I'm not going to leave you here!" Becky said. She sounded jittery.

They looked at each other and their eyes welled with tears. Tom could barely comprehend the insanity he had just witnessed. Becky hugged him, holding him close for a long time.

Tom watched an ambulance pull up near them. He beckoned to two students nearby and asked them to help him get to it. When he put his arms around the students' shoulders, he told Becky again that he would be fine, that she should go write her story. She gave him another hug, tears still streaming down her cheeks. She gave him one more look and left.

Tom briefly remembered how he'd been carried off the football field in a similar way after each one of his Achilles injuries. The scenes around him were so shocking, he could barely think.

He hopped with the students to the ambulance, and the emergency team made room for him. He then watched in horror as they lifted a student on a stretcher into the ambulance who had a gunshot wound in his side. Tom breathed rapidly, shocked at all the blood. He hoped the student was not going to die. He couldn't grasp that he had just witnessed the shooting of innocent human beings standing not far from him. The day had begun with protesting the war and yet, he felt he was looking at the aftermath of a war.

The ER was full of patients, and Tom waited as those with gunshot wounds were wheeled away on stretchers. A nurse pushed him in a wheelchair to an orthopedics room on another floor. The doctor, after taking an X-ray, informed Tom he had a severe ankle sprain that had most likely torn the ligaments that held the bones together. Tom closed his eyes momentarily, then stared silently at his enormous, swollen ankle. The doctor put a cast on his lower leg and foot, and told him he would need to be on crutches for four weeks. The reality then hit him. He had been worried about Becky, concerned about the student in his ambulance who had been shot, and overwhelmed by everything that had happened. But now Tom thought again about football. He felt a mounting sense of despair.

He sat stiffly in the waiting room, periodically trying to reach Kevin on the phone, the images from the day still swirling through his mind. People came and went around him. Kevin finally answered and promptly arrived at the hospital to pick him up. When he saw Tom in a cast, he grew serious and came to sit down next to him while Tom described what had happened. Kevin told him that the Guard had tried to arrest him, but he ran away, afraid he would be shot in the back. He helped Tom up, and they were silent the entire drive home and for most of the rest of the evening, overwhelmed by what they had seen. The phone rang repeatedly, but Tom didn't pick it up.

———

Tom was still shaken when he woke the next day. He planted himself in front of the TV to watch the news, wanting to hear every perspective on what had happened. He was angry. The shootings confirmed everything he'd been thinking about for the past year: the dominant American culture was sick and violent. Twenty-nine guardsmen had fired sixty-seven rounds, killing four students and wounding another nine.

Tom answered a call early that morning, guessing it was his mother. He had thought of phoning her the night before, but everything had been too fresh, and he didn't want to know whether his father had somehow played a role in what the National Guard had done.

"We've been worried sick about you!" his mother said. "Kara has been calling us since last night. Were you not at home?" She sounded like she'd been crying. "I hope you weren't anywhere near those shootings!"

"I was standing not far from where students were killed. I saw them fall," he told her, his eyes still on the TV.

"Oh, Tom! Are you alright? If it happens again, please stay in your house—please stay safe!"

Tom hesitated before asking her the inevitable question. "Was Dad here? Was he involved with the Guard?"

"No," she said. "His company wasn't mobilized. But he knows people in Company C who were."

Tom lay back on the couch, relieved. He couldn't bear to think of his father with the troops on the Commons. "The shootings by the Guard were unbelievable," he said.

"We heard that a sniper fired the first shot at the Guard, probably some outside radical," she said.

"No, that's a lie." He immediately sat up. "There were no outsiders, and no one shot at the Guard."

"But nothing probably would've happened if students hadn't rioted," she said. He was shocked at what he was hearing.

"The Guard murdered four students, Mom! And now Nixon is bombing Cambodia!"

"I know terrible things are happening. But Tom, we need to be loyal to our country. Rioting isn't going to help."

Tom pressed his lips together, fuming. He was sure that his mother was parroting his father. He imagined his father was standing near her, listening to their phone call.

"I need to go," he said, disgusted. "I'm not sure about classes—they may close the university. I'll come home sometime, probably after I get the cast off my ankle."

"What?" she gasped. Without emotion, Tom explained that he had tripped and sprained his ankle, then he ended the call quickly without adding the details.

Tom continued to closely follow the news that day and over the next few days. He was comforted somewhat by the national outrage over the shootings. In the aftermath, demonstrations occurred at many universities, and he learned that more than thirty ROTC university buildings had been burned or bombed. But when he read in a newspaper that a Gallup Poll showed that 58 percent of Americans blamed the students for the shootings, he threw the newspaper across the room. Something had to change.

———

A couple of days after the doctor had put a cast on Tom's leg, Kevin drove him to the athletic training facility. Jonesy looked sad, having already read Tom's medical record describing the sprain.

"Do we need to do the same therapy routine as before?" Tom asked.

"Yeah." Jonesy paused.

Tom feared what he would hear next. He leaned against a locker. "What about football next fall?" he asked.

Jonesy looked at him, shook his head, then looked at the floor. "You've had a ruptured tendon, a strained tendon, and now torn ligaments, all on the same foot. Your foot is a mess, Tom. If you try to play football, it might result in an injury that will never heal. If you don't get therapy right now, you may limp for the rest of your life."

Tom's stomach dropped as he realized that his days of playing football were over. Jonesy put his hand on Tom's shoulder, and then moved on to the next injured player.

That night, Tom stared into the darkness of his room. He was in a place he'd been before, but it had never felt as bleak as it did now. He looked back on all the football games he had played, his elation after applying the skills he'd worked so hard to develop, using his strength to help his team move the ball down the field.

Without football, Tom again had no direction—and this time, it was permanent. He needed to find a new purpose. He spent the next few days smoking pot and listening to music, taking his mind off the reality—the enormity—of his loss.

———

In the weeks after the shootings, Tom and Kevin smoked pot on their porch, drove around listening to music, and talked a lot about what was wrong with society. But Kevin soon grew tired of talking. Late one night, he said he wanted to act.

"We need to escape," Kevin said.

"Where to? And what would we do?" Tom glanced at his crutches.

"Lucas is thinking of going to Hawaii. He has a friend on Kauai," Kevin said. "There's a commune named Taylor Camp there with treehouses. I'd love to see how they're living."

Kevin went on to explain how the camp had begun with thirteen hippies settling on public land. The population exploded when Elizabeth Taylor's brother offered beachfront property he owned as a refuge to people ousted from the public land by the state.

Tom was intrigued. A commune wouldn't be corrupted by all the ills of society. If he stayed in Kent, he'd continue to be part of a society that didn't work—he would need to make some tough choices about his future and how he'd participate in that society. Tom couldn't see himself contributing to it, and he didn't want to be part of the problem. If he could leave this behind and help build something better, why wouldn't he? But he thought of Becky, Woz, and Jack, and their views of the future.

Kevin was suggesting a monumental change—moving thousands of miles away, leaving behind his family and familiar Midwestern way of life. He needed more time to think about it. "I'd be interested," Tom said, "but that's a big move."

Two days later, Kevin appeared in the doorway of Tom's room and broached the topic again. "What are you going to do?" he asked. "The university is probably going to be closed for a while, so you may not be able to take your summer classes anyway."

Tom looked up from his magazine. "What did you decide?"

"I'm going to graduate in June, and my father's giving me some cash for a graduation gift." He grinned. "I want to go to Hawaii."

Tom thought of Thoreau, living in the wilderness, at peace with nature. Maybe Hawaii *would* offer an alternative way of living, a way to help create a culture opposed to the destruction he'd seen on campus and on the news. He was warming up to the idea of taking a risk, given the uncertainty of his other alternatives.

He probably had enough money saved from his summer carpentry job to get there, and he was sure he could find a job that would pay him enough to live on. Financial worries were minor, compared to the significance of leaving.

Kevin put up a poster in the living room with an enlarged picture of a naked woman seen from the back sitting in a lotus position on a beach, her long blond hair falling to her waist as she faced the sun rising over breaking ocean waves. The phrase "Come to Hawaii" was scrawled along the top.

———

Kevin was right; Kent State decided to close for at least six weeks. Students received credit for the remainder of their spring classes and were not required to take finals. Tom chose to stay in their house in Kent for the four weeks he needed to wear a cast. He lived alone while Kevin visited his father in Chicago. He tried reading books from his courses on American society and watched the news daily. But often, he just stared out the window, thinking about his lost football career and his disappointment in his country. He was sinking deeper and deeper. Something had to change.

When Kevin returned from Chicago, he dropped his bags onto the floor of the living room and asked, "Are you going to go to Hawaii with me or not?"

Tom looked up at the poster. "I think I will," he said.

Kevin's face broke into a broad smile. "It's your best alternative, O'Brien.

Losing football is a bummer, but you can only mope around for so long. It's time to act."

Tom didn't know if Hawaii was really the answer, but he knew he didn't want to go to summer school, regardless of when the university might reopen. He didn't want to look for a job, whether it was in a corporation, government agency, or the university—he despised those institutions. And he didn't want to return to the mind-numbing drudgery of manual labor like his carpentry job. He felt more alone than he ever had, completely alienated from his family and his friends Jack and Woz. All the while, the threat of the draft was a sword hanging over his head. He listened to "Helpless" by Neil Young repeatedly, the melody and lyrics a perfect expression of how he felt. He'd been low before—his Achilles rupture, his arrest, and the losses of Cindi and Becky—but none of these compared to his current misery.

23

Once he had his walking cast, Tom packed his things, and Kevin drove him to the Kent bus station, where he bought a ticket to Massillon. Kevin planned to pick him up in Massillon when his ankle felt better—hopefully in a week—and then they would drive to Chicago to catch their flight to Hawaii. While Tom was in Massillon, Kevin would pack his things and turn their house over to the new renters. With everything in motion, Tom was excited, except for one thing. He dreaded telling his parents about his Hawaii plans.

Kara, having arrived home from college the day before, surprised Tom by picking him up at the bus station. She began to tear up when she saw Tom's walking cast and asked if it was definite that he would not be able to play football again. He got a lump in his throat and, unable to speak, nodded. She seemed to understand and changed the subject.

Tom's mother embraced him at the front door, as his father stood behind her. He'd known it would be awkward to be around his father for the first time since the Guard shootings. His father greeted him warily.

Both his parents stared at Tom's walking cast. His father asked, "Football?" and Tom shook his head. His father lowered his head and closed his eyes. Tom's mother bit her lip and reached for Tom's arm.

It was fortunate that Kara was there. She lightened the atmosphere by telling everyone that Woz—she called him Ron—had invited her to his graduation ceremony in June, where she would meet his parents. He planned to start his job as an Arthur Andersen trainee in Chicago on July 1. She asked her mom to cook an early dinner, since she wanted to shop for a gift for him that evening.

"That's wonderful news about Ron's job," Tom's mother said as they sat down to eat. "Have you decided on your plans, Tom?"

Here it comes, he thought. He put down his fork and took the plunge. "Actually, yes. Kevin and I are going to Hawaii."

"Wow," Kara said slowly, her eyes darting back and forth between their parents. "I'd love to go there." She seemed concerned but gave Tom a supportive smile.

His father stopped chewing, and Tom could see his familiar disapproving look.

"But what about your studies?" his mother asked. "When will you graduate?"

Tom listened to the ticking of the clock in the family room. He cleared his throat and said, "The university is closed because of the shootings. I'll take courses later." His father's eyes narrowed at the word "shootings."

"So, you'll go back to school in the fall?" his mother asked.

"I don't know yet. I'll figure it out."

His father cast his eyes around the room, looking like he was preparing to say something.

"You have no plan?" he finally managed to say. His tone was accusing.

"I said I'll figure it out."

"You're this close to graduation, and you're off to Hawaii?" His father gestured into the air, then let his arm drop to the table. The water in Tom's glass shook. Tom hesitated, but he felt his face begin to flame, and he got ready to defend himself.

"The university wouldn't be closed if the Guard hadn't killed the students," he said.

His father frowned deeply. "If the students hadn't rioted, they wouldn't have been shot."

Tom's heart beat faster. "Are you kidding me? That's just bullshit! There was no reason for the Guard to fire their rifles." He saw a look of alarm come over his mother's face.

"Let's not talk about it. It was unfortunate for everyone," she said.

"Mom, it was much more unfortunate for the students who got killed than for anyone else. They were murdered right in front of me." His mother's lip quivered.

"We're just so glad you're alright," she said.

But he *wasn't* alright. He couldn't answer his mother. Kara, keeping her eyes on her plate, put her hand on her forehead. Tom's father was silent, and neither he nor Tom looked at each other. After several long seconds, his mother stood to clear the dishes.

Tom stood also and stepped outside, wishing he had a joint. He sat down on the front steps. He remembered carrying Grandpa, in his wheelchair, up these very steps with his father. It felt like forever ago. His heart ached.

Kara soon appeared next to him with their father's car keys, ready to go into town to get a graduation gift for Woz.

"I think you should come with me," she said, putting her arm around his shoulders. "You know, get out of the house for a bit."

Later that evening, Tom and Kara returned home with an expensive tie for Woz to wear to his new job. Tom found his father watching the Indians game, with a bottle of Grandpa's favorite whiskey and three glasses on the coffee table in front of him.

"Come on in," he said, appearing relaxed from the whiskey he'd had. "Get yourself a glass and help me cheer for this miserable baseball team."

Tom and Kara looked at each other. Their father only drank on occasion, and it was rare to see him like this. They sat on the couch, and Tom poured himself a glass of whiskey. Tom offered Kara a glass but she declined, looking at their father.

"Your grandpa invested a lotta hours rooting for this team," their father said. "He wasn't rewarded for it much, other than some successful seasons in the 1950s."

Tom couldn't fathom the change that had come over his father. It had gotten ugly at dinner, and this had to be due to more than just a little whiskey.

"The Indians frustrated him, that's for sure," Tom said, taking a sip from his glass.

"I miss your grandpa's optimism," his father said. His eyes misted over for a second.

Kara hugged a couch pillow. "I wish he could have seen more of my field hockey games," she said.

"Yeah, he loved watching you kids play." Their father's glass was empty, and he sat quietly in Grandpa's chair, with his head back and his eyes on the game.

They watched the next batter come up to the plate. Tom felt the whiskey relax him. He looked at his father and felt his anger dissipating.

His father took a long look at Tom. He closed his eyes for several seconds, and then opened them. "You and I disagree about Vietnam, Nixon, and the future of our country, and that's not going to change."

Tom immediately tensed up, but he held his tongue.

"But you're right about the Guard at Kent State," his father said. "It was a gigantic screw-up."

Tom did a double take, then slowly sat back and took a sip of whiskey, not knowing how to respond. He watched his father, who surprised him by wiping tears from his eyes.

"I've given so many years to the Guard," his father said, his eyes still on the TV. "I love its purpose, and I love its mission. But what it did to those kids was wrong." He shook his head, but before Tom could reply, his father stood up and left the room, walking toward the stairs. "I'm tired," he said over his shoulder. "Let me know how the game ends."

Tom and Kara stared at each other on the couch.

"I've never seen him like that," she said. She seemed choked up.

She went upstairs shortly afterward, but Tom remained on the couch, watching the game, not knowing what to make of it all. He was relieved—and strangely vindicated—by what his father had said. If only his father could open up more. Tom had ached for that for as long as he could remember. He would have liked to have heard his father reminisce for longer about Grandpa.

The game ended. The Indians lost.

———

Tom spent the week in Massillon packing, catching up on magazines, reading a Kauai guidebook, and resting his ankle. He also, as best he could, helped Kara practice, driving her each morning to the high school field, where he timed her sprint repetitions and helped her practice her stickhandling by throwing the hockey ball on the ground to her right or left.

Tom's father didn't bring up the conversation they'd had about the Guard again, and Tom took that as a sign that he shouldn't ask. Instead, his father let him know more than once that he wished Tom had a plan for the future instead of traveling to Hawaii. Tom tried to refrain from fighting with him, though he came close several times.

Kevin picked up Tom as planned. On the driveway, Tom hugged his mother and Kara goodbye, who both cried, and his father stiffly shook his hand. Tom didn't know when he might see his family again, and this added to a gnawing sense of uncertainty. He watched them in the sideview mirror as he and Kevin drove away.

Unsure if he had made the right decision, Tom was silent for the first hour of the drive to Chicago. But Kevin chattered excitedly and didn't seem to notice.

At the airport, Tom wrestled with his doubts. He already missed the Midwest and his family and friends. What were he and Kevin going to find in Hawaii? Was it possible to create a culture based on peace and love? He knew what they were rejecting, but what were they embracing?

PART III:

1970-1972

24

On the Fourth of July, Tom and Kevin flew to Los Angeles, changed planes, and then flew over endless miles of ocean to Honolulu. Kevin said that it was their Independence Day; they were leaving behind a sick society for a culture of peace and love. They transferred to a smaller plane for the short flight from Honolulu to Lihue, and Tom watched through his airplane window as they approached the island of Kauai. He marveled at the contrast between the dark green foliage covering the island and the surrounding blue ocean. Drawing closer, he could follow waves moving toward the shore on a long beach. Tom knew that Lihue had around 3,000 people. Unlike metropolitan airports, landing in Lihue felt like descending in a clearing, with an airstrip in a small town surrounded by a jungle and the ocean.

As they walked toward the gate, they were caressed by a warm breeze unlike any he'd felt before. The colors were so vivid, the sky overhead so blue. Tom couldn't believe he was there.

Lucas had arrived in Lihue three weeks earlier and met up with his friend Scotty, who said they could all crash in his apartment until they figured out what they wanted to do. Tom and Kevin waited at the curb until an old Toyota pulled up, and Lucas got out and greeted them. Lucas still wore a Fu Manchu mustache, but now it was connected to bushy muttonchop sideburns. Memories of the acid trip with Lucas returned to Tom; he greeted Lucas cautiously as he set his bag in the trunk.

The Toyota was Scotty's—Lucas had borrowed it to drive them the short distance to the apartment. They stopped in front of an old building that was two stories high and about three times as long. Tom noted the wooden plank siding covering the building, at one time painted gray, but now faded and discolored. The roof had only enough slope to let the rain run off. It was a dingy, aging structure; the only amenities were some benches and picnic tables under a palm tree on one side of the building. "Home, sweet home," Lucas said. Tom wondered what kind of situation he was getting himself into.

Lucas parked in a lot filled with used cars like Scotty's, some with surfboards tied to their roofs. Tom looked around the neighborhood. There was another similar apartment building nearby, at least two bars, a car repair garage, and a tire shop. The people he saw walking on the street—there were no sidewalks— were primarily Islander and Asian, with few whites. Lucas led them into the building and through a hallway of stained carpeting and walls needing paint.

Lucas knocked on a first-floor apartment door and entered before being invited in. He introduced them to Scotty, who was lying on the couch drinking a beer. He stood, wearing shorts and a buttoned shirt with its sleeves cut off. His hair was a dirty blond color, slicked back behind his ears, and he had a three- or four-day beard growth.

"It's the football players!" Scotty said, but he didn't smile. "We need *haoles* like you to protect us." Tom guessed him to be two or three years older than he was.

"What's a *haole*?" Tom asked.

Scotty studied him a moment. "White people from the mainland," he said. "The locals don't like us. They think we're stealing their land and their jobs." Tom remembered reading about this in one of his guidebooks—white Christian missionaries as far back as the 1800s who colonized Hawaii at the expense of the native populations.

"Scotty's right," Lucas said, sitting with his arms crossed on a barstool. "You don't want to be alone at night around here, or you'll get beaten up. They call our building the 'Haole Hotel' and think we're all rich white kids."

"So, what's the arrangement, Lucas?" Scotty asked. "Are you all crashing here tonight?" Scotty had a long neck, prominent Adam's apple, and deep-set eyes. He stared at Tom and Kevin as he talked. His arms and legs were sinewy, not muscular. Tom had rarely been around someone so intense.

"Yeah, if that's okay." Lucas rested his elbow on the countertop next to several unwashed cups. One of the cups had a cigarette butt in it.

"It's all right as long as I get the bedroom, and you each give me five dollars a night. You can use the couch or yoga pads for the floor."

Tom and Kevin looked at each other, shrugged, and nodded. There wasn't much else they could do.

"I don't have to go to work for another couple of hours, so how about a joint?" Scotty said. Tom watched his Adam's apple go up and down as he spoke.

"I've got one already rolled," Lucas said, feeling around in his pockets.

Lucas lit a joint and passed it around, and Scotty put on an Allman Brothers album. Tom sat on the floor next to a stain that was shaped like one of the Hawaiian Islands. He looked at it as he settled into a mellow state, nodding his head to the music.

Scotty's intensity lessened, and he explained how he'd advanced from busboy to waiter to bartender. Lucas had started work a couple of weeks earlier as a dishwasher. They said jobs were available at the resorts near Kalapaki Beach.

"What do you guys know about Taylor Camp, the commune where they live in treehouses?" Kevin asked, taking another toke.

"The hippie place on the North Shore?" Scotty asked. "They're pretty far out. You could find out more from Jeanine upstairs—she used to live there."

"Really? Can you introduce us to Jeanine?" Kevin said. "Maybe we could borrow your car to get there?"

"Sure. You can use my car when I don't need it, but you have to fill it up with gas and give me five dollars each time," Scotty said, putting his dirty feet up on the coffee table.

Tom nodded at Kevin. "How about we go look around?" he said. "Check out the area or walk to the beach."

"Good idea," Scotty said. "I came here for the surfing and the girls—that's where you'll find them."

"Some food would be good after that pot," Kevin said, standing up.

Tom, Kevin, and Lucas walked to Tiki's, a nearby bar and restaurant. Lucas pointed at the bar across the street and warned them not to go there—it was only for locals, and risky for haoles to even walk by it. Kevin asked if the locals were Native Hawaiians. Lucas said they were but also included immigrants from other islands like Samoa and from Asia. The Samoans interested Tom because he knew of Samoan football linemen recognized for their size and strength.

While they waited for their burgers and fries, Lucas said hi to another guy from their building named Barry and invited him to bring his food over and join them. Barry was almost as tall and broad-shouldered as Tom, but much slenderer, carrying himself comfortably. He smiled warmly, his white teeth contrasting with his tan face and neck. His hair was over his ears but trimmed and combed back.

"This is a table of athletes," Lucas said, running his fingers through his sideburns. "Barry played basketball at UC Santa Barbara, right?" Barry nodded. "Kevin and Tom played football at Kent State."

"Kent State?" Barry asked, his face growing serious. "Were you guys anywhere near the shootings?"

Being reminded of the shootings sobered Tom. It was jarring to suddenly have the images of the rally and National Guard go through his mind with the backdrop of the bar in Lihue. "We were there and saw kids being shot," Tom said. "I was tear-gassed and sprained my ankle, and Kevin almost got arrested throwing canisters back at the Guard."

"That's horrible," Barry said, furrowing his brow. "A friend and I came here about a year ago to get away from the insanity. I have a high lottery number—you too?" Kevin nodded, but gestured with his head toward Tom. Tom said his number might still be selected for the draft, and Barry shook his head grimly.

The food arrived at the table.

"Do you think you're going to go back to the mainland at any point?" Kevin asked Barry.

Barry took a bite from his burger and looked thoughtful. "Maybe . . . next year for graduate school. This is a beautiful place, but I'm not going to be a waiter for the rest of my life."

Tom thought that even here on the island, people had to face reality. "What will you study?" Tom asked.

"Maybe an MBA." When he said that, Kevin looked down at the floor and then over at the people at the bar. Tom knew how strongly Kevin felt about the destructive nature of business and capitalism, but Barry seemed to him like a reasonable guy. Barry finished eating, put some money on the table, and got up to go meet a friend.

"My roommate is headed back to California next month, so if you or anyone you know want to share my apartment, I'll have an opening then," Barry said. He grinned and strode out, giving some of the people at other tables a wave as he left.

Tom dug into his fries, looking around the bar and at Kevin and Lucas. He could've been back in Kent, getting ready for summer classes in construction management and watching the news of everything gone wrong, but instead, he was in Hawaii. However small, he had a place to live and a group of people his age that he wanted to get to know better. He looked forward to getting settled and exploring the island.

——

The next day, Lucas, smoking a joint in the back bedroom, gave them directions to the beach; it was about a mile away. There was a store they could stop at on the way back to get groceries and any needed items.

Tom and Kevin walked down the street on Tiki's side, peering curiously at the bar for locals across the street. It was unnamed, with a sign that only said "Bar." The street had a blacktop surface with scattered potholes and no curbs. Tom noticed a couple of stares and heard muttering as he and Kevin went by. Two guys kept their eyes locked on Tom.

"This neighborhood is a bit shaky—we don't seem to be wanted," Kevin said. He pulled his hair back into a loose ponytail and kept walking.

"It makes sense. We're just more white people who take their jobs." Tom kept his head down to avoid provoking the two guys.

"I want a peaceful community," Kevin said. "I can't wait to visit Taylor Camp." They got to the end of the street and turned toward the beach. As they passed some palm trees and several chickens, Tom said, "We need to figure out some real living quarters soon. That apartment is going to become a pigsty with four guys in it."

"If we can live in Taylor Camp, that's what I want. How about you?" Two of the chickens skittered out of the way.

"I'll have to see what it's like first. I'll need a job to make it here, and from what I can tell, the jobs only seem to be near the resorts."

"But we might not need jobs if we can live off the land—farming and fishing."

They found the store on the way to the beach and stopped to buy beach towels. Tom loved the smell of the ocean air. He stepped onto the sand, gazing at the blue of the water before them. They spread their towels out and sat down, looking up and down the beach.

There were several young women lying on the beach, their lean, tan bodies covered by tiny bikinis. Young men, both white and locals, sat a short distance away from the women, competing for their attention. Four girls arrived shortly after Kevin and Tom sat down, and before long, Kevin was in a conversation with them. They were from California and planning to stay the summer before returning to college.

When, after moving closer to the girls, Tom stood up to take off his T-shirt, one of the girls said, "Who are you? Hercules?" The girls laughed but kept looking at Tom's body. One of them asked him if he'd help her with putting suntan oil on her back.

Kevin went to swim with a couple of the girls, and Tom entered the water after him. Like the breeze, it was warm but refreshing. He, Kevin, and the girls moved beyond the breakers to ride up and down on the incoming swells. Tom loved it, looking back at the wide beach and the tree-covered hills in the distance. He felt a million miles away from Kent, and that was okay with him.

When they finished swimming and sat in the sun, one of the girls suggested they come to the house they were renting for dinner. They all walked to the store to pick up hamburger meat and salads. Kevin, laughing, also bought six-packs of beer.

They walked on the other side of the street from the locals' bar, but four guys came out of the bar. "Look at the fucking haoles with our women," one of the locals said loudly.

The girls, still in their bikinis, immediately stopped talking. One of them stepped behind Tom, and another one folded her arms over her chest. Tom stared at the guys, his adrenaline rushing and face reddening.

"Yeah, I mean you, big guy," the local said, squaring his shoulders.

One of the other girls took Tom's arm. "Keep walking," she said. "These guys are always after us and will fight anyone who gets in their way. They beat the shit out of a boy from California last week—he had a broken cheekbone and had to be hospitalized."

Tom, Kevin, and the girls kept walking while the locals laughed at them. Tom only managed to relax after they turned the corner and arrived at the girls' house several blocks away. On the back patio, Kevin offered everyone a beer, while Tom fired up the grill and helped the girls make hamburger patties, and soon everyone was smiling and laughing. One of the girls came out of her bedroom and opened her hand to show three joints. Kevin smiled broadly. "Now, it's a party!" he said. Everyone was soon swaying to the music.

After dinner, Tom sat on the couch, and two of the girls sat down by him. One of the girls had her hand on his shoulder, and the other had her leg pressed against his. In his mellow haze, Tom could see the two girls were competing for him. They continued to drink and smoke until sometime later when one girl took his hand and stood up. She led Tom to her bedroom, past another bedroom where Kevin and a girl were undressing each other. Tom and the girl clumsily took off each other's clothes. The girl ran her hands over Tom's chest and arms, then pulled him down on her bed.

He awoke the following morning lying sideways on the bed, the girl asleep beside him, still naked. He remembered her leading him through various sexual positions he'd never experienced before. He put on his swim trunks and walked to the kitchen, where Kevin sat at the counter with the other two girls. After having coffee and joking a little about the night, Tom and Kevin left, thanking them for the party and asking them to thank the girls still sleeping.

On their walk home, Kevin kept saying, "That was incredible." Tom felt he'd participated in a sensory overload of beer, pot, food, and sex. He kept smiling at the pleasures he'd experienced, but a part of him wondered how long he could live that kind of life.

When they entered the apartment, Lucas looked up, surprised. Kevin and Tom told him about their night. He laughed and said it was "Hawaii living up to its reputation."

Scotty, when he got up a short time later, said, "It's not hard. Girls come to Hawaii to escape their problems and have fun. Just like you guys did."

"We didn't come just to have fun," Kevin said. "We came to see Taylor Camp."

"Right," Scotty said.

"What about Jeanine? Is she like the other girls?"

"No way. Jeanine's a mystery, hard to get close to. You'll see her this afternoon."

"Did she come to Hawaii to live at Taylor Camp?" Tom asked.

"I don't know. I heard she came with a guy, and it didn't work out. Lucas may know more than me—she buys pot from him every now and then."

Tom went to the kitchen to make a sandwich, first washing a plate from the stacks of dirty dishes. He was eager to see what Taylor Camp was like, but he was also curious about why it hadn't worked out for Jeanine. "What does Jeanine do since she left Taylor Camp?" Tom asked, locating the dish soap next to the toaster.

"Works in a resort shop. She loves swimming in the ocean—with the most beautiful legs on the beach, in my opinion," Scotty said, pausing, as if to picture her. Tom tried to imagine a mysterious Jeanine with beautiful legs. He was intrigued to meet her.

———

Later that afternoon, Scotty and Lucas brought Kevin and Tom to a picnic table under the palm tree outside, where Scotty had arranged to meet Jeanine. Scotty greeted her when she arrived, introduced her to Tom and Kevin, and motioned for her to take a seat. Tom noticed that Scotty and Lucas had combed their hair and both smiled when they saw her. He could see why. She was tall—he guessed five foot ten—and she wore her hair shorter than most girls, a mixture of brown and blond strands; her bronze tan was accentuated by a pale-yellow halter top and cutoff jean shorts. She was stunning.

After Scotty's remark about her legs, Tom avoided looking at them, but he sensed her well-proportioned frame. She confidently gazed at them. Her dark brown eyes enhanced her beauty, but her expression was matter-of-fact, betraying no emotion. She looked at Tom steadily, and he turned away first.

Scotty began the conversation, saying that Kevin and Tom wanted to hear about Taylor Camp. Jeanine asked what they wanted to learn, looking only at Scotty. Kevin jumped in with several questions about how long she'd lived there, and why. Her answers were succinct, directed at the questioner with no emotion. Jeanine had come to Taylor Camp the previous summer with her boyfriend because they wanted an alternative to the destructive American culture. She described Taylor Camp as a community with positive goals: peace, solidarity, and an absence of rules. Tom watched her from the side as she faced Kevin—her sharp cheekbones; her long, dark eyelashes; her melodic voice. He asked her why she'd left, and she turned and looked at him fully and silently, until he started to feel uncomfortable. "My boyfriend and I split up, and I didn't like the politics," she finally said. Tom nodded, wanting to know more. Kevin asked how they could visit the camp, and she hesitated.

"I haven't been there since I left in February, and I'd like to see a couple of friends. I'll go with you and introduce you to Ramona, one of the camp's leaders."

"Great," Kevin said. He gave Scotty five dollars to use his car, and they all settled on Tom, Kevin, and Jeanine meeting in two days to drive to Taylor Camp. Jeanine stood up to leave and Lucas quickly followed, saying he would walk with her. He closed the door behind them.

"You were right about her legs," Kevin said. "She's gorgeous."

"A lot of guys have tried to take her out, including me, but she stays to herself," Scotty said.

Tom didn't say anything. He kept thinking about her dark brown eyes and penetrating gaze.

25

The Hawaiian morning was beautiful—sunny but not too hot, with a comfortable trade wind. Jeanine walked toward Tom and Kevin, and they got up from the picnic table bench. Tom said he'd drive, so he and Jeanine got into the front seats of Scotty's car while Kevin climbed in the back. She directed Tom out of Lihue to the Kuhio Highway, a two-lane road.

Kevin kept up an almost nonstop chatter as they headed north, asking Jeanine about the island. Tom sensed her presence next to him, and he thought she felt his, but they didn't look at each other as he concentrated on driving and she answered Kevin's questions. He was conscious of her tanned legs and had to work at not looking at them.

"Have you seen the whole island?" Kevin asked Jeanine, sticking his arm out the window.

"I have. There's a lot to see. We're coming up on the Wailua River, where I've kayaked. There is a beautiful waterfall not far from the ocean." Jeanine's hair was blowing with the breeze. She reached up to brush it off her cheek.

"What's your favorite spot?"

"Hanalei Bay. I can show it to you on our way."

"What do you like about it?" Tom asked.

"You'll see," she said. Tom sensed she was more outgoing with Kevin and more reserved with him.

They could often see the ocean on the right while they drove north, with waves breaking either on sand beaches or rocks. They crossed the Wailua River and then drove slowly through the town of Kapa'a, with its shops and tourist hotels facing the sea. As the settlements grew sparser, they traveled past green-covered mountains on their left and saw higher mountains ahead, their peaks sometimes obscured by fast-moving clouds. Jeanine said they were nearing the North Shore, where short bouts of rain were common.

After descending from the hills, they drove over a one-lane bridge and then into the town of Hanalei, where the Kuhio Highway ended and became Hanalei's main street. Tom asked Jeanine if she knew the town's population, and she guessed two to three hundred people. She directed them through the residential areas toward Hanalei Bay.

They parked and walked through large pine trees to the sand beach. Tom surveyed the crescent-shaped bay that looked two or three miles long, with a vast beach that stretched almost the entire length of the bay. Scattered clusters of people were on the beach and in the water. When he looked up at the mountains on the western end, Jeanine told them they were the beginning of the Na Pali Coast, where cliffs rose to four thousand feet. She turned to the mountains that rose over Hanalei on its south side and pointed to small silver strips lining the mountains, explaining they were waterfalls caused by heavy rains.

"I think this is the most beautiful place in the world," Jeanine said.

"It's amazing," Tom said. Their eyes met, and Tom felt his face and neck grow warm.

"Look at the surfers," Kevin said, drawing Tom's and Jeanine's eyes away from each other.

"Some world-class surfers have grown up here and gone on to win competitions in Oahu," Jeanine said.

They returned to their car and drove slowly along the northern coast, often encountering one-lane bridges, until Jeanine pointed to an area where they should park. Tom caught Kevin's eye in the rearview mirror, and they both sat forward, craning their necks to look ahead. They spied a series of treehouses not far from the beach. "They really do live in treehouses," Kevin said, laughing. A naked woman their age was bent over in a nearby garden, gathering vegetables. Tom resisted saying anything in front of Jeanine, but from over his shoulder, he saw Kevin looking at the woman with wide eyes. He parked the car and two muscular men wearing only shorts and with long beards down to their chests walked toward them, looking concerned. Jeanine said they were Vietnam vets who helped keep order in the camp.

"Look who's here," one of the men said, slowing his gait when he saw Jeanine get out of the car. "We thought you might be gawkers."

"Hi, William," she said, resting her hand on top of the car. "I have some friends I'd like Ramona to meet. They're interested in learning about the camp." William was almost as tall as Tom, his back and chest covered by his shaggy hair and beard, slender with a washboard stomach. Tom guessed he was three or four years older.

"I'll let her know." William left, and Tom looked at their surroundings. The trees and bushes were an intense green, contrasting with the light blue sky. Sunshine filtered through the leaves, casting shadows on the beach, as a gentle warm breeze fanned them.

The structure of the treehouses was so different from the apartments Tom had helped construct with Dan and his crew back in Massillon. They were made from an assortment of materials, including various woods, planks, and bamboo poles, thin metal siding, and mesh screens. Some had sloping rooflines with clear plastic tarps over them, others had porches with hanging blankets, and most had wooden ladders or steps leading straight down to the sand.

A large woman walked toward them, carrying a child on her hip. She wore shorts and a blouse unbuttoned almost to her waist. Tom imagined she had been nursing the child, a sight he had never seen. Jeanine strode over to her and they hugged, though it seemed perfunctory. She then turned and introduced Tom and Kevin. Ramona had a confident presence, and she appeared to take in Tom's size before she invited them to sit at a table near the steps of one of the treehouses.

Other people from the camp appeared and greeted Jeanine, most of them—both men and women—wearing shorts with no tops. Tom tried to only look at everyone from the neck up. He didn't want to seem like a gawker.

"Aloha. This is my little Lela," Ramona said, turning the child to face them. Lela looked at them with large eyes, then stretched her arms toward Jeanine. "She was born a couple of months after you left," she said to Jeanine.

"She's beautiful," Jeanine said. She gave her full attention to the baby, not looking at Ramona.

"It's cool that you're raising children here," Kevin said.

"We're all one big family. Lela has many parents and many brothers and sisters." Ramona's unbuttoned blouse hung open.

"I'm going to go catch up with friends," Jeanine said to the group. Tom watched her leave, and another woman immediately ran toward her. They hugged for several seconds.

Kevin moved closer to Ramona, looking eager to find out more about the camp. "You seem to be creating an alternative life here," he said.

She smiled at Kevin, then directed her gaze to the camp. "We reject the violence of America," she said. "Everyone here wants to live a life of peace and love and to be at one with nature. We want to live freely with few rules to follow, trusting in each other."

"That's far out," Kevin said, nodding. A tanned, topless girl went past them holding a guitar, her long blond hair almost to her waist. Ramona stood up and started walking toward a treehouse, and the group followed.

"We reject the violence also," Kevin said. "We were at the Kent State riots."

Ramona's eyes narrowed. "Those shootings were the ultimate expression of America's violence," she said. "Were you in danger?"

"We were near students who were killed," Tom said quietly, suddenly recalling the chaotic scene in the ambulance when, in the gurney next to him, the emergency team fought to stabilize the student with the gunshot wound in his side.

Ramona studied Tom for a moment with what he felt was a combination of pity and superiority. Her gaze was sympathetic but also condescending. Given his size, was she trying to demonstrate that she was in charge? Jeanine had said she didn't like the politics at Taylor Camp.

"So, you're able to live off the land, with fishing and gardens?" Kevin asked.

Lela squirmed toward Ramona, and Ramona opened her blouse wider to let Lela find her breast.

"As much as we can. Some people work part-time in Hanalei, but we use any outside income for the good of everyone."

"This seems to be a spiritual place," Kevin said.

Ramona walked farther into the treehouse community. "Here is our church," she said. "We call it 'The Church of the Brotherhood of the Paradise Children.' It's not part of any religion, but we use it to meditate and talk about spiritual topics."

Kevin seemed enthralled. "Are drugs part of your spiritual life?" he asked.

Ramona smiled. "You are full of questions! Yes, we believe drugs can open our consciousness. The weed we have here is far out. We also trip with psilocybin. I think some people are going on a shroom trip today."

Kevin leaned toward Ramona. "Could I join them?" he asked eagerly.

"We'd love to have you," Ramona said with a smile. "What about you?" she said to Tom.

The two of them looked at him, and he hesitated, assuming Jeanine would not be going with them. "I'll pass on the trip, but I'd smoke some dope if that's possible."

Ramona shifted Lela to her hip and told them to follow her. The sand was soft beneath Tom's feet, although he kept stepping on bits of harder bark or leaves. She introduced Kevin to Terry, who gave Kevin a few mushrooms for later, and told William that Tom would join him if he was going to smoke pot.

They met some other people from the commune and ate a rice and vegetable dish for lunch. Tom and Kevin sat on a cushion on the ground at a low table with a dirty tablecloth. Kevin chatted with a couple who had their arms around each other, and Jeanine, who had shown up, continued visiting with friends. Tom gazed at her, then out at the beachfront toward the ocean. The rolling waves soothed him. Could he experience the peace he sought with nature here, living like Thoreau?

After lunch, Kevin disappeared with Terry, and Jeanine went into one of the treehouses with friends. William approached Tom, lit a joint, and passed it to him.

"This is pot from Kauai seeds," he said. "Be careful—too much of it can cause hallucinations."

Tom studied the joint between his fingers. "I smoked some pot in Lihue. So, this is different?"

"Yeah, I know Lucas. He probably got that pot from The Company—the Hawaiian mafia—out of Honolulu. Who knows what they mix with it; it's much weaker. He might also have small amounts of Kauai pot from local sources, but he and the mob make their money from the Honolulu pot."

Tom took a small toke and could immediately feel the effects of the Kauai pot—he was more alert than he had been from Lucas's pot.

William took a hit, put the joint in an ashtray, and looked at Tom. "Ramona said you were at Kent State during the riots." Tom nodded. "That could have been me shooting those students. I was gung-ho to kill Vietnamese and hated student protesters." He looked disgusted with himself.

"What made you change?"

William shook his head while he stroked his long beard. "The war was insane." His eyes seemed to go somewhere else.

"I have a friend who lost his arm in Vietnam—he feels like you do."

William appeared uncomfortable and looked toward the ocean. "Why don't you help us fish."

Tom joined William and three men to take the fishing net out into some water protected from waves by rocks. Tom held his section of net and followed the group. When they got there, the others stripped down, so Tom did, too, since he hadn't brought a swimming suit. He felt conspicuous and looked back toward the cluster of treehouses, wondering if Jeanine watched them as they pulled the net into the water.

A short time later, they hauled the net onto the sand and there were several fish flopping in it. They let the smaller ones go and put the larger ones in a basket to be cleaned for supper. They put on their shorts, and William invited Tom to some hammocks strung between trees, where he said he would nap.

Tom lay down in one of the hammocks, feeling the warm breeze dry the water from his body, still mellow from smoking pot. William closed his eyes, and Tom looked at the clouds. The large green leaves overhead set against the deep blue sky took his breath away. He dozed under the trees to the sound of birds chirping and the crashing of the surf.

———

Tom was sitting at a table chopping pineapple with William when Kevin and Terry returned from their mushroom trip. They had their arms around each other as they walked, and appeared to be deep in conversation. They were of similar height, but Terry's thinning hair and pudgy body contrasted with Kevin's long, thick hair and athletic build.

Kevin shouted ecstatically when Ramona and Jeanine came out to meet them: "This is so cool—I want to live here!" Terry chuckled and looked at Ramona. "I think he'd fit right in." Tom was reminded of Kevin's enthusiasm for the acid trip he and Kevin had taken in the spring near the river in the Kent city park.

Jeanine said they needed to get on the road back to Lihue since she had to work that evening. Ramona looked at her and Tom and said they would be welcome to live in the camp as well. Tom thanked her for the invitation, saying he would consider it, while Jeanine kept silent. Kevin told her he would be back with his bags as soon as possible. Tom wondered if Ramona, observing Jeanine's friendships and conversations that day, wanted to give her a second chance at living in their community of love.

As Tom drove them back to Lihue, Kevin continued to chatter, and Jeanine remained silent. Tom sensed that the Taylor Camp visit had affected her deeply, and he wanted to talk to her about it. But Kevin, still coming down from his shroom trip, kept talking about his hike into the hills on the trail toward the Na Pali Coast. He marveled at what he had experienced: the singing birds, the misty warm rain, and the views of the ocean, which through the mist often included colorful rainbows.

Tom glanced at Jeanine while Kevin talked. She either looked straight ahead or turned her head to look out her side window, her eyes covered by large, dark sunglasses. During one of Kevin's few lulls, Tom asked Jeanine if she would ever consider living at the camp again. "It seems like you have a lot of close friends there," he said. But Jeanine kept silent, only shaking her head from side to side as she stared straight ahead. This sparked a new theme for Kevin—how great it would be for all three of them to live there. "The people were amazing!" he said, leaning forward to try and catch Jeanine's eye. "And everybody kept saying how much they miss you! We should all move there together!" But Jeanine, looking out her side window, suddenly yelled, "No! I'm done there!" and then returned to being silent and motionless for the rest of the drive. This made Tom even more curious about her experience there, but she clearly didn't want to talk about it.

Tom parked the car by their apartment building and thanked Jeanine. She turned, finally looking at him without her sunglasses. He could have continued looking into her deep brown eyes forever, but she nodded and got out of the car. Kevin apologized for upsetting her and then thanked her several times and hugged her. Tom stood awkwardly, not sure if he should hug her also, but she made it easy by saying goodbye to the two of them and turning to enter the building.

That evening, Tom thought long and hard about Ramona's invitation to live at Taylor Camp. Kevin's enthusiasm was contagious, but the drugs didn't excite him as they did Kevin. Part of him was tempted to stay in Lihue to see if he had a chance with Jeanine, but he had left Ohio to find an alternative to the violence and destruction he had experienced, and here was a choice—he could escape from that past and join a loving community focused on peace and enlightenment. Why not make that choice?

This life-changing decision brought to mind the draft, another life-changing event, but one that did not give him a choice. He was tired of worrying and waiting to hear if his draft number would be reached. He called his draft board in Ohio the next morning while Kevin slept. Scotty and Lucas had already left for work.

The phone rang nine times, until Tom heard a recording tell him he was being put on hold. He stared out the window at the gray apartment building across the way, his palms sweaty. After several minutes, a draft board official answered.

Tom quickly cleared his throat. "My lottery number is 189," he said as clearly as possible to the man. "The last time I checked to see whether you'd reach it, it was too early to tell. Can you tell me how it stands now?"

"Hang on." Tom could hear muffled voices in the background. A dog barked outside. Kevin turned in his sleep. Then, the voice came back. "We don't anticipate needing additional draftees from our board given President Nixon's withdrawal of US troops."

Tom's heart leaped. "Okay, okay—let me confirm. Are you saying I won't be drafted?" He gripped the receiver in his hands, pressing it into his ear.

"Not according to our July numbers. It could change if there is an escalation of the war, but that's highly unlikely," the man said.

"Thank you, thank you!" Tom said. His voice echoed in the kitchen, and Kevin stirred. "Yes, sir. Thank you." Tom tried to bring down his enthusiasm, recognizing that the draft board official probably thought of being drafted as an honor. But the official seemed to understand, saying, "Have a good life," before hanging up.

Tom gazed out the kitchen window. A huge load had been removed from his shoulders. His thoughts again turned to Taylor Camp. He decided he would move there with Kevin. His life was moving in the right direction. It was more critical for him to join a community with a positive culture than to pursue an uncertain relationship with Jeanine.

Kevin got up and poured himself a cup of coffee. "That sounded like an exciting phone call," Kevin said as he sat down.

"Very exciting. My draft board isn't going to reach my number."

"That's tremendous!" Kevin said, reaching over and giving Tom a high five. "Now what are you going to do about Taylor Camp? Come on—you have to go."

"I'm in!" Tom said.

A huge smile appeared on Kevin's face. "That's it then. Let's ask Lucas to drive us to Taylor Camp tomorrow to move in."

"I'm ready." Everything was falling into place.

"Great—tomorrow night we'll sleep in a treehouse," Kevin said. "Ramona said there was an empty one we could live in; it was used last by Jeanine and her boyfriend."

Tom wasn't sure what he thought of that.

26

It didn't take long for Tom and Kevin to pack up what little they'd brought to Hawaii. Lucas dropped them off at Taylor Camp in the afternoon, giving them a nod as he pulled away in Scotty's car. Tom had wanted to say goodbye to Jeanine, but she had gone to work, so he asked Lucas to tell her he was going to try living at Taylor Camp.

Kevin stripped off his shirt as soon as they arrived, and William walked them over to the empty treehouse they could use. It was small, with a flat, corrugated tin roof, mosquito netting for the windows, and plywood along the bottom. Several boards were propped up at an angle against one of the posts.

William went up the ladder first, followed by Tom. The inside mostly consisted of a low bed along the wall, some planks for shelves, and several overlapping rugs across the wooden floor. William suggested that they could add a room. Jeanine's former boyfriend Leroy, he said, had started gathering boards for an addition before he left. Tom agreed. He would want his own room.

Ramona and Terry welcomed Tom and Kevin while they were unpacking and told them the camp would celebrate their arrival at dinner. Word had spread that the newcomers had left the destruction of the Kent State shootings to seek a new culture of peace, and camp members were eager to meet them.

That evening, about thirty people went to the large treehouse room that was used for meals. A few lit joints and passed them around, offering them to Tom and Kevin when they introduced themselves. Most of the people gathered were minimally clothed. After a few minutes of smoking dope and meeting camp members, Tom felt more at peace, relaxing in the warm haze in a room full of smiling people.

"Welcome, everyone," Ramona said. "We're happy to have Kevin and Tom join us in our life of peace and love. Let's hear a few words from the newcomers." Tom and Kevin looked at each other, not prepared for this request. But Kevin nodded and surveyed the room.

"I'm so happy to be here," Kevin said. "I joined Terry on the shroom trip two days ago, and he talked about the quest for the Buddhist state of nirvana, where there is a release from the cycle of death and rebirth. I want to devote myself to this spiritual quest and growth." Terry and several others nodded their heads in approval.

Tom was glad Kevin had gone first, giving him time to formulate his words. "I came here to find an alternative life that can be a model for changing the American culture built on capitalism and greed. I want to learn from you and help you create a peaceful, loving community."

Everyone broke into applause, and Ramona invited them to the buffet table, where fish, vegetables, and fruit were ready to be served. As they moved toward the table, William, looking very stoned, gave Tom a quick embrace. Tom and Kevin took their seats on a low wooden bench, and a short topless woman introduced herself as Donna and sat next to them. Tom recognized her as the woman weeding in the garden when they first drove into the camp. She asked Tom and Kevin numerous questions about football and the Kent State shootings, contributing to the conversation and fellowship that vibrated the room. As community members finished their meals, they stopped by Tom and Kevin, bent over, and hugged them around their shoulders.

"I'm in heaven," Kevin said when they returned to their treehouse. Warm breezes blew gently through the open windows, and Kevin, looking completely stoned, stood in front of them with his arms outstretched.

"Yeah, quite a welcome," Tom said, feeling the promise of a community of loving people. It would take some adjustment, but he was optimistic. He had found the alternative he was looking for.

He gave the bed to Kevin that night, sleeping on a yoga mat on the floor instead. He didn't want to sleep where Jeanine had been with someone else.

———

Tom and Kevin were outside examining the wooden boards for an added room when Terry stopped by to talk about their contributions to the camp.

"We have no written laws. We're a community guided by a spirit that creates order without rules."

That was exactly what Tom wanted. "How can we help?" he asked, straightening up.

"We have rotating duties for everyone: gardening, fishing, picking fruit, cooking, and cleaning. When we're low on cash, people also take odd jobs in Hanalei."

"We'd be glad to jump in," Kevin said.

"What if someone fails to take his or her turn?" Tom asked.

Terry's friendly face disappeared, replaced by a concerned look that made Tom feel he shouldn't have asked the question. "We give feedback and hopefully correct their behavior."

"Who decides when corrective action is needed?" Tom asked.

Terry again seemed annoyed by the question. "We rotate leadership of the camp. Ramona replaced me this past year. We convene a council of leaders to address issues."

Tom nodded, thinking of Jeanine's comment about the politics of Taylor Camp. But his curiosity about how the camp functioned was satisfied for now.

Tom and Kevin started their rotational assignments that afternoon. Tom began by pulling weeds next to Donna in the garden, while Kevin joined the fishing team. Tom was not ready to go naked, but he took his shirt off to be like most of the men.

Donna looked at him and smiled. "Nice body."

"Thanks," Tom said slowly, not knowing whether her remark was meant to be a sexual invitation. He was uncertain about whether he wanted to have sex with her, but he sensed this was the way of life here.

———

Tom and Kevin followed a similar daily routine, carrying out their duties and eating meals with camp members. Tom completed the construction of the additional room in their treehouse and enjoyed the camp tradition of playing volleyball on the beach after supper. But after three weeks, he began to tire of the daily chores. He also grew tired of Kevin's exclamations after every shroom trip led by Terry. Tom had no interest in joining them, although camp members had started referring to Kevin as a holy man on par with Terry, given his pursuit of nirvana and his visions of what the camp could become. Instead, Tom occasionally smoked pot with William. The high felt good, but when he came down, his boredom returned.

One afternoon, a thunderstorm moved through the camp. William covered his ears at the sound of thunder and ran to his treehouse. Tom grew concerned when William didn't come out the next day.

"What's going on with William?" Tom asked Terry.

"The sound of thunder reminds him of Vietnam."

"But the storm is over."

"I imagine he's on a drinking binge—he's an alcoholic. The camp has been good for him, but he'll occasionally sneak in a bottle of whiskey."

At night, Tom and Kevin talked privately about what they observed in the camp. Tom felt he had seen another side of Terry. They were both surprised about William's alcoholism. Tom also wanted to hear Kevin's thoughts about Donna.

"I think she is ready to take me to bed anytime I want her to," Tom said. "It's tempting, but I'm also not sure it's a good idea."

"She already did it with me," Kevin said, lying in the bed with his hands behind his head. He'd been going around naked the entire time.

"You're kidding!" Tom sat up from the yoga mat he'd been reclining on.

"No, we picked fruit together, and on the way back, she took me to her room in her treehouse and asked me to choose a condom from her collection in her drawer."

Tom couldn't picture Kevin with Donna. "It's hard to know who's with who around here," he said. "Do you think Terry is Lela's father?"

"I don't know. I don't think it matters. Taylor Camp is a place of free love."

A quick thought flashed in Tom's mind. Maybe Leroy was Lela's father?

That night, Tom lay awake in bed thinking about the people he had met in the camp. He had discovered things that were not evident in their warm welcomes. He believed their intentions were good, but he needed more time to see how he fit into this community.

———

One morning, Terry approached Tom and asked him if he had any cash to contribute to the central fund for camp expenses. If not, Tom could take a turn working in Hanalei. It would entail signing in early at a manpower office and waiting to be chosen for odd jobs, such as distributing flyers or maintaining the city's parks and neighborhoods. Not wanting to part with his cash, Tom got a ride to the manpower office the following morning and sat down to wait on a bench with other men looking for work.

"Nice hair. What, are you one of those Taylor Camp hippies?" a grizzled older white man asked.

"I live there," Tom said, holding his head higher.

The man sneered at him. "Then why aren't you naked?"

Another guy, sitting at the end of the bench, said, "Come on—you know if he was naked, he wouldn't land a job, and he needs to earn money to buy his drugs." Tom hadn't expected this attack, and he looked at them steadily.

A young Hawaiian man sitting with two other Hawaiians spat on the floor toward Tom. "Fucking haole hippies." Tom stared at the bubbles from the saliva on the ground.

A white man, about fifty with a crew cut, came from his manager's desk to stand in front of Tom. "We don't want Taylor Camp hippies in Hanalei. You're selling drugs to children and spreading diseases from your orgies."

Tom froze. He didn't know this would be the kind of reception he would receive outside of the camp. "I just want to work," he said, his face reddening.

The man stood over Tom, his arms crossed. He appeared to study Tom's larger build. "Fine," he said, still scowling. "I've only got one job for you today—emptying trash into a garbage truck. Don't leave the truck, and keep your orange vest on."

Tom spent the rest of the day riding on the rear of a garbage truck and stopping at residences and businesses to empty garbage cans. The driver, a city employee, didn't talk to him. The nauseating stench of the garbage was worsened by the warm temperature. Then, a rainstorm hit, different from the daily, short bursts of rain common on Kauai. For the last hour, Tom picked up and dumped cans in the rain.

"Holy shit," Tom said to Kevin that night as he toweled off after a swim. "I already knew locals don't like us if we're white, but it turns out if we're from Taylor Camp, the whole town hates us."

"Don't worry about it," Kevin said, looking stoned. "They have no clue how to live in peace and love. What we have here is special."

"But the idea is to be a model of an alternative life for others. How can we make any progress if people hate us?'

"Just concentrate on your own spiritual growth." Kevin started descending the ladder. "Teach others by showing them who you are," he said, before he disappeared. Tom shook his head—Kevin didn't know what he was talking about.

Tom had no problem standing up for ideals he believed in, but he didn't yet know how to live them out at Taylor Camp. He thought of his father, who would strongly disapprove of Taylor Camp, and his mother, who would worry if she knew even half of what went on here. He hadn't called his parents once since arriving in Hawaii and still didn't plan to until he was more settled and had an update he was willing to share with them.

———

At Kevin's urging, Tom started attending the Om circle at the treehouse named The Church of the Brotherhood of the Paradise Children. He wanted to see if he too could find peace and enlightenment. In the Om circles, he learned to meditate, focusing on his breathing and letting go of thoughts. This relaxed him, but he didn't see how his enlightenment at Taylor Camp could influence the creation of an alternative model for broader society.

One morning, as Tom returned from fishing, he walked by a woman sitting against the side of a treehouse. She was smoking a joint, with her naked four-year-old son beside her. The woman closed her eyes and swayed back and forth while her son grabbed her leg, yelling, "Mommy!"

"What are you doing?" Tom asked the woman in a loud voice. "Can't you see your kid wants you?" The woman looked at him through half-closed eyes and said, "Leave me alone."

Tom was appalled. How could she treat a child like this? How could an alternative community be built without adults providing guidance and structure for children? Tom only saw people trying to grow spiritually themselves or seek pleasure through drugs and sex.

When Tom took his seat in the Om circle one afternoon after having a joint with William, Donna came to sit beside him. The leader asked everyone to hold hands to unite their spirits. Donna reached over and squeezed Tom's hand. Her touch made him feel close to her, but he was confused in his stoned state, not knowing if it was spiritual or sexual closeness. When the meditation ended, the sun was setting, and Donna led Tom behind a tree in the shade. She moved closer to him, making him feel warm and relaxed, not unlike being in a meditative state. But he was startled when she put her hand down the front of his shorts. He pulled away.

"What's the matter?" she asked, looking surprised.

"I was feeling relaxed just holding you—I didn't expect that," he said. For some reason, he felt disloyal to Jeanine.

Donna smiled and moved in to pull his head down for a kiss. "It's okay. I want more," she said softly. "Let's go to my room."

"No."

She stepped back, her eyes narrowing. "This is a community of peace and love."

"I'm just not ready."

Donna took a step back and put her hands on her bare hips. "I saw you ride up here with Jeanine. You looked like you were ga-ga over her."

"So?"

"Her boyfriend, Leroy, didn't have any trouble fucking me, or Jeanine's friend, Alice."

Tom tried to clear his head from the effects of pot. "Leroy slept with the two of you while he was with Jeanine?" He blinked a few times to focus better.

"Of course he did. It's okay to love someone here and still have sex with others."

Tom remembered how upset Jeanine had seemed on the ride back from Taylor Camp. Maybe she had been reminded of what she saw as a betrayal by Leroy, even though the camp condoned it. "Is Alice here?" he asked, trying to recall all the women he'd met.

"No, she left." Donna shifted her weight in the sand, looking unhappy. "Not long after Jeanine left. We heard she had a nervous breakdown."

Tom tried to piece it together. "What about Leroy?"

"When Jeanine found out he was having sex with Alice and me, she went into a rage—we all heard it—and kicked him out of their treehouse. She threw all his stuff outside and stayed holed up for days. Leroy asked Ramona to help get them back together."

"What did Ramona do?"

Donna seemed impatient. "She told Jeanine—like I said—that this is a camp of peace and love. We can love each other without being owned by one person."

Tom shook his head. No wonder Jeanine was upset.

"So Jeanine left? And Leroy?"

"Jeanine disagreed with Ramona and stormed off to Lihue. We were glad to be rid of her negative vibe. Leroy returned to California. After they both left, Alice was in a deep depression—a real mess—and her parents came for her."

Tom thought that Donna had relayed all this without any remorse or sympathy. She seemed instead to blame Jeanine for all that had happened. His mind raced. "I need to go," he said, backing away from the tree.

Donna looked offended. "Okay, go," she said. "I don't think you belong here." Tom went to his treehouse, turning back once to notice Donna studying him from a distance.

He drank some water, trying to finish coming off his high, then put on a T-shirt and walked to where the stream flowed into the ocean. He found a spot and sat there for the rest of the evening, thinking that living at Taylor Camp might have been a huge mistake.

———

Tom had trouble sleeping that night, and he stayed in bed the next morning, avoiding his chores. When Kevin returned around noon, he said that the gardening group had missed him and that Ramona wanted to see him.

That afternoon, he went to Ramona's room, where she eyed him quietly and poured him a cup of sun tea.

"You hurt Donna yesterday," she said.

"By not having sex with her? Don't I get to choose who I sleep with?"

Ramona took a drink of tea before she answered him. "We don't take sex that seriously here. People should feel free to pursue pleasure without hang-ups."

Tom didn't pick up his cup. "I'm not going to have sex with just anybody."

Ramona smiled. "You remind me of Jeanine. She wanted an exclusive relationship. Maybe your living in her treehouse is rubbing off on you."

"Donna told me about Leroy. I imagine Jeanine felt incredibly betrayed."

"She had nothing to feel betrayed about," Ramona said. "That's not the culture we have here."

Tom almost asked whether Ramona had also betrayed Jeanine by sleeping with Leroy. He stared at the floor for a few seconds and then looked up. "I'm not sure if I'm meant for this culture."

"I'm not sure you are either." She nodded and squinted, as if to say this didn't surprise her.

Tom stood up. "Let me think about it," he said. He spent the rest of the day walking on the trails, thinking how naïve he'd been. How could he have been so blind to not see the destructive side of Taylor Camp? He had believed that it was a community of peace and love, ignoring Jeanine's experience and comments and overlooking the caution he felt when he first met Ramona. How could he be so stupid? He tried to gain some clarity about what he was going to do, but it was hard to think in a drenching rain that lasted longer than usual.

———

"I'm not sure I want to keep living here," Tom said after dinner that night as he walked with Kevin back to their treehouse.

"Why?" he asked, turning to face Tom. "This is why we came to Hawaii."

"Yeah, but is this what we dreamed of? I want something more challenging than gardening or emptying garbage cans."

Kevin looked puzzled. "We're living a spiritual life, like monks! What we *do* is not that important. It's what we *become* that matters. *That's* how we influence change."

"I don't think it's for me. We're expected to have free love, but we don't know who the fathers are of the camp's children," Tom said. "Is this a model for a new culture?"

Kevin stopped walking. "You seem to be talking yourself out of living here."

Tom looked toward the hills and sighed. "I'm not into drugs like you are. I'd like a deep relationship with a woman, not free love. And I don't want to be seen as a disease carrier when I'm outside the camp."

Kevin was quiet for the rest of the walk. At the base of the ladder, he stopped and looked at Tom, his expression one of sadness. "We've been through so much together," he said. He hung his head, his hair extending all the way down to his navel, and when, after a few moments, he once again lifted his head, Tom could see that his eyes were red-rimmed. "I knew this was coming. I could tell," Kevin said.

Tom nodded. His decision to leave might cause Kevin more pain than he'd thought. He grew quiet, remembering their first meeting in their dorm room at Kent State, football practices, their double dates, conversations they'd had that led to Tom's political awakening and participation in protests, their experimentation with drugs. Kevin had come to Grandpa's funeral and been there for him as he healed from his football injuries. He felt guilty about leaving him.

"I'm just moving to Lihue; I'll only be an hour away," Tom said. Tom had not thought out his next steps, but he knew he wasn't ready to leave Hawaii, and Lihue was where he'd already met some people. In particular, Jeanine was there. Having lived in her treehouse and learned more about her made him feel closer to her.

Kevin kept looking at Tom and then finally nodded. "All right," he said, putting his hand on the ladder. "When are you leaving?"

Tom didn't see much point in staying longer. Ramona and Donna had been acting icily toward him; he didn't have any outstanding obligations to the camp, and he didn't really feel connected to anyone else besides William. He'd learned some things in the Om circles, but overall, Taylor Camp wasn't the new culture he wanted to help build, and it didn't seem to hold any answers for him.

"I'm going to Hanalei tomorrow to call Barry and ask him if he'll come pick me up," he said, his plan unfolding as he spoke. "Maybe he's still looking for someone to share his apartment."

———

Barry picked Tom up from Taylor Camp two days later. As Kevin helped carry his bags toward Barry's waiting car, Ramona stood watching beside a picnic table. She made no effort at a farewell, only saying, "Good luck chasing Jeanine," and then turning away as they walked by. Terry was watching from a treehouse. Tom waved to him, but Terry stood motionless.

"Terry can't understand why you're rejecting being one of the paradise children," Kevin said.

"He still has you," Tom said. "The camp sees you as a holy man—you're becoming as influential as Terry."

When they reached the car, Kevin turned to Tom and held out his hand. Tom took it and pulled Kevin toward him, hugging him like Kevin usually did to close friends.

"You take care of yourself," Tom said.

"You, too."

A wave of feelings came over Tom—he sensed a finality with this parting, a loss of a close friend. Kevin's eyes again became red-rimmed.

As Tom turned to the car, a voice said, "Wait." William was walking quickly toward him.

"You be good," William said, reaching out to embrace Tom.

"You, too, man," Tom said, giving William a bear hug. "Keep this place in order."

Tom got into the car, where he could see Barry staring at William and Kevin and the treehouses beyond. Kevin was wearing nothing except a necklace. Tom and Barry drove off, and when Barry reached the main road, he looked at Tom. "Wow, that's . . . quite a place."

"Yeah. It's not for me," Tom said. He stared out the window at the gravel road but did not look back at Taylor Camp. He felt sunburned, thirsty, and extremely tired. Barry turned up the radio, as if understanding Tom might not be ready for a long conversation. Tom kept his face turned toward the window for much of the trip, much like Jeanine had on their drive back from his first visit.

The closer they got to Lihue, the more reality seemed to set in for Tom. He appreciated the beauty of Kauai—the joy of swimming in the ocean, the green wooded hills and mountains, and the comfortable temperature and ocean breezes. It was a wonderful escape, but what was his purpose in living here? His immediate need was to find a job. He would pursue one that used his skills as a carpenter, probably paying more than a job as a dishwasher or busboy. But that would be to survive, to earn a living—not to advance some purpose that would improve society. He'd thought Taylor Camp might hold what he was looking for, but all that had flopped. He had more questions than answers.

Kevin seemed to be pursuing the vision in *The Electric Kool-Aid Acid Test*—the discovery of a new religion. But having now lived in Taylor Camp for almost two months, Tom knew that vision was not for him. He thought of another book that had influenced him, Fromm's *The Sane Society*. How could he figure out a way to work toward something closer to Fromm's vision?

Tom pondered these questions as they drove south, looking out the window at waves crashing on the beach. But his thoughts were interrupted by other questions that had nothing to do with improving society. He kept returning to images of Jeanine sitting next to him in Scotty's car, and walking with her at Hanalei Bay. He thought of the times she had looked at him directly, with eyes he wanted to dive into.

27

S oon after Tom moved in with Barry, he knocked on Jeanine's door. She lived at one end of the second floor, and Tom and Barry lived at the other. She opened the door only halfway, and her face became still when she saw it was Tom. She wore the pale-yellow halter top she wore on the day he first met her, drawing his eyes to her bronze tan.

"How about having lunch?" he asked. "I'm no longer at Taylor Camp."

"I heard." Tom thought he detected a hint of satisfaction on her face.

"I'd like to hear your thoughts about it."

"I don't want to talk about it," she said without emotion. "And I've had lunch."

He leaned closer to the door. "Can we maybe just go for a walk sometime?"

"Maybe later." She shut the door on him, leaving him staring at its chipped paint.

Tom walked back to his room at Barry's, kicking himself for his stupidity. Why had he opened with his desire to hear Jeanine's thoughts about Taylor Camp? A place where she had had her heart broken?

Tom hesitated to approach Jeanine directly again. Instead, he hoped to run into her at a social gathering, like at one of Scotty and Lucas's parties.

Scotty owned the best stereo and the best collection of albums in the building, and Lucas had a steady supply of marijuana. On Scotty's nights off from bartending, he often threw parties in his and Lucas's apartment. Their friends from the building and girls he met at the bar all piled in with packs of beer and bottles of rum, and they all bought the drugs that Lucas sold from his bedroom. Lucas supplemented his supply of regular pot with small amounts of strong Kauai pot and, occasionally, psilocybin.

Tom and Barry enjoyed the music and the social atmosphere of these par- ties. Tom also kept one eye on the door, hoping that Jeanine would show up, as Lucas had said she had in the past. He watched people come in and out all evening, partaking of beer or pot and listening to Scotty's albums. Some people sat alone in a corner, their eyes closed and heads bobbing to the beat. Others, like Tom and Barry—a little drunk and maybe a little high from occasional hits on Lucas's joints—talked and laughed. But Tom saw no sign of Jeanine.

Tom also hoped to run into Jeanine at the apartment building. He once saw her in the hall with another girl. Their brief greeting, especially when their eyes locked, did nothing to discourage him. A flush came over his face after they passed each other.

He tried to figure out his attraction to her. It was sexual, even though she didn't seem to be trying to be sexy. Yet, there was something else, something that went deeper—to a more spiritual place—and he wasn't sure why he felt this about her. He wouldn't know unless she gave him a chance to talk to her.

———

Tom had better luck finding a job, looking in earnest after too much partying during Labor Day weekend. When he inquired at the carpenter union headquarters in Lihue, he was only one of a few white men in the waiting area. Tom sensed that he would have been quickly dismissed that day if he hadn't been able to demonstrate that he qualified as an apprentice or higher-level carpenter. But once they saw his card, the union signed him up right away— carpenter apprentices were apparently in demand on Kauai. He paid a union membership fee and was told to call each day to see if a job was available.

His first job was to help construct a townhouse in Lihue. When he arrived at the site, the foreman and workers were either Asian, Islander, or a combination. They all studied him as he stood there, and one of them said loudly to the group nearest him, "Look at the haole hippie." A couple of the workers, who were about as big as Tom, squared their shoulders and stared him down. It wasn't until he showed his carpentry skills that the crew members stopped glaring at him or saying rude things.

During their coffee break, he did his best to be friendly, but he made sure to be aware of the distance between himself and the other men. He didn't want any trouble. When one of the more talkative islanders found out that Tom had played college football, a few other carpenters became interested.

They told him about Samoan linemen they knew in the NFL, and Tom was glad to have the opportunity to talk about something familiar. Still, many of the carpenters never looked at him, probably because they resented him taking a job away from a local.

The pay was good though, and after learning that the highest demand for carpenters was in Kapa'a, about ten miles away, Tom decided to invest in an old Datsun, heavily rusted from the salt air. He found work most days, and all the foremen in the area soon came to appreciate his skills and work ethic.

Manual labor wasn't something he wanted to do for long. He had called it drudgery in the past. But in the setting of Kauai, where he was uncertain about his future, he preferred carpentry over working in a restaurant or bar, and he earned higher pay than those workers. He was grateful that he had a good way to support himself for now.

———

At one of Scotty's parties, Tom smoked a joint with Lucas, who had just sold some Kauai pot to a girl in a bikini. Tom, feeling relaxed, revealed that he'd been wanting to get to know Jeanine better but didn't want to intrude on her or push her too hard. Lucas took a long toke. "Jeanine smokes Kauai grass," he said, his voice pinched. He exhaled a huge plume of smoke that slowly dissipated around them. "She's been smoking a lot more lately." He went into a coughing fit, then asked Tom what they'd been talking about.

"Jeanine," Tom said.

"Oh, right," said Lucas. "She's a private chick, man. I've never even been in her apartment. She just opens her door a little and slips me some dough for the pot. Hardly even says hello. Scotty helped her move in after she left Taylor Camp, but she's never invited him back. He told me she has some sort of small Buddhist shrine in the corner of her apartment where she meditates." Before disappearing into his bedroom with a couple of new customers, he added over his shoulder, "If you want to talk to her, your best bet is to catch her at Coco's resort shop. She usually works evenings at the end of the week."

Tom was intrigued to hear that Jeanine had a shrine. On a Friday evening a week later, he walked to the resort, where he spotted a cluster of shops that included Coco's, a store that sold children's clothes. He could see Jeanine through the window, talking to a customer, an older woman holding up tiny colorful sundresses. Jeanine's brown hair hung down slightly above her shoulders, the blond strands glistening in the store's light. As she smiled at the woman, Tom's heart quickened. Jeanine was beautiful in her light blue sundress. She looked relaxed and unguarded. When the woman left, Jeanine noticed Tom outside, and he gave her a small wave.

Jeanine came to the open door with a look of surprise. "What are you doing here?"

"I heard you worked here." He scanned her face, searching for any kind of negative reaction, but was glad to see a faint smile.

"Do you need any sundresses?" she said.

He laughed. "No, I came here to see if you wanted to do something with me."

She hesitated, then grew serious. "I'm not looking to date anyone."

He smiled and shrugged his shoulders. "We won't call it a date. We could go to a restaurant, the waterfalls you told me about, or whatever you like. No pressure."

He thought he saw her tearing up a little, but a mother and daughter came into the store and she quickly turned away. He stood there awkwardly, unsure of what to do. He waited until Jeanine finished pointing the mother to a rack of dresses, and then told her he would catch her later. He glanced briefly at her as he left, and she met his eyes.

He walked down the resort hallway thinking of her look; he didn't know what to make of it. She could have just said goodbye with a quick glance away from the mother. But she had looked deeply at him with some emotion. Was it possible she could be interested?

He had been so passive with Cindi and Becky, each often in charge of their relationship, including breaking up with him. If there was a chance with Jeanine, he wanted to engage with her in a better way than he had in his previous relationships. He decided to continue to take the first step, given her uncertainty.

Tom put a note under Jeanine's door on the day of a party at Scotty's, saying he hoped to see her that night. He felt he had nothing to lose. She didn't come, but she surprised him another night by arriving late in the evening. She was wearing shorts and a tank top, and she looked directly at him as she entered the apartment, but she walked over to Lucas, where he sat on the couch. She looked down at him, pointing to his bushy muttonchop sideburns and laughing, and then they turned to go into the bedroom.

Tom wondered just how much she was smoking these days. When the bedroom door opened a little while later and she came out, she walked right toward him, her smile and eyes on him all the way, an extra bounce to her step. Other guys paused and watched her as well, just as drawn to her long bare legs as Tom was.

"I got your note," she said, smiling. Her eyes were bloodshot.

"You're in a good mood."

She smiled and leaned closer. "Lucas has the best dope. Do you want to try?"

Tom couldn't believe how near she was to him. He loved her attention but had mixed feelings, knowing much of it was the effect of the Kauai pot. "I'm going to pass," he said.

Jeanine turned to greet Scotty, who was walking toward them. He had the same stoned look that Jeanine had.

"Can I get anything for you two?" Scotty said.

"No. This music is fabulous," Jeanine said, bobbing her head to the beat of Deep Purple.

"Let me know if you have any requests."

Scotty walked away to greet other guests. His cheeks seemed sunken, and the creases in his face were like those of an older man. Tom turned back to look at Jeanine, wondering what was next.

She stared at him, continuing to smile. "You wanted to be with me. Here I am."

Tom wanted to talk to her away from the people, loud music, and pot. "Let's go outside where we can hear each other." She nodded and followed, waving goodbye to Lucas as they stepped out into the hallway. Downstairs, they sat down at a picnic table along the side of the building, Jeanine sliding in across from Tom.

"Why exactly are you interested in me?" she asked, immediately growing serious.

Tom was surprised at her directness. She gazed at him in the moonlight with complete confidence. He decided to try to be as direct as she was. "I like you," he said, his palms a little sweaty. "I want to know more about you."

"What do you want to know?" She rested her forearms on the table.

"Well, why aren't you open to going out on dates?"

She paused. "I had a bad experience with my boyfriend."

"I heard a little about it at Taylor Camp."

Jeanine hesitated, seeming to wonder how much Tom actually knew. "Then you probably heard Leroy took the idea of free love literally. He fucked my friends."

Though her tone was sharp, Tom sensed she still seemed wounded. "Yeah, and Ramona and most everyone else there seems to think that is okay," he said.

"A lot of people ridiculed me for being upset, telling me I was wrong. I lost Leroy, and I lost a lot of friends I considered my family."

Jeanine's confidence seemed to lessen, and she appeared to be getting anxious. "So, you left?" Tom asked gently. A warm ocean breeze rustled the palm trees overhead.

"Eventually. I tried to be open—like Ramona said I should. But I was depressed and angry. I kicked Leroy out and stayed alone in the treehouse. The others blamed me for disrupting their big happy family. I felt betrayed by Leroy and my friends . . . and then poor Alice freaked out." Jeanine looked down. "I don't want to talk about it anymore."

"How about we just take a walk together," he said. She nodded, and they went slowly up the hill, away from the beach. Tom was quiet, feeling protective of her. When she seemed to recover from talking about Taylor Camp, he turned to her and said, "I'd like to take more walks with you."

She took a step away from him. "I like you, but I can't risk a new relationship."

He nodded. "I've been in relationships that didn't end well. I won't push you."

She stopped walking, something in her expression softening. But then, she turned away and said, "I need to get back to my apartment." She walked half a step in front of him all the way back.

When they got to her door, she paused to look at him. He was motionless, not wanting to show any desire or expectation of a kiss. He didn't want to do anything to jeopardize what they'd begun. She gave him a brief smile, put her hands on his shoulders, drew him close for a hug, and then let him go. She began to turn toward her door.

"How about if I meet you at your shop on Monday and walk you home?" he asked, hoping she would at least agree to a twenty-minute walk.

She stared at him, her eyes searching his, and then finally nodded before going into her apartment and closing the door. He stood still for a moment, feeling excited, and then went back to his place, thinking of her hands on his shoulders, drawing him close to her.

28

Tom started walking Jeanine home from her job at Coco's as often as he could. Each time their conversations deepened—Tom first wanting to know more about her and then Jeanine asking about him. He was cautious, not wanting to push or pressure her, as he had promised. When they reached their apartment building and arrived on the second floor, Jeanine would turn left to her apartment, and Tom would turn right to his. He was deliberate in not proposing that they do anything else together, except confirm the next time he would walk her home.

He learned that her last name was Carter. She was born in New Jersey but grew up in Seattle, where her family owned a clothing company. She described her family as chaotic, her father's repressed English emotions clashing with her mother's Greek and Irish passions. The Greek in her, Tom thought, explained her dark eyes and olive skin.

Jeanine told him she'd always felt closer to her father and hated how her mother attacked him. By the time Jeanine graduated from high school, she didn't know what she wanted to do other than move out of their house, away from family tensions and her mother's criticism. She loved rock music and tried singing in a local band, modeling herself after Grace Slick of Jefferson Airplane. She almost joined the hippies in San Francisco, but her father persuaded her to apply to college, and she wound up at UC Berkeley. As she described the Berkeley scene, Tom pictured her rebelling against the life of her parents—going to concerts and antiwar protests and experimenting with drugs.

"Were your parents freaked out over your changes?" he asked as they walked. They passed some surfers carrying surfboards, walking slowly after what had probably been a long day at the beach.

"Oh, yeah. My mother almost kicked me out of the house when I came home for spring break with a headband, wearing bell bottoms and a braless top."

Tom pictured his own parents and their reactions when he first showed up at home with long hair. "What about your father?"

"He dealt with it alright until my sophomore year, when I started going with Leroy."

Tom was silent. He was deeply curious about their relationship, but he didn't want to show too much interest.

She kept talking. "Leroy was two years older than I was, with long hair and a beard. We went to the love-ins and acid tests in San Francisco. My parents visited me at Berkeley and met him, and I could tell my father was shocked."

Tom thought about how each of them had gone to Taylor Camp influenced by another person—Kevin in his case and Leroy in hers.

Jeanine, who seemed to relax with Tom the more they talked, began to ask him about his life during their walks. She'd heard from Lucas that he'd been quite a football player. He told her of his dreams to be a college and pro football player, and how close he'd come. When she learned about the rupture of his Achilles tendon, she exclaimed, "Of course!" and looked up at the evening sky.

"What?"

"Here you are, this perfect body, like a Greek god. But you're vulnerable. You know—the story of Achilles?"

"What do you mean?" Tom felt his face warming—she had complimented his body.

As they walked, the back of her hand swung and gently touched the back of Tom's. "Achilles was the greatest Greek warrior," she said. "The legend says that his mother dipped him in the river to protect his body, but she held him by one of his heels. He was eventually killed by a poisoned arrow shot into that heel."

"So you're saying I'm like the greatest Greek warrior?" Tom grinned at Jeanine.

"I'm saying no one is invincible," she said. "That rupture was your fate. You were destined to be shot by that poison arrow. You can't fight fate, Achilles."

Tom grew serious, thinking he had been shot by several poison arrows. Jeanine also became quiet. She took his arm, and Tom looked at her. They walked several steps, with her gazing down at the sidewalk. She leaned into him, appearing strangely vulnerable. Eventually, she turned and faced him. "Talking about your fate makes me think about my own poison arrows."

"What are they?" Tom asked, feeling her warmth.

"I can't bear to be hurt by someone I thought loved me."

Tom wondered who had hurt her the most—her mother or Leroy. "Do you think that's because of your mother's criticism?" he asked.

"Probably. But I think most about what Leroy did to me."

The flag went up again for Tom. He was silent, hoping she would say more.

"I fell totally in love with him and was ready to follow him anywhere. I dropped out of college to come to Taylor Camp after he graduated. I was blinded by him."

Tom nodded, continuing to wait.

"Talking to you makes me realize I try to protect myself—like Achilles's mother dipping him into the river," she said. "I try to do it by smoking pot. I feel more confident after that, but my heart isn't protected, like Achilles's heel isn't."

For some reason, Tom immediately thought of his grandpa and his love of Irish whiskey. He glanced at her face, noticing that she seemed to struggle with her emotions. They had arrived outside their apartment. "Would you mind holding me?" she asked.

He brought her next to him, thrilled by the warmth of her body against his. He kept trying to think of holding her as a friend, not as a lover, but it was difficult. He stood motionless, feeling her soft breasts on his chest, wanting to kiss her neck. She finally moved away and looked at him, her eyes glistening. "Thank you," she said. He nodded, his heart pounding. He was falling in love.

Jeanine continued to ask him questions on their walks. He told her about his family, tension with his father, and the loss of his grandfather. She wanted to know about his previous relationships with Cindi and Becky.

One weekend, Jeanine suggested they take a drive up to Hanalei Bay, her "most beautiful place in the world." He was excited she'd initiated that next step. After parking, they walked to the beach and picked a spot to spread their towels. When Jeanine took off her swimsuit cover-up and walked in her tiny black bikini to the water's edge, Tom was stunned by her beauty. They decided to take surfing lessons that afternoon. Jeanine outperformed Tom, the elite athlete, by learning surfing techniques more quickly than he did.

"Looks like you need to step up your game, Achilles!" she said, her hair wet

and droplets of water on her body. She stood triumphantly in her bikini, waiting for him to catch up to her. He walked out of the surf smiling and carrying
his board, not sure if he'd ever felt this way about anyone before.

——

Scotty continued to host parties, with invitations to Tom, Jeanine, and others,
but the number of girls he invited from the bar decreased in the fall as the tourist
season slowed. Tom showed up at most of Scotty's parties, drinking beer, listening to music, and bantering with Barry, Scotty, and Lucas. Jeanine was more
selective in her appearances, more likely to attend when there was a small group
of people she knew. When Tom walked her home one day after her afternoon
shift, she told him she might see him at Scotty's party that night.

She arrived at about ten o'clock in a black tank top and denim mini-
skirt, took a cursory look around the room, and walked tentatively toward
the couch, where Tom was. Tom knew that the others were aware that he and
Jeanine were spending time together, but he didn't know if she knew they were
aware—maybe that was why she was tentative. She stopped to talk to Scotty,
who offered her a hit on the joint he was passing around.

When Lucas came out of the bedroom, she greeted him with a smile,
and her tentativeness disappeared as the two of them laughed together. They
made a strange pair, with Jeanine, a towering beauty, looking down on pudgy
Lucas. His face was difficult to distinguish behind his bushy sideburns and Fu
Manchu mustache, but they treated each other as good friends. Lucas turned
to the bedroom, and Jeanine looked at Tom, holding up a finger to indicate
she'd be with him in a minute.

Twenty minutes later, she came out of the bedroom with a big smile and
strode confidently toward Tom. He could tell she was high on Kauai dope
and wondered what she would do. She sat down on the couch and slid next to
him, looking into his eyes with unveiled enthusiasm.

"Hi, Achilles," she said, and his heart skipped a beat.

"Hi," he said. "Feeling okay?" She smelled like a mixture of coconut sham-
poo and pot. He put his arm around her, and she nodded happily and settled
in closer. He was aware that people were watching.

Scotty, who'd been drinking a beer next to the stereo, called out, "There's a
handsome couple." He toasted them with his bottle. "Any requests, Jeanine?"

"Jefferson Airplane," she said. "Definitely Jefferson Airplane."

When "White Rabbit" started, Jeanine stood up, taking Tom's beer bottle out of his hand and pretending it was a microphone as she sang along with Grace Slick. Tom had never heard her sing before and was mesmerized. Her voice blended well with the record, but there in Scotty's apartment, it was both sweeter and stronger in tone. She closed her eyes at times, consumed by the music, but then she would open them and gaze directly at Tom. Everyone had turned to watch her, nodding their heads or moving their bodies to her performance. When Jeanine ended the song on the long last note, she thrust her beer bottle in the air, and everyone applauded, some raising their beer bottles. Scotty jumped to his feet, a joint pressed between his lips as he led a standing ovation.

Jeanine, flushed with excitement, took a drink of Tom's beer and grabbed his arm.

"Let's get out of here," she whispered into his ear. She waved goodbye to Scotty and Lucas as she and Tom walked out into the hallway, where the air was cooler.

"That was amazing," Tom said.

"It was for you." She took his arm and linked it with hers, leaning into him.

"Where are we going?" he asked.

"Upstairs to my apartment." She smiled.

Jeanine opened her door, turned around to face Tom, and led him inside. He noticed immediately how simply she lived. Her small studio had only a single bed in one corner and colorful Indian tapestries covering her walls. A small statue of a meditating Buddha rested on a low table in another corner, along with two candlesticks, an incense holder, and a few rocks and seashells.

With the door closed behind them, Jeanine put her arms around Tom's neck and brought her lips close to his. He'd envisioned this kiss ever since he met her and circled his arms around her. But he could tell her actions and confidence were driven by her high. He hugged her, resisting his desire to lean down and feel her mouth against his.

"You've been so good not to push me," she said, her head against his chest. "But I know you want to be close, just like I do." She looked up at him, then pressed against him more. Her eyes were wide.

As aroused as he was, Tom said, "I don't know if I'm ready to do this right now. I'd rather wait until you're not on that strong pot." He couldn't believe he was stopping this. Her breasts were against his chest.

"Come on, Achilles—pot makes sex wonderful," she murmured.

"But would we have sex if you weren't high?" he asked. They'd walked for weeks, and she'd just started to show him who she was. He needed to make sure she desired him the way he desired her. He wanted what they had to be real, without the influence of drugs.

She pulled back suddenly, and a fierce look of anger came over her face. She seemed about to make a retort, but then her look of defiance left as quickly as it had arrived. She lowered her head and let her forehead fall against his chest.

Tom was quiet, continuing to hold her. He had been so careful with her; he didn't want to do something they would regret. But the warmth of her body excited him.

"Show me your shrine," he said, dropping his arms from their embrace. Jeanine lifted her head, her eyes half-closed. He again felt protective of her, as he had the time before when she had become anxious. She took him over to the corner, and they sat down on the floor in front of the shrine.

"Let's light the candles," he said. Jeanine found matches and lit them, moving to lean against him. They sat still, watching the candles burn. Tom liked that she'd created a sacred space in her home, even though that meant not always letting others in.

"Your apartment is beautiful," he said. "Just like you."

"Really?" Her eyes found his. "You turned me down."

"Yes, really," he said. "Let's do something together without pot."

She looked at him with disappointment, but then she again turned her attention to the candle flames. She rested her head against him, and her breathing seemed to slow and deepen after a while. "You're tired," he said. "I'm going to leave so that you can sleep." He brought his head down and leaned in, slowly kissing her cheek, close to her mouth. Her face was soft and warm, and an electricity shot through him. She gazed at him silently.

He helped her climb into bed, pulling a blanket over her, then walked to his apartment still thinking of the warmth of her cheek against his lips. How might she feel about him in the morning without the effects of the Kauai pot? He knew he could have had an incredible night with her, but he didn't question his decision. If either of them had regrets the next day after sex, wondering if the pot interfered with their true desires, that could ruin what they'd started.

He tried to sleep, but he tossed and turned all night, thinking of her down the hall.

When he picked Jeanine up at Coco's the next evening, she stood waiting for him just outside the entrance with a sheepish look on her face. "You've worked at not pushing me," she said. "But then I end up being the pushy one."

"Trust me," he said, smiling to ease her worry. "I wanted to be with you, and it took everything I had not to." He was relieved she'd talked first about it, knowing that avoiding it could cause a strain in their relationship. Her eyes became wet. "I wondered," he said, "would you like to go out with me on Saturday night—on a date?"

She reached out and took his arm, almost shyly. "I'd like that, Achilles," she said. "It's a date."

Before walking home, they strolled along the beach, the setting sun giving the sky an orange glow. Tom breathed deeply the ocean air. Who knew his life circumstances would bring him to Kauai? The troubles of his past seemed so far away—this was a paradise where a girl like Jeanine wanted to be with him.

Jeanine had said his Achilles rupture was his fate. He had joined Kevin in escaping a destructive society and going to Taylor Camp to create a new culture, but that culture had its own politics, dysfunction, and drugs—possibly as destructive as the society they had escaped. Had his fate now led him to Lihue, to right here at this moment with Jeanine?

———

Tom took Jeanine to the nicest seafood restaurant in Lihue, and the hostess seated them at a table among palm trees in an open courtyard. Jeanine wore a flowery sundress and seemed to be in a calm, relaxed state. They looked out on the ocean and felt a warm breeze as the sun went down.

Tom had been curious about Jeanine's shrine. He asked her if she was a practicing Buddhist. "I'm not," she said. "But I took some Eastern religion courses at Berkeley, and I tried meditating in yoga classes. I set up the shrine for meditation when I'm feeling confused or depressed, especially after what had happened with Leroy."

The server brought them mahi-mahi and ahi, and Tom said he too was drawn to Eastern religions, but he really didn't know a lot about them. "I used to feel a lot of peace from repeating Hail Marys after confession," he said. "I've been wondering if I could experience that with Eastern religions." Jeanine told him what she knew about the Buddha's noble truths. Tom loved having this conversation with her.

After dinner, they walked home slowly, his arm around her shoulders, and hers around his waist. They were quiet as they climbed the stairs in their apartment building, and stopped on the second floor, smiling at each other.

"Would you like to come to my place?" she asked, laughing and appearing embarrassed at the formality of her question, especially after only nights ago, she'd pulled Tom there in a drugged state.

"Yes, thank you," he said with a smile, and they walked arm in arm to her studio.

Inside, she lit the candles in her shrine and dimmed the light over her table. They moved slowly, as if trying to savor their passion. She pulled an Indian print bedspread down to the bottom of the bed, and Tom, almost unable to contain himself, gently undressed her, and then she undressed him. They moved together to lie down on the bed and began to slowly caress each other. Tom marveled at the sensation of her bare skin. They looked at one another and brought their mouths together for a long, deep kiss. He'd waited for this moment and felt lost as she moved her lips to his cheeks, his eyes, and back to his mouth. They kissed each other's bodies, taking turns, and finally joined together, hugging each other tighter and tighter, feeling that they couldn't get any closer. Tom pressed so close that he felt he was inside her skin, forming one body as everything released, feeling a physical and spiritual ecstasy he had never experienced before.

They slept that night on Jeanine's single bed, intertwined tightly so they would fit. They woke up early in the gray morning light and made love again, then stayed in bed for hours, talking and kissing and touching each other. When they eventually got hungry, Jeanine, naked, made some scrambled eggs and toast, and they ate, still undressed, at her small table, after which they went back to bed. Tom felt drawn by her magnetism whenever she moved close to him, instantly aroused and desiring her. They made love throughout the day, and in the evening, they showered together, dressed, and walked over to Tiki's for dinner.

———

Tom continued to pick up Jeanine at Coco's and walk her home every evening she worked. They ate together, and he often stayed overnight at her apartment. This pattern continued for weeks—they were either working or together, making love frequently. When Jeanine worked days, they often went to the beach after work. On weekends, Jeanine took Tom on tours of the island.

Tom had never been so deeply in love. He felt no need for any other companionship. He also felt no drive to define his purpose as he always had in the past—that had been put on hold. He lived day to day with the love of his life. He enjoyed seeing Barry, and occasionally invited him to join them at Tiki's, but he stayed more nights at Jeanine's than at his apartment. He now felt no desire to attend Scotty's parties.

Jeanine was also happy to spend her social time alone with Tom, with one exception: she wanted to continue singing at Scotty's parties. Whenever they arrived at a party, Lucas seemed overjoyed to see her, and she would go with him to the bedroom to smoke the Kauai pot. She would then return and sing a Grace Slick song or some other song that she and Scotty had selected. And always, she was met with cheering, a standing ovation, and looks of admiration or jealousy from the partygoers.

Each time, Tom joined everyone in clapping—she was magnetic when she performed—but he knew also that the Jeanine everyone enjoyed would soon lose her euphoria, and he alone would see what that was like. His goal was to get her upstairs to her studio before she became anxious or lethargic. As time passed, it became a tiring duty that he dreaded. He hated to see her like that and came to not only lack the desire to attend Scotty's parties but also to dislike them.

29

Tom and Jeanine hiked the Kalalau Trail two miles through the Na Pali Coast mountains to Hanakapi'ai Beach. They frequently stopped to take in the beautiful views of the ocean and mountains as they ascended and descended steep sections of the trail, which often crossed streams flowing down the mountain valleys. Standing on the beach, Tom was tempted to dive through the waves to cool off after their strenuous hike, but Jeanine pointed to the danger signs warning of strong currents and the count of swimmers who had drowned there.

"I know a better place," she said, and led him upstream for another mile or more on the challenging trail to the Hanakapi'ai Falls and its pools. Tom had never seen such a spectacular waterfall, which Jeanine said dropped about 300 feet from the top of the cliff. People were swimming in the clear pools beneath, and Tom and Jeanine joined them. Afterward, they spread their towels on a grassy area to eat the lunches Jeanine had packed.

"I could stay in Hawaii forever," Jeanine said, gazing up at the surrounding cliffs covered with moss. Tom moved closer to hear her over the sound of the waterfall, brushing his lips on her shoulder. He didn't know if he could imagine Jeanine in another setting, and this suddenly caused his stomach to tighten. He thought of his life on the mainland.

"It's beautiful. But I keep wondering what's next," Tom said.

"How can you look at this waterfall and worry about what's next?" She laughed, poking Tom with her chopsticks.

"I just know I don't want to be a carpenter forever."

"What did you want when you came to Kauai?"

"Kevin and I wanted to be part of a new culture—to help create something better than the rest of society offers. Didn't you? Isn't that why you lived at Taylor Camp?"

Jeanine opened her pack to get a carton of fresh pineapple that she had cut into chunks. The look on her face turned more serious. "Leroy wanted that. I followed him."

"From what I can tell, Taylor Camp must not have met his needs, either."

She looked at him, appearing to want to end the conversation. "It met his needs for communal sex."

"What about you?" he asked quickly, trying to redirect the focus. "Don't you feel a need to work toward something?"

"I like what I learned about Lao Tzu from my college days. He says that the way to do is to be, and that letting your life flow keeps it on course."

"I don't know," Tom said. He doubted he could be the kind of person who just let his life flow. How would he arrive at his true purpose in life if he didn't have goals in mind? With football, it was always so clear. "I wish life was like sports. You commit, work hard, and try to win. In football, I had a purpose and goals."

Jeanine smiled and took a bite of pineapple. "I don't think Lao Tzu would say life should be like football—he wouldn't believe that life should focus on a result. He would say you need to find who you are and let life flow through you."

"Are you able to do that?"

Her face became still. Some nearby swimmers splashed one another. "My life is chaos," she said, watching them. "I rarely sense that it's flowing, but I want to get to what Lao Tzu is talking about."

"So, what does this mean for you and me?" Tom asked.

Her smile came back, and she caught his eye. "We'll see. Let's finish this pineapple before we figure out all of life."

After lunch, they packed their things and got ready to go. Jeanine walked to the pool and rinsed her hands, and Tom followed her. When she stood up and saw him, she put her arms around his neck and kissed him. Tom felt her pull; he loved her. But he also felt pulled toward an unknown future, one that might not be in Hawaii.

———

The beginning of the Kalalau Trail was close to Taylor Camp. Tom had suggested they stop to visit Kevin before or after their hike to the Hanakapi'ai Beach, but Jeanine had no interest. He left a message for Kevin, telling him he would stop by the following weekend. It had been almost six months since they last saw each other.

Tom pulled into Taylor Camp in his rusty Datsun and Kevin came to greet him. Kevin wore only shorts. His hair and beard were longer than Tom had ever seen, and he was incredibly tan. Tom was ready to shake hands, but Kevin immediately embraced him, and Tom returned the hug. They sat down at a small table near a treehouse.

"So, is this working out the way you wanted?" Tom asked, looking at his friend. Kevin's face had deep creases in it, and he looked tired.

"It's far out. I'm in a spiritual place."

Kevin was staring at him—he looked more intense than Tom had ever seen him. "Are your shroom trips helping you feel spiritual?"

"Yeah, I take a trip every week. I've seen myself, how I was on a destructive path. I'm correcting that now." He didn't seem like the old Kevin Tom had known in college.

"Sounds like it's what you wanted."

"Ramona says we can be a model for the world."

Tom nodded, his eyes briefly scanning the camp for Ramona. He would not want to follow her model.

"What about you?" Kevin asked. "How is Lihue?"

"I'm working as a carpenter and spending a lot of time with Jeanine."

"Jeanine! That's great. People here still talk about her." Kevin shifted his eyes toward the beach, staring at it for several seconds.

Kevin's outgoing personality had seemingly disappeared, especially when he left the conversation. He recovered quickly, though, when Ramona approached from the dining hall.

"Kevin, remember it's your turn to help prepare lunch today," Ramona said, arriving at the table. She wore a head scarf, a long, flowy skirt, and a very wrinkled T-shirt. Her looming presence made Tom think she had gained weight. Was she pregnant?

Kevin looked up at her, nodding twice. "Guess what? Tom and Jeanine are together."

Ramona turned to face Tom then, her eyes narrowing as she looked down on him. "I hope you both found what you're looking for." She walked away before Tom could reply.

Tom and Kevin talked for a while longer. Tom spoke of their Kent State memories—football, antiwar demonstrations, and the student shootings. Kevin seemed to have difficulty shifting from one topic to another, often stopping to look at the ocean. "Those things all happened in my previous lives," he said at one point.

When Tom stood up to walk to his car, Kevin walked with him and hugged him goodbye. But Kevin's distance, his trance-like spells, stayed with Tom on his drive home. He felt more than ever that he'd lost Kevin—the energetic and passionate friend who had meant so much to him, the friend who had persuaded him to come to Hawaii.

Before Tom got to his car, William appeared. They smiled and gave each other high fives. Tom sensed that William was taking care of Kevin, which he was grateful for. As Tom pulled away, he wondered what life would be like for Kevin in the future.

———

Tom did not have contact with his family for weeks after arriving in Hawaii. He had recalled several times the awkward goodbye in their driveway, with his mother and sister crying and his father barely looking at him. When he thought of communicating with them, particularly letting his mother know he was okay, he knew she would ask for his address. He wasn't about to tell her he was living in a commune with no address.

However, when he moved in with Barry at the end of August and started working as a carpenter, he sent a short letter to his family, saying that he was fine and giving them Barry's address and phone number. Not long afterward, he received a long letter from his mother, beginning with how worried they had been. She said they would call but the long-distance cost was exorbitant. Instead, she reported on family activities, much of it on Kara's preparation for the upcoming field hockey season. Tom closed his eyes when he finished the letter. He missed his family, despite its craziness.

When he returned from visiting Kevin at Taylor Camp, he decided to write a short note to his family saying he would call them on Christmas Day. He told them it would be his Christmas present—he had saved money to pay the cost.

Tom called on Christmas morning, and his mother answered—it was the afternoon in Massillon. They had just finished their turkey dinner, and they wished he was there.

"I wish I was there, too," Tom said, and he meant it. He remembered the smell of his mother's turkey roasting in the oven, the satin-threaded Christmas ornaments on the tree, carols playing on their stereo, and the chair Grandpa used to sit in. His mother told him she would put his father on the line while she found Kara. There was a rustle, and then he heard his father breathing on the line.

"Is Ohio State going to win the Rose Bowl?" Tom asked to break the silence.

After about a five-second pause, his father answered, "They should be able to beat Stanford." His voice sounded lower over the phone.

Tom felt the burden was on him to keep the conversation going, so he asked about football at Kent State and Massillon. They exhausted all the football updates and then fell silent. Tom was relieved when he could hear his sister talking to someone.

"Remember to write your mother," his father blurted out before saying goodbye.

There was another rustle, then Kara said, "How's Christmas in Hawaii?" She sounded cheerful, breathless even.

"Not the same," Tom told her. He looked at a palm tree against the blue sky outside his window and smiled to know his sister was on the other end of the line. "How's Christmas in Massillon?"

"I have a surprise for you," she said.

"What's that?" Tom asked. There was silence.

"Hey, man!" It was Woz's voice. "Didn't know I'd be here, right?" Hearing his friend brought back a flood of memories about football and meals together at Kent State.

"Woz! Good to talk to you."

"So, are you enjoying Hawaii's beautiful beaches and women?" Woz said. Tom heard Kara hit him and whisper, "What?" She and Woz laughed.

"It's nice here," Tom said. "Definitely beautiful. But eventually, I need to figure out what I'm going to do."

"What about Kevin? How's he?"

"He lives on the North Shore in a place called Taylor Camp. He's sort of freaked out right now. It wasn't for me."

"I wouldn't think so," Woz said. "But Kevin . . . he never did anything halfway." Tom smiled, then heard Tony Bennett's Christmas album start to play in the background. "Merry Christmas, O'Brien," Woz said. "I hope we get to see you soon. Here's Kara."

There was silence again as Tom waited. He had enjoyed hearing his friend's voice and was glad Woz was there to liven up the family Christmas in his absence this year. He sensed stability in Woz's success and integration into the O'Brien family.

"I wish I could celebrate Christmas in Hawaii," Kara said, coming back on.

"Yeah, but I'm missing your winter snow. How was field hockey?"

"We finished second in the Big Ten, and I started every game as sweeper!" Kara said. "That's my girl!" Tom heard Woz say in the background. She giggled.

"Good for you!" Tom stopped talking as emotions overcame him. He was proud of his sister and wanted to be with her to experience her enthusiasm. Instead, he watched the fronds on the palm tree outside sway a little in the breeze.

"I want you to come and watch me play next fall. For my senior year," she said.

"You can count on it. I assume Woz—excuse me, Ron—will be there also?"

"Yeah, he has assignments in Columbus, so we see each other a lot. He's planning to transfer from Chicago to the Columbus office this spring."

"I'm happy for you, Kara."

She thanked him, and Tom could tell that she was beaming. He heard the Christmas music continue to play over the line and Woz talking to one of his parents. He pictured the snow-covered pinecone decorations his mother had probably set around the house and his father using the poker to turn a log in the fireplace.

Tom's mother came back on the phone and told him to look for a box of

Christmas cookies. She told him how much she loved him and reminded him to write.

Tom hung up and took a deep breath. He felt homesick, thousands of miles from his family. He had Jeanine, but not much else, other than beautiful scenery and weather. He went to get a drink of water and stared at himself in the bathroom mirror, wondering who he was and what he was doing. He saw a healthy young man, fit and tanned, but his eyes showed struggle and uncertainty. He knew the desire to help start a counterculture to replace the destructive American culture was no longer a priority for him. He could contribute as an individual with his behavior and choices, but he was unsure how to do that in his life in Hawaii.

Tom went downstairs to check the mail. The cookies had not yet arrived.

———

Tom could tell that his friends in Kauai were also affected by the holidays, some saying they had island fever. They all envied Barry, whose parents decided to celebrate their thirtieth wedding anniversary in Lihue during the holiday season.

Jeanine proposed welcoming Barry's parents with a Hawaiian-style meal at the picnic tables by their apartment building. Tom loved her idea and appreciated her caring for his good friend. They invited Scotty, Lucas, and some of Barry's friends who were waiters at the restaurant where he worked. Everyone brought a dish that was part of a traditional Hawaiian luau. They even had roasted pig from a friend who worked at luaus.

When Barry introduced his parents, Jeanine placed a lei of beautiful flowers around each of their necks, saying "Aloha," and everybody applauded. Tom wondered if the way everyone treated Barry's parents showed how much they missed their own parents and homes, even though many of them had escaped to Hawaii from family conflicts.

During the meal, Barry's father, who was a high school basketball coach, turned to Tom and said, "You started as offensive guard at Kent State?"

"Yeah," Tom said, swallowing a bite of macaroni salad. "We didn't have a great team, but our offensive line was pretty good."

"Mid-America Conference football is tough, just below the Big Ten. You must have been a dedicated athlete to achieve what you did."

Tom nodded and blinked, absorbing the words of praise. Something stirred in him. The words from Barry's father reminded him of his father and grandpa.

"Your parents must have been proud and enjoyed watching you like we enjoyed watching Barry play basketball."

Tom cleared his throat and began to unwrap his steamed laulau. "They were," he said, keeping his eyes on his paper plate, so Barry's father wouldn't see they'd become red. "My grandfather, too—he played football on Massillon's first undefeated team."

"You *and* your grandfather played at Massillon?"

"My father, too."

Barry's father put down his plastic fork. "That's the top high school football program in the country!" Tom smiled and then Barry leaned in with one of his friends to ask his father a question. Tom noticed that Jeanine, sitting next to Lucas, had been watching him.

Later, as Tom and Jeanine were leaving, Barry's father grabbed Tom's arm and again shook his hand. "You should be proud of what you accomplished," he said. Tom nodded, thanking him, and turned to join Jeanine.

As they entered the building, Jeanine looked at him closely. "What was Barry's father saying? You're emotional."

"He congratulated me on my football accomplishments." Tom felt his eyes watering.

Jeanine smiled at him and put her hand on his shoulder. "He validated all your years of hard work."

Tom thought again of his father and grandpa—he hadn't realized how much he missed their support and encouragement.

——

During the holiday season, the pace in Lihue and other Kauai destinations increased considerably. Tom's carpentry work remained the same, but the hotels, shops, and restaurants teemed with customers during the peak tourist season, causing Jeanine, Scotty, Barry, and Lucas to spend several weeks working overtime. Tom was left with more time alone on the weekends. He decided to use it to read a couple of Eastern religion books Jeanine had saved from her college days: *The Way of Life According to Lao Tzu* and *The Teachings of the Compassionate Buddha.*

The introduction to *The Way of Life* intrigued Tom, calling Walt Whitman and Henry Thoreau disciples of Lao Tzu, the Chinese poet who lived twenty-five centuries before them. Tom, sitting on a straw mat at the beach one morning, thumbed through the book and found the poem Jeanine had cited, which said, "There is no need to run outside . . . The way to do is to be."

Tom lay down on his stomach on the mat and looked out at the ocean, his chin on his forearm. Was traveling to Kauai "running outside," leaving the center of his being? For the next several hours, he thought about what he might do—what purpose he could pursue to find his center. He watched tourists arrive and set up on the beach. He rolled up his mat and walked along the edge of the water with his book. He found some boulders and sat down and leaned against them, his face turned to the sky. He didn't come up with answers, but he felt he could understand why Jeanine turned to these readings to help her when she felt lost.

In the coming days, Jeanine, tired from working long hours during the tourist season, didn't seem to have time or energy for reflection, and she wasn't available to talk with Tom about his own thoughts. She said she needed to use her time off to decompress, and he watched her increasingly do it with Scotty and Lucas, listening to music and laughing with them while getting high. She wanted Tom at her side, so he reluctantly went with her, but always quietly sat on Scotty's couch with his beer, wishing she would cut back on smoking Kauai pot. When she laughed, it sometimes didn't even sound like her.

30

The new year, 1971, brought changes to Scotty's parties. The mix of people attending included people who had recently moved into the apartment building—often college dropouts. The turnover was noticeable, with current tenants hearing new voices through the thin walls and smelling new cooking odors.

Tom found Scotty's parties even less enjoyable with the new people there, and Barry agreed. If Jeanine was working and couldn't attend a party, Tom instead went to eat at Tiki's with Barry. They liked to talk about growing up as all-state athletes. Tom learned that Barry had hoped to play basketball for a PAC-8 conference team like Tom had hoped to play football for a Big Ten university. Tom was also intrigued by Barry's plans to return to California for graduate school and ultimately find a professional job, reminding Tom of Jack and Woz. Barry told Tom that he saw living in Kauai as a fun break before settling into the reality of a career. Tom continued to contemplate his own path.

One evening Jeanine planned to go to a Scotty party, and Tom suggested they go eat with Barry—she said that sounded boring. She wanted the music and laughter. When they arrived at Scotty's, Jeanine embraced Lucas and laughed before following him to the bedroom. Tom thought she seemed as excited to see Lucas and smoke his dope as she was to sing a Grace Slick song. Given the distance he had been feeling, Tom wondered if their relationship was changing or if she was becoming dependent on Kauai pot, or maybe both.

In early March, one of Scotty's parties attracted more people than usual. Tom and Jeanine showed up a little after nine, and the party was in full swing. The room was smoky and crowded, with some people standing in line outside the bedroom where Lucas sold drugs. Tom moved through the crowd with Jeanine, spotting several new people who had recently moved into the apartment building.

Lucas, followed by a heavy-set guy with red hair and a small, wild-eyed girl, came out of the bedroom just as Tom and Jeanine arrived. Lucas was excited to see Jeanine and said he had heard from Scotty that she would sing "Somebody to Love" that night, one of his all-time favorites. Scotty's stereo was turned up loud, playing the *Let It Bleed* album.

Tom watched the red-haired guy talk loudly to Scotty while the girlfriend scanned the room anxiously, clinging to his arm. She seemed overwhelmed by the noise and activity, and Tom wondered if she was hallucinating from too much Kauai pot. He watched them start dancing to the Stones, but she slowly twirled, out of sync with the music.

Jeanine and Lucas came out of the bedroom, and Tom saw the familiar confident look on Jeanine's face. She yelled past everyone, "Achilles, let's dance!," took his hand, and pulled him to his feet. She danced in front of Tom, throwing her head from side to side, her hands on her hips or up in the air, but she didn't seem to be dancing *with* him.

They stopped dancing when the album ended, and Scotty placed the Jefferson Airplane album on the turntable, moving the needle to "Somebody to Love" and giving Jeanine a wink. Jeanine moved to the center of the room and sang along with Grace Slick, with people joining her on the chorus. Tom smiled, watching how absorbed Jeanine was in the song—she did have an amazing voice. She moved smoothly with the music's beat, comfortable with showing her emotions—aware of the audience, but in her own world.

When the song ended, everyone cheered and applauded. Jeanine had amped up the room, and Tom could see some of the new guys in the building watching her. The album continued to play as Jeanine started to make her way back to Tom. But along the way, the redheaded guy came close to Jeanine and said with his loud voice, "Let's dance!" Jeanine, flush from her performance, started dancing with him. Tom watched closely to make sure she was okay. The redhead's girlfriend stood alone, her mouth open, looking confused.

"Why are you dancing with her?" she suddenly screamed, putting her hands on her head. Her voice was shrill, causing others in the room to look at her, but her boyfriend ignored her, his eyes on Jeanine. The girlfriend ran at him and hit his back with her tiny fists. Jeanine's eyes widened, and she stepped back. The guy grabbed Jeanine's hand and said loudly, "Don't stop," while he pushed his girlfriend away with his other hand.

Tom had watched all this unfold with irritation, but something in him snapped when he saw the guy grab Jeanine's hand. He jumped up, his face red, and stepped between Jeanine and the guy.

"Get away from her!" he ordered. The guy, though shorter than Tom, turned and shoved Tom. Tom shoved him back, causing him to reel backward a few feet. Lucas yelled for them to stop, but while Tom was looking at Lucas, the guy recovered and tried to throw a punch. Tom drove the guy across the living room, leaning his weight into him like the all-state blocker that he was. He pushed him over an easy chair that caused the guy to flip and land on his back. Tom then straddled him and slapped him across the face twice.

The girlfriend screamed, "No! No!" and Tom looked up at her. He got off, and the redhead slowly sat up, a shocked expression on his face. Tom was prepared to knock him back down if necessary.

"Take her and get out!" Tom said. People backed up as the two left quickly.

Tom walked back to Jeanine. She stood with her arms crossed, upset, as he expected she would be. Still, he was surprised when he realized she was upset with him.

"What are you doing?" she yelled, glaring at him. "I was just dancing with the guy. Why did you get so violent?" She stared at him, appearing to be both furious and overwhelmed by what she had seen. The music continued to blare from the speakers.

Tom stayed silent, not wanting to argue in front of everyone. Jeanine stormed away from him, found Lucas, and went into the bedroom, slamming the door behind them. Tom looked around, noticing the stares and whispers. Feeling unappreciated, Tom left, observing on his way out that Scotty was dancing by himself in the corner, waving his arms with a huge smile and closed eyes.

Upstairs, lying in his bed that he had rarely slept in, Tom replayed what had happened over and over, feeling deeply wounded by Jeanine's anger. Hours passed, and she didn't come to find him. He heard Barry come home from work.

Tom only dozed briefly during the night. When he was staring at the ceiling from his bed in the morning light, there was a soft knock on the apartment door. He got out of bed, still in the same clothes from the night before, and opened the door. It was Jeanine. Her face was washed out, and she was wearing the thin shirt she used for pajamas. She looked at him with a combination of fear and anxiety. Tom was on guard, not wanting to get hurt again.

"I'm sorry," she said.

He looked at her silently, his hand still on the doorknob.

"It was the pot," she said. "I felt invincible and wanted to dance."

"I didn't think you would do it with that guy grabbing you and his girlfriend screaming."

She sighed. "It just added to the excitement."

He heard a door open down the hall but didn't look. They both stood silently while the footsteps made their way down the stairs. Tom feared that Jeanine might be addicted to Kauai pot. He knew marijuana was not physically addictive like heroin, but he had read there could be psychological addiction. He thought of his grandpa, a fun-loving and caring person, but an alcoholic. Was Jeanine like his grandpa?

"Do you think you can you live without pot?" he asked, looking at her.

"Of course—I just like to be high now and then." She avoided his eyes. He kept looking at her, unsure about what to say or do, still feeling hurt. She moved toward him, tilted her head up, and kissed his lips gently. Her lips lingered on his, and then she hugged him. He put his arms around her, feeling her against him, her breasts through her shirt. She pressed into him more, and he grew warm with desire. His breathing quickened.

Jeanine turned toward her apartment, preparing to leave, but she kept her arm around him and pulled him with her, her eyes locked on his. He shut his door, and they walked quickly together to Jeanine's studio, holding and caressing each other along the way. Once inside, they made love with a hunger Tom had never experienced, their bodies seeming to meld into one another.

Afterward, he felt healed—comforted—but as he gazed at Jeanine lying beside him, the dark circles beneath her eyes, the worry that was still on her face, he was afraid that her drug use would separate them.

———

A few days later, Tom met Barry for dinner at Tiki's on a night when Jeanine was working. "Lucas said you somersaulted a guy over Scotty's furniture," Barry said as Tom was sitting down.

Tom still couldn't believe he'd slapped the guy's face. "I went overboard—I should've just escorted him and his girlfriend out. She couldn't handle what-ever drugs she was on."

"I also heard from Lucas that Scotty freaked out."

"Yeah," Tom said, looking at Barry. "He was in ecstasy, dancing in his own world. What was that about?"

"Lucas has a supplier of cocaine—it's getting popular on the West Coast and in Honolulu. He told me Scotty's been trying it, mixing it with pot to get a more intense high,"

Tom sat back in his seat, thinking of the way Scotty had looked—dancing wildly, unaware of others, out of control. He worried that Lucas was introduc-ing some drugs at the parties he wouldn't want Jeanine to be around. "I heard at Taylor Camp that Lucas gets his drugs from The Company, the Hawaiian mob," Tom said.

"He might actually get his coke from somewhere else," Barry said. "He's not advertising it now, but he told me he expects a growing market in Hawaii beyond Honolulu, including Kauai."

Tom thought of Jeanine, disappearing into the bedroom with Lucas at Scotty's parties. "It's pretty dangerous, right?"

Barry nodded. "Yeah, people die from coke overdoses."

Tom felt a foreboding about Scotty's parties. They seemed to be getting more dangerous, with new people and riskier drugs—no longer just the casual gatherings of friends to relax and listen to music. Tom didn't want Jeanine to take drugs, but if she did, he hoped she would stick with pot and stay away from cocaine. The thought of it scared him.

———

Jeanine's hours at Coco's decreased in May, as the tourist season slowed, but Tom was still busy. He was now a journeyman carpenter, in demand by more than one construction company, and he began saving the money he earned, often thinking of Barry's plan to return to college.

"I think we should stop going to these parties," Tom said to Jeanine one evening when they were getting ready to leave for Scotty's.

"But I like seeing Lucas and the others, and listening to the music with you," she said. She was slipping into some platform sandals.

"I'll go if you stop singing."

"What? Why?" she asked, straightening up.

He paused. "I think it leads you to want more pot." Her lips became thin and she looked at him, seeming to struggle.

"I'll stop singing, if that is what it takes for you to come with me." She didn't look happy. But Tom quickly agreed and put his arm around her.

———

One Saturday night when Scotty's party was at its peak around eleven o'clock, three Native Hawaiians arrived whom Tom had not seen before. They loomed just inside the doorway, filling the space with their presence and their menacing stares. A couple of them kept their hands conspicuously inside the deep pockets of their cargo shorts. Scotty, who didn't seem as if he knew them either, approached to greet them, but looking cautious, he hung back several feet away. Several of the guests moved toward the far wall in the opposite corner.

"Where's Lamb Chops?" the biggest guy asked. He looked around the room, his eyes coming to rest on Tom, who matched him in size. He gave Tom an extra-long stare, and Tom felt a threat had been issued, perhaps signaling him not to move.

"You must mean Lucas," Scotty said with what Tom knew was a forced smile. "I'll get him." Scotty went quickly into the bedroom, and a moment later, Lucas followed him out. When Lucas saw the men, he froze where he was.

"Why are you here?" he asked. His eyes raced from one man to another.

The shortest man had his long hair tied in a ponytail. "We want to see if your customers are happy," he said. "What are you selling them?" Scotty motioned for Jeanine to turn down the music, his arm waving to get her attention.

"Your pot, as usual," Lucas said. Tom saw his Adam's apple bob up and down as he swallowed. "Also, as we agreed—small amounts of Kauai pot and mushrooms from local sources. We're fine, so there's no problem here."

"What about cocaine?" The big man and the third guy, still with their hands in their pockets, moved closer to Lucas, coming to stand on either side of him.

"No," Lucas said, his voice a little higher.

The big man grabbed Lucas's arm and bent it behind his back, causing Lucas to cry out. Jeanine and a couple of girls near the speakers gasped. Tom stood up and moved near Scotty, locking eyes with Jeanine and willing her not to move. However, any thought of rescuing Lucas disappeared when the third man took a pistol out of his pocket and pointed it at them. Everyone in the room became extremely still.

"Don't try to be a hero," the ponytail man said to Tom. "Or you'll end up dead. Your friend is lying."

The big man raised Lucas's arm, causing him to cry out again. "I only have a little cocaine," Lucas said, grimacing in pain.

"Where did you get it?"

"From a friend in Vegas."

"You know that we're your only source of drugs. We do you a favor by letting you sell some local products, and this is how you thank us?"

"This was just one time." The guy holding the gun turned his eyes from Tom to the man with the ponytail. Tom could tell that Lucas's answer was not satisfactory.

"You make us come from Honolulu to stop something that puts our Company at risk," the ponytail man said. "The Feds are on our case in Oahu. We'll decide when to expand cocaine to the other islands—not you."

"It won't happen again," Lucas said. He winced, turning his face toward the ceiling as the big man raised the angle of his arm.

"You're right about that." The ponytail man then nodded to the big man, who brought Lucas over to the coffee table. He took Lucas's arm from behind his back, stretching it out on the table between some cigarette butts. Holding Lucas's wrist down with his left hand, he took out a wire cutter from his pocket with his right.

Lucas squirmed to get away. "What are you doing?" he asked, his voice panicked.

"He said he'll never do it again!" Tom said. Scotty's head jerked to Tom, then back to Lucas. The man pointing the gun at them slowly shook his head at Tom, narrowing his eyes. Tom saw Jeanine's anguished look and heard her quietly say, "No, no."

The big man leaned in to put his weight on Lucas's hand and keep it steady. Then he opened the handles of the wire cutter and positioned Lucas's pinky finger between the blades. Lucas flailed, his feet flipping around helplessly behind him. He screamed as the man clamped down and closed the handles.

Blood spouted on the table and floor, and Lucas screamed and screamed as the man cut his pinky off. Several people turned their heads away or screamed also; one girl ran into the kitchen and vomited into the sink. The big man reached down into the pool of blood on the table, picked up the severed finger, and held it in front of Lucas's face.

"This is for my dog," he said. Lucas sobbed and groaned.

"Don't ever cross us again," the ponytail man said. "You'll lose more than your fingers next time."

The big man looked at Tom again, seeming to challenge him to act. But Tom remained silent, his mouth dry, his eyes narrowed. He was careful to remain motionless until the three men nodded to one another and left, leaving the door open behind them.

Everyone stayed quiet until the footsteps in the stairwell had receded, a few people with their hands over their mouths. Then Jeanine jumped up, tears streaming down her face, and went to hold Lucas, crouching on the ground next to him. Tom yelled to Scotty to get a towel to help stop the bleeding, and he went to grab Lucas's elbow to elevate it above Lucas's head. Jeanine had blood dripping down her arm, and she helped Tom pick Lucas up.

Tom and Scotty managed to get Lucas downstairs to Scotty's car, Lucas stumbling along as they lifted him between them. Jeanine kept shouting to Lucas that he would be okay in between her sobs. They sped to the emergency room, the car flying up onto the curb as Scotty turned the last corner.

While they waited for Lucas to be treated, Tom held Jeanine and stared at the dried blood on all three of them, including on his own hands.

———

After that, Scotty stopped throwing parties. Lucas continued selling drugs from The Company and his local sources, but he was more discreet and selective with his customers. Scotty started inviting smaller groups to stop by, usually no more than four or five people, who quietly enjoyed smoking pot while listening to music. Jeanine was always invited, and Tom went with her if she decided to go, given her agreement not to sing. However, he grew increasingly uncomfortable with any participation by Jeanine, even though she assured him she would only take a small toke of Kauai pot. While she was in the bedroom, he would wait for her on the couch, staring at the secondhand coffee table Scotty had picked up from a friend to replace the first one. A frayed rug on the ground covered the area where the bloodstains wouldn't come out.

When Jeanine wanted to stop by Scotty's on a night that Barry had invited Tom and Jeanine to join him and his friends for dinner at Tiki's, Tom was torn. He preferred being with Barry but didn't want to leave Jeanine alone with Lucas and his drugs.

"I promised Lucas I'd stop by," Jeanine said, after Tom tried to persuade her in her apartment to join Barry's dinner.

Lucas. It was always Lucas. Tom looked down, shaking his head. "Do you want to be with Lucas, or me?"

"I want to be with both of you," she said, sliding a bracelet up her arm.

"Well, I don't want to be with Lucas, I don't want to be with Scotty, and I don't want to be with their friends."

Jeanine twirled around to face Tom, her jaw clenched. "Then don't go with me. Go with Barry!"

Tom stood up, walked to the window, and looked down at the street. How long could this go on? Jeanine hadn't attempted to understand him or meet him halfway. Tom turned to look at her, and her angry dark eyes confirmed her position. His heart sank. He strode to the door, stepped rapidly down the stairs, and left for Tiki's.

After spending the evening with Barry and his friends at Tiki's, Tom returned to Jeanine's, but she was still out. He was tempted to go down to Scotty's, but instead, he went in and rested on her bed.

Jeanine came back an hour later. When she saw him, her face lit up with a big smile and supreme confidence—all signs Tom was familiar with. She lay down beside him, kissing him and starting to take off his clothes. He knew she loved to have sex when she was high, but he had no desire. He felt he was being used.

"I don't want to," he said, taking her hand off his shorts.

"But I'm ready for you," she told him, her lips on his neck.

"It's only because you're high."

She stopped kissing him, pulled away, and stared at him, glowering in anger. "Fuck you, then!" she said, turning her back to him and facing the wall.

Tom closed his eyes and compressed his lips, hating how she shut him out. He waited, hoping she would speak after a few moments, but he found himself just looking at her back. He finally decided to get up and go to his apartment. He didn't think Jeanine was asleep, but she didn't look at him or say anything when he left.

There was no knock on the apartment door the following morning—no attempts by Jeanine to see Tom. He knew she worked the evening shift that night, and he decided to pick her up to walk home if he hadn't heard from her during the day.

When Tom arrived at Coco's that evening, Jeanine turned to him with a blank look. She locked the shop's door, and they began the walk home. He realized he was going to have to start the conversation.

"Why did you get so angry last night?" he asked.

She stared straight ahead, continuing to walk. "You rejected me," she said.

"No. I just wish you wouldn't get high on pot."

"I don't want to be told what to do."

Tom turned to her. "I love you—I want to be with the *real* you."

She turned to look at him briefly, and he felt a slight thawing of her coldness. "Then I need you to help me stop smoking pot so much," she said. "If I go to Scotty's, I want you to go with me."

Tom's eyes widened to hear her actually ask for his help. "Okay," he said. "I'll go with you. But will you leave when I'm ready to leave?"

She paused. "Yeah."

As they made their way home, Tom debated whether to ask her to go into treatment for psychological addiction. But he kept his mouth shut, knowing how she hated being told what to do. He decided that they were making progress, and he didn't want to jeopardize it with more words.

31

Jeanine held to the pledge she had given Tom, only taking a small hit of pot at Scotty's parties and leaving early when Tom asked her to, much to Lucas's disappointment. Scotty looked older every time Tom saw him, his face gaunt and dark circles under his eyes.

Tom was happy Jeanine was holding to her pledge and felt they were becoming close again. He tried to talk to her one evening about their future, feeling that he'd put his life on hold in his time in Hawaii. He told her that he wanted to be with her, but he needed a direction, a purpose. He felt it was time to stop partying and grow up, time to take steps to define his future, like Barry was. But when he brought all this up with Jeanine, she laughed like she had when they'd hiked out to Hanakapi'ai Falls. "I don't understand why you can't just live in the present," she said. He smiled and said he didn't know why either, but this didn't take away his feelings of frustration. Afterward, lying in bed while Jeanine slept, he thought of Woz, Jack, and Becky and wondered what they were doing in their careers.

One day, Tom traveled to a new construction site in Kapa'a while Jeanine had a day off from work. Rain began to fall as he drove to the site. The crew worked most of the morning, but the rain increased shortly before noon, and the foreman dismissed everyone.

Tom drove back to Lihue and, not finding Jeanine in her apartment, went to his to shower, where he still kept his clothes. Before he showered, Barry arrived with bags of groceries—he said he had run into Jeanine downstairs as she entered Scotty's apartment.

Tom went downstairs to Scotty's after his shower to see if Jeanine was still there. He knocked on the door, but no one answered. Hearing music from an album by the Grateful Dead, he tried the door; finding it unlocked, he stepped inside. He saw Jeanine in the easy chair and Scotty and Lucas on the couch, their heads nodding to the music, looking at each other with big smiles and half-closed eyes. They all turned to stare at him, their looks of euphoria disturbed by his entrance. Jeanine moved her lips, trying to say something, but Tom couldn't understand her mumbling. Scotty gazed at Tom with wide eyes and a crazy grin, and Lucas's euphoria turned to panic. Tom guessed they were high on a mixture of cocaine and pot, based on what Lucas had described to Barry. He quickly went over to Jeanine.

"Hey," he said gently, leaning down and putting her arm around his neck. "It's time to go." He began to help bring her to her feet, but her body was slack. From the couch, Scotty waved his arm in protest, uttering a long, drawn-out "Noooo . . ." but didn't move, his body also slack. When Tom put his hands under Jeanine's shoulders to lift her, she struggled, and her eyes widened in fear, but she was too weak to resist. He brought his arm around her, lifted her, and then guided her out of the apartment, with Scotty and Lucas, still sitting, mumbling after them.

Upstairs, he lay her on the bed, and her eyes looked wildly at him and around the room. "Stop the demons!" she yelled. Tom guessed she was hallucinating—he felt her pulse and found it was beating rapidly. Worried about an overdose, he debated whether to call an ambulance. But her pulse slowed, and she dozed on and off as the effects of the drugs wore off. He stayed by her bedside for a couple of hours, monitoring her and staring at the rain outside. Eventually, her eyes flickered open. She looked around at the room.

"Why am I here?" she asked.

"I brought you here from Scotty's. You were drugged out, and I was worried."

As Jeanine became more alert, furrows appeared on her forehead, and the corners of her mouth turned down. "I told you to let me do what I want."

Tom stared at her in disbelief. "Do you want to kill yourself?" he said. "You mixed cocaine with pot, didn't you?"

"So what?"

"You told me you were only going to smoke a little pot at Scotty's, and you'd do it when I was with you. I can't trust you if you're going to do this."

"Then don't! It's my life!" She scowled, with a look Tom didn't recognize.

"Let's go to Tiki's. You need some food." He tried to brush her hair off her forehead.

"I don't need you to take care of me," she said, moving his hand off. She clenched her teeth.

"What do you want?"

"I want to be alone," she said, her eyes looking out the window. The sky and the room were gray.

Tom took several deep breaths. He was unnerved by what he'd seen and didn't know what to do. "Jeanine, we love each other."

"Leave me alone! I don't want to be with you!" She pulled her Indian print bedspread over her.

He kept looking at her, but she didn't meet his eyes. He got up, standing near her for several seconds, but she continued looking away. "Okay," he said finally. He walked out of her apartment and closed the door behind him.

———

Tom slept at his apartment that night. When he got up and prepared to go to work, all he could think about were Jeanine's words about not wanting to be with him. Tom hoped this was produced by her drugged state, and that she would think differently when the drugs wore off, but he didn't hear from her that morning. When he returned from work, he went to her apartment and found her door locked. He had a key, but he decided to knock first.

"What?" Jeanine said from behind the closed door.

"Can I come in?"

"No. Get away from me."

He stared at the chipped paint on the door, as he had the first time he'd come to her apartment. She hadn't let him in then either. "Jeanine, I want to talk."

"Get away!" she yelled.

He knew the walls were thin and imagined people listening. Feeling anxious, he turned and walked back to his apartment. She worked the evening shift that night, and he decided he would pick her up at ten o'clock, although he was apprehensive about what she would do when she saw him. When he arrived, she glared at him.

"Don't you get it? I don't want to see you," she said.

"What the hell?" he asked. "Are you serious? Are you ending things between us?"

She narrowed her eyes. "I told you to stay away from me." She stopped locking the shop door and stood inside, waiting for him to leave.

Tom turned, walked in the opposite direction she'd be walking home, and sat down in the resort bar. He leaned his forearms on the counter, feeling numb. The bartender asked what he wanted, and Tom stared at the bottles on the shelves behind the counter. He ordered an Irish whiskey. When it came, he looked down and held his head in his hands.

——

Tom's world fell apart without Jeanine. He didn't realize how much he'd depended on her for his happiness. He kept hearing her words, "Get away!"— feeling he'd been pierced with knives. The eight hours of work he had every day helped take his mind off of his misery, but he felt lost, merely going through the motions. He went to the beach when he came home, ignoring the young girls who flirted with him, and tried not to look down the hallway toward Jeanine's studio. After drinking beer, he'd go to bed early, usually drifting in and out of sleep for hours. The weekends were worse, especially if Barry was working.

When Barry was free, the two of them would often eat at Tiki's or go to the beach together. Barry had been accepted for graduate school at UCLA and would be leaving Labor Day weekend. They talked a lot about Barry's plans, Tom's breakup with Jeanine, and their experiences of living in Hawaii, including the drug scene around them. Tom was grateful to have Barry, a good friend, to lean on in his heartache.

"Kauai *is* beautiful," Barry said one night when Tom was drowning his sorrows with whiskey at Tiki's. "People come here to escape. They have big expectations—I know I did—but I've seen too many just end up drifting, hooked on drugs."

Tom thought of the scenic beaches and falls around the island. He'd never been to a more breathtaking place, especially Hanalei Bay with Jeanine. But he agreed with Barry—the beauty of the island was no longer enough.

"You should visit me in LA," Barry said, drinking the last of his beer. "Or if you're done with the Hawaii thing, we could rent a place."

"Maybe," Tom said. Barry's invitation intrigued him. He realized he'd been so in love with Jeanine that he stopped thinking about leaving Kauai, other than his failed attempts to talk about their future. A fresh wave of sadness hit him, and he ordered another whiskey.

When Barry said he was ready to leave, Tom told him to wait until he finished his whiskey, and then he ordered another one. As his drunkenness increased, Tom stopped talking. He looked straight ahead, gritting his teeth, with both hands holding his glass and saying only, "I can't believe she's left me."

"C'mon, man," Barry said, eventually convincing Tom that it was time to go home. Barry reminded Tom of Jack or Woz, friends who knew him well and took care of him in subtle ways. Tom stumbled toward the door, and as he stepped outside, he looked across the street at the bar for the locals. It was a hot evening with high humidity, and Tom could feel sweat dampening his shirt.

"I'm sick of not being able to walk in front of that fucking bar," Tom said loudly. He started to walk across the street, zigzagging in his drunkenness.

Barry quickly grabbed his arm and swiveled him around. "Not a good idea. They don't like us, remember?—let's go home."

Tom wrenched his arm away and walked toward the bar. Just then, two locals came out, music blasting behind them before the door closed again.

"What you do, haoles?" one of them asked, jerking his chin at Tom and Barry. "You think you can walk by our bar?"

"You're damn right," Tom said. He swooned a little to the left.

"I don't think so." Two more men came outside, frowning when they saw Tom and Barry.

"We're leaving," Barry said, retaking Tom's arm. "My friend drank too much."

Tom's eyes squinted, and his mouth hung open as he stared at the men. "I'll go when I'm ready."

"Why don't we show him he's ready now?" one of the guys said to the others. They laughed. Then all four moved closer to Tom and Barry with clenched fists.

The door to the bar opened again, this time harder, and the guys turned to see who else was joining them. A Native Islander who probably weighed at least 300 pounds ambled toward the four men, his eyes narrowed.

"This Samoan bouncer won't leave us alone," the local said to the others. "We're already outside!" he said to the bouncer.

The bouncer noticed Tom and slowed his gait. "I know about you, Mr. Football."

Tom looked at him, taken aback by his size. "Did you . . . play football?"

"Yeah," he said, his face a little less stern. "But my cousin was the best. All-American at Michigan State."

Tom's head was spinning at the collision of two worlds. "Who?" he asked.

"Bob Apisa."

Tom broke into a wide smile, his attention turning from the four locals. Barry's eyes went back and forth between Tom, the Samoan, and the locals. "I remember him," Tom said loudly. "A fullback. He helped Michigan State win the national championship."

Barry, seeing an opening, grabbed Tom's arm again. "We're just leaving," he said.

The bouncer nodded. "Good, because these guys will kill you if they have a chance. Go back to your haole hotel, and don't come close to this bar again, got it?" The four locals glared at Tom, throwing out profanities and spitting at his feet.

Tom kept smiling drunkenly. He felt a kinship with the Samoan and resisted Barry's pulling on his arm. "Good luck to you!" Tom said to the Samoan, who stood there with his arms crossed. Tom finally turned to leave with Barry. "Did you hear that? Michigan State!"

The following day, when Tom stumbled out of his room around noon, Barry told him how close he'd been to getting beaten, maybe even killed. Tom didn't care; he needed aspirin. When he was a little more clear-headed in the evening, he wished that he'd fought the locals. He wasn't afraid of getting hit. He would have liked the excuse to turn his grief into rage.

———

Tom received a letter from Kara in mid-August with the Ohio State field hockey schedule enclosed. She wasn't going to let him forget his promise to watch her play in her senior year. She suggested he come to watch the team play its archrival, Michigan, in early October.

Kara's letter and Barry's invitation to join him in LA accelerated Tom's thinking about the future, even though he was still deeply depressed about the loss of Jeanine. He missed everything about her—her dark eyes, laugh, beautiful body, athleticism, and intimacy. But if he and Jeanine were done with their relationship—he had not seen her or heard from her—there was no reason for him to stay in Kauai. He was tired of his treatment as a haole, sick of the drug scene in his apartment building, and ready to do something besides carpentry.

Yet, he suffered without Jeanine. He drank every night to help him get to the next day of work, where he hammered nails and sawed boards like a robot. He had experienced feelings of aloneness and abandonment before, but they were nothing compared to his loss of Jeanine. He felt that he was at the bottom of a deep hole of darkness, overcome, with no way to get out.

32

The restaurant where Barry worked invited Tom to a going-away happy hour for Barry a few days before Labor Day weekend. Barry told Tom that he'd asked them to invite Scotty, Lucas, and Jeanine. "Maybe this will give you a chance to talk to her," he said. Tom's heart stopped. He hoped so. He couldn't believe he still hadn't seen her since that night three weeks ago, not even running into her around the building. He couldn't accept that their relationship was over. He wanted her to consider getting back together. If she agreed, he would return to Kauai after seeing Kara play field hockey and forget about going to LA to live with Barry. He wanted her to know that she was everything to him.

But Jeanine didn't show up at Barry's party. Tom watched the door for over an hour, his stomach dropping every time the door opened to admit someone new. When he realized she wasn't coming, he drank whiskey and stared out the restaurant window facing the ocean. He saw Lucas standing at the bar by Scotty and went to him. Lucas looked at him warily, probably knowing why Tom had approached him.

"I need to talk to Jeanine," Tom said.

"I don't think she wants to talk to you." Lucas, appearing uncomfortable, took a drink from his bottle of beer, and Tom stared at the nub of his pinky.

"I'm thinking of going back to the mainland," Tom said. "And I'd really like to see her before I go." He felt his throat get tight and cleared it.

Lucas took in this news. "I still don't think she would want to see you."

"Do you see her? How's she doing?"

"I see her," Lucas said. "I'd say she's depressed."

Tom took a deep breath. He felt his shoulders droop. "I have to see her. She trusts you, Lucas. Can you arrange a time when we can meet?"

Lucas paused, a slight frown beneath his Fu Manchu mustache. "Only if you promise not to tell her what she should do. She won't forgive me if you do that."

"I promise."

Lucas nodded and left. Tom sipped his whiskey, and Scotty approached him.

"You're dying, aren't you? This breakup with Jeanine is killing you," he said.

"Yeah, that's how I feel."

"You need to understand. Jeanine is drawn to the dark side—that's why she and Lucas are so tight," Scotty said. "I know it well myself—it's self-destructive."

Tom stared at Scotty's Adam's apple, taking in his words. He felt he had experienced the dark side himself, whether due to football injuries, the strife with his father, the breakups with Cindi and Becky, the loss of Grandpa, or the disappointment of Taylor Camp. Tom knew Jeanine had her issues with her past, painful circumstances leading to her emotional dependence on pot. He was confident that their love for each other could help them both avoid self-destruction. But Jeanine didn't want help from him.

Tom's eyes began to sting—he didn't want to continue the conversation with Scotty. He quickly said goodbye and left, only realizing later that he hadn't talked to Barry all night.

———

Tom took Barry to the Lihue airport on Saturday of Labor Day weekend. He tried to shake off his feeling of melancholy and drummed his fingers to the music on the radio, though he wasn't matching the beat. He thought of how close he and Barry had become, and how he would miss him.

"I hate leaving you all alone in your misery," Barry said at the curb.

"I'll get by," Tom said, forcing a smile while helping Barry unload his suitcases.

"I'm serious about living together in LA," Barry said. "I have some college friends there, but I won't know anyone in graduate school." He held his plane ticket in his hand, and the corners flapped a little in the breeze.

"I might take you up on it," Tom said. He still held onto hope of convincing Jeanine to get back together. She was a West Coast girl—perhaps she would be open to coming to LA to be with him. Maybe a change of scenery would be good for them.

Barry stuck out his hand. "Do it. I'm serious," he said, clasping Tom's hand. "I'll look for a two-bedroom apartment and call you."

Tom watched his friend enter the terminal and the doors close behind him. He envied Barry being able to move on to the next part of his life, his next steps known and planned.

On the way home, Tom grew uneasy thinking about his own next steps. Whether Jeanine was with him or not, he felt directionless when he considered the possibility of leaving Kauai. His thoughts about what to do next raised questions from the past. He remembered when he and Kevin had arrived with dreams of creating a new culture. That experience did not provide answers to his questions: What was his purpose and path? How could he help build a better society? And now a new question: Would it be with Jeanine?

———

Tom waited for over a week before Lucas got back to him about seeing Jeanine. It had been agonizing. With Barry gone, he was lonely in his daily routine of working, going to the beach, drinking beer, and eating in front of his TV. He had thought about looking for a roommate, but he preferred to be alone, and his carpentry wages were enough for him to rent the apartment by himself.

Tom held back his urge to ask Lucas if he'd talked with Jeanine, not wanting to push things too hard or seem too desperate. Finally, Lucas stopped by one night and told him he could pick Jeanine up at Coco's in two days. He said he'd promised her Tom wouldn't tell her what she should do with her life. Tom's heart leaped.

The next two days took forever. Tom paced around his apartment in the evenings. He stopped drinking beer and did push-ups and sit-ups to feel more fit. He studied himself in the bathroom mirror, imagining how to show his love for Jeanine through an expression of patience and care.

When Tom arrived at Coco's at ten o'clock, Jeanine looked cautious and uncertain. Her eyes had circles under them—he wondered if they were from lack of sleep or crying, or both. Tom, his palms sweaty, suggested they find a place to sit and talk. She started to shake her head, but he told her it wouldn't take long. They walked to the outdoor balcony near the resort bar and sat down at a table across from each other. It was a slow night in the middle of the week, and Tom was grateful that only a few other people were there. He ordered a beer when the waitress came, and Jeanine chose sparkling water, though she made no move to drink it when it arrived.

"Thanks for seeing me," Tom said, searching her face.

Jeanine looked at him silently.

"I'm thinking of leaving the island," he said. She didn't react. "But not if there is a chance of us getting back together."

"I can't be with anyone right now." She looked out toward the beach.

"I can wait. I'll wait forever."

"No," she said, her face still turned toward the darkness of the ocean. "You should get on with your life."

Tom felt like he'd been struck by another blow. "But I want you in my life." He swallowed, his eyes watering. He tried to control his facial expression, but it was no use.

"I need to fix myself," she said. "I can't believe I mixed cocaine with pot—it made me realize how messed up I am."

"I want to help you."

She looked at him now with her dark eyes, the eyes he had wanted to dive into the first time he saw her. They were filling with tears. "I know you want to help, but you can't—I need to do this alone."

He started to reach across the table to take her hand in his, but she pulled back from him abruptly. "Tom, you need to listen to me once and for all. We can't be close. I need you to stay out of it."

Tom felt the finality of her words and closed his eyes. He wanted to break down but went ahead and said what he had planned. "I think I'm going to live with Barry in LA." His voice shook. "When you're better, I'd like to come back to be with you, or have you come to LA."

"I can't promise anything. I just can't."

A tear ran down his cheek and he quickly wiped it away. He looked down at the table, blinking repeatedly to prevent other tears from forming.

"I'm so sorry I'm hurting you," she said.

"You're not hurting me," he said with a lump in his throat. "You're the best thing that ever happened to me."

"I need to go," she said.

He looked at her silently through his tears.

She stood up, looked at him for a long moment, kissed him on the cheek, and left without turning around.

Tom held up his hand to the bartender, his eyes blurry. When the server came, he ordered a whiskey and sat for an hour listening to the ocean waves break in the darkness. He wanted to walk into the waves and never come out.

He returned to his apartment and felt Jeanine's presence as he looked down the hallway at her door, but he couldn't go there anymore. He barely slept that night, feeling physically and emotionally devastated. His heart ached, and he wouldn't have been surprised to have had a heart attack; he felt so weak. When he got up in the morning to shower, he let the warm water run onto his body for over thirty minutes, moving his head under the pulsating spray.

The following day, he bought plane tickets for a flight from Lihue to Cleveland, and a flight five days later to Los Angeles. When Barry called, Tom confirmed he was coming to live with him, telling him he would arrive in October after visiting his family in Ohio. Barry was glad to hear this news. He didn't ask about Jeanine.

Tom didn't try to see Jeanine again. After working another week, he quit his job, sold his car to a used car lot, and began packing things he would take to Massillon and LA. A moroseness came over him. He kept himself busy, carrying out the steps necessary for his departure. He was tempted to drink steadily and sleep around the clock, but his old sense of discipline allowed him to focus on the tasks he needed to finish.

———

A couple of nights before his flight to Cleveland, Tom woke to the loud sound of a siren coming from the parking lot. He looked out the window and saw the flashing lights of an ambulance and a police car. Was it Jeanine? He threw on some clothes and ran downstairs. In the downstairs hallway, Scotty and Lucas's apartment door was open, and a police officer and two paramedics were inside. With his heart in his throat, he asked what was going on and tried to enter to see if Jeanine was there, but the officer barked gruffly for him to stand back. Tom backed into the hallway, his eyes wide with fear. Other residents had gathered outside their apartment doors or were standing in clusters in the hallway.

One of the paramedics was leaning over someone. The officer yelled at Tom to move out of the way. He went outside, his hands shaking, and stood by the front walk, where he knew the paramedics would come out. He had goosebumps on his arms and felt he might vomit.

After several minutes, the paramedics came out the door, carrying a stretcher with a person on it. A sheet covered the head and body. Panic overcame Tom, and he moved in step with the stretcher from a distance, staring at the sheet in the moonlight. Other residents of the building stood in small groups, some by the picnic table where Tom had first met Jeanine.

The paramedics slid the stretcher into the ambulance. From several feet away, Tom heard the medic say on the radio, "We have an overdose."

"Who is it?" Tom interrupted. His voice cracked. "Who is it?" He then turned to see the police officer bring Lucas out with his wrists handcuffed behind his back. Lucas was sobbing.

"What happened?" Tom yelled to Lucas, running over. The police officer held up his hand, commanding Tom to stay back or face arrest.

"Scotty's dead!" Lucas blurted. Tom felt cold inside, but at the same time, a wave of relief washed over him. Wild-eyed, he looked around for Jeanine.

The police officer led Lucas to his car, and Tom heard him say, "We've been watching you." More people emerged from the apartment building, and then Tom spotted Jeanine coming down the steps with a frantic look on her face. She was barefoot and wearing her thin pajama shirt. When she saw Lucas, she ran to him, but the police officer forcefully pushed her away, threatening to arrest her, too. Tom called her, and she came quickly to him.

"What's happening?" she asked, her voice shrill, her face stricken. "Tell me!"

Tom didn't know what to say, other than to just give her the facts. "Scotty's dead from an overdose, and Lucas has been arrested."

"No! No!" Jeanine screamed, her face crumpling. She fell into Tom's arms, and he held her tightly as she wailed, which made him cry.

Tom looked at Lucas in the back seat of the police car, but Lucas looked straight ahead. The police officer appeared to be taking a few statements from residents. After a few minutes, Jeanine's sobs began to subside. She seemed to regain control, and let him hold her, but she appeared numb, her eyes closed, her body motionless, in shock. The policeman walked over to the ambulance and talked with the driver. "I thought the Feds had contained coke in Honolulu, and we only had to worry about pot," he said, shaking his head. "This is going to spread to all the islands."

After the ambulance and police car left, their lights flashing, the residents started to go back inside. Tom took Jeanine back up to her apartment—she moved slowly up the stairs with her head down. He felt her shudder. Then, standing at her door, he tried once more.

"Jeanine, this place is insane. Come with me." He couldn't stand the thought of leaving her in such a dangerous place. But his plea again went nowhere.

"I can't," she said, her eyes closed. "I need to be alone." He looked at her and asked her one more time, but she was silent, keeping her eyes closed. He walked toward his apartment and heard her door close behind him.

Later that night, as he lay on his mattress, he kept thinking of how it could have been Jeanine on the stretcher. He wanted to get her out of this place, to show her things could be different, to help her see a future with him. But he knew, as he lay there staring at his ceiling, that she didn't want him, and that he didn't have a clear view of the future.

He turned onto his side and saw that it was 3:48 AM. He closed his eyes against the glow of the alarm clock, thinking back to the first time Kevin had mentioned Hawaii after the shootings. He replayed events from his time on Kauai over and over again—wondering how he'd gotten to this place and what he should have done differently. He thought of Kevin, one of his best friends—now addicted to psilocybin trips and just a shell of the vibrant leader he used to be. He pictured Jeanine going into the bedroom to get high with Lucas every time she went to Scotty's parties. He remembered Lucas being forced to his knees and having his pinky cut off, his screams piercing the air. He recalled the moment he found Jeanine incoherent and almost unconscious, high on pot and cocaine with Scotty and Lucas. He saw again the stretcher being pushed past him, the sheet pulled up over Scotty's body. He knew he couldn't have prevented these things from happening, but the fact that they had made him feel helpless. He urgently needed to get away from this life. He longed for normalcy—safety, predictability, no dependence on drugs or alcohol, and steady relationships. He missed his family in Ohio and hoped to rediscover these things when he went home, and he hoped to start a more normal life in LA.

When he got up, he trimmed his hair and shaved. He took a walk on the beach, feeling the ocean breeze on his neck. He sat down with his back against a boulder and spent the rest of the morning looking out at the water, knowing that across that great expanse, somewhere to the northeast, was Los Angeles.

As his plane took off, he looked out the window, marveling at the contrast between the dark green foliage and the surrounding blue ocean. He knew he was leaving a piece of himself on Kauai. Would he ever be the same?

33

Tom felt uncomfortably cold in his sweatshirt and wished he had put on his jacket before sitting down in the driver's seat. Early October in Ohio was colder than he remembered. His father, in the passenger seat beside him, appeared unbothered and turned the vents up. Tom's mother, in the back seat, wearing a scarlet and gray scarf, had been chatting happily for most of the drive to Columbus. She was pleased to have Tom home and to be taking this trip together to Kara's game, where their family would be reunited. She passed a thermos of coffee to Tom's father and then touched Tom's hair for a quick moment.

"I can't get over how nice it is to see your face and ears again," she said. Though this statement about his hair annoyed him, he looked at his mother in the rearview mirror and offered her a smile. He knew he'd worried his family, and in spite of their bothersome comments, he was relieved to have this time to be home with them before his move to LA.

He didn't blame his parents for their comments—they meant well. They couldn't possibly know or understand what he'd experienced. He guessed from their concerned expressions and quick glances to each other over the past few days that they could tell he was sad, although he hadn't mentioned Jeanine. They appeared to be treading carefully, perhaps to avoid prying too much or doing anything that might create distance again.

When Tom had arrived at his Massillon home, he'd immediately absorbed the familiar settings—the small well-maintained yard, the mailbox he'd installed, Grandpa's chair in the family room, his bedroom with posters of football players still on the walls. He loved the smells of home cooking from the kitchen—his mother had served him brownies shortly after he'd entered the house. He felt he had returned to stability. That night, after closing the door to his bedroom, he'd collapsed onto the bed with his shoes still on and slept for hours.

Once he was rested, he felt serene in this stable home setting. He let his mother pamper him—feeding him his favorite meals and taking care of his laundry. His father made attempts to talk to him, starting, as usual, with sports. Although he calmly listened, Tom heard everything from a distance. Without Jeanine, he felt as if he were underwater. He moved slowly and felt weightless. He wanted to rise to the surface to take a breath, to see Jeanine or at least talk about her. But he hadn't spoken a word about her to his parents, and he didn't plan to. There was no way to express the emptiness he felt without her.

Entering the vicinity of the Ohio State campus, Tom spotted the stadium, the huge horseshoe-shaped structure he'd always loved. He continued to gaze at it as they got closer. He felt excited, as if about to be reacquainted with a long-lost friend. When he pulled their car into a parking spot and they all got out, he took a quick moment to collect himself. This was a world he knew and remembered.

"O-H-I-O! O-H-I-O!" some fans yelled as they crossed the parking lot.

Tom and his parents met Woz at the stadium gate. "You're so tan!" Woz said, giving him a firm handshake, but then pulling him into a hug. "And your hair! So clean-cut!" Tom watched Woz hug Tom's mother and shake hands with Tom's father. His father seemed relaxed and happy to see Woz, like he always was with Jack.

Woz led them to their seats, and they sat down in the bright afternoon sun. Woz pointed to where Kara was warming up in her scarlet and gray uniform; she found them immediately, waving with a big smile and mouthing Tom's name.

The game against Michigan was close, but the Buckeyes won 3–2. Kara made several plays that kept Michigan from taking shots on the Buckeye goal. Woz stood up and cheered whenever she made a good play, then would turn excitedly to Tom and Kara's parents to explain what she'd done and how it was critical for her team's defense.

"Big win today!" Tom said to Kara when they picked her up to go to dinner. She gave him a long, warm hug, and he grew emotional. He cleared his throat.

"Yeah, it's always great to beat the Wolverines," she said, studying him for a moment. Her eyes went to Woz, then back to Tom. Could she detect the sadness he was trying to conceal? "They'll be gunning for us in the tournament," she said, and smiled. There was a competitiveness and maturity in her that Tom hadn't seen before; his little sister was now an experienced senior and a team leader. Woz and his father looked at her with admiration and he imagined they felt the same—men like himself who had devoted significant parts of their lives to sports.

Their dinner conversation was lively, with Kara teasing her father, pulling him out of his serious shell. She sat next to Tom, and he felt she was helping bridge the gap between him and his father. She put her arm reassuringly around him at one point, giving him a quick squeeze. Tom's mother was all smiles, and Woz was just like a member of the family.

After dropping their parents off at their hotel, Woz suggested that Tom join Kara and him for a drink at a campus bar. They sat down in a booth, and Tom noticed college students laughing next to them. They seemed so young, so naïve and inexperienced. They had no idea what they would face after leaving the protected world of college life.

"So . . . you enjoyed Hawaii?" Kara asked, once again studying Tom's face.

Tom didn't know how to answer that question, not even for himself; there was no way to represent what he had experienced in words. He struggled with what to say, then finally landed on "Kauai is a beautiful island." Kara and Woz exchanged a glance.

"How's Kevin?" Woz asked.

"I think Kevin is a bit lost," Tom said. His hands were around his beer, but he did not feel like drinking it. He was a bit lost, too. "Kevin got into too many drugs." As Tom said it, he felt a sharp pang in his heart, and the images of Jeanine strung out in Scotty's apartment and then of Scotty's body on the stretcher were in his mind.

"You guys were going to change the world," Woz said.

Tom looked at him. He didn't sense any criticism or mockery from Woz, so he said, "Kevin lives in an alternative world, one I decided I don't want to be a part of."

"For what it's worth, I think you made the right decision," Woz said. Kara nodded.

Tom didn't feel he had made any kind of decision, other than escaping danger and insanity, but he didn't know how to talk to Woz and Kara about that. To avoid answering, he took a sip of his beer.

"Mom said you've decided to live in Los Angeles," Kara said. "I know she wants you to come back to the Midwest."

"I know, but I like warm weather and living near the ocean," Tom replied. He didn't say he also hoped that the love of his life would join him there.

"What will you do?" Woz asked.

So many questions. "I'll be in good company with my friend Barry," Tom said. "You'd like him. He played basketball for UC Santa Barbara. And I think I'll start with a carpentry job—it pays well and has kept me afloat all these years."

Tom wanted to shift the focus of the conversation away from his life. "What's up with you guys?" he asked, taking another sip of beer.

Kara and Woz looked at each other and grinned. "I think Kara might marry me after she graduates." Woz reached out to take Kara's hand.

Tom erupted in laughter. "You think? What about it, Kara?"

Kara looked at Woz mischievously. "If he behaves, that might be true. But we haven't set a date." Still grinning, she slid closer to Woz.

Tom kept asking them questions about Kara's graduation, Woz's job, and their plans for marriage and the future, and he felt happy for his sister and good friend. He was also glad to deflect any attention from himself. But after Woz and Tom dropped Kara off at her dorm, Woz turned to Tom in the darkness of his car.

"Kara thinks you were in love over there," he said.

The heaviness returned to Tom. "I was," he said, looking outside at the shadows on the sidewalk. "I am." It was quiet.

"That's a bummer," Woz said, turning his head to look at Tom.

"I'm eager to get to LA—to start a new life."

"We wish you the best. We'll be thinking of you."

Tom looked at Woz and nodded, his lips pressed together. "Thanks," he said.

In his remaining days in Massillon, Tom tried to decompress from the intensity of Kauai. He slept a lot, sprawled on the couch, watched TV, and read magazines. The news articles about the withdrawal of US troops and increased attacks by the North Vietnamese Army made him glad he wasn't in Vietnam.

But overriding everything were his feelings of grief. He couldn't stop thinking of Jeanine. He imagined walking with her along the beach, lying with his arms around her in bed, kissing her softly on her lips. He wondered what she was doing and if she thought about him as much as he thought about her.

——

Barry picked Tom up at the Los Angeles airport, and they greeted each other with a handshake and big smiles. After almost a week of being with his family, who had never been to Hawaii and could not understand what he had experienced, Tom was overjoyed to see Barry, who knew exactly what Tom had left behind in Kauai. When they pulled up to Barry's apartment building and moved Tom's things into his bedroom, Tom felt at home in a well-constructed building with a large backyard lawn and patio. They celebrated that night at a local restaurant that reminded them of Tiki's.

Tom's first priorities in Los Angeles were to get a vehicle and find a job. He bought a used Ford Pinto with the money he had saved in Kauai. Since he had never failed with carpentry, he registered as a journeyman carpenter at the LA carpenters' union. He soon had multiple temporary opportunities that paid well. Because he had the immediate need to make a living, he put aside his goal of working toward a noble purpose that improved society. But he enjoyed no longer being treated as a lower-class haole, and he poured himself into work with dedication and discipline. By November, he landed a permanent job with Johnson and Sons Construction, a company that built high-end homes, apartments, and condominiums.

After a week on the job, Tom's supervisor, Gabe, a Johnson and Sons foreman, told him he was impressed with his carpentry skills. He also asked if Tom had played football given his size, and soon they were engaged in frequent conversations about their favorite football teams. After a couple of months, Gabe began asking Tom to help check blueprints and monitor project schedules. He was again impressed with Tom's skills and asked how he had learned the business side of carpentry. Tom told him he had studied construction management in college, which made Gabe raise his eyebrows and smile. One day, Gabe said that the boss wanted to see him the following day. "If you want to be considered for a promotion, you should wear something business-like," he said.

The boss, Wendell Johnson, was the older of two sons of the company's founder. The father was still president, but the foreman told Tom he was turning more responsibilities over to his sons while he increased his time leading funding campaigns for political candidates. Wendell mainly focused on managing projects, while his brother, Larry, concentrated on marketing and business development.

Wendell's office was large, but without any frills. He appeared to be in his mid- or late fifties, with a slight build and graying hair combed to the side. Wendell was looking at Tom's job application as he sat down in front of Wendell's desk.

"You're an experienced carpenter. You've proven that to us in addition to showing your previous carpentry work on your application," Wendell said. "Gabe tells me you studied construction management in college? You didn't include that in your application."

Tom felt large and out of place in the office chair. He was used to working outside, and the button-down shirt he wore was tight around his neck. He described his major at Kent State, saying that he didn't list it in his application because he was responding to an ad for carpenters. "I was two courses short of graduating," he said, "and then right around that time, the school shut down after the student shootings."

"So you don't have a degree?" Wendell asked.

"No, sir." Tom thought that this might bring their meeting to an early close, but Wendell seemed unbothered.

"I've heard good things about you from Gabe and others," Wendell said. "I could have our personnel director find local college courses that would meet Kent State requirements. Would you be willing to take the courses needed to get your degree?"

"Is that possible? I'd love the opportunity to do that." Tom was surprised. He hadn't expected to receive this kind of attention from a vice president. He'd simply assumed he would work his forty hours each week as a carpenter, and then ultimately pursue something more meaningful when he could.

Wendell grew quiet. "That Kent State thing must have been a mess," he said after a few moments. "Did you go to Hawaii to get away from it?"

"Yes, in part. School was closed, and my roommate wanted to see Hawaii." Tom hoped that would be the end of that question—he didn't want to talk about their desire to change the American culture.

"Gabe mentioned that you played two years of college football. Why did you stop?"

"I tore my Achilles tendon." Their conversation had gone to a more personal place, and Tom was nervous about letting his boss know about past struggles he'd faced. He didn't want to be seen as weak or incapable.

Wendell was silent for several seconds. "It's none of my business, but I think you've had some hard knocks and overcome quite a bit."

How was it that Wendell, someone he'd just met, seemed able to see Tom so clearly within the span of one short conversation? Tom nodded slightly. "I've tried to do my best. I feel lucky to have this job and try to learn things every day."

"When I was in my twenties during the war—around your age—I had dreams of glory and victory before I went off to fight," Wendell said. "But I quickly learned that war is no game, and there are no rules. Friends of mine were killed." He stopped and looked out the window. "Life can be brutal, and I think you've seen some of that already. But when I came back, I recovered by working for this company, using my skills every day and constantly learning like you are." Wendell stood up then and shook Tom's hand. "The personnel director will be in touch."

Tom felt a new sense of hope as he rode the elevator on his way out. For some reason, Wendell wanted to take a chance on him. He felt a connection with this man, who'd offered him guidance and kindness, something he hadn't had since playing football for Coach Peters at Kent State.

———

By January, Tom was enrolled at a local college in courses that Kent State had approved, and Wendell had surprised him by promoting him to foreman of a construction crew. It seemed that Wendell had taken Tom under his wing. Wendell's expectations and belief in him motivated him to work even harder. Between his courses and job, he had little time for anything else, which at least kept him from being depressed about Jeanine. He thought of her frequently, still hoping they would get back together. After getting his job, he'd written her a six-page letter to share the news and tell her about life in LA. But he never received a reply.

Tom completed his courses that spring and received his diploma in the mail from Kent State. Despite all his misgivings about construction management, he was proud to have earned a bachelor's degree. He knew his mother and father would be proud also, but he wasn't ready to tell them yet. He had made a quick trip to Ohio a couple of weeks earlier to watch Kara graduate and celebrate her engagement to Woz. He decided to surprise his family by showing them his diploma when he returned for the wedding in August.

Tom told Wendell that he had received his diploma, and Wendell took him out for a steak dinner to celebrate. Their drinks arrived, and Wendell made a toast, congratulating him on his achievement. He then leaned in and asked Tom some questions about his impressions of the company up to that point.

Tom found this curious and looked at Wendell, who nodded at him encouragingly. "This is the most professional place I've ever worked," Tom said. It was easy for him to say this after his experiences with Dan's crew in Ohio and the small Kauai companies.

Wendell smiled. "That's good to hear, because I want you to look for ways to make us even better. Next week, I'd like you to start testing an IBM package to see if it can improve our project management."

Tom worked extra hours to implement the IBM package and received praise when he presented it to project managers at Wendell's request. He had never felt so challenged by a job, and so recognized. Some of his fellow foremen predicted that Tom would be promoted to project manager soon. He was amazed at how his life had changed so rapidly—a year ago, he'd still been in Lihue, reluctantly attending Scotty's parties and occasionally getting spat on by locals at work.

Everything seemed to be moving fast. Tom's plans of defining his life's goals were being overtaken by daily events. He enjoyed his job and wanted to help the company. But he still felt he was searching for a larger purpose. He also was continually aware of the absence of Jeanine. He would have loved to have her with him on the new journey he seemed to be starting. He'd written her a second letter, this one a little shorter in case the first one seemed like too much. But again, she didn't write back.

———

When Tom arrived in Massillon for Kara and Woz's wedding, he felt his age more than he had in previous visits. He became aware that he was observing his family through a different lens on this trip home. He was twenty-four now, advancing in his career, and his parents were approaching fifty. Standing next to them in the kitchen one day, Tom sensed his parents saw him as an adult—he felt they treated him as an equal for the first time. He'd also come to feel more mature than Kara and Woz, having learned that life can be brutal, as Wendell had. The hard times he'd gone through had shaped him and given him perspective. However, he was still not over his heartbreak from losing Jeanine.

Kara and Woz arrived in Massillon to prepare for their wedding that weekend. As everyone gathered for dinner, Tom announced that he had a surprise. He took his diploma from Kent State out of his bag, which he'd had framed. His parents looked at each other, their eyes wide. His mother immediately embraced him, practically jumping up and down, while Woz said, "It's about time!" He shook Tom's hand. Kara said, "No way!" and came to hug Tom as well.

Tom's father held the diploma quietly in his hands. Everyone turned to look at him. He read, ". . . conferred upon Thomas Michael O'Brien the degree of Bachelor of Science in Construction Management . . ." He looked up and gazed at Tom. "Very impressive, Tom," he said. "And your job is going well?"

Tom nodded and tried to stand taller. "I'm a foreman," he said. "But my boss plans for me to become a project manager."

"Do you like it?" his father asked. "Are you happy there?"

"Yeah, I think so. I have a great boss."

His father's face softened. "I'm proud of you."

Tom's breath caught in his throat. His father's words took him back to memories of Pop Warner games when he was ten, with his father cheering for him on the sidelines. Tom had always enjoyed the approval of his father and the crowd rooting for him and his team. This made him want to perform better, play harder, and achieve more.

Later that night when he was helping Kara and Woz stuff wedding rice bags to throw after their reception, he learned that Kara had accepted a physical education position in the Columbus school system, and Woz was already looking for a house. Tom envied how their lives were coming together.

With so many months gone by, and no word from Jeanine, Tom began to let go of false hope. He needed to focus on his new life in LA, like Kara and Woz were in Columbus. Still, at the wedding, he wished Jeanine were there to see his sister and Woz start their life together. He wanted what they had.

PART IV:

1973-1979

34

om and his teammates paddled furiously, competing with other canoes in the five-hour race off the California coast. He sat in the center of the outrigger canoe, where his size and strength contributed most to the team's speed. Over and over, he dipped his paddle deeply into the water and pulled, straining his upper body to propel the canoe forward. His team finished the race in second place and then gathered with the others at the bar on the beach, celebrating their hard work with cold beers.

He had begun working out again after settling in as a project manager for Wendell. He was careful to avoid stress on his right foot—first by biking, then switching to a new sport that he grew to love: outrigger canoe racing, a team sport requiring strength, technique, and endurance like football. By the summer of 1973, his world evolved to consist primarily of two activities: work and canoe racing.

Tom viewed his life in a new way. He felt that it was difficult to predict or control what would happen. He often thought of his Hawaii experiences, seeing them as part of a chaotic time that couldn't last, in contrast to his stability in LA. Tom was now living a good life, where his income allowed him to have his own apartment after Barry got married, buy a new car, and participate in the canoe club's races and social activities.

He wondered at times if he was betraying his ideals—his goals to improve society, to develop alternatives to the destructiveness of corporate America. He was glad to be helping build housing, where families could settle and grow and become productive citizens. But he was not satisfied—he was still searching for a purpose, even though he didn't struggle with it as frequently as he had in the past.

One evening, Kara and Woz called him to share the news that Kara was pregnant. It sparked Tom's imagination. He pictured meeting his new baby niece or nephew for the first time, visiting him or her in the toddler years, maybe even cheering from the sidelines during sports events. He found himself paying more attention to parents with children. When he saw a father building a sandcastle on the beach with his two children after a canoe race, he stopped and watched. The kids giggled as they ran back and forth with small buckets of water. The father added a tower and together, they built a moat and carved some steps. It triggered thoughts that increasingly occupied Tom's mind—maybe it was time for him to settle down and start a family.

———

The canoe club held an awards ceremony dinner at the end of every season in the late fall, which Tom attended for the first time with his teammates. As he stood alone at the bar waiting for a drink during happy hour, he was approached by an attractive woman in a halter-style sundress. Her dress, tight and trim at her waist, revealed powerful and shapely hips and thighs, and she had tan broad shoulders and well-defined triceps.

She looked at him intently with blue eyes, her face framed by mid-length blond hair swept back, and introduced herself as Darlene.

"How long have you been with the club?" she asked, sipping from her glass of wine.

"This is my first season. How about you?" He was facing the bar, but Darlene was fully turned toward him.

"I've rowed a lot, but this is my first season with this club." She smiled, reaching to touch one of her diamond-studded earrings as she spoke. Tom couldn't help but notice her triceps again.

"I really like the club so far," he said. "I haven't been in shape like this since college."

A waiter rang a bell to indicate the end of happy hour. Darlene took his arm and walked toward the dinner tables, moving with confidence and ease. "Let's sit together," she said.

He was surprised at how direct she was but went along, giving his teammates at a table across the room a smile, and sat down next to her at another table.

"What made you so fit in college?" she asked, sliding her chair closer.

"I played football for Kent State."

She asked him if he was there during the shootings, then, as drinks and dinner were served, what position he played, where he came from, and how he ended up in California. He kept his answers brief and factual, skirting over details about Hawaii. Her hand brushed his when she reached for her salad fork.

"What about you?" he asked. "How long have you been rowing?"

"Since I was fourteen. I was on the UCLA rowing club in college."

"Impressive." He was curious to know if there was more to her than her athleticism and pretty face.

Then, she added, "I almost qualified for the 1968 Olympic team in single rowing, but I injured my back and had to stop rowing for six months until my disc healed."

Tom looked at her closely. "I know how that feels," he said. "My coach thought I would be drafted by the pros until I tore my Achilles tendon a second time."

She lowered her glass of wine and searched his eyes. "It was one of the worst times in my life. I don't know if I ever went through anything harder." She briefly described what those six months were like for her and the subsequent therapy and reconditioning. She wasn't emotional about it, but Tom nodded, feeling strangely drawn to her. He hadn't expected to find someone who understood so much of what he'd been through himself. Had he found a kindred soul?

Darlene didn't linger on the topic of shattered dreams, which Tom appreciated, but she leaned toward him after hearing how close he'd come to reaching the highest level of football achievement, seeming to feel the same bond he felt. They continued asking each other questions about their lives, laughing after a second glass of wine.

He learned that she was a year older than he was. After graduating from college, she had worked for a commercial real estate company and had recently taken courses to get a commercial real estate license. She had heard of Johnson and Sons and knew that her father had had dinner with Wendell's father on political funding campaigns.

They walked to their cars when dinner was over, reaching his first. "That was fun," Darlene said. She stepped closer, reached up with her hand, and pulled his head down to kiss him. Her lips were warm and pressed his with extra firmness at the end. "Let's get together this weekend," she said as she released him.

This was the first time he'd kissed anyone since Jeanine. It felt different but still excited him. "That would be great," Tom said. They exchanged numbers, and as he drove down Sepulveda Boulevard, he thought about their conversation, how she looked in her dress, her kiss. He had never dated a girl who seemed equal to him in athletic ability and desire. Even though he hadn't been interested in beginning a relationship with anyone, he realized he had no trouble following Darlene's lead.

They were soon spending every weekend together and often weeknights. They worked out together at the rowing club, but Darlene also liked to plan activities for them outside of rowing. They went on long bike rides up the mountains overlooking Los Angeles. They bodysurfed on beaches along the coast. Darlene wore short shorts that showed off her tan muscular thighs or bikinis that revealed her sculpted abdominal muscles, and Tom was aware that their athletic figures often drew looks from others.

Their enjoyment of physical activities carried over to the bedroom. They made love on their second date when Darlene invited Tom into her apartment, leading him to her bedroom, then pushing him back onto the bed and getting on top of him. Tom found her beautiful and returned her passion. As their physical intimacy increased over the next few months, Tom enjoyed Darlene's playfulness—she would surprise him by initiating sex at unexpected times and in unexpected places—under pine trees in a secluded area of a state park one afternoon, on the beach late at night.

As Tom grew closer to Darlene, he thought how different their relationship was from his relationship with Jeanine. His connection with Jeanine was romantic—a deep attraction, passionate, spiritual, but also irrational and uncertain. Darlene met his practical needs—companionship, stability, and working toward goals. Sex with Darlene didn't reach the mind and body connection he'd had with Jeanine, but his relationship with Jeanine had also wrecked him. He came to believe that romantic love was overrated.

He loved Darlene's beauty, playfulness, and self-assurance. So he agreed with her when, after about six months of going together, she brought up the topic of getting married and having a family. It made sense to him, and he didn't see why he shouldn't move on to that next stage. This is what people did in life, he reasoned, and he did really care about Darlene. They became engaged in August.

———

One fall evening, Tom groaned when they watched President Ford on the TV news.

"I can't believe he pardoned Nixon."

"Why?" Darlene said. "Nixon got us out of Vietnam."

Tom looked at Darlene, who was perched on the other end of the couch. "He killed a lot of American soldiers, and he broke the law with Watergate."

Darlene's eyebrows arched. "The Democrats started the war, and they were out to get him," she said, her voice rising.

Tom stopped, realizing that he and Darlene had never really discussed the war. He was troubled by what she said but was also wary of a fight. His passion for politics had lessened after his Kent State and Hawaii experiences. He now wanted to be able to engage people calmly and rationally. Rather than say anything, he smiled, moved over, and gave Darlene a kiss.

But Tom learned more about Darlene's political beliefs at a dinner later that fall with her parents and some of their friends. Her father, a wealthy dermatologist, finished his bite of quail and stressed the need for Republicans to continue their leadership of California after Governor Reagan stepped down in 1975. Darlene wholeheartedly agreed, adding that Reagan should run for president. Her father nodded and put his arm around her shoulders.

Tom took a drink of water, feeling a little warm. He knew Kevin would have been appalled to hear Darlene's beliefs, but Tom wanted to keep his opinions in check. He and Darlene had many things in common that could override their political differences.

"You and your dad seem close," he said on the way home. He sat in the passenger seat because Darlene had wanted to drive her car, saying it was a nicer car for the occasion.

She smiled and said, "My father was a great college tennis player—he's driven to win in sports, in politics, in everything." She signaled right and changed lanes. "That's how he raised me. I would never have succeeded in rowing without his constant support."

Tom liked that she felt this way about her dad. Still, as they pulled into the parking garage at her apartment, he wondered if any of their differences—political or otherwise—would ever become a problem.

——

Tom let their wedding planning unfold as Darlene desired. They made a whirlwind trip to Ohio to introduce Darlene to his family, spending a couple of days in Massillon, where Tom showed Darlene the neighborhood and schools, and especially football fields, that were part of his growing up. His mother was polite and respectful to Darlene, though he could tell she was not acting as she normally did. He wondered if she would have been like that with any fiancée he brought home. His father talked to Darlene about her rowing competition. As Darlene sat on their family room couch in a long elegant black dress, looking overdressed for Massillon, Tom wondered if her answers were maybe too boastful for Midwestern values, but his father was also respectful to her.

They then spent a night in Columbus to visit Woz and Kara, whose daughter, Isabella, had recently had her one-year birthday. Woz and Darlene seemed to hit it off by talking about her competitive rowing, not unlike Tom's father. But what Tom had thought would be the best relationship—Darlene and Kara, two successful female athletes—did not have a good beginning. They seemed to be competing with each other in conversations.

The highlight of the visit for Tom was his niece, Isabella. He loved to hold her and rock her to music. Darlene said she was envious, and Kara beamed. Woz said he hoped he would be an uncle soon. On the plane ride back to Los Angeles, Darlene assured Tom how much she enjoyed his family. Tom had his doubts, but he pushed them aside.

Tom also followed Darlene's lead in looking into houses for sale, especially in the top school districts, thinking of their future children. He was more ready than ever to become a father. Barry had recently become the father of a baby boy, Johnny, whom Tom enjoyed holding when he visited them at their small home in Pasadena.

Tom had wedding invitations sent to his aunts, uncles, and cousins, but he doubted if any would take the expensive flight from Ohio to California. He could tell from talking to his mother on the phone that she was nervous about participating in what looked to be a fancy wedding at a country club, especially with such a small group on the O'Brien side. Tom assured her everything would be fine, and she would enjoy seeing California. Tom also invited Jack and Lynette, who Tom had learned had gotten married when he was in Hawaii. Jack responded that he would attend, but that he and Lynette were separated.

Tom and Darlene were married on a sunny June day in 1975. Darlene, looking stunning in her backless wedding gown, gracefully greeted a large crowd of her relatives and family friends after the ceremony. Many of them commented on Tom's size or build. Tom, feeling restricted and uncomfortable in his double-breasted tuxedo, introduced Darlene to his friends, Wendell, and some of his coworkers. He was glad when the formalities were over, and he was free to spend time with Woz and Jack, whom he introduced to Barry. The four of them stood together, looking out over the grounds of the country club, each with a small plate of hors d'oeuvres.

Jack was the most direct about Tom's marriage. "She's a looker," he said, glancing over to where Darlene was chatting with her father and one of the LA City Council members Tom had met. "Hope you have better luck than I did."

Barry's wife approached with their son Johnny, and Tom offered to hold the baby while they went to get some wine.

"You're a natural," Woz said, smiling.

After Barry and his wife returned, Tom went to be with his mother and father, who were standing alone while Kara showed Isabella to the bridesmaids.

"It was a beautiful wedding," his mother said. She seemed dazed, perhaps from being out of her element. "Darlene looks so gorgeous and so . . . ." A group of Darlene's cousins started yelling and cheering by the bar, and his mother's voice trailed off. Tom sensed a questioning in his mother, maybe more with her distant look than her words. "I hope you'll both be very happy," she finally said.

"You'll probably buy a house next?" his father asked. He too looked uncomfortable in his suit. He held a plate with several uneaten appetizers, including a crab-stuffed mushroom with only one bite taken out of it.

"We're looking at starter homes in Glendale," Tom said. He knew they had no idea where Glendale was, but he wanted his plans to sound concrete. He hoped it would make them a little less worried.

"And you still love your job?" his mother asked, looking up at him.

"It's going well."

"It seems like everything is lining up for you now," his father said.

Tom couldn't tell what he detected in his father's voice. Was it doubt? Displeasure? He decided to take it at face value. "I think we're doing pretty well." He wished Grandpa were there.

After dinner, toasts, and clearing the tables, the band began to play, and Tom and Darlene performed the traditional wedding dances. When Tom went to say goodbye to his parents, who were taking Isabella back to the hotel, he overheard Kara say to his mother: "She sure is in charge." He waited another split second before appearing next to them, pretending he hadn't heard anything.

Darlene joined him in saying goodbye, then said, "Can you go find the wedding coordinator? It's almost time to do the cake." Darlene fed Tom a large piece of cake and frosting stuck to his lip. He wiped it off with his hand and then saw Kara looking at him from across the way.

The next day, Tom and Darlene flew to Banff National Park in Canada for their honeymoon. When Tom settled on the plane and looked out the window, he thought of his family's reactions to Darlene. Their looks and comments had bothered him, and he'd tried not to think about them at the hotel the night before their flight. But neither the visit to Ohio nor the wedding had gone as well as he'd wanted.

Tom concluded that his family needed to get to know Darlene better. Unlike his former girlfriends, Darlene brought him stability. This allowed him to focus on his job and canoeing while joining her in her desires for a home and a family. He appreciated that she wasn't afraid to take charge, and she continued to excite him. As soon as they got their tent up during an overnight hike in the Banff mountains, she turned to him with a playful look. She took his hand, led him into the tent, undressed him, and then crawled naked with him into their sleeping bag in the cool air.

———

With their combined income, Tom and Darlene soon had enough money saved to buy a small house in Glendale. It had a brick-lined walk leading up to the front door, two bedrooms and two bathrooms, and several apricot and citrus trees in the fenced backyard. Darlene stopped taking the pill the same day they moved into their new house. In the coming weeks, she made it clear she was already planning for them to get a larger home after they had a child and said she had the scoop on some new housing developments through her real estate connections.

"But this is going to require you to earn a higher income," she said one night when they were getting ready for bed. "If I stop working and stay home as a mother, we're going to need to make some adjustments in our spending." Darlene finished brushing her hair and studied herself in the mirror. "Although there's so much money in real estate right now—I think I could make more money than you if I got my license."

Tom, already in bed, looked at Darlene. "I thought you wanted to be a mother."

"Sure, but it's frustrating seeing you make peanuts while so many other people we know are getting rich." She walked over to the bed, wearing only a long T-shirt that once belonged to Tom. "But I know you'll think of a way." She pulled the T-shirt up over her head, smiled at Tom, and turned off the light. Tom did want to start a family and would find a way. That's what people did, he said to himself, as Darlene found him beneath the covers.

———

At Tom's next performance review, he let Wendell know that he and Darlene were trying to start a family and he was interested in seeing if he might be able to do more to get a raise. From the other side of the desk, Wendell smiled at him and said he thought Tom would make a fine father. Wendell agreed that income was a big deal for a growing family, and he suggested to Tom that he think about how to help grow the company.

"I've already been giving some thought to that," Tom said. He'd been considering alternatives ever since Darlene started telling him he needed to earn more money.

"What are your ideas?"

"I think there's a growing demand for multi-family units, especially condominiums, and we have an opportunity to position ourselves before developers prepare proposals."

Wendell's eyebrows went up, and he sat forward. He had Tom share his observations around this, and Tom cited some data he'd prepared just in case. After a few moments, Wendell said, "I'd like you to focus on that market,

Tom. If you're successful in going beyond our current condo construction level, I'll have no problem pushing for a promotion and a significant raise for you."

Tom began working longer hours on business development while continuing to manage his current projects. His approach was to use his knowledge, organization, and people skills to earn the respect and trust of developers, who came to value his ideas for condo construction on the properties they hoped to acquire. Johnson and Sons was awarded three new condo projects through Tom's efforts to have them included in developer proposals, and Wendell promoted him to senior project manager, a role that came with a significant raise. Darlene started looking for a bigger house and even bought a crib.

One night, Tom worked late to finish condo plans that a developer was including in its proposal due the next day. He arrived home after Darlene was already in bed and sat down on their couch in the darkened family room. Resting his head against the cushion, he wondered about his current success. He'd struggled for many years to figure out what he wanted to do and who he wanted to be. He realized that he had become confident of his skills, that he'd learned how to work and enjoy it. He had a balance he'd never experienced before, enjoying his job and looking forward to raising a family.

But he still had unanswered questions. How long would a rewarding job and a family last? It didn't last for Coach. And how satisfied was he with his purpose and goals now? He knew he was living a good life by society's conventional standards, but was he pursuing goals like his father had stressed? Or was he pursuing more money because Darlene pressured him? He worried that his company's profits sometimes got in the way of its goal of providing homes for families. Although he felt closer to having a clearer purpose than he had before, Tom couldn't shake the feeling that he was still missing the mark.

———

By Tom and Darlene's one-year wedding anniversary, Darlene had still not become pregnant. Their material success continued to grow—she'd gotten her commercial real estate license and shared in commissions; Tom won new projects for his company, and they were actively searching for a bigger house. But Tom could see that the longer they went without Darlene becoming pregnant, the more tension they experienced in their marriage.

Unprotected sex at first was a thrill for Tom, no longer having worries about impregnating a girl before he or she was prepared for it. It seemed to excite Darlene, too. For a while, she played a game of seducing Tom every other day, not telling him where or when it would happen. She often pulled him down to make love on the plush carpet in their living room.

When there were no results, they read about ways to track the calendar each month and make sure they had sex during Darlene's ovulation. When there were still no results, Tom noticed that they both began to seem less enthused about sex and got frustrated with each other more easily.

"What's going on? We're at our peaks, and we're having plenty of sex," Darlene said.

"I don't know. Your periods seem unpredictable."

"So, you're going to blame me? Maybe you're the one with the problem."

Tom winced. Darlene often became competitive in their disagreements before he even was aware there was anything to compete over. He suggested they see a doctor.

Two weeks later, they checked in for their appointment with a fertility doctor and sat down together in the sterile waiting room. Tom felt awkward, anticipating talking about their sex life with a doctor they had never met. Next to him, Darlene sighed impatiently. Finally, a nurse led them to the exam room where they met the doctor, an older man with silver hair, who beckoned them to sit down.

"Are you having frequent sex?" the doctor asked. He sat on a rolling chair and faced Darlene.

"We have no problem with that," Darlene said.

The doctor made notes on his clipboard. "Are you under stress? Do you have ideas about why you've not gotten pregnant?"

"My job can be stressful," Tom said, looking at Darlene. "But I don't feel it's affecting our sex life."

"My job can be just as stressful as his—maybe more." She seemed defiant. "I need to develop relationships as a new real estate broker."

This was news to Tom. He knew Darlene wanted to be a successful broker, but he thought that was secondary to wanting to be a mother. He looked at her questioningly.

"What?" she said loudly. "Do you think I don't have stress like you do?"

"I just wasn't aware being a broker was that important to you at this point."

There was silence as the doctor observed them. His forehead wrinkled, seeming to signal criticism, maybe about the conflict he had just watched, or maybe about Darlene's desire to be a broker when she should be focusing on motherhood.

"What about your periods?" the doctor asked.

Darlene was silent, and Tom jumped in. "They seem irregular," he said.

The doctor looked at Darlene. Darlene looked back at the doctor and then looked at Tom, possibly feeling these two men were ganging up on her.

"I've had unpredictable periods for years, maybe related to my rowing workouts."

"She almost went to the Olympics," Tom said, trying to offer Darlene a smile.

The doctor made additional notes on his clipboard, seeming to value this information. "Olympic athletes often engage in extreme exercise, which could impact ovulation and affect fertility. Do you still row competitively?'

"Yeah, but I don't work out as much." She crossed her arms.

"I suggest you stop competing and only do light workouts, and we'll see if that results in more regular periods. We'll also take a blood sample from you before you leave and see if that tells us anything," the doctor said. Tom was happy to hear this recommendation, even though he could tell Darlene was becoming irritated.

"What about Tom?" Darlene asked. "What if he has a low sperm count?"

The doctor stood up. "That could be possible, but I think your exercising might more likely be the reason for not conceiving."

Darlene clenched her jaw. "I want him tested!"

The doctor looked down at her, seeming to grow impatient. "Okay, I'll also order a semen analysis." He made additional notes.

Darlene nodded vigorously, looking at Tom.

When Darlene got out of the car in their garage after a silent ride home, she slammed the door shut and looked at Tom.

"This could be a problem with you as much as with me!"

"Yeah, but the doctor blamed extreme exercise." Tom stood there with the car keys.

"I didn't believe that a bit, the sexist old fart. He wasn't even going to test you!"

Tom narrowed his eyes and pressed his lips together. "Let's do what the doctor said and hope you'll get pregnant." He wanted to go inside and get away from her anger.

Darlene cut down on her workouts, but she still entered the rowing competitions she loved. Tom had always watched these races when he could; he enjoyed seeing her compete. Now he had mixed feelings, since the doctor had recommended she stop. But he felt he had said enough, especially after they learned that his sperm count was normal. They kept having sex during Darlene's ovulation, and he hoped for the best.

But Darlene missed some ovulation dates because of weekend campaigning for Ronald Reagan. When she missed more dates, saying she was tired after spending evening hours at work, Tom began to wonder whether her commitment to having a child was wavering.

35

Darlene earned her commercial real estate license and decided she wanted to leave her company for more lucrative opportunities. Her father put her in touch with some investors, and Tom encouraged her to go after what she wanted. She was hired by a small company whose CEO, David Phillips, had a track record of earning large commissions.

Tom hoped Darlene was successful in her new job, and that it would lessen the strain in their relationship. She now had work responsibilities like he had. Hopefully this more satisfying job would help them regain the intimacy they'd lost. He also had thoughts of proposing they adopt a child if she couldn't become pregnant; he still hoped they could become parents.

Darlene soon had her first success in helping a developer outbid its competitors for a valuable piece of property. Tom was amazed at the size of Darlene's share of the commission, more than a third of what he earned in a year. He took Darlene out to dinner to celebrate her success, but she was quiet on the drive to the restaurant and continued to be even after their drinks and appetizers arrived.

"I know we've had our frustrations," he said. "But this job seems like a new direction for you."

"Yeah, I like it," she said, while dipping a shrimp into cocktail sauce. She looked for the waiter to order another drink.

Tom hesitated, but then took the plunge. "I'm hoping you feeling good about your job will help us enjoy each other like we used to." His eyes searched hers.

"What do you mean? We're fine," she said, dipping another shrimp into the sauce.

Tom nodded, but he stopped talking. He followed her eyes to look at the people at the bar. She seemed nonchalant, not ready to intimately engage with him. He wondered if their jobs and their uncertainty about their future as parents had changed her views of their marriage. He missed when things were simpler with her. He missed her playfulness—it seemed like years since she had initiated spontaneous sex with him. They passed the rest of the evening by making small talk over dinner about the real estate market.

Despite appearing happy with her new job, Darlene remained distant. Tom grew tired of being the only one trying to improve their relationship. He still dreamed of raising a family and thought a child, even if adopted, could maybe bring them back together. But her distance made him feel awkward about bringing it up. He feared that she no longer wanted the same things he did, so what was he working so hard toward? What were he and Darlene building together?

Increasingly, their interactions seemed transactional. He made her coffee in the mornings before she headed out the door. She ordered them Chinese food for dinner. He took care of the bills. She dropped their clothes off at the laundromat. But he realized at some point that he could do all these same things with a roommate. Where was the additional closeness and intimacy that a marriage was supposed to bring?

Tom was surprised one morning to see Darlene's open purse on the kitchen counter. She'd come home late the night before and immediately fallen asleep after crawling into bed next to him. Even with his back to her, he could smell that she'd been drinking. She was still sleeping soundly when he got up in the morning to make coffee.

Her purse was next to the coffeemaker instead of stored as usual in the closet. The corner of an envelope was sticking out of it. She must have dropped it there in her drunkenness. He opened the purse to see more. "My Darlene" was scrawled on the outside of the envelope. Something grew still inside him.

He put the bag of coffee beans on the counter. Mockingbirds called from the trees in the backyard, but it was quiet from the bedroom. Frowning, he took the envelope out of the purse and opened it to find a card with a large dark-red heart on it, surrounded by embellishments in gold foil. Inside the card were the handwritten words "I love you! D." in the same scrawl as on the outside. The only name starting with "D" that Tom could think of was David Phillips, Darlene's boss. He racked his mind for other Ds and other possible explanations—a friend or relative?—but he had none.

Tom stared at the floor, feeling as if he'd been struck. He had believed Darlene's excuses for coming home late: the fundraisers, the business meetings, the drinks with clients. Were those false?—a cover for when she was really with Phillips? How could he have been so blind? He carefully put the card and envelope back into the purse, closing it with the zipper.

What should he do? He made the coffee as usual, but in his anger, accidentally slammed his thumb in the utensil drawer. He could confront Darlene with the card when she got up, but he couldn't be absolutely sure that the "D" was Phillips, and he didn't want to admit he had been prying in her purse. He heard her alarm clock go off and decided to look for more evidence of an affair before confronting her. He took his open mug and left quickly for work. He didn't want to see her, and as he pulled out of their driveway, he thought bitterly that she probably would prefer not to see him either.

He worked that day and the next in a daze. A draftsman asked him if everything was okay when Tom pressed the wrong button for their floor in the elevator and then cursed.

Two mornings later, Darlene told him as they left for work that she would be attending a client meeting dinner that evening. She had on a crimson-colored dress Tom hadn't seen before, and he suspected she was lying. He got into his car at the same time she got into hers, and as he started the engine, he watched her pull down the driver-side visor in her car and use the mirror on it to apply lipstick.

Tom worked hard that day to complete his parts of a project bid ahead of time, and he sped through two meetings. He left work early to drive to Darlene's office building and confirmed that both Darlene's and Phillips's cars were in the parking lot. He parked on the street at a distance where he could still see their cars but they weren't likely to see him. Phillips and Darlene came out of the building at about five o'clock and got into Phillips's car, a black Mercedes. Tom's breath caught in his throat.

He followed them as they drove away, feeling outside of himself, as if he were an actor in a movie and he would either lose the suspects or they would see him. But neither happened, and ten minutes later, with his heart beating erratically, he watched them pull into a motel parking lot. Tom again parked on the street a distance away. Phillips left the motel office and opened Darlene's car door. He put his arm around her as they walked to a room, and Tom felt like he was slowly sinking. When they entered the room, Tom's stomach dropped. He pulled away from the curb, narrowly missing a passing Ford Granada, whose driver honked his horn loudly.

Tom felt humiliated. How many times had Darlene deceived him? And what was he going to do about it? As he sped down the freeway, his eyes stung, and a pit opened in his stomach, one born more of pain than anger. Catching a glance of himself in the rearview mirror, he thought he looked like someone else—maybe again an actor, only this time, one who had caught his wife in an affair. He didn't understand how his life was unfolding like this. And he didn't see how their marriage could be saved.

Darlene came home around ten that evening, her hair unruly in the back. Tom was waiting for her on the couch, anxious about the conversation they were about to have. She appeared about to brush past him, but he told her they needed to talk and gestured for her to sit in the chair across from where he was sitting.

"Can't this wait until the morning?" she asked impatiently. "I've had a long day, and I'm ready to go to bed."

Tom took a deep breath. "No, we have a problem." At this proximity, he could see that her lipstick was smeared.

She slowly sat down across from him, looking at him defiantly. "You mean our 'frustrations'?" He thought of the dinner to celebrate her commission and his attempt to address their relationship. She was mocking him. Her red dress was wrinkled, as if it had been wadded up or left in a heap.

Tom stared at her through narrowed eyes, his heart thumping in his chest. "You didn't go to a client dinner tonight."

Her eyes flickered for just half a second. "I certainly did, downtown at the Hilton."

"No. You went to a motel with Phillips."

A shocked look came over her face. She seemed to be searching for ways to deny it. "You followed me?" she asked, rising to her feet.

Tom felt his face get hot as his anger rose. "Yeah!" he shouted. "I saw Phillips put his arm around you and take you into a room."

Darlene crossed her arms angrily. "How dare you," she said. Then, she sputtered, "I would never have done it if you'd been a better husband."

"What are you talking about? I've been good to you, and look what I get in return?" He looked at her furiously. Was she really blaming her infidelity on him?

"You're so nicey-nice," she said, waving her arm at him derisively. "But there's nothing underneath your smile."

This stung. Was she questioning his love for her? He'd tried to make her happy, following her lead from the very start. He'd pursued advancements in his career for her and their future family. How could she say he'd been anything less than a devoted husband?

"It must be different with Phillips," he said. "He must be a perfect man for you."

She stared at him. "It is different. We've talked about me getting a divorce." She let her hands drop to her sides.

Tom's eyes widened. Although he'd had little hope for their marriage in recent months, he hadn't imagined she would go this far so fast. "You're telling me you're ready to end our marriage? Before we even make it to our second anniversary?"

Darlene sat back down in the chair. She looked pale. "I never felt you fully loved me after we got married," she said in a serious tone. She hesitated, looking at the floor. "You took care of me, and we had fun, but I think you've always viewed me as just a means to your ends, a way for you to have the kind of wife and family you wanted."

A wave of pain came over him. Despite Darlene's betrayal, they had tried to build a home and family together. "You wanted it, too!" he said, stumbling on his words.

"Yeah, but you haven't been there for me like you think you have. You just like the idea of me." She pulled a pillow in front of her chest. "I wanted to be loved by a man who wanted to be with me, not by someone who only cares about work and canoe racing and a perfect family. I've hardly ever felt the love that I wanted from you."

Tom choked back his tears and shook his head, wounded by her attacks. "I guess Phillips will solve all your problems then." His anger grew as he glared at her.

"Don't try to make *me* feel guilty! You're the one who broke this marriage!" She stood up, threw the pillow on the floor, and abruptly walked to the guest bedroom, slamming the door behind her. The pictures they'd hung on the wall rattled.

Tom stared at the guest bedroom door, unable to believe how the scene had played out. In all the ways he'd imagined the conversation going, not one of the scenarios involved Darlene blaming him for the root of their troubles.

He went to the kitchen to get a glass of water and stood in the kitchen doorway, not knowing what to do. He looked around their living room, at the photos from their wedding on the mantle and the artwork that he and Darlene had chosen. His life had just come apart—it had happened so suddenly. His mind was buzzing, and his thoughts were scattered—he kept replaying her words over and over. He decided to go to bed, even though he wasn't tired. Feeling heavy, he slowly undressed and got under the covers. He lay still while the pain grew in his chest, the heartache of not being loved. He never fully fell asleep that night. He just dozed on and off, thinking about how he'd been rejected once again.

An hour or so before his alarm was set to ring, Tom heard Darlene in the bathroom. She came into the dark bedroom, her footsteps slow and quiet on the carpet, and got some clothes out of the closet, the hangers sliding just barely along the wooden rod. He pretended to be sleeping, keeping his breathing deep and rhythmic, like he'd done on so many other nights. He heard her close his bedroom door, then she was in the kitchen, where dishes clattered. Moments later, the garage door opened, she backed her car out of the garage, and the garage door closed. Tom got out of bed, went to the window that looked out toward the street, parted the curtains, and watched her drive away.

He took a long shower, letting the water run over his head and face for a good fifteen minutes, and then put on his robe. He looked at the plush living room carpet where he and Darlene had made love as he walked to the kitchen. She'd left a bowl in the sink. Drinking a cup of coffee that Darlene had made, he called work, saying he didn't feel well and was taking the day off. He brought in the newspaper and read it at the kitchen table for over an hour, numbing his mind with trivia. He moved to his study, sat down in his easy chair, and thought about their confrontation the night before.

Darlene had had the luxury of imagining being divorced for months, while it had all hit him within just the past few days. And yet, their troubles had started well before that. He wondered if this was how it had happened for Coach—or for Jack. He thought again of how naïve he had been. He'd never had any suspicions about Darlene having an affair, even though now, looking back, he could identify signs of her unhappiness.

He kept hearing her words about how he could have been a better husband. He hung his head, realizing there may have been truth to her accusations. He did love Darlene, but it was more for her companionship, their shared interests, and the stability she offered him than it was for a deep or romantic bond. He realized he should have listened to the part of himself that needed tenderness, closeness, and a spiritual connection. He couldn't help but recall the love he'd had with Jeanine—chaotic, but romantic, deep, and intimate. He remembered thinking after their breakup that the idea of romantic love was overrated, but he now realized he probably didn't have enough of it with Darlene. His decision to marry her had perhaps been influenced too much by his desire for stability and the fear of being wounded again.

He looked at his wedding band, blinking back tears. Darlene had accused him of being the one who didn't hold up his end in the marriage. On some level, he recognized that he might have been unfaithful to Darlene, never giving her his heart, and only going through the motions. But he was sad that he hadn't been able to make it work. Would he ever find a woman who would make a life together with him in a loving relationship?

That night, Darlene came home around eight. She had a fierce look on her face when she entered the house, but when she saw that Tom was no longer angry, she softened.

"I need to figure out my next steps," she said to him from the edge of the family room. "I want to stay in the guest bedroom until we settle things."

Tom, sitting in the same place as the night before, looked at her. "I never knew you were so unhappy," he said gently.

"I wasn't that aware either until I met David. He understands me and knows how to give me what I need."

Tom was silent, feeling hurt. "There doesn't seem to be much hope for us then."

They looked at each other, both knowing this was true. Darlene's eyes filled with tears, and Tom closed his.

"How should we do this?" Darlene asked after another few moments, her voice hoarse. "I don't want it to get ugly."

Tom rubbed his forehead. He'd had all day to think about things, but it was still so unreal. "I think we can find a lawyer to be a mediator for us," he said. Darlene nodded.

"What about the house?" Tom asked,

"I've thought about this," Darlene said. "You keep the house but pay me some support until I don't need it."

Tom was surprised. "Okay," he said, studying her face to make sure she really meant it. "I'll find a lawyer who we both can meet with." Again, she nodded.

Tom stood up, and Darlene looked at him. Tears ran down her cheeks. He moved to hug her, halfway expecting her to push him away, but she pressed herself against him for a long time. Then she went to the guest bedroom and closed the door.

That week, Tom walked through the motions at work, feeling numb. He told Wendell that he was getting divorced and saw instantly that he wasn't surprised. "You're welcome to take all the time off you need," Wendell said.

Tom heard nothing from Darlene in the evenings until she came home late, often after he was in bed. It was painful to have her living in his house, knowing their relationship was over. The mornings were the worst, when they had to coordinate time for using the bathroom, the closet, and the kitchen. They each tried to stay out of the way of the other as much as possible. One night, as Tom sat alone, he thought of his grandpa and poured himself a glass of Irish whiskey. That was how Grandpa got through tough times. But Tom knew better, remembering his indulgences in his younger years, and he only had one drink.

Tom and Darlene met with a lawyer the following week to begin drafting their papers for a no-fault divorce. Three weeks later, the divorce petition was filed, and she moved out of their house to live with Phillips. Darlene's final departure, directing movers to load a few furniture items, was a solemn undertaking. When Tom and Darlene matched eyes briefly, he guessed she was as close to tears again as he was. He left before that happened, spending hours reading at a coffee shop but not really focusing on the words.

Tom threw himself into work after Darlene moved out. Coming home to an empty house was difficult for him. He had a beer a couple nights, but he didn't want to get into that habit again. Instead, he joined a fitness club and focused on getting into better shape. He settled into a routine similar to his life four years earlier, before he'd met Darlene, with a focus on work, fitness, and canoe racing, especially after hearing that Darlene had joined a different rowing club. At a certain point, Tom realized that he felt freer and lighter than he had in years, which said something about how exhausting it had been to try and make their marriage work. The court finally approved the divorce papers in February 1978, right before his thirtieth birthday.

———

After the turbulence of Tom's divorce calmed and he was fully engaged at work, he began to think once again about his future. His salary at Johnson and Sons had grown each year during the housing boom, and he'd received large end-of-year bonuses, which he had saved for college expenses for the children he and Darlene had planned to have.

Wendell decided to retire in the spring of 1978, and his younger brother, Larry, took over the company. Wendell told Tom he had recommended to Larry that he promote Tom, and Tom could tell that Larry was testing him.

But Tom was testing Larry also, who was increasing the company's urban business. Developers were buying downtown buildings that served as rental properties, and then contracting with Johnson and Sons to convert the buildings into condos for young professionals. Tom was uncomfortable with his role in the gentrification of these neighborhoods, where poor and minority populations were being pushed out.

This discomfort raised old questions for Tom: What was he really meant to do in life and how was he to carry out his purpose? He knew he wanted to help improve society, but was he? His thinking was accelerated when he stopped by one of the urban projects he was managing, converting three stories of rental apartments to newly constructed condos. When he approached, he saw a group of Black activists who were carrying signs and picketing the property. "Stop stealing our homes," they chanted. Tom remembered his days of picketing against the war at Kent State. But he realized he was now on the wrong side.

36

The fire in the forested hills overlooking Los Angeles moved slowly toward outlying towns, threatening the small communities and the homes on the hillsides, and a thick, gray haze hung in the air. Tom parked his federal pickup truck at a fire station in one of the towns used as a headquarters by the state and local firefighters and stepped onto the gravel. He found his counterpart from the State Fire Marshall's office standing off to the side.

They looked up the hill and saw firefighters clearing brush and putting out small fires. "It seems to be under control," Tom said. He could smell the smoke in the air and soon he could taste it in the back of his mouth.

"Not if the wind kicks up," the man said, squinting toward the west.

"What would happen?" Tom asked.

"I think we could lose this town, plus a lot of surrounding homes. You may have business tomorrow."

Tom had already alerted federal disaster assistance staff about the potential need for immediate federal assistance. He planned to monitor developments overnight and assess the situation in the morning.

He had worked as an emergency management specialist for the Federal Disaster Assistance Administration for about four months since his career change in July of 1978. After his dissatisfaction with gentrification projects pursued by Johnson and Sons, he had submitted several job applications to public-sector agencies, knowing he would most likely have to take a pay cut. He didn't hear for weeks about his federal applications, and he assumed he didn't meet their requirements until he got an enthusiastic call from a federal personnel manager. They liked his experience as a project manager since much of their work involved coordinating projects and contracts in response to emergencies. When they learned that he was willing to accept the required pay cut, they were excited to have someone with his experience join them.

The winds kicked up in the morning, and Tom could do nothing except wait and see what damage the fire caused. The winds finally subsided in the afternoon, and firefighters made their way through the burned areas. They announced the following day that the fire had killed three homeowners and destroyed a small town nestled among the trees.

Tom's heart sank when he surveyed the damage and talked to some of the homeowners. One man told him he and his wife had tried to use a hose to keep the fire from reaching their house, but a large burning branch from a nearby tree had fallen on their roof. The fire spread quickly throughout their house, and they rushed to their car to leave the area. His wife sobbed as the man talked because they hadn't found their two cats. Tom closed his eyes, imagining the cats had not survived given the pile of ashes where their house used to be.

Tom turned to a state official who was calling him to come to another damaged house. His adrenaline rushed as he planned how to respond to the couple and other homeowners. He would help people who had lost everything apply for federal aid, including temporary housing and federal grants. He planned to stay near the site at a motel or in a trailer for a few days.

Tom frequently reflected on the differences between his federal job and his work at Johnson and Sons, where he had dedicated himself for eight years. Why did he feel less stressed in this role, even though he worked as hard, or harder, and was more actively involved in crisis situations? Wendell had taught him how to be a professional, applying the discipline he had learned as a successful athlete. But his work at Johnson and Sons had not given him the same sense of purpose provided by his federal job, through which he felt he contributed more meaningfully to society. He now had the power and resources to improve people's lives by lessening their suffering caused by disasters. The urgency of responding to crises excited him, like competing in football—although with much more at stake.

———

Tom had not been home to Massillon since he and Darlene made a quick trip for Christmas in 1976. He'd been glad that trip was only for a few days because the tension between Kara and Darlene was so uncomfortable. And as much as his parents tried to accept and include Darlene, he could see them exchange quiet glances. From their point of view, he supposed Darlene did seem more brash and outspoken than what they were used to. He had often tried to smooth over or soften things Darlene said.

But Tom's trip to Massillon two years later, the first time seeing his family since his divorce, was quite different. Though he hadn't wanted to face them after the breakup—thereby confirming that their concerns about his marriage had been valid—he grew excited as his plane descended and Cleveland came into view. His mother fussed over him at the airport, giving him a long hug at the baggage claim area. She felt smaller than he remembered, and her hair had gotten grayer since the last time he was home. Tom's father shook his hand firmly. His hair was grayer as well. He gave Tom a small nod and reached down to pick up one of his bags. Was this the beginning of a new stage in their relationship?

His mother chatted happily on the drive home. When they arrived, Kara, Woz, and Isabella were already there, having driven up from Columbus to spend a few days. The front door opened, and Isabella, now four years old, came running down the steps to meet her uncle Tom. He lifted her high and hugged her. He couldn't get enough of her that day—twirling her, chasing her around the house, and doing funny voices with her. She sat on his lap when he was on Grandpa's chair and asked him to sing Christmas carols with her. That moment alone would have made his trip home worthwhile.

There was very little said about Tom's divorce that day, though as Tom ascended the stairs to read Isabella a bedtime story, he overheard his mother tell his father, "I can't see how Darlene could leave her home and marriage." Though Tom knew his parents didn't approve of divorce, he felt that they understood and supported him. And he thought, on some level, that they may even have been relieved.

After his mother and father had gone to sleep, Tom, Kara, and Woz sat around the kitchen table to catch up over extra Christmas dessert with eggnog and brandy. Woz was enjoying his work in Columbus for Arthur Andersen, and Kara was thinking of looking into coaching once Isabella was in kindergarten.

"Coaching?" Tom asked, leaning forward and resting his elbows on the table. "I'd love to do that." He imagined himself standing on a football field cheering on the team, the green grass beneath his feet, the sun shining on him. Tom had not been on a football field in a long time, and he realized how much he missed it.

"How's your new job going?" Woz asked him.

"I feel good about it," Tom said. He filled them in on his federal work and said that although he couldn't picture himself doing it forever, it was a good fit for now.

"Are you still living in the same place?" Kara asked. "By yourself?" When Tom nodded, he saw her look at Woz, then take a deep breath.

"We never thought Darlene was good enough for you," Kara said.

Tom looked down. "We weren't a good fit," he said. "I'm to blame as much as she is." It was quiet.

"Well, you're a free man now," Woz said, offering a smile.

Kara swiveled to face Woz. "You better be careful." But then she laughed and kissed him on the cheek. "So are you seeing anyone?" she asked Tom.

Tom shook his head and took a drink of eggnog. Truthfully, Tom was lonely, and it was hard for him to live in the same house where he'd lived with Darlene. Though Darlene wasn't the answer, he knew he still wanted to have someone to love and to be loved back. He wanted a connection with a woman—romantically—the same way he'd had with Jeanine. But he didn't know if that was possible twice in one lifetime.

The night before he flew back to Southern California—after Kara and her family had returned to Columbus—Tom and his father watched a football bowl game together. They each had a glass of Grandpa's favorite Irish whiskey. When Tom got up to refill his glass, he spotted one of Isabella's stuffed animals behind the couch. He smiled to himself, thinking of her wide eyes and big laugh every time she hid it from him.

"You've got quite a granddaughter," Tom said, picking up the stuffed animal and waving it at his father.

His father smiled. "We sure do. She's pretty high energy."

"Probably a challenge for Kara and Woz when she gets older," Tom said.

"They'll get through it, just like we did with you and Kara." Tom looked at his father to see if there was unspoken resentment in his statement, but he didn't register any. Tom thought of the night his father picked him up at the police station.

"You seem to enjoy your new job," his father said, his eyes on the TV.

Tom grew wary, expecting to be judged. "I do," he said carefully.

"That's good, although I don't know if I could work for the federal government, other than a military branch."

Here came the critic. Tom tried to control any defensiveness he felt and attempted to change the subject. "What about you? Have you begun thinking of retirement?" he asked.

His father's face dropped, the corners of his mouth turning down. "That's at least ten years away for me."

Tom realized his mistake. "Well, I admire your dedication," he said quickly. "And the way you've always worked hard to take care of our family." His father remained silent, watching the TV.

Tom studied his father's profile. In spite of their tensions and disagreements over the years, Tom knew his father had done a lot for him. "You know," Tom said after a few moments, "you taught me a lot about the need for purpose, goals, and discipline. I think I'm almost there."

Tom's father turned and looked at him. "I had that kind of impact on you?"

"Yeah," Tom said. On the TV, the team they were rooting for scored, but his father was watching Tom.

"Well, that's something—I never thought you heard me," his father said. His voice had a softer quality to it.

"I did," Tom said. "I heard you." He knew his father's opinion of him had always had a tremendous impact, for better or worse. He'd meant it when he told his father that he thought he was almost there. He was closer to figuring out how to make something of his future from all the good and bad of his past.

———

Tom shook hands with his father and hugged his mother at the curb outside the airport. His mother said, "I hope you can find a good woman." He thought about his mother's words after settling into his seat during the plane's ascent.

Tom had considered pursuing a new relationship after his divorce. He had opportunities, with canoe racing teammates trying to set him up with dates. But he ignored their proposals. He not only wanted to avoid an experience like he'd had with Darlene; he also found himself thinking about Jeanine more often than not, the warm memories mixed with painful ones. He wasn't ready to put himself at risk emotionally, so instead, he'd devoted his time to his job, staying fit, and canoe racing. Still, on the flight back to LA, he allowed himself to think about Jeanine. When the plane began its descent at the end of the flight, he imagined breaking through the clouds and Kauai coming into view.

Memories of Hawaii often came up when he got together with Barry, whom he still kept in touch with. They met periodically for a beer after work, or—before Tom's divorce—for dinner occasionally with Darlene and Barry's wife, Stephanie. Tom saw them more frequently after his divorce, in part because he enjoyed playing with their three-year-old son, Johnny, who ran to Tom when Tom arrived with his arms outstretched, wanting to be lifted high in the air.

After Tom returned from visiting his family in Ohio, he spent a quiet New Year's Eve at Barry and Stephanie's house. Johnny was a bundle of energy and took Tom's hand after dinner, saying, "Let's play." Tom sat on the playroom floor and pushed a toy bulldozer with Johnny and tried to play tunes on the colorful toy xylophone. Tom already missed his niece Isabella, so playing with Johnny made his heart feel especially full.

"You'd be a good father," Stephanie said, picking up some toddler puzzles Johnny had grown bored with. Stephanie was tall and slender, similar to Barry. But she was quiet, in contrast to Barry's beaming extroversion. Tom paid attention to her when she spoke.

"Yeah," Barry said, tossing a rubber ball to Tom. "It's time you found another woman."

Tom looked at him and shrugged. "You know I don't have a great track record with relationships."

"Well, all I know is there's more to life than working and racing canoes. Why don't you try to reconnect with Jeanine? I've always thought you were at your best with her."

Johnny pushed over his box of small wooden blocks in front of Tom. Tom smiled and helped Johnny build a fort using the blocks, but he had a small pang in his heart. "It's been over seven years," he said. "The odds of that happening are slim."

"Think about it," Barry said. "A trip to Hawaii is worth it regardless of what you find out."

Tom silently dismissed Barry's suggestion. Jeanine would either be with someone or have no interest in seeing him. But the idea of searching for her didn't leave him. The following week, Tom asked a coworker about assignments in Hawaii and learned that he could volunteer if they needed help responding to Hawaii disasters.

The thought of finding Jeanine was exciting, but he didn't know if he could handle being rejected again.

37

When Tom learned in the spring that heavy rains had flooded several homes in Oahu, he offered to help provide federal disaster relief. He was scheduled to start the week-long assignment in April and reserved his return flight for the following Monday. He had few expectations of finding Jeanine but knew that if he somehow did, he wanted to have extra time if—by some miracle—she wanted to see him.

As Oahu came into view from his seat on the plane and he saw the brilliant blue of the water against the coastline, his stomach was in knots. Though he had not lived in Honolulu, a huge and vastly different city compared to Lihue, he felt himself grow emotional. His time in Lihue had been chaotic. He'd been lost and disillusioned, but he recognized that something in his spirit responded to Hawaii.

After checking into his Honolulu hotel, he grew excited to begin his search for Jeanine. He sat down at the small desk in his room and looked for her phone number, using a directory that included a section for Kauai. His heart raced as he turned the thin, crinkly pages and then ran his finger down the list of Carters, finally finding "Jeanine Carter" at a Hanalei address. His breath caught in his throat. *This has to be her*, he thought.

He sat looking at his phone, its coiled cord twisted and its buttons gray. What if she was married but had kept her last name? What if she was living with someone or had a long-time companion? What if a man answered the phone?

Tom stared at his hands. Jeanine could have started her life over in Hanalei, with no desire to be reminded of those crazy times in Lihue. Or, he feared, she could be uninterested in talking to him. Her words from years ago still reverberated in his memory: "Leave me alone!" He wasn't ready to face any of those possibilities. He closed the directory, slid it away from him to the far side of the desk, and stood up to find a restaurant.

That night, he went to bed still not knowing what he would do. He lay in the darkness, thinking of Jeanine's phone number across the room from him. He didn't remember falling asleep, but the next morning, an urgent call from the federal disaster office jolted him awake. They needed his help immediately. After hanging up, he looked once again at the phone directory, then quickly began to get ready.

———

Tom met federal staff that morning at their Honolulu office. Sue, a stocky emergency management specialist, asked Tom to ride with her on the half-hour trip to the Windward area, near the town of Waimanalo, where over fifty homes had been damaged by flooding from torrential rains. This community was populated mainly by people of Hawaiian descent, many of whom farmed in nearby agricultural fields. On the drive there, Tom observed the effects of the rains along the coast and asked Sue how the town's residents were doing. All she knew was that they needed a lot of help.

They met up with state and local staff at a school where they had set up a disaster recovery center. People with damaged homes, many of them looking distraught and exhausted, stood in a long, wavy line to find out how the federal and state government could help them. Tom saw families with federal blankets wrapped around them, who had slept outside because their homes had been wrecked or were unsafe. He passed mothers holding crying children. He was ready to help however he could.

"We have an older woman who is still refusing to leave her home," a local planner for the community told Tom and Sue after hurrying over. "The flood moved her house off its foundation. It's unstable and dangerous, but she won't listen to us."

Sue asked Tom to help the planner, while she worked with the people in line on their aid applications. The planner, a young white man who had grown up on Oahu, offered to take Tom to the woman's house, saying she was known only as "Grandma." Tom asked if he knew how to say "Grandma" in Hawaiian—"Kupuna Wahine," the planner said.

The planner parked their car and approached Grandma sitting in a chair in the front yard of her house, a small structure that was tilting and full of mud. She was a tiny native Hawaiian with a weathered face of wrinkles, and she had mud on her feet. She looked at them with penetrating eyes, shaking her head at them.

"Grandma, we're here to help you," the planner said.

"You're worthless—get away from me." She turned her eyes to Tom, as if challenging him. Tom guessed that she was in her late eighties or early nineties. "You haoles aren't taking my land," she said, scowling.

Tom looked at her, remembering how insulted he used to feel when called a haole. But it didn't bother him now. Worried her home would collapse behind her, he was focused only on helping her. "No, Kupuna Wahine," he told her. "I will not let them."

She paused, studying him silently, her gaze intense. She narrowed her eyes. "Who are you?"

"I'm Tom O'Brien. We need to find you a place to stay while we fix your house."

She continued to stare at him, looking fiercely into his eyes, trying, it seemed, to determine if he was trustworthy. He relaxed his face and looked back at her openly, his eyes not leaving hers, waiting patiently for several more seconds. He was relieved when she finally said, "You take me?"

"Yes," he said, not sure what had made her trust him, just knowing he had tried to be respectful to her. She nodded once, then slowly stood up, her back hunched over. Her gaze was softer, and she held onto her shell necklace. Tom gently helped her toward the planner's car. They drove her to the recovery center, where Tom filled out her applications for her. They then took her to a motel designated for people with damaged homes. The planner told her he would stop by later with food, but she looked only at Tom, who assured her everything would be all right.

The following morning, Tom got a federal truck from the vehicle pool in Honolulu and drove to the center to help other home and business owners. The planner told him that they needed Grandma to come to the center again to fill out more papers, but she had refused to come, asking for O'Brien. Tom felt honored that she wanted him to help her.

He drove to the motel and knocked on her door, announcing his name. A moment or two later, she opened it and silently nodded toward his truck, holding onto her necklace. He stayed with her for most of the day, making arrangements for a contractor to repair her house using a federal grant, and bringing her food and drink at various times.

"Kupuna Wahine, I'm going to have to leave and take you to your motel, but I've told him what needs to be done," Tom said late that afternoon, gesturing toward the planner. "He'll take care of you. Both of you can call me if needed."

Grandma, who was sitting in a chair Tom had secured for her, looked at him for a long time. "Good," she finally said. She allowed Tom to help get her up and into his truck. He drove her to the motel, walked her to her room, and opened her door. She looked up at him, rested her hand on his arm for a moment, and turned to go inside.

That evening, Tom thought about Grandma—the way she had relied on him and looked to him during this catastrophe. This fierce, defiant woman, who had likely survived a lifetime of haole discrimination, had allowed him to help her. He knew what he'd done was what the job required, but he was surprisingly moved that she'd opened herself up to him, and he'd been able to find a way to get through to her.

Tom had chosen his federal job because he hoped it would give him the sense of purpose he had been searching for. After two days with Grandma, he realized his real purpose, regardless of where he worked, was to help people and improve their lives. Hearing Grandma say "Good" was more satisfying than any of his football, construction, disaster assistance, or other achievements. He realized that was what mattered to him most.

—

After a full day helping Grandma, Tom ate dinner by himself at his Honolulu hotel and then went to his room. He walked back and forth between his desk and the window, thinking of Grandma but also of Jeanine. He'd had a good day—maybe that would carry him through any disappointment he might experience by talking to Jeanine. He studied the street four floors below, looked at the cover of the phone directory, and finally decided to call her. He tried to calm his nerves as he dialed, but his throat was dry. The phone rang three times. Then, there was a rustling, and she was there.

"Hello?" she asked with a melodic tone that was relaxed and familiar. A lot of time had passed since the last time he'd seen her, but he pictured her look-ing the same. His heart pounded.

"Jeanine. This is Tom O'Brien." He had practiced this greeting, deciding to keep it simple, but he felt his voice sounded weak, almost shaky. He wished he could do it over. His breathing was shallow.

The line was silent for a few seconds. "Tom? What a surprise! Where are you?" He couldn't tell if she sounded pleased or not.

He swallowed. "In Honolulu—on a work assignment." He closed his eyes and plunged ahead. "I wondered if I might be able to see you in Kauai." She didn't respond right away, and Tom immediately thought he'd been too forward. He should have preceded this with more conversation. He pictured her looking out the window with her dark eyes, wondering how to end this awkward call. He steeled himself for rejection.

"I'd love to see you."

His eyes widened, and he quietly let his breath out, relief flooding over him. His heart continued to pound. He wanted to go to her immediately, but he still didn't know her situation. He needed to check his excitement, reminding himself that, so far, all that had really happened was a short phone conversation between old friends. She could have a husband or lover in the same room for all he knew.

"My work will wind down at the end of the week," he said. "What if we meet Saturday night for dinner if you're free?" *Please, be free,* he thought.

"Saturday's great." She suggested they meet at a restaurant called Tahiti Nui in Hanalei at seven.

"Good," he said, deciding to hold the conversation until then. Though he sensed she might like to talk more, he didn't want to betray his eagerness to see her or say anything that might cause her to suddenly change her mind. "Seven o'clock. I'll see you then," he said, sounding more businesslike than he'd intended.

He hung up the phone and stared at it. It was the closest he had been to Jeanine in over seven long years. A lot had happened in his life since the last time they'd seen each other, and he had no idea where their dinner might lead. Maybe that would be all—one night of old friends reminiscing over a meal. He needed to assume that, to limit his expectations, and he needed to make sure his face didn't register disappointment.

Tom flipped to a different page in the directory, running his finger down a listing of hotels. He didn't want it to be awkward on Saturday; he needed a place to retreat to in case things didn't work out as he hoped. He reserved a hotel room in Princeville, near Hanalei, and for the rest of the night, his mind raced with nervous excitement.

———

Walking out of the terminal into the warm ocean breeze in Lihue was just as transcendent as it had been when he and Kevin had landed there years ago. He had time to spare before traveling north to Hanalei, so he drove to the neighborhood where he used to live. His run-down apartment building— the "Haole Hotel," as the locals had called it—had been replaced by five stories of condominiums. He stared at the condo landscaping, imagining the picnic tables that used to be near the apartment building, where he and Kevin had sat while Scotty introduced them to Jeanine, and where he and Jeanine had first talked alone. Tiki's was still down the street, and now had seating under umbrellas on a new deck. The locals' bar across from Tiki's— the scene of his near-beating—had been replaced by a sushi bar.

Tom had only lived in Lihue for about a year and a half, but he had a lifetime of memories from that intense period, ranging from blissful times with Jeanine to the tragedy of Scotty's death.

He arrived at Tahiti Nui early and sat down at a table. He ran his fingers through his hair, sipped his glass of water, and tried to relax his shoulders. He was adjusting his shirt when Jeanine entered. She caught his eye and smiled. Tall and gorgeous, she still took his breath away. Her angular features had softened and matured, but her eyes were the same—dark, expressive, and animated, drawing him to her, as they always had. Tom stood up, but he didn't know what to do—whether to kiss or hug her or shake her hand. She continued to smile as she made her way over and ended the uncertainty by pulling him toward her with her hand on his shoulder for a quick kiss on his cheek before sitting down.

Tom's heart leaped as he sat down. He was thrilled to be near her, still feeling her warm lips on his cheek. "So, you're living in the most beautiful place in the world," he said.

"I am. I can see the waterfalls in the mountains out of my bedroom window. I couldn't love it more." She looked at him quietly, as if comparing the younger version of him with the man before her. Her arms, tanned and smooth, rested on the table, and she played with two silver bracelets made of intertwining circles on her wrist.

"I'm glad you're happy," he said, wishing he could reach out and touch her arm. He wondered if his arrival also made her happy. Was his presence tonight actually welcome? He needed to clear his throat. He took a drink of water. "What do you do for a living that allows you to stay in this paradise?" he asked.

"I bet you can guess," she told him, smiling. "I still sell children's clothes, but not at Coco's. I have my own store now—on Main Street in Hanalei, right down the block."

Tom's eyebrows raised. "You started your own business? That's impressive. How did you build it to become the owner?"

Jeanine's face grew serious, and she looked at Tom in earnest. "After Scotty died and you left, I needed to change my life. I went into treatment and told Coco's that I wanted to work toward a management position. They increased my hours, and I found another apartment and saved money. I needed to focus on my job in those days. It became my only priority."

Tom remembered how he too had wanted to change his life after Scotty's death, to start fresh and work toward stability after the chaos of Lihue. He wondered what she'd meant by the words "after you left." She'd told him to leave her alone. Was she glad he'd left, allowing herself to seek treatment; or was she heartbroken, as he had been?

"After becoming assistant manager at Coco's, I realized I could run a store myself. I had to rent a space for several years while I grew the business, but I finally bought the building two years ago." The waitress arrived to take their orders, and Jeanine smiled at Tom. "What do you drink these days?"

"An occasional beer or a glass of wine, but I'm fine if we don't have alcohol." He didn't want to propose an alcoholic drink if she had given up drinking in her treatment.

"Let's have a bottle of wine." She chose one, and the waitress left. "I stopped doing drugs after Scotty died, and I stopped drinking for quite a while," she said. "But I like a glass of wine for special occasions."

Tom was relieved to hear her say that. Part of the heartbreak he'd experienced for so long, even after moving to LA, had been in knowing she struggled with addiction but not being able to help her.

"This is a pretty special occasion," he agreed. "I'm glad you were free this evening." She nodded, and her lively eyes drew him in again. His face and neck were warming.

She leaned forward, closer to him. "Now, I want to hear about you."

Tom tried—poorly, he thought—to summarize his life in LA after leaving Lihue. Jeanine nodded and probed him, wanting to know more, but he felt like he kept stumbling over his words. He still didn't know if she had a partner, and he didn't want to say anything that would be awkward or presumptuous. In the end, he decided to be honest and spoke matter-of-factly about his jobs, marriage, and divorce.

If Jeanine was bothered to know he'd been married, she didn't show it. She listened with kindness, meeting his eye and nodding her head. But as he continued to talk, he realized how vulnerable he'd made himself; she knew a lot about him by this point, but he had no idea what she thought about his phone call . . . this meeting . . . him. When she filled his glass again with wine, Tom took a drink and made up his mind to ask her his burning question. He just had to. "So, are you in a relationship?"

He watched her react—first with a smile, then with curiosity, and then with what seemed to be caution as she sensed the seriousness of his question. She studied him for a few moments.

"No," she said softly. "I ended one about two years ago—a guy from San Diego who wanted me to move there." She set down her glass of wine. "He took me on business trips around the world. Not something I needed, but it was okay." Tom saw that she was trying to offer him honesty, as he'd offered her.

"How long were you together?"

"We saw each other for about three years. He owned a condo here in Princeville and also his home in San Diego."

"That's about how long Darlene and I were together," Tom said. She looked down at her glass of wine. She was comfortable with silence and did not need to look at him. He realized that the friendliness he was feeling from her was not necessarily an indicator of how she really felt—she had depths that had always been mysterious to him.

But the wine gave him courage and loosened his tongue. "I've never forgotten you telling me to leave you alone when we broke up. It crushed me."

Jeanine arched an eyebrow, looking surprised and puzzled. "I don't remember saying that—I was probably high. I do remember realizing I needed to be alone."

"But was that the end of us for you—when you realized that?" Jeanine sat back, and he immediately regretted asking her. Of course that had been the end for her—and his question now sounded thoughtless and needlessly confrontational. He prepared himself for whatever she might say.

But she just looked at him for a long time, her face impossible to read. The silence grew unbearable, and he looked toward the people at the bar. He began to sweat. He was so stupid. The conversation had been going fine before. He closed his eyes and felt them fill with tears. He'd blown it—she would end their dinner early and wouldn't want to see him anymore.

"Tom—are you okay? You seem upset."

He looked at her through his moist eyes, humiliated that she could see his tears. He pressed his lips together. He didn't know what to say.

"I never meant to hurt you," she said quietly. "Really." She lowered her voice even more. "I had to be alone to confront what I had become—a drug addict. I thought about you all the time during my treatment; I talked about you a lot with my therapist. She thought I should contact you, but I was too scared after all I'd put you through. I thought you left because things had gotten too crazy for you."

"But I wrote you letters."

"I know," she said. Her lip trembled, just barely. "I cried when I got them, and I saved them. But I didn't know what to write back. I was a mess."

He looked at her and then looked down, preparing himself for the end.

Jeanine took a deep breath. "Your phone call this week brought back so many memories—good memories for me."

Wait. What? Tom lifted his head, not sure where this was going, but he felt a glimmer of hope.

Jeanine hesitated, seeming to struggle with what she wanted to say. "Do you . . . want to try to be together again?" she asked, looking at Tom. Her dark eyes were full of emotion.

Tom stared at her. His heart was in his throat. "That's why I'm here," he said. He could hardly breathe.

An almost imperceptible smile appeared on her lips. Then, she pulled it back in and said, "We would probably have challenges."

Tom smiled. "Probably." It was all he could do to keep from lunging across the table to embrace her.

But she reached across the table first and put her hand on his. He turned up his palm and held her fingers. He was amazed at how warm and tender her hand was, the same as when he had held it years ago.

"I still go to therapy—just so you know who you're getting. It would be good if you could join me sometime. That is. . . . if you wanted to."

"I want to." He squeezed her hand and looked into her eyes, ready to do anything she wanted. They were quiet, gazing at each other. Tom couldn't believe this was happening. He didn't want the moment to end.

A table of diners next to them got up to leave, after which Jeanine finally broke the silence. "So, okay, what happens now?"

Tom laughed, feeling a welcome release of emotions. Seven-plus years of being away from Jeanine. He wanted to kiss her—to hold her and never let her go—but he was cautious. "I don't know. Maybe I should go to my hotel room tonight, and then we can get together tomorrow."

"That reminds me of you walking me home from Coco's before we were lovers; how careful you were!" She laughed and brought her other hand up to hold his.

"I just want to do this right," Tom said.

Jeanine smiled at him, "All right. At least walk me home."

Tom paid the bill, and they stood up at the same time, grinning at each other. They walked under the streetlights holding hands in the dark, and Tom, feeling the warm evening breeze and listening to the sound of waves crashing on the Hanalei Bay beach, was conscious of Jeanine next to him at every step. He couldn't believe how wonderful it felt to be close to her again. Following her lead, they turned onto Weke Road and came to a stop at her house, one of the smaller homes across the street from larger homes that faced the ocean. She turned to him at her doorway with a smile and took a step closer to him.

"Okay, Achilles, you've proven how disciplined you are." She put her hand on his chest. "I want you here."

"Now?" He was excited to feel her warmth pull him toward her.

She tilted her head up toward his. "Yes," she said softly. "You can cancel your room reservation."

He cupped her face in his hands, and they kissed deeply. They said little as they entered Jeanine's house. She moved him to the bedroom, where they undressed each other in the darkness. Her warmth and tenderness overwhelmed him, and Tom kept reaching out to hold and touch her, feeling her face, her neck, her back, her thigh. He wanted to feel and know she was there—that she was real. They kissed and made love and kissed and made love as if it were the first time. They were one body, connected by their souls. When, sometime later, she curled up next to him, her head on his shoulder, he pulled her toward him and felt something inside him finally begin to relax. It was a tension, a turmoil, that had been in him for years.

"I'm glad you found me," she whispered against his chest.

His mind raced ahead to what might come next for them, but he knew there was still more to figure out. He willed himself to stop, wanting to concentrate instead on the pleasure of holding her close and being with her now. As much as possible, he wanted to allow things to flow naturally.

They slept together in a tangle of arms and legs, as they'd used to in Jeanine's single bed. They made love again in the gray light of morning, after which Jeanine opened her bedroom window to let a warm breeze blow in. Tiny strips of silver sliced through the green forests in the mountains, the waterfalls that Jeanine had pointed to when she first showed Hanalei Bay to Kevin and him. They had a view of paradise.

———

They dressed a little later, and as Jeanine scrambled some eggs for breakfast, Tom stood at her kitchen window, looking out again at the waterfalls. "Do you know what happened to Kevin?" he asked. He'd heard from Barry that Taylor Camp was burned down, but he hadn't known who to contact to find out about Kevin.

"Kevin's here," she said, setting down her spatula and turning to face him.

"Really? In Hanalei?" Tom thought of seeing his friend, but knew, on some level, he'd lost Kevin a long time ago.

"Yeah, he moved to Hanalei after the state condemned Taylor Camp," she said. "William and his girlfriend let him live in their spare bedroom."

Tom thought back to his days at the camp, and his conversations with William. "Somehow, I always knew William would watch out for Kevin." He got up to pour the coffee and help serve the eggs, reflecting on how Kevin had seemed to have gone past a point of no return. "Is he working?"

"Sort of. Kevin's father helped William and Kevin buy machinery for making tie-dye T-shirts after Kevin refused to return to Chicago. I sell them in my store."

Tom tried to picture it. "To be honest, I'm surprised Kevin can function," he said. "He was in pretty bad shape when I last saw him."

Jeanine lowered her eyes, then looked at Tom. "He can't function without William's help," she said. "He has trouble with flashbacks from too many years of shroom trips, and now he's been diagnosed with dementia."

Tom stared at Jeanine in amazement as he received this sobering news. Kevin was still young—Tom remembered how passionate, sharp-minded, and promising he'd been in college.

"But," Jeanine said, "William is a faithful friend after Kevin—in his role as a holy man at Taylor Camp—helped him deal with his trauma from fighting in Vietnam."

Tom was silent, thinking about the unpredictable turns in a person's life. In his time in Hawaii, he'd seen more than one life ruined, and he was frustrated to think of all that had been needlessly lost.

"What about Lucas?" he asked. "Are you in touch with him?"

Jeanine sat down at the kitchen table, cupping her mug in her hands. "He was sentenced to ten years in prison on the mainland for drug trafficking. I wrote him a couple of times, but never heard from him."

Tom thought of how close she and Lucas had been for a time, and he shook his head. The last time he'd seen Lucas, he was in the back of a police car, and Jeanine had been sobbing. Tom swallowed. "We're lucky we survived," Tom said. "We're not dead or in prison, and we haven't lost our minds."

"I know," Jeanine said, reaching out to take Tom's hand. "I'm grateful every day."

Tom looked at the waterfalls. He thought of his years of searching for a direction. He had tried to follow what had been written in books, explored new realities through drugs, escaped to paradise in Hawaii, and tried living in a commune of peace and love. It was a desperate search, full of danger. Both he and Jeanine could have ended up like Kevin, Lucas, or Scotty, friends who stepped off the path too far, their dreams leading to self-destruction.

———

Tom and Jeanine spent the weekend catching up on each other's lives and discussing their future. Tom knew that she would not move from her house and clothing store in her beloved Hanalei, and he wouldn't ask her to. The decision didn't seem hard to him—he would move to Kauai to be with her.

Jeanine questioned Tom about his decision while walking on the beach one evening. She was worried that he would be giving up his career for her. He told her that he would initially look for a construction job. Then he would search for a career with more purpose. He explained that as much as he appreciated helping with disaster assistance, there was something about it that was short of his purpose. He believed he was intended to pursue something that more directly helped people improve their lives.

"I'm not giving up on doing what I'm meant to do," he assured her. "I hope I'm closer to finding it now. But there is one thing I'm confident I have found—that's you, the love of my life." She looked at him with her dark eyes, smiled, and threw her arms around his neck.

38

The week after Tom returned to LA, he asked a realtor friend to look over his house, advise him on preparing it for showing, and develop a for-sale listing. Within two weeks of its posting in mid-May, Tom received an offer. Before accepting it, he called Jeanine. "Are you sure you're ready for me?" he asked.

"I can't wait." He could tell by the way she said it that she was smiling.

"Okay, I'm accepting the offer tomorrow, and there's no going back. You're going to have me—right?—for better, for worse, till death do us part?"

"That's my pledge."

"Good!" Tom wished he could sign the papers that moment. He and Jeanine stayed up late on the phone, making plans for when he would move into her house. His closing date in late June allowed him time to make arrangements.

That night lying in bed, Tom looked around at the walls and ceiling of his Glendale house. It had been part of his and Darlene's dreams to start a family. After those dreams had crashed with their divorce, he had stared at these same walls and ceiling on countless nights, feeling alone and lost and wishing he could have avoided that pain.

But he'd gone through other hard times since high school, often wishing they'd never happened. How different would his life be if he hadn't been injured, if he hadn't gone to Kent State, if hadn't met Coach Peters, Kevin, or Woz? Would he be the same person if he hadn't witnessed the shootings, and if not, would he and Kevin have left conventional society for Hawaii? As he lay there, he recognized that some of the pain he'd gone through was good; it had made him more of who he was meant to be and helped him understand what was important to him.

One of the hardest things he had experienced—his breakup with Jeanine in Kauai—had helped spark his growth in LA: meeting Wendell, advancing at work, investing in other activities, broadening his perspective. And now, remarkably, here he was, able to begin a new chapter with Jeanine, wiser and more assured of his direction.

Tom signed the papers to accept the offer on his house the next evening after work, then called his family and Barry to let them know.

———

Tom missed Jeanine so much that he took a week of vacation in mid-June to fly to Hawaii to see her. He also wanted to look for a new job in Kauai while he was there, to see what his options were. Before leaving, he gave notice that he was resigning from his federal job.

At the airport, Jeanine walked to him swiftly and gave him a long kiss. He held her and was struck again by the circuitous journey of his life that had led him to meet her, and then to return to her. He didn't know exactly how the journey would continue in Hanalei, only that it would be with her, and that excited him.

Tom borrowed Jeanine's car in the middle of the week to call on a couple of construction companies he found in the yellow pages, one in Lihue and one in Kapa'a. The Lihue company dismissed him quickly, probably thinking something was wrong for him to leave his federal job. But the Kapa'a owner—Buddy—seemed intrigued. About ten years older than Tom and a head shorter with a round belly, he looked at Tom through squinted eyes, curious and confident.

"You've got a good job with higher pay," Buddy said. "Why do you want to go backward in your career?" Tom was honest. "At this stage, being with the woman I love is more important than having a perfect job."

Buddy seemed mildly amused. But then he shook his head and appeared to challenge Tom with a scowl. "We don't have work for another project manager right now, and I can't afford to pay someone based on their potential."

Tom sensed that Buddy was interested in him, and he thought of what he could do to make it work. "How about if I help you develop proposals for bids?" Tom asked. "If we bring in new work, then you could hire me to manage it."

Buddy put his hands on his hips and continued to study Tom for several seconds. He peered down at Tom's resume and appeared to be working something out in his head. Finally, he smiled and said, "That's fair. I'll look for some projects wanting bids, and you can prepare our proposals."

Tom extended his hand to shake Buddy's. It was a start.

——

When Tom returned to LA, he packed the few things he was shipping to Jeanine's and invited Barry, Stephanie, and Johnny out to dinner at Johnny's favorite Chinese restaurant. Tom ordered an extra plate of noodles, which Johnny loved, and helped Johnny coil them around his chopsticks. Tom realized how much he was going to miss Barry and his family, especially Johnny. After they'd cracked open their fortune cookies, he told Johnny that he wouldn't be able to see him for a while.

Barry invited Tom to their house after dinner, and Tom spent the evening talking about their times together and tickling Johnny, who hid from him behind the couch. Tom held Johnny up as high as he could when he got ready to leave, so Johnny could touch the ceiling with his fingers. "You're growing so fast that next time I may not even be able to lift you," he said. Tom hugged all of them before leaving and promised to keep in good touch. That night Tom teared up when he told Jeanine on the phone how much he was going to miss Johnny.

In the next few days, Tom shipped off the last of his boxes, did a final row with his canoe racing team, and found himself alone in his empty home after a secondhand store bought his furniture. The place seemed cavernous. As he made his way from room to room, he was glad someone would have a fresh start here, filling the space with their things, bringing their experiences, perspectives, and hopes. When he was ready, he stepped outside and closed the door behind him.

——

As he got up from his seat on the plane and prepared to get off, he thought, *This is it—the beginning of the rest of my life.* But then some of the tourists in rows ahead of him took a long time to get their bags, and he stood there waiting in line to deplane, looking at their straw hats, their Hawaiian shirts, and the cameras that hung around their necks. He was grateful when the line finally started to move.

Jeanine drove him to her house—*their* house, he corrected himself—with the windows down. She wore sunglasses and smiled at him, one hand on his leg as she drove. He let the warm breeze blow on his face and extended his arm out the window.

He spent his days following his arrival figuring out the new shape of his life. He was used to having the structure and routine of a job and some sort of plan around what he would do. He contacted Buddy immediately and helped him prepare proposals for three projects wanting bids. While waiting to hear back about the bids, he walked each day to Jeanine's shop to have lunch with her while her assistant minded the store. Tom was impressed to see the way Jeanine managed her store, her customers, and her suppliers. She was smart and purposeful, and he could tell how much she enjoyed her work. For some reason, this made him feel listless.

Tom was relieved when Buddy informed him that his company had been awarded one of the projects that Tom had prepared a proposal for. That night, Tom prepared supper after Jeanine got home from work, and then they walked down the Hanalei Bay beach, holding hands as the sun set.

Tom met Buddy at his office and learned that the project was a large remodeling job for a Kapa'a hotel facing the ocean. Buddy and Tom agreed that Tom would start work as its project manager in late July. Tom also alerted Buddy that he planned to take a few days off over Labor Day weekend to visit his family in Ohio. Buddy, behind his desk, stood up and reached across to enthusiastically pump Tom's hand as Tom was getting to leave. "By the way, I've been meaning to ask you," he said. "Did you play football?" Tom, used to this question, was about to give his usual cursory reply, but based on the way Buddy was looking at him, he detected more behind the question.

"Yeah, I did. Kent State offensive guard."

"Really." Buddy grew quiet. "I thought so, with your size," he said. "Maybe you can help me check out our Kapa'a High School football team this fall."

High school football? Tom smiled. It had been years since he last thought about high school football. "You sound like a football fan," he said.

"I'm at every game," Buddy said, "though the team's only been okay every season. I always think the boys have promise though."

Tom smiled and nodded. "Promise can take a person a long way," he said. Maybe he would check out a game or two.

One day in mid-August, Buddy stopped by the construction site, pulling his truck up to the fence. Tom looked up from his blueprints as Buddy approached.

"You've made a lot of progress on this project," Buddy said, glancing around.

"Thanks. Things seem to be going well so far."

"I'm hearing that's because you've headed off some problems—one with the owner who wanted a design change, and one with a carpenter who came to work drunk."

Tom nodded. Those problems were nothing compared to his experiences in LA.

"You just took care of them and kept going," Buddy said. "Good work." He appeared to have more to say, so Tom just smiled and continued to look at him. "So . . . I talked to the high school principal, Bruce Ackerson, and the football coach, Roger Bradley, about you."

That wasn't what Tom expected to hear.

"Would you be willing to be a resource for the football team, maybe speak to them when practice starts next week?" Buddy asked.

"Sure. I mean, I don't have a problem with that if the coach doesn't," Tom said. "He's okay with it?"

"Yep. We had a losing record last year, and he could use some help. I'll set up a meeting, so you can meet Bradley and Ackerson." Buddy seemed pleased and headed back to his truck, surveying the work site as he left and giving Tom a wave.

Tom turned back to his work, thinking about how much Buddy seemed to care about the team. What kind of advice might the players need? He was curious to see them practice. The last time he'd done anything like this was in college for his younger teammates, and before that? Kara's high school field hockey team. He was looking forward to meeting the Kapa'a High players.

Tom came up behind the end zone and spotted the coach, Mr. Bradley, a history teacher at the high school whom Buddy, Tom, and Mr. Ackerson had met with a week earlier. It was a warm gray day with an occasional drizzle of rain, and Tom stood and watched him address the players. Mr. Bradley looked up and, noticing Tom, waved him over.

Tom faced the players sitting on the practice field and watched them joke with each other or stare across the field at the cheerleaders' practice. When Mr. Bradley introduced Tom, only a few looked up, and Tom could see that he was going to have to earn their attention. He remembered how Coach Peters engaged with his players by asking questions.

"What do you guys think of your team this year?" Tom asked. The players all looked at him with silence. One of them chewed gum. Another scratched his chin. "Are you playing well or are you just an average team?" One of the guys seemed like he might be insulted, but then he went back to looking at the cheerleaders.

"We have the potential to be a good team," a player in front said after another moment or two. Several of the guys looked at him, then back at Tom.

Tom asked them what it would take to be a good team. They talked about needing more training and to be in better shape.

"No kidding," one of the players said, nudging his friend. "You could run a lot faster." The group laughed, and Tom could see they were beginning to engage with him better.

"What else?" he asked. "What does it take to be a good team?" He made eye contact with them and waited several seconds before a player spoke up.

"We need to want to be good."

"Right," Tom said. "So do you? Coaches can improve your skills and give you workouts to get you in shape, but desire has to come from within you." The players looked at him more seriously than they had at the beginning of practice.

As Tom was leaving, Mr. Bradley asked him to join the team on the sidelines for their first game the Friday after Labor Day. "I'd love to," Tom said. Being on the field with the players had electrified him, awakening something in him he hadn't felt in a long time. He would never have guessed he'd be involved with football again, especially in Hawaii.

———

Tom and Jeanine reached the baggage carousel in the Cleveland airport a few days before Labor Day weekend. Woz, Kara, and Isabella were waiting for them. Isabella was hopping up and down.

"It's been too long!" Kara said, embracing Tom. Then she turned to Jeanine and studied her, smiling warmly in a way that looked genuine. Jeanine extended her arm to shake hands, but Kara brushed it aside and pulled her forward for a hug instead.

"Look at this five-year-old!" Tom said, bending down to hug Isabella. Isabella beamed, and when Tom introduced Jeanine to her, she reached up and gave Jeanine a long hug. Jeanine, who'd bent down next to Tom, seemed touched, almost speechless.

They picked up their bags and walked to the parking lot to Woz's van. Their drive to Massillon was full of chatter, with Kara asking Tom about his job and Jeanine about her clothing store, and Jeanine asking Isabella about kindergarten. Tom gazed out at the familiar Midwestern landscape. He couldn't have been more thrilled to have them all together. He and Isabella sang along to a tape Woz popped into the cassette player.

They pulled into the driveway of his parents' home, which was freshly painted and surrounded by neatly trimmed bushes and a lush lawn. The mailbox he'd installed was still there, a little more weathered but apparently standing strong. His mother came rushing out the front door to greet them, followed by his father. Tom quickly got out of the car and strode toward her, and she moved into him, hugging and kissing his cheek before resting the side of her face against his chest. "Tommy, it's so, so good to see you," she said.

He held his mom, then said, "Mom, this is Jeanine." Jeanine approached and surprised Tom by giving his mother a quick hug.

His mother seemed pleased by this and looked at Tom, and then at Jeanine. "I haven't seen Tom this happy in a long time," she said to Jeanine. "You have a good effect on him."

Tom's father had more wrinkles on his face and neck—he was older and smaller—but he still carried himself with presence. Before Tom could address him, Tom's mother said, "Come meet Tom's girl, Jeanine." His father walked toward Jeanine, and she extended her hand. He shook it, smiling slightly.

Jeanine looked closely at his father. "So, you're the one who taught Tom to be so organized and disciplined," she said. "I think that you've had a huge influence."

His father smiled, bigger now. "I hope that's a good thing."

"It is," Jeanine said, touching Tom's arm. "I don't know a better man."

To Tom's surprise, his father said, "I don't either."

———

The evening went by quickly, with everyone catching up over dinner and in the family room. Woz told Tom he'd been promoted to partner in Arthur Andersen's Columbus office, and Kara, Tom learned, had just started as an assistant coach for the girls' high school field hockey team. Tom filled them in on his construction job. When he mentioned that he'd been asked to advise a high school football team, he noticed his father listening intently.

A little later, everyone went to bed, but Tom and Jeanine, who were still on Hawaii time, decided to take a walk, as they often did on the beach at home. They held hands, and Tom wondered what Jeanine thought of his family. The warm August day had cooled down quickly in the evening, the weather unpredictable as it often was in the Midwest as the summer neared its end.

"Your mom—she's incredible. So kind," Jeanine said, as they neared the end of the street. "She sure loves you and Kara."

"All of us," Tom said. "She's always been like that."

"You're lucky, you know. All I got from my mother was criticism."

Tom squeezed Jeanine's hand, and they walked quietly together. "For me," he said, "all the criticism was from my father."

Jeanine gave Tom's hand a squeeze this time. "Well, at least from what I can tell now, I think he's proud of you—he observes you without you knowing it."

"Really?" Tom was surprised. "I've never seen him observing me."

"Maybe he's too proud to be caught. But I noticed him doing it today," Jeanine said. They turned the corner onto the next block. A dog barked in the distance. "And you know what else," Jeanine said, "I see you observing him too."

Tom raised his arm and placed it around Jeanine's shoulders, pulling her toward him. It was good to have her there with him in Massillon. He cared what she thought about his family, and he was glad to see that his family had so warmly and easily embraced her. "I think my mother's right," he said. "You have a good effect on me."

———

Tom was watching out the window when Jack and his wife Carol pulled up the next day to join the family for dinner. Jack had gotten new glasses and was dressed more casually than he used to, though he still buttoned his shirt all the way up to the top. His new wife was as he'd described to Tom over the phone—pretty, with brown shoulder-length hair. She had tinted sunglasses, which she placed on top of her head when she shook hands with Tom.

"So you're Tom's oldest friend," Jeanine said to Jack during dinner. "What was he like as a boy?" Tom was wary about what Jack might say. Jeanine seemed to enjoy learning about Tom's youth, having spent part of the afternoon with his mother looking at old photos of Tom. Tom's father had shown her a few of Tom's old football trophies.

Jack put down his fork. "You may have heard about Tom getting his first football from his grandpa when he was four. But you probably haven't heard how he cried all through Sunday school because his mom wouldn't allow him to take it to church!"

Everyone laughed and Jeanine said, "That sounds like Tom." Tom looked around the table, smiling and nodding, glad that Jack had not chosen a more embarrassing incident, although he wondered which part of the story Jeanine thought sounded like him—his crying?

"Of course," Jack said, "Tom and I didn't have much in common for a while after high school. But now we do—both with successful rebounds, in love with beautiful women." Jeanine and Carol exchanged glances. Tom guessed that both were disguising the urge to roll their eyes.

After dinner, Tom invited Woz and Jack down to the basement to hang out, like old times. Jack asked Woz about his job as a partner for Arthur Andersen, and he and Woz chatted about Jack's role as manager of mechanical engineering with his second company.

"I have six engineers under me," Jack said, which made Tom smile and look down. He remembered Woz and Jack having a similar conversation in the same room after Grandpa's funeral. Kevin had looked at Tom then and silently mouthed, "Boring." Tom wished Kevin were there with them.

"What about you, Tom?" Woz said. "You left your government job. What's next?"

"I'm doing project management work for a construction company right now," he said.

"What? You were doing that after your first years at Johnson and Sons," Jack said. "You could be helping run that company now."

"Maybe," Tom said. "But I wanted a change, and I was making more of a difference through my federal job."

"That sounds like your old hippie philosophy talking," Jack said, smirking a little. When Tom didn't smile at this, Jack moved on. "So, what else are you going to do?"

"I'm going to enjoy living with Jeanine in Hanalei."

"More power to you," Woz said quickly. "There will be days when I wish I was in Hawaii." He patted Tom on the back.

"You're right about that," Jack said.

Tom smiled to himself. He, Woz, and Jack had, at various points in the past, all stormed out of conversations like this that had gone awry. They had different viewpoints and goals, but they'd come a long way. People could disagree and still accept one another. He raised his beer to his friends and toasted them. "Come visit us," he said. "You guys have money."

———

Woz had started his van to drive Tom and Jeanine to the airport, and Tom grew emotional as he watched Jeanine hug his family in the driveway. His mother and Kara cried when he approached them to say goodbye, and he held Isabella and hugged her close.

"We'll be back at Christmas," he promised, loading the last suitcase into the van. His father closed the rear door, and then he and Tom looked at each another. Tom shook his father's hand and thanked him for hosting their visit, and his father nodded. Tom didn't know what else to say, so he turned to go, but his father stopped him, holding his arm.

"Let me know how it goes helping that football team," he said. Tom met his father's eyes.

"I will," Tom told him. Jeanine, who'd been watching, raised her eyebrows at Tom and smiled, and next to her, Kara laughed and took Jeanine's arm.

As Woz reversed the car, chatting with Jeanine, Tom looked at his family through the front window. They'd all come a long way.

39

Kapa'a High was still behind by two touchdowns near the end of the fourth quarter. Standing on the sidelines next to Mr. Bradley, Tom saw the dejection on the players' faces, their parents sitting emotionless in the stands, and Buddy shaking his head and frowning. The other team wasn't trying that hard; its players laughed and joked around during a timeout. Tom had watched Mr. Bradley continue to call the same plays repeatedly, which the opposing team had quickly grown to expect, and he had watched him yell at his team when they gave up touchdowns instead of adjusting their defense. In the end, Kapa'a High lost its opening game of the season by three touchdowns.

Having attended several practices and gotten to know the players, Tom found the game incredibly painful to watch. When it was over, the players walked to the locker room with their heads down. Mr. Bradley yelled at them some more, then sent them to the showers. He told Tom that the team had things to work on, but Tom thought that Mr. Bradley himself needed the most work. How long would he be able to assist a man with so few coaching skills? But then Tom saw the young faces of the players and couldn't help but give them words of encouragement after they showered. He decided he'd stick with the situation and help as much as he could.

—

The following week, Buddy stopped by the construction site again, parking his truck by the fence as he normally did. He got out and walked with his hands in his pockets, gazing at the progress of the project as he approached Tom. They talked briefly about the remodeling, but Tom quickly deduced that what Buddy really wanted to talk about was the football team. Tom was still mid-sentence, when Buddy said, "I've heard great things about you teaching the kids in practice, but last week's game was a disaster. Don't you think we could have played better?"

Tom was careful. "I think the team can play better, but it was just their first game."

Buddy looked at Tom closely. "Let me cut to the chase," he said, waving his arm. "The players, their parents, people in town—none of us are happy with the coaching."

Tom could understand why, but he just listened, not sure where Buddy was going with the conversation. Tom knew that if he wanted to keep working with the team, he'd need to be diplomatic with Mr. Bradley.

"Look," Buddy said. "Would you consider the head coach position? If I get support from the school's community council and persuade Ackerson? We would work your job around it."

Head coach position? Tom's jaw dropped. He remembered Grandpa's words about helping kids grow through sports, where they learn to work hard and to deal with winning and losing. "I might be interested," he said. "But I don't want Mr. Bradley to think I've sabotaged him."

Buddy's face lit up. "Let me worry about that. You just keep showing up to practices to help the team, and Ackerson or I will get back to you."

Two days later, Mr. Ackerson called Tom in the evening, right as he and Jeanine were about to start dinner, and offered him the head coaching position. "If you want it, it's yours," Mr. Ackerson said. "We think you'd be great with the team."

When Tom asked about the current coach, Mr. Ackerson said Mr. Bradley had come to him all on his own and told him that he couldn't make the kind of headway he wanted to with the team. He preferred to concentrate on his teaching.

Tom covered the mouthpiece on the receiver and whispered to Jeanine, "They're offering me the job." She grabbed his hand, and he told Mr. Ackerson he accepted his offer.

When Tom hung up, Jeanine laughed and leaned over to kiss him. "Congratulations, Coach O'Brien," she said.

Tom spent the rest of the evening jotting down practice plans for the coming week.

——

As he'd done when he played football himself, Tom showed up for practices early. When he led the team through drills and plays, he praised and reinforced good performance. He treated poor performance as an opportunity to teach—never criticizing anyone. And he worked the players hard. Tom asked the assistant coaches to stress conditioning and techniques, which made many of the players complain of exhaustion. Tom told them that was what would make them better players.

Gradually, as the practices went on, the mood of the team changed, and Tom not only heard less complaining but also saw more improvement. He jogged in the rain with them, lifted weights with them, and constantly encouraged them. He gave them advice, taught them new techniques, and showed them how to support one another.

They won their next game by two touchdowns. Buddy leaped to his feet, and the parents and other fans cheered loudly. But Tom knew the players had their work cut out for them if they wanted to keep winning. He turned from praising them to telling them what he wanted them to work on in the next week.

——

After practice one day, an assistant coach told Tom that the players wanted to know more about him. He suggested Tom have a session where they could ask him questions.

The players settled on the benches in the locker room, and it was quiet for a moment as they looked at Tom and one another. Finally one of the juniors asked Tom how he had become a good football player, and the players leaned forward with interest.

Tom smiled. "I worked hard, and I stayed disciplined. Football meant more to me than anything else for a long time. Even as a boy, I made it my goal to be the best." He described playing in the Pop Warner League and the influence of his father and grandfather.

One of the seniors, likely thinking about his own future, wanted Tom to compare college football to high school football. Tom told them about the kind of dedication he found he needed in college to combine studying with practicing football, reminding himself of his high school and college struggles.

He looked around the locker room at the young faces turned toward him and wanted to prepare them for life's twists and turns.

"I tore my Achilles tendon when I was a senior in high school," he said, seeming immediately to get the players' attention. "Before that, I thought I was going to be playing for a Big Ten school in college, but I couldn't recover in time, and all my scholarships were withdrawn." Even the assistant coaches watched him closely. "It pretty much ended my dreams," he said. "I thought football was over for me."

Another player asked Tom how he got over it, and Tom told the team that he'd had a hard time. He lost his girlfriend and struggled with what to do with his life after graduation. As Tom talked to them, he gained greater clarity about his experiences himself. He openly shared that he'd been charged by the police with a misdemeanor for underage drinking. The locker room grew even more quiet.

"If not for my grandfather and a construction boss who took a chance on me, I don't know that I would've had the encouragement I needed to move past that time," Tom said. He told them how he unexpectedly came to play for Kent State, which wound up being where he was meant to go all along, although he had struggles there also. "I was still figuring out a lot in my college years, and thankfully, I had a coach there who was a great mentor."

The players continued to ask questions, and they learned about his other injuries, what it was like to be in college during the Vietnam War, and how the protests and shootings had affected him. Tom thought about his continuous search for purpose, and the disappointments and disillusionment he'd faced in life.

"Yeah, I've been knocked down a lot over the years," Tom said to the players, looking around at them. "But I can see now that all that stuff is what helped me learn how to get back up."

As the players watched him, Tom was struck by the fact that he had a story to tell that could help them. As their coach, he bore a responsibility to help shape them. It was an honor he hadn't felt before, even with all his former football accolades and career success.

———

The rest of the season went well, with the team continuing to improve, winning more games than it lost. They won their last game on a broken play, when their punter recovered a snap that had gone over his head and threw a long pass for the winning touchdown.

After the game, several parents came down from the stands to shake Tom's hand and thank him for the impact he'd had on their sons. Tom knew he'd taught the players to work hard and deal with the ups and downs of competing in sports, but it was especially rewarding for him to hear that what he'd taught had made a difference in other parts of their lives.

Buddy was already at the construction site the following week when Tom arrived. He was direct, as usual, saying that Tom had tamed some of the wild boys on the team. Tom didn't know what he meant, and Buddy explained that several of the football players had been disrupting classes and challenging teachers. Their negative behaviors had apparently eased up after Tom became their coach.

"Ackerson wants you more involved with the school," Buddy said. He'll be in touch with you soon to get your thoughts on something." He looked at Tom for a long moment, a slight smile on his face. Then he left, muttering, "I might lose a project manager, but that's okay."

A week later, the secretary escorted Tom into Mr. Ackerson's office.

"You've had a remarkable impact on our football players," Mr. Ackerson said, standing up enthusiastically to shake Tom's hand. "And I'm not just talking about winning more games."

"I've really enjoyed it," Tom said. "I appreciate that you gave me the opportunity." He looked at Mr. Ackerson's nameplate, his pencil holder, and his in-basket on the desk and waited to see where this meeting was heading.

Mr. Ackerson surprised Tom by offering him a teaching position, one that was opening because the business teacher was retiring. Buddy had told him that Tom had a degree in construction management, and Mr. Ackerson believed Tom could cover fundamental business concepts. He dismissed Tom's concern about a teaching certificate, saying they would figure that out. He also asked Tom to be an assistant coach in other sports at the school, in addition to staying on as the head football coach.

Tom tried to picture himself as a teacher. "I hadn't anticipated this," he said. The thought wasn't unappealing, but he wasn't as sure about his skills in the classroom as he was on a field or court. Was this opportunity in keeping with what he was meant to do?

"If you have doubts, let me just say that you're a natural when it comes to developing students, and you have a quiet leadership presence that everyone respects, including me," Mr. Ackerson said. "You'd be good for this school and our community."

Tom was flattered. "I'll have to think about it." They agreed to discuss the offer again in a week. Tom walked slowly down the school hallway, noticing students in classes through the small rectangular windows of the closed doors. He felt a sense of belonging and purpose as he made his way through the school, not unlike when he took his disaster relief job. But this was much closer to his heart and his goal of helping people, as he had felt when he had helped Grandma. He believed he could help these kids.

———

That evening, he went on his usual walk with Jeanine. Waterfalls flowed down the sides of the mountains in the distance. Clouds covered the mountaintops, moving and changing shapes, some dark with rain and others light in the sun.

"He told me I'm a natural at developing students," Tom said as they reached the beach, taking off their flip-flops. "I just don't know if that applies to the classroom."

"He's right about you," she said. The breeze gently blew her hair to the side, and she tucked part of it behind her ear.

"Doing this would mean my salary will be cut again," he said. "It's been going down steadily ever since I left Johnson and Sons."

Jeanine looked surprised. "We don't need the money," she said. "You sound like Woz and Jack when you talk like that. You don't need to worry about advancing upward and living the typical American dream. That's not who you are."

Tom thought about his walk by the classrooms in the school hallway earlier that day. "I just want to do the right thing," he said. "I think I can help those kids, but maybe I'm looking for some other type of confirmation."

"This is meant for you," she said. "I think it's your fate."

"How do you know?" he asked. He looked out at the surf. "I sure didn't plan it. I've been searching for what to do ever since playing football was no longer an option for me."

"Remember when we hiked out to Hanakapi'ai Falls when we first started seeing each other, and we talked about Lao Tzu's poem? You told me you wished life was like football."

"Yeah. I've learned that life is definitely not like football."

"The poem says that the way to do is to be," she said. "Don't you think that's what you've done? This is your next stage of being now."

Tom thought of his father. "My father was all about the rules of life— purpose, goals, and discipline, like what's needed for football. I know he also thought of it in terms of a career. But when I've tried to apply it to broader life, I've always needed more. It's not enough for dealing with my ups and downs."

Jeanine turned and looked at him intently. "I think you've found *your* rules of life, and they go beyond having goals. It's what the school sees in you—a person who has let his life flow, whose fate is to help people. And now you're here to do it."

Tom slowly exhaled, feeling the breeze against his face. He hadn't always let his life flow. He'd hung on to his hardships and questioned everything. But even the most painful circumstances had enabled him to see a bigger world and helped him grow. Jeanine was right—he should accept who he was and let his life flow in the direction meant for him.

He searched Jeanine's eyes as she continued to look at him. "I'm going to take the job," he said. The decision filled him with excitement and peace—it was his fate. He drew her to him and kissed her, and she cupped his face with her hands. When he released her, her eyes lingered on his, as if she had something on her mind.

"What is it?" he asked, immediately concerned.

"All this talk about the future—I've been thinking a lot about my own fate. I keep having these feelings, and then I push them aside, but they're still there."

Tom looked at her quietly, unsure of what to expect. Her hair blew against her cheek.

"I never really thought I would consider anything like this, until I saw how much you care about Isabella and Johnny. I've been noticing the kids who come into my store lately—the way they light up when someone shows them attention. I don't know. I'm wondering about having a child together. I mean, would you want to?"

Tom's heart began to pound. He could think of nothing he'd want more. But before he could answer, Jeanine continued, "The thing is, I never really wanted to be a mother. My mom was not a good role model, and I was messed up for a long time—I still am in many ways." She grew quiet, turning her body slightly to the side, as if she felt she'd said too much.

Tom was tearing up. "You'd think differently if you could see yourself the way I see you," he said.

"You've always taken the best and worst parts of me," she said. "No one else loves me the way you do, Achilles. But as a mother—I need to be a worthy one, deserving of that child."

Tom reached out to hold her to him. "I think you're deserving—a child would be lucky to have you. I know I am." She put her arms around his waist. "Why don't we just take it a step at a time," he said.

Jeanine pulled back and looked at him, smiling. She intertwined her arm with his, and they continued their way down the long beach—quiet, reflective, each taking their own steps but walking together. Tom felt the sand beneath his feet. He looked again at the clouds drifting over the mountains and took in the sound of the rolling waves.

ACKNOWLEDGMENTS

Although I've always loved reading novels, I wasn't interested in learning about literature until my mid-twenties when I began taking courses at the University of Iowa, eventually earning a master's degree in English. I'm thankful for all my brilliant English teachers, with special memories of Sherman Paul, who helped me see my life through literature, and David Morrell, whose seminar on Ernest Hemingway and the novel *First Blood* helped plant the seed "I could write fiction."

That seed lay dormant in me for forty years, when my only activity related to creative writing was keeping a journal. I finally acted by taking courses at the Loft Literary Center in Minneapolis, a wonderful organization that welcomes and supports writers of all levels. I'm forever grateful to one of my first Loft instructors, Patricia Hoolihan. Under her gentle coaching, we all gained the courage to read our writings aloud and have them discussed in class. I am also thankful for another Loft instructor, Maya Hlavacek, whose course required each of us to write a short story that we discussed in class. My eyes watered as I listened to the positive comments from Maya and my classmates about my first story. What a milestone!

The Loft courses led me and other students to form a writing group facilitated by Maya. I can't thank Judy Anderson, Kolina Cicero, Dan Satorius, and Maya enough for their many insights and suggestions that have strengthened this novel. I also want to thank Amy Friebe, Mary Carroll Moore, and Leslie Wells for helping shape this novel in its early stages.

I'm grateful to the outstanding team of Greenleaf professionals: Daniel Sandoval, Morgan Robinson, Brian Welch, Adrianna Hernandez, Neil Gonzalez, Madelyn Meyers, and Tiffany Barrientos. I am especially indebted to Jessica Choi for helping bring this story and its characters to life with her creative developmental editing, to Aaron Teel for bringing the scenes and characters closer to the reader with his superb copy editing, and to Anna Jordan for her magic in creating a compelling design.

I am also thankful for the support of my sisters—Nancy Swearingen, a writer of family histories, and Bethany Johns, an extraordinary book designer—and of my brother, David Johns, who inspired me with stories from his life in Hawaii. Finally, and most importantly, I want to thank my family—Linda, Anna, Adam, Charlie, and Sophie—for all their love and support.

ABOUT THE AUTHOR

Always dreaming of writing, Robert Johns began his literary adventure in 1976 with a master of arts in English from the University of Iowa. After a career in academia and the public sector, he became active in the Loft Literary Center in Minneapolis, participating in Loft writing groups and conferences and writing fictional stories for publication.

The inspiration for his novel, *O'Brien's Broken Play*, was influenced by his years of growing up in a Midwest family, his competition in high school sports, and his coming of age during the political turbulence and societal change of the late 1960s and early 1970s.

During his undergraduate years at Iowa State, he vividly recalls watching the televised riots at the Chicago 1968 Democratic Convention, participating in antiwar marches, and hearing protest leaders announce at a campus rally that four Kent State students had been killed by the National Guard. These and other experiences influenced his search for an alternative purpose that would help change the American culture.

In addition to *O'Brien's Broken Play*, he has written three novellas, including stories about an Iowa farm girl who is radicalized by the Vietnam War, a local government manager trying to live up to his 1960s ideals, and an immigrant's son caught between cultures. He lives with his family in the Twin Cities.